Passion's Poison

Poison's Passion

BY

LEXI POST

Passion's Poison

Lexi Post

Beatrice Rappaccini is tired of the one-night stands that keep her alive. Tired of the illness she causes when she releases her sexual poisons into her partners. But when she meets Zach Woodman, everything changes. Desperate for what she can't have, she puts her heart and life on the line, ignoring the anonymous letters warning her to stay away.

Zach Woodman, logger turned chainsaw artist, has the perfect life, but no one to share it with after the deaths of the women he loved. Fascinated by the sexually experienced yet naïve Bea, he promises himself he will end their hot relationship before fate takes another beautiful woman from the world.

But he discovers Bea has no idea how to have a relationship, and he is perplexed by her strange behavior, hippie mother, six fathers and her request to give him every man's sex fantasy. It is only when he might lose her that he realizes he must make a decision that will break his heart either way.

Acknowledgments

To Bob Fabich for showing me what happily ever after truly means. For my sister Paige Wood, whose endless creativity and help has been so amazing.

For my mom, Jo Brous. Thank you for all your love and support.

And thank you to my critique partner Marie Patrick, my agent Jill Marsal and my wonderful editor Grace Bradley. You are all the best.

Author's Note

Passion's Poison was inspired by Nathaniel Hawthorne's short story *Rappaccini's Daughter*, first published in 1844. In Hawthorne's story, Giovanni Guasconti, who is going to the university in Padua, Italy, falls in love with Beatrice Rappaccini. The lovely Beatrice is the daughter of Dr. Giacomo Rappaccini, a scientist known for his work in producing beautiful but poisonous flowers that even he cannot touch, though Beatrice can. Giovanni realizes he has become poisonous as well by being with Beatrice and enlists the help of a friend, an enemy to Rappaccini, to find an antidote. Giovanni convinces Beatrice to drink the antidote, but because the poison is so prevalent in her body, when the antidote kills the poison, it kills her too.

But what if Beatrice had a daughter? How would the daughters of Rappaccini survive today?

"What have you done? You've killed her, the most beautiful flower of all my creations! I will not allow your triumph. Nay, for from her poisonous body I will bring forth her child, and never again will you or your kind love a daughter of Rappaccini!"

Signor Dr. Giacomo Rappaccini in the year of our Lord 1845

Chapter One

Present day

Zach Woodman was too local to be her lover.

Beatrice Rappaccini reminded herself of that fact as she drank in the sight of the shirtless man using a chainsaw in the forest clearing. The stark muscles in his arms and back danced with the movements of the machine as he angled it through a massive log standing on its end. His jeans stretched against straining thigh muscles braced in a slightly bent position, his construction boots encased in mud.

Bea tried to breathe, but the heat infusing her flesh overwhelmed her. What was happening? She had released her body poisons less than two nights ago down in the city, but this desire making her heart beat as fast as a hummingbird's wings felt different. This couldn't be good.

She gulped in air, desperate to control her breathing even as her high-heeled boots sank deep into the mud of the forest floor.

Zach moved to the side of the log and carved out a deep groove. Bea watched his pectorals tense under the layer of dirt covering his chest as he held the machine steady.

Mesmerized, she tried to take a deep breath but her lungs constricted, refusing to allow in the cool forest air. Her head spun as darkness encroached on her peripheral vision. Oh damn. She pulled her feet from the muck and sat down hard on a stump nearby. Dropping her head between her knees, she closed her eyes and focused her attention on inhaling.

As oxygen flowed into her lungs, the clearing grew quiet and unease replaced her near panic. She opened her eyes to find two boots standing in front of her. Silently, she wished she could crawl under the granite rock lying between those feet.

Since that wasn't an option, she lifted her head. Zach's sweat-streaked six-pack abs came into view above the edge of his blue jeans. Her stomach clenched. It tightened even more as his muscled chest, complete with wood shavings caught among the short, dark hairs, seized her attention. She took another calming breath, ignoring the growing warmth between her legs, thankful she remained seated.

Her gaze reached his angular face, where she found he had taken off his goggles. His green eyes, filled with curiosity, stared at her. His mouth quirked. "Are you okay?"

She shivered as his baritone voice slid through her like an otter through water, leaving ripples of weakness suffusing her body. She swallowed a groan. Mentally, she reached for the hospitality professional she'd trained to be. "Yes, I just need a moment." The breathy answer was anything but professional.

His scrutiny didn't leave her face. "Can I get you something? A bottle of water? A beer?"

She nodded, not trusting her voice.

His grin pulled the corners of his dark lips, moving the stubble of his unshaven face to form black arcs around the sides of his mouth. He turned and strode toward the log cabin she'd come upon at the end of the dirt driveway, his confident swagger demanding her attention.

She wrenched her gaze from his tight ass to give her body a chance to cool. She was here on business and her libido had to behave. Her body's attraction to this man didn't make sense. She had released her debilitating sexual toxins in a one-night stand on Saturday and had reached orgasm three times. It was only Monday. She should have a whole week of relief. Somehow, she had to gain control of herself.

By the time Zach returned with water and a beer, she hoped she appeared normal. He silently held out both. She accepted the water bottle while he opened the Bud Light and took a couple gulps. She stared as his Adam's apple bobbed along the corded muscles of his neck. Desperate to dampen the heat in her body, she raised her drink and sipped.

He gestured toward her with the half-empty beer. "Feeling better?"

She swallowed the cool water and cleared her throat. "Yes, thank you. I'm not sure what happened. I probably should've had breakfast this morning."

He looked at the sky before returning his attention to her. "Breakfast? It has to be about lunchtime."

She tried a slight smile but feared it came across more as a grimace, so she offered her hand. "I'm Beatrice Rappaccini from the Lakeside Inn in Meriden."

He grasped her hand in a strong grip, causing fire to shoot through her arm, across her body and straight to the juncture of her thighs. She almost squeaked in surprise.

"I'm Zach Woodman, but I imagine you already figured that out. What can I do for you, Ms. Rappaccini?"

Oh, the possibilities were endless. She looked at the zipper of his jeans and wished it open. He could strip and push his hard cock into her hungry body and make her come until she screamed. She'd never screamed before, but she had a feeling she could with him.

"Ms. Rappaccini?"

She started and pulled her gaze from his crotch. Had she seen a bulge growing there or was it her imagination? What was happening to her? "Please, call me Bea." Oh that sounded way too husky. She really needed to get a hold of herself.

She stood, wavering a bit in her heels. He grasped her arm and steadied her, getting wood shavings on the sleeve of her green dress, but she didn't think he noticed. Did he notice anything about her, such as the fact her body reacted to him like wildfire to wind? With the constant smirk on his face, it was hard to know.

She tried to find a semblance of composure as she removed her arm from his grip. "I'm here to commission a carving for one of the Larsens' inns, specifically, the Lakeside. The Larsens would like something unique."

He took another swig of beer, but his gaze never left her. "Hmm, something unique, as in abstract, or just different from my other carvings?"

Bea shook her head. "Definitely not abstract. The Larsens prefer rustic to fit in with the environment. I wandered through your shop," she pointed back toward the log cabin with the sign "Zach's" burned into it, "but nothing there is quite right."

He wiped his forehead with the beer bottle as he contemplated, staring at her with his brows drawn together in concentration.

Did he think about the carving or her? She blushed. Since when couldn't she read a man? Her very survival depended on her ability to find men who were attracted to her. So why was he different? And why was she so affected?

He drained his beer and smirked. "I think this will take some time and I need to wash up. Would you mind staying for lunch while we work on it? You could use some food and I need a break."

She shrugged. "Sure, I'd be happy to." She'd be happy to do whatever he wished, take off her clothes, sit on that log, let him— ugh. She had to stop this.

He turned away from her. "Great. This way."

As he headed for the opposite side of the wooded clearing, she hesitated. "Isn't this your shop over here?"

He looked over his shoulder. "Yeah, but you won't find any food in there. The house is this way."

She swung her gaze back and forth from the cabin to where he said his house sat. Could she trust herself to go farther into the woods with him? Did she have a choice? She was being silly. This was business.

She picked her way along what appeared to be a continuation of the dirt driveway. There was a bit less mud and a lot more trees, which made for easier walking, if anything could be easy in four-inch heels in the middle of the backwoods of New Hampshire.

She was only ten feet behind him when they came to another clearing. Her gasp made him turn.

He grinned. "You like it?"

His home was a mansion, if an enormous log structure could be called that. The size of a hunting resort, it sat upon a cliff overlooking a serene valley. Its three-story windows came to a point above a massive deck that ran the full length of the house.

"It's beautiful," she breathed.

And so was he as the sun lit his hair, proving it a dark-chocolate brown as he pointed to the view. "You should see it in the fall. The leaves in this valley look like a painting and in the winter, the snow gives you the feeling of being the only person in the world."

A strange emotion flitted across his rugged face. Was it wistfulness or loneliness?

He started walking again. "Come on. We'll enter through the basement so I can get out of these dirty clothes."

Hmm, she liked the sound of that. Giving her libido a mental slap, she followed him as he took a short path to a door under the long deck.

The basement was made for coming in dirty. A large mat for shoes lay at the entrance and the wall had hooks for coats. To the right she could see a bathroom. Log stairs beckoned to the left.

He gestured toward the steps. "If you want, you can go on up into the kitchen. I have lunch meat in the fridge and bread on the counter. I'm going to shower down here first."

She wanted to ask if he needed help, but resisted. "Should I take these boots off here?"

He nodded and motioned to the bench at the edge of the shoe mat. He sat himself, pulled the rugged ties from his Timberlands and stepped out of them.

She tried to remove her own boots, but they wouldn't budge.

He stood in front of her. "Can I help?"

She looked up to reply, but at the thought of him touching her, her voice stuck in her throat. She nodded instead.

His hands came around her foot and he tugged at the black leather knee-high boot. She wiggled her ankle and the boot glided off into his hands. He held it up for inspection. "It's a shame they're so muddy, or you could wear them in the house."

An image of herself in a black leather teddy wearing her tall black boots and standing at the end of a bed with him tied to it flashed before her eyes. The erotic scene had her taking short breaths, and she glanced at his face to see if he noticed her heat.

He met her gaze, his eyes twinkling before he dropped the boot on the mat. He put his hands out, now covered in dry mud, and waited for her to place her other foot in them. She complied and her boot was off sooner than she wished. "Thanks," she squeaked.

"No problem." The huskiness of his voice sent a shiver gliding along her skin.

But he turned toward the bathroom and strode in, his back muscles rippling with his walk. He flicked on the light and started to undo his belt, leaving the door open.

Fascinated, she stared, her body drinking in the sight of his sexy, massive shoulders while her mind conjured what his ass would look like.

He pulled the belt from his jeans, his biceps flexing as he reached down to his zipper. He paused and glanced over his shoulder to catch her staring.

Bea froze. The intensity of his green eyes sent lightning through her veins that converged between her legs in a shocking burn. She snapped her gaze away before she made a fool of herself and jumped him. Grabbing her water bottle, she sprinted up the stairs, but paused at the top to look back. Did he chuckle? She listened, but the only sound was the water from the shower.

She turned around to find the living room the size of the Lakeside Inn's lobby, except taller. The view calmed her, cooling her enough to appreciate the scene despite the barren trees and gray boulders that announced the end of winter. How could he afford this place? His carvings were expensive, but buried in the woods as he was, miles from civilization, he couldn't have that many orders.

To her right stood a river stone fireplace with a six-foot mantle and a chimney that rose through the ceiling. She couldn't help running her fingers over the smooth rocks. There were sheepskin throws on the floor in front of the hearth surrounded by warm, wood couches with soft, russet covers. The whole room spoke of casual comfort, manly.

To her left she found the kitchen with its black appliances and charcoal granite countertops. Shuffling over the smooth pinewood floor made her want to skid across it in a pair of socks as if she were eight years old again, but she refrained.

She opened the giant refrigerator and found sandwich makings, which she piled on the center island. The counter was the perfect height for making lunch, or perhaps making love. If she sat on the island, she'd bet it would put her at a nice height for Zach to lick her—

"Did you find everything?"

She whirled around to find him strolling toward her in nothing but a pair of jeans, his bare feet warming the wood floor. His wet hair appeared darker and very thick, but his shoulder and chest muscles had her throat closing with anticipation. Her fingers itched to run through the damp curls that covered his overdeveloped pectoral muscles and tease the nipples already hard from the cool air.

"Bea?"

"Yes?" She gulped.

"Are you okay?"

The look in his eyes wasn't lust but concern. She gave herself a mental slap. "I'm fine. I wasn't sure where you kept the bread."

A loaf sat next to the toaster. He picked it up and placed it on the island. His body, no more than six inches away, caused hers to overheat again.

She smirked. "I guess I didn't look very hard."

He studied her, making her squirm.

Did he see how hot she was for him? How embarrassing. She retreated to a safer distance and stood before the three-story window, her body attuned to the man taking plates out of the cupboards behind her. She tried to focus. "The view is even more breathtaking up here."

"That's why I built here. It's secluded."

Bea turned to look at him. "Where did you live before here?"

Zach had the bread loaded with roast beef and sliced tomatoes and had turned to set the knife in the sink when he stopped. "Maine."

She padded across the floor to the counter and sat on a stool. "That's more remote than Tamwick. I would imagine you could find a lot of isolated acreage there."

He picked up the condiments. "Mustard or mayo?"

"Mayo, please."

He slathered on a good helping. Obviously his slim waist and hips weren't affected by calories. But his dietary habits didn't hide the fact he hadn't answered her. Then again, it wasn't any of her business.

She took the hint. After all, she was here for the Larsens, not herself. He was off-limits in so many ways. "So, how many carvings do you do a month?"

He turned to put the food back in the refrigerator, which gave her the opportunity to enjoy the scenery of his back. He had a scar that ran from his left shoulder blade to the right side of his waist. She wanted to know what had happened, but didn't ask.

He closed the fridge, a beer under his arm, and balanced the plates as he walked. "It depends. If I have orders, I fill them. If not, I make a few extras to have on hand. Sometimes people want one yesterday."

She followed him to a large rustic pine table. He placed her food to his left as he deposited his at the head. She sat facing the view, but found him more interesting.

He picked up his sandwich. "When do you need the one for the inn?"

"By Ice-Out."

He chewed his food, but raised his eyebrows.

She shrugged, it was an unusual deadline, but Sharon Larsen had set the date. Her bosses could be a bit eccentric. "I know, I know. Who's to say when Ice-Out will be? I did some research and the earliest the lake was clear of ice for the M.S. *Wavemaster* boat to make its five scheduled ports was March 24, but the latest was May 12."

He took a swig of beer. "It's March 26th and this warm spell is melting the ice pretty fast. All we need is a good rain and the lake will clear, as least enough for the boat."

She nodded, her mouth full of roast beef.

He sat back in his chair. "Well, I have to admit it's the strangest deadline I've ever had."

She swallowed and licked her lips before she spoke. "I know it's a bit unusual, but I'm sure the Larsens will pay top dollar if you can produce a carving in time."

"I'm not worried about the money. It's the time factor. However, I've never been one to shy away from a challenge and this one is definitely unique." He smiled with anticipation.

Bea's heart did a little sidestep. Oh no, this wasn't good at all. Lusting for this man was bad enough, but liking him would be dangerous for both of them. The sooner she left his house the better. "So, what could you do for the inn? I have a brochure about it in my car."

He pushed back from the table and walked into the living room where he grabbed a pad of paper and a pencil that sat on an end table. "I've actually seen the Lakeside Inn. Had drinks in the bar there once or twice."

How could she have missed that? Her body reacted like radar to him.

He strode back to the table, a secret smile on his face. "Mostly during bike week, so I wasn't there long, but I do remember it."

That explained why she hadn't seen him. She always took that week off to help her dad Gerry at his bar.

Zach nudged his empty plate aside.

As he began to sketch, her curiosity piqued. She finished half her sandwich and pushed her plate away so she could lean forward for a better view. "I saw a sketch of raccoons in your shop. Can you do something that nice?"

He didn't look at her, his attention fixed on his drawing.

Her gaze wandered from the paper to his face. His brows moved inward, revealing deep lines of concentration. His eyes were a dark green and heavy-lidded, which to her mind was a winning bedroom combination. He had a straight nose, strong and masculine, but his lips were to die for. They were dark with a lot of stubble around them and supported by a square jaw. Thankfully, he had no cleft in his chin. She despised that model look.

He turned the pad toward her. "Here are a few options. If I stay with the lake theme, I could do fish jumping, or reeds, or a mermaid, though I admit to being less than stellar with female faces. The chainsaw doesn't like them."

His quick grin had warmth spreading from her neck to her toes. His eyes shone with good humor and she wanted to revel in their merriment. But he broke eye contact and pointed to a few other rough sketches.

"Or I could do beaver, black bear, or…" He hesitated.

She leaned closer to get a better look at the pad. The faint scent of musk floated toward her.

He met her gaze, their faces mere inches apart, and all she wanted was for him to kiss her.

His eyes were full of excitement, but for her or the carving? She couldn't read him, which drove her crazy. Her own attraction overrode all her normal senses.

He grinned. "How about a birch tree? I could have a beaver at the bottom in the process of gnawing it down while a downy woodpecker yells at him from a branch above. I think it would blend well with the inn's surroundings and yet stand out as a story in itself."

Bea swallowed. His face glowed with energy and vitality. She couldn't resist.

She leaned forward and kissed him.

~~*~~

Zach's brain took a second to realize the gorgeous woman across from him had her lips firmly planted on his. But as soon as he did, he took control and wrapped his hand behind her neck to pull her closer.

Her soft lips parted at his movement.

He slipped his tongue inside and explored the sweetness of her mouth. The blood rushed from his slow brain to his groin. The need to bring her body against him grew so strong, he groaned.

She pushed herself away.

He let her go, but he wanted more, a lot more. His cock straining against his jeans attested to that fact.

She wouldn't meet his gaze. "I'm sorry. I didn't mean to… I just thought your idea was so brilliant… I don't usually… I mean—"

He smiled at the blush reddening her high cheeks. If he could capture that look in wood, he'd be famous. "No need to apologize. I didn't mind a bit. In fact, anytime you feel the need, I'm at your disposal."

It was the wrong thing to say. He realized his mistake two seconds too late. Her face went from pretty in pink to white.

She stood, overturning her chair. "I should go. Again, I'm very sorry."

She made it to the top of the stairs before he caught her, grabbing her hand. "Hey, are you okay?"

Bea took a deep breath before she turned to meet his gaze.

When her moist brown eyes stared up at him, he cursed himself for a heel.

She attempted a smile, but failed miserably. "You've asked me that a lot since I got here, but yes, I'm fine. Just horrified at my behavior."

Though her lashes were wet as she blinked to hold back her

tears, he couldn't ignore the beauty of her face, the silkiness of her hair, or the barely controlled need to take her in his arms and comfort her. He didn't know what to say, but he had to see her again. "Listen, I'll work on a few sketches. If you come by Wednesday, we can choose one so I can get started."

She hesitated before she shook her head. "I'm sure whatever you decide will be fine. After all, you're the artist."

She tried to remove her hand, but he held tight. "No, actually, I'm a logger by trade. I started this whole carving thing for kicks. Really, I'll need your help to decide what to carve."

Her shoulders slumped and his gut twisted in response, but his groin tightened the moment she nodded.

"Very well. I'll be back Wednesday after I go over the books with Mr. Larsen."

He smiled and let her go. "Good. I'll see you Wednesday."

She started down the stairs.

Unwilling to lose sight of her yet, he leaned over the railing, watching until she reached the basement. Crossing to the windows, he waited to catch sight of her as she left the house. He heard the door close and she came into view as she picked her way through the trees in her ridiculous high-heeled boots, her hips swaying with each cautious step. How he'd love to see her naked except for those boots, sprawled across his bed, wrists tied above her head. The thought of her boot-clad legs wrapping around him while he pumped inside her had his cock hardening again. He wanted this woman.

He spoke to the windowpane. "Turn around and look up, Bea."

She kept walking, but when she reached the edge of the clearing, she stopped.

He held his breath.

She took another step, looked back, then continued out of sight.

Zach smiled and strode into the kitchen. She was as attracted to him as he was to her and he couldn't have been more surprised. He cracked open another beer and leaned on the counter. Professional women like Bea usually didn't go for him. He was too rugged. But if she was interested, he certainly wouldn't put up a fight. He'd never had a gorgeous woman kiss him the day he met her, but a fast-and-furious relationship would be perfect. He'd learned all too well, long-term with him was a death sentence, literally. Three times together and he would end it.

He grabbed his pad of paper off the table and sat in the living room. He sketched long, black flowing hair, a slim body and legs that went on forever. Detailing the face, he added almond-shaped eyes that tilted up slightly, erotically. A soft stroke added a slender nose that was followed by full, sensuous lips. He paused, remembering the feel of them on his own. His cock stirred as he drew full, naked breasts, the smallest of navels and a hint of shadow between her legs. Then he added the boots, filling in the black leather. Holding the paper up, he looked his fill. She would be delicious.

He closed his eyes. Was it Wednesday yet?

Chapter Two

"Bea, calm down. There has to be another way." Her mom's voice came through her cell phone and ascended another octave on the pitch scale.

"I am calm, Mom. I've thought this through. I've tried your way and it hasn't worked. The only way I'm going to get pregnant is to have in vitro fertilization."

"No, you haven't tried 'my way'. Did you ever think the reason you haven't become pregnant is because you're always with different men? I didn't get pregnant with you until I was down to sleeping with the same six. That might be the answer."

Bea's attention was drawn by a customer with suitcases trudging into the lobby. "Mom, I have to go now. I'll call you later."

"Come over for dinner Saturday night. I think we need to talk more."

"Okay, I'll see you then." Bea sighed as she ended the call. Ever since meeting Zach, she couldn't shake the feeling that she had to do something and fast. She just wished she knew what it was she should do.

As the customer approached the front desk, one of the bellmen offered to take his luggage. Bea stepped around the corner into the office and tapped Kayla on the shoulder. "You have a check-in."

Kayla set down her cup of coffee and pasted on a smile. "Got it."

As she sauntered past, Bea stopped her to brush away a little white powder near Kayla's lips.

Kayla rolled her eyes. "Thanks."

Bea took Kayla's seat in the back and pushed aside the jelly donut on the desk. Blindly, she faced the window. Her mom didn't understand, and Bea had no idea how to explain it to her. It wasn't her biological clock. It was her need to stop hurting the men she had sex with, her "poison-release vessels" as her mom referred to them. But Bea couldn't think of them like that, wouldn't think of them like that. Every one of them had a life, and the sickness she caused them had started a self-loathing inside her that had grown beyond the bearable. She needed help.

Bea pulled her phone from the pocket of her jeans and dialed. "Hello, Grandma."

"Ah Bea, how nice to hear from you. Did you have a satisfying weekend? How many hunks did you shag?"

She flushed. "Grandma! Only one, but that's partly why I'm calling. I can't do this anymore."

There was silence and a long sigh. "I know how you feel, honey, but you have to. If you don't, your poisons will build up inside and kill you."

"Are you sure?" She knew she sounded desperate, but she didn't care.

"That's what happened to my mother."

Bea leaned forward in her chair, her heart slowing. "I didn't know that. I thought she died in prison."

"Yes, she did, because she had no men available that she could release her poisons into. You were wondering if it was true, weren't you? Even though you may have only felt lightheaded and drained sometimes, you wondered if the toxins in our bodies would really kill us. I'm sorry to say, they will."

Bea swallowed. Her grandmother had leapt ahead of her own thought process. "I understand. Mom told me once that if I have a baby it would lessen the need for release. Is that true?"

"Absolutely. Before I had your mom I had to have sex at least seven times a week, but now I only need it four or five times."

"Wait. How do you get that in the assisted living community where you are? I mean…don't men start to lose… Isn't it—"

Her grandmother laughed. "I can see you blushing from here, Bea. The short answer is I have my regulars and Viagra has done wonders for my health."

"Oh gosh, I never thought about getting old. How did we survive all these generations?"

"We didn't. I am the oldest Rappaccini so far. Aren't you the lucky one?"

Though her grandmother said the words in jest, Bea felt her heart constrict. "I *am* lucky. If I didn't have you, I wouldn't know what was true. I just got off the phone with Mom. I told her I wanted to try in vitro fertilization."

"Oh, I bet your mom was excited."

Bea shook her head. "No, she wasn't. In fact she freaked. I don't get it."

"Well, blow me over and sweep me under the rug. She's still holding out for you to get married."

"What? How can I marry when I need to have sex with multiple men?"

Her grandmother's mumbled words didn't quite make it through the phone.

"What did you say?"

"Never mind, dear, I'll explain your mother to you another time. So you want to get pregnant to lessen the need to have sex?"

Her grandmother made it sound as if she'd just lost her mind. "I'm not looking to become a nun or anything. I just can't keep making all these men sick. It's wrong. But I also don't want to have a child that must go through what I have to. I can't do that. I just can't. Is there any way to know if my child would have the same genetic poisoning? I mean, it's been generations since Giacomo did this to us. Is there any chance my child could be normal?"

"There's always a chance, honey. That's why we've all had daughters. We keep hoping. So how many times do you need to orgasm on a man to make it a week?"

"Three." It was her magic number and one she'd lived with since she'd hit puberty, or rather since Phillip.

"Oh, that's good. Your mom only needed five, so there is a good chance your daughter would be none or one. *She* could definitely have a husband. Oh Lord, just thinking about having a great-granddaughter to cuddle has got my blood pumping. Are you serious about this, Bea?"

Was she? "I don't know. It's a lot to think about."

"I think— Hold on, honey, there's someone at my door."

Bea leaned back in her chair again as she listened. A male voice could be heard along with her grandmother's.

"Honey, I have to go. Why don't you start processing this and come for a visit so we can talk this out some more. Okay?"

She raised her brow. Since when had her grandmother started talking like a psychiatrist? Must be one of those lectures they provided for the people in the retirement community. "Okay, I will. You have fun, Grandma."

"I plan to, honey."

Bea smiled as she ended the call. She may not have all the answers she had hoped for, but talking with her grandmother always made her day brighter. She couldn't imagine what it must have been like growing up in the fifties and sixties with the Rappaccini poison, but Grandma Beatrice had managed and her mom had too. So did that make her a wimp for feeling bad about the men she used to survive?

She glanced at the half-eaten donut and on impulse took a bite. Kayla wouldn't mind. The sweet grape jelly slid across her tongue like thick Chambord, reminding her of Zach's tongue exploring her mouth. She shook her head to dispel the memory. Since Monday when she met him, she'd been torn. Her attraction to him had nothing to do with the poisons in her body and everything to do with him as a person. At least that was her best guess since she'd never been attracted to a man in that way. Usually she assessed the available men, eliminated any who had wedding rings and determined who would be the easiest to get into bed and last the longest. But with Zach, she wanted to be with him in a way she couldn't because she didn't want to hurt him. The fact was, she didn't want to hurt anyone anymore.

Every man she had sex with became sick, though she'd never witnessed the extent of the illness since they were men only in the big city for conferences. That's why she traveled so far. She wasn't anxious to run into them again after making them ill. Still, she was careful to have no more than three orgasms with one man. There had to be a way around her predicament. If there was, she would find it.

With her determination in place, she focused on the scene outside the inn. She didn't like what she saw. The sky had turned a stormy gray, and despite it being just after noon, it looked as if it were dusk. Her stomach knotted. She had to get up to Tamwick and back before the snow began to fall.

"Beatrice?"

She started and looked around to find her boss behind her. "I'm sorry, I didn't hear you."

Craig Larsen dropped a printout on the desk. "I think you're right. I forgot to add the plowing expense for the last month. It's been so warm lately, it's hard to believe we were buried in four feet of snow a couple weeks ago."

She pointed to the window and the thickening clouds. "And it looks as if we might get buried again. I really should head up to the artist's place before it gets too bad. This might help delay Ice-Out, but it could also delay his work on the carving. His tool of choice is a chainsaw."

"A chainsaw?" Craig's thin red eyebrows rose in disbelief, reminding her of a squirrel with an empty nutshell.

"Yes, and I don't think he'd be willing to start work on it in the middle of a storm."

Craig picked up the paper again. "You're right. Why don't you get going? You found the biggest mistake I made with the books. I'm sure I can find the smaller ones. Thank you for your help with this. I'll see you tomorrow."

"Okay. And don't forget to tell Kayla she can have Friday off."

"Right. Will do."

No sooner had he left the office than Bea hit the car starter on her key chain, threw on her wool coat and stuffed her hands into her black gloves. Grabbing her purse, she strode out the door. She was torn between her wish to see Zach and her fear of giving in to her attraction for him, which would only hurt him. She shouldn't go, but it was her job, at least that's what she told herself.

Once the car warmed, she pulled onto the road and headed north. She glanced up at the darkening sky and gritted her teeth. "Please don't snow. Please don't snow. Please don't snow."

She tightened her hands around the steering wheel as she inspected the windshield for small flakes that might be the harbingers of larger ones. Though no white dots appeared, the sky was almost dark when she pulled into Zach's driveway. Her heart rate sped at the sight of him, causing her palms to sweat in her warm gloves. The man could only be described as a work of art in the flesh.

He stood on the front porch of his shop. Had he been waiting for her? He wore an old black bomber jacket and blue jeans. His blue-and-black flannel shirt complemented the whole mountain-man look. He was off-limits, a business associate, too local for a one-night stand and too kind to risk a relationship with. She had to control herself this time.

As she stepped from her car, he approached. She sensed the tension in his strides.

"I wasn't sure you were going to come."

He'd been worried she wouldn't return? Her heart melted and she had to clear her throat. "I'm sorry, Craig kept me longer than I expected. Do you have the sketches?"

He linked his arm with hers and started to walk her around the shop. "Yeah, they're up at the house."

His touch, despite their respective coats, had her heartbeat increasing and her body tingling, anticipating his next demand. She pulled away from him. "You don't have them here?"

He faced her, the ever-present grin on his face. "No, I didn't know what time you would arrive, so I left them in the house. Is that a problem?"

Bea glanced back at her car. The possibility of going into his house again shot pure fear as well as need racing through her veins. There was something about his humble talent and appreciation for nature that had her heart skipping. She didn't want to hurt him, but she craved having sex with him. No, she couldn't trust herself in his house. "I can wait in my car while you get them."

He raised his eyebrow and stared at her. "Why? You have much better shoes for walking in the woods today and you know it's not far. Besides, it's snowing and I don't like the thought of you sitting in your car by yourself."

She glanced beyond his dark-green eyes to see it had indeed started snowing, heavily. Damn, she was doomed. A little place inside her jumped for joy and she squelched it. "Fine, but let's make this quick. I don't want to be driving in this if it gets too deep."

"Right." He grabbed her hand and they started walking for the house.

The warmth of his palm seeped through her glove despite the fact he'd been outside with his coat unzipped. "Aren't you cold?"

He chuckled. "Cold? It's only thirty degrees out. We had below-zero temperatures this winter. How did you ever survive?"

She shrugged. "I have an automatic car starter to make it toasty before I get in. Other than that, I stay inside as much as possible."

He gave her hand a squeeze. "You live up here, but don't go outside to enjoy the winter activities?"

She shook her head in response but slowed as they approached the house, awed by the sight of the snow falling into the valley.

He let her go, allowing her to look her fill.

She sighed. "It's truly magnificent."

He smiled. "Oh, you haven't seen anything yet."

She tore her gaze from nature's beauty to look into his eyes and found appreciation there.

He took her hand again. "Wait 'til you see it from inside."

She followed him into the basement where they both took off their outerwear, then went upstairs. She walked to the great windows. The barren trees already sported a coating of white, but the snow appeared to fall strictly in the valley and not from the sky since the cloud cover and snow were the same color.

She sensed him step behind her before his words brushed her ear. "It's breathtaking, isn't it?"

She nodded, not trusting her voice as shivers ran down her arms and across her chest, sensitizing her breasts. That this rough man could appreciate the natural beauty was endearing and so sexy.

He remained behind her, not touching, but she was fully aware of him. He wanted her to be aware. Her muscles tightened as her body prepared itself for complete capitulation. She swallowed the groan that threatened to slip from her throat and stepped away. "So, where are the sketches?"

He didn't hide his disappointment fast enough, and she steeled herself against the need to give in to him. He picked up a small pile of paper from the living room and brought it to the table. As they sat, she couldn't help but remember the kiss they shared and her gaze riveted to his lips.

They moved. "If you keep looking at me that way, I'm going to have to kiss you."

She jumped as if slapped and brought her gaze to his. Desire, pure and simple, shone in his eyes. Her body started a slow burn as moisture swelled her pussy and her nipples strained toward him. "I'm sorry."

"Don't be. In fact, I'd rather you weren't."

She was in his house on business, but her brain refused to focus because all her blood had rushed to the juncture of her thighs. She licked her lips, trying to hold on to her sanity, but she wanted to touch him so much that deep inside she ached.

A man could only take so much and Bea's expression far exceeded Zach's breaking point. "All right, that's it."

He reached across the table with both hands and brought her face to his. Her quick breath brushed across his lips, so when she didn't pull away, he kissed her. She moaned as he pressured her to open for him, and he swooped his tongue inside to stroke hers. She tasted like fresh honey. Her citrusy scent enveloped him. He wove his hands through her hair, bringing her closer. When her tongue pushed between his lips, he growled in hunger.

She tugged away and he let her go, cursing himself for ruining the moment.

She bent her head and stared at the pile of sketches.

Zach silently demanded she meet his gaze, but she didn't. Staring at her swollen lips, he repositioned himself in his seat to make his growing cock more comfortable, if that were possible. It throbbed with wanting, its tip already moist and ready to conquer. Taking a deep breath, he forced himself to concentrate on his drawings and spread them out before her. "I designed a number of variations on the theme we talked about the other day."

Her flush faded as she focused on his work.

"Here is the basic premise with the state flower and forsythia thrown in." He pointed to the sketch on her left.

She appeared to study it, but he wasn't sure she actually saw it. Good. He hoped she had a hard time concentrating because he sure as hell did. All he could think about was how smooth her skin felt. How much he wanted to cover her curvaceous body with his and sink his cock deep inside her pussy.

He counted to ten and moved another drawing in front of her. "This one brings out the wildlife, so the focus is on the beaver and the woodpecker, but I've also thrown in the Monarch butterfly, wooly caterpillar and a raccoon. On this third sketch, I've kept everything in life-size proportion, but had to leave off the insects because the chainsaw can't do that type of detail."

She perked up. "That's the one. It's perfect. And I just know Sharon will love it." She looked up at him, her eyes shining with excitement.

He grinned. People's reactions to his work still surprised him. He was just a logger and it amazed him to find someone like her energized by what he did for fun. Did she know her eyes sparkled when she was happy? "You're sure?"

She peered at the sketch again. "Oh yes, absolutely. Can you really do this with a chainsaw?"

He leaned back in his chair, crossed his arms and raised an eyebrow. "You doubt I can?"

She flushed. "No, I mean a chainsaw appears to be a bit unwieldy for such small detail."

"Actually, a chainsaw is an amazing machine if you respect it. In comparison to the trees it can fell, it's a small tool, yet it brings down giants in the forest. Don't get me wrong, it can be a pain in the…uh. Jamming, not starting and kicking away can occur, which is frustrating as hell and dangerous. But if you take care of it, watch where you put it to work and prepare for the worst at all times, you can accomplish a lot."

Bea focused on every word he uttered. Her absolute attention caused a warmth to spread through his chest that he had experienced only a couple times before. He leaned forward. "Some people see it as a loud, cumbersome machine. Many lifetime loggers curse it. But my father taught me to respect it. If you ignore its look and sound, you can use it as finely as a paintbrush, though I admit I haven't achieved that level yet."

Bea touched his arm. The connection sent blood racing to his groin, but she appeared innocent in her enthusiasm. "You may call yourself a logger, but you're an artist at heart. When did you start logging?"

He placed his hand on hers, needing to feel her bare skin. "I was nine. That's when my father first took me to the sites. I wasn't allowed to do much at first. Frankly, I was too small, but as I grew, he allowed me more responsibilities."

She sat back, pulling her hand from his hold. He resisted the urge to take it back.

She cocked her head. "How old were you when you took down your first tree?"

He smirked. "Let's put it this way, I was too young for it to be legal."

Her face flushed. She had to be as affected by their mutual attraction as he was.

He pushed back his chair and rose. "I have a photo of me with that tree. It's not that impressive because the tree is down, but I remember how tall it was."

He walked into the living room to the corner between the fireplace and great windows where a small photo in a black frame hung on the log wall. He pointed. "That's me and my first pine."

She moved closer. "You look maybe fourteen. That tree is huge. It doesn't even fit in the photo."

Zach stepped up behind her and pointed to another small person in the left corner of the picture. "That's Josh, my best friend. He's a doctor at a research hospital here in New Hampshire. He only did logging during his summer breaks from school."

His breath whispered past her ear and he witnessed a tiny shiver flow down her skin.

She turned, boxed in by his body. "Why, um, did you stop?"

He gazed into her eyes and saw caution mixed with desire, but he let her see his naked need for her. "I was made an offer I couldn't refuse."

"Oh."

He had to touch her or go insane. Lifting his hand, he moved her silky hair off her shoulder before cupping her neck. Every inch of his body tightened with anticipation, his cock no exception. He bent his head forward, holding in check his raw desire. "I can't refuse the invitation of your lips either, Bea."

She caught her breath and her mouth opened.

As his lips touched hers, she reached her arms up to twine around his neck. Her hold set his body on fire. He wanted to consume her. He enveloped her in his arms, pulling her against him. A heady sensation coursed through him as he played his lips over hers, his teeth nibbling, his tongue invading.

She wiggled, fitted herself to him, her breasts crushing against his chest, burning him.

He moved his hand to behind her head, tilting it so he could taste the side of her neck while his other found her ass and pulled her pelvis tight against his granite-hard cock.

She sighed in surrender and played with the hair at the back of his neck, caressing him.

He bent her backward, licking his way down between her breasts. He could see hard nipples through her blouse and bra as they anxiously waited for his attention. His blood pounded at the sight, straining his control. He murmured against her chest. "Beatrice, I want you."

Bea's brain kicked into gear at Zach's words. She wanted him too, but not for just a night. Her pleasurable heat turned frosty. How could that be? She didn't even know him, but her heart already named him hers. She pushed against his chest to break his embrace.

He let her go.

She staggered back, her knees shaky, her breaths coming fast. "I'm sorry if you got the wrong idea," she rasped.

He stared at her quizzically. "What idea would that be? That you're as attracted to me as I am to you? That this," he motioned with his hand pointing between them, "is great?"

She shook her head, trying not to look at the large bulge in his jeans. "I-I don't know. It's too fast."

He stared into her eyes. "You mean too hot, don't you?"

She gulped as his words sent fire racing through her veins. She nodded.

He took a deep breath and jammed his hands into his front pockets. "Yeah, I guess you're right. But it's not something we can ignore."

His gaze changed from polite to possessive. "I want you, Beatrice Rappaccini. I want you naked in my bed. Once you're there I want to taste you, smell you, feel you and pump into you until I lose myself."

At his words, Bea's legs turned to slush and she sank into the nearest chair.

He hunkered down in front of her and took her hands. "Bea, is there any reason why we shouldn't get together?"

Oh, was there. But none she could tell him. He wouldn't believe her if she did. Her last long-term relationship back in high school ended with her boyfriend in a coma. Despite his eventual recovery, she still carried a pile of guilt around with her. As much as she wanted Zach, she couldn't be happy with one night. This wasn't about her need to cleanse the toxins she produced. This was about the idea of having one special man in her life. The only obstacle standing in her way was her deadly body.

Zach dropped her hands. "What is it? You hesitated for too long." He stood abruptly. "Are you already seeing someone?"

She jerked her head up, surprised by the anger in his tone. "No, I'm not. It's complicated."

He walked away from her and stood behind the other couch. "Why do people always have to make things complicated? This is simple human nature, two adults who are attracted to each other. What's so complicated about that?"

She straightened her shoulders. "First, I'm supposed to be here on business. I don't think it appropriate to kiss a vendor on company time. Second, I don't know anything about you except that you can create amazing statues with a chainsaw and you used to be a logger from Maine. I like to know a lot more about a person before I have sex with him."

How little she knew about her one-night stands stabbed at her conscience, but she ignored it.

He grinned and came around to sit on the couch perpendicular to her chair. He took her hand again. "If those are your only concerns, I can work with that. You're being very reasonable and I'm being impatient. Forgive me. You're so damn beautiful, it's hard for me to control myself."

Heat rose in her cheeks and she looked down to see his big calloused hand holding hers. She wished it were so simple.

He raised her chin with his other hand. "Bea, I'll try to be patient if you're willing to give it a chance."

She stared at him, this incredible man who her body and her heart seemed to crave. A man who would suffer if she gave in to her own needs, but she was weak. Her head nodded of its own accord while her mind screamed no.

He leaned forward and brushed a featherlight kiss upon her lips.

She wanted to cry at his tenderness and she silently cursed her deranged ancestor again for the poisonous nature he had inflicted on her, on so many Rappaccinis. "I better go."

He stood with her hand still in his. "I'll walk you to your car."

She let him help her up, wishing she could figure out some way for a relationship to work, but a deep-rooted fruitlessness settled deep in her stomach.

He let go of her hand to cup her face in his palms. "You look as if you're going to cry."

She put her hands on his chest. "No, I—oh no."

His brows drew together in concern and his hold tightened on her face. "What's wrong?"

She stared at the scene over his shoulder. "I don't think I'm going anywhere now."

He turned toward the great windows, his arm coming around her, but he remained silent. He squeezed her waist.

Outside the snow fell hard, and on his massive deck a foot of the beautiful white flakes announced her imprisonment. The Tamwick roads would be impassable. How could she stay in his house overnight without sleeping with him? "Maybe, it's not as bad as it appears. You must have gusts up here, right?"

He raised his brow. "Study the snow. It's falling straight down. There's no way you'll make it back to Meriden in your vehicle."

She stared at her silent jailer, unable to fault the large, white flakes defined against the dark grayness outside. He was right. In his home with the snow piling up, it was as if they were the only two people on Earth. But if that were the case, he would be dead within the week.

She shook herself and the foreboding that flooded her body. They weren't the only two people in the world. In fact, she needed to call Craig. "I better make a few calls. Let people know where I am."

He stepped away, the energy in his body palpable. "Sure, I'll go downstairs and get wood for the fireplace. I'm thinking it's going to be a cold one."

Zach gave her a reassuring smile that did everything but reassure her. Then he headed downstairs, leaving her body in jitters, her heart aching and her mind frantically searching for answers like a chickadee caught inside a house, desperate to find a way out and accomplishing nothing but harm to itself.

Chapter Three

Zach reached the basement and went straight for the door to look through its window. Flipping on the outside light, he grinned. The snow fell faster than an eighty-foot pine. It must be fate. To have a beautiful, passionate woman stuck with him for the entire night. He never believed in that "meant to be" garbage, but tonight he'd won the jackpot. Poker with his friends would never be the same.

He switched off the spotlight and strode to the pile of logs in the corner. Heating with wood warmed a man three times. When he cut it down, hauled it in and burned it. He would add a fourth to that list, getting hot with a sexy woman on sheepskins in front of the fire. Yup, he could feel the heat already.

He pulled four large logs from the pile. Balancing them, he trudged upstairs and dropped them into the wood box next to the fireplace. He paused to enjoy the view of the woman on the phone before heading back downstairs. She was hot for him. He could feel it. And the feeling was mutual. Hell, if she wanted to get to know him better, he'd tell her his life story.

Grabbing the log sling from the hook on the basement wall, he piled it with smaller logs, branches and kindling, slung it onto his shoulder and made his way back upstairs. He dropped his load near the hearth.

Bea faced the valley-side windows, so he walked to the edge of the sliding-glass door and flipped on the spotlight above the deck. The bright light lit up the falling snow, making it a sparkling, silent moving picture against the black night, as if they were trapped within a snow globe.

Her eyes widened in awe as she gazed at the beauty outside before turning her attention back to her conversation.

At least she could appreciate nature's serenity. Many women he'd known focused on how much his place was worth and didn't get his world.

He returned to the fireplace and crouched before it to brush aside the old ash. He piled on the wood according to size, lit the newspaper and let the kindling catch flame.

Bea's conversation drifted over to him. "But Mom, I can't."

Silence reigned as Bea listened to her mother. This wasn't a conversation he should hear. Standing, he resisted the urge to gaze at her and jogged upstairs. His guest might need a few items for her unexpected stay tonight, and he didn't want to be a poor host.

Bea covertly watched as Zach left the room and breathed a relieved sigh. She had a hard enough time concentrating on her conversation with him in the room, but the huge logs he carried upstairs had brought back the image of his naked torso, which silenced all other thoughts.

"Bea, are you still there?"

"Sorry, Mom. He's such a distraction."

She could almost see her mother smile on the other end of the phone. "Honey, all I'm saying is don't end it before it begins. It's been over fourteen years since the episode with Phillip and that was my fault. You know what your limits are now. Get creative. I know in my gut you can have a happily ever after."

Bea pulled out a chair and sat at the table, her grandmother's words about her mom and marriage at the forefront of her mind. "How can you know that, Mom? *You* didn't get one. Unless you believe long-standing relationships with four of my possible six fathers is happy."

"It is, honey, but yours could be better. The poison in our bodies dilutes with every generation. You have a chance."

Bea rolled her eyes. "Yeah, so does my lottery ticket."

Her mother sighed. "Just give it some time, that's all I'm saying."

Bea stared as Zach's jean-clad legs came into view on the stairs, followed by his plaid shirt and big smile. "I have to go, Mom. I'll call you when I get home."

"Okay, honey. Love you."

"Love you too." She ended the call and dropped her phone back into her purse.

Zach crouched in front of the fire and adjusted the logs with a poker.

How could she possibly have a relationship with him without killing him? Even now she wanted to eat him up, body and soul.

He joined her and faced the window. "It's stunning, isn't it?"

She tore her gaze from him and focused on the falling snow. Though it came down fast, it fell in graceful disorganization like feathers. "Yes, it is. It's so bright in the lights compared to the darkness outside."

"That's why I throw on the spotlight. It makes the snow feel like nature's blanket instead of a menace."

She stood, the need to be close impossible to resist, her body destined for his as sure as the ice on the lake would melt. She stared at him. This logger viewed snow in such unique ways. She'd never met a man like him and she'd met many.

Zach must have sensed her scrutiny because he turned his head. The green depths of his eyes were uncharted territory she hoped to investigate. But at that moment, her stomach growled.

He gave her a self-depreciating smile. "I guess I'm being a poor host."

She averted her eyes and covered her stomach with her hand. "I'm sorry. I didn't have a chance to grab lunch today."

"You do a lot of skipping meals, don't you? That must be why you're so thin. Let me see what I can find for dinner. But I warn you, I'm not a great cook."

She shrugged. "That's okay, maybe I can help."

"Great." He grabbed her hand and led her to the kitchen.

Her heart skipped a beat at the naturalness of his action and warmth spread up her arm into her chest.

He released her as he opened the refrigerator and searched. "I wasn't expecting company. I'm not sure what we have to work with. I have a few eggs and some shredded mozzarella. I have pepperoni slices, mushrooms, tomatoes, carrots, but no lettuce. I guess a salad is out. I have more food in the freezer, but I'm not sure your stomach can wait that long."

Bea looked over his shoulder from the safety of the other side of the island counter. "Hmmm, do you have any macaroni and cheese?"

He closed the refrigerator and squatted to open a cabinet. "Just the Kraft kind. I also have some canned mushroom soup, tomato sauce and applesauce. I think mixing those together won't be very appetizing."

Bea came around the counter. Zach's position put his face even with the juncture of her legs and her heart started to race. She stepped back a few inches. "Perfect. Grab the mac and cheese box and the tomato sauce."

He obeyed and rose with the items in his hands.

She stepped back farther in an effort to concentrate on dinner instead of him, not an easy task. "Okay, I'm assuming you know how to make that." She pointed to the box of mac and cheese.

He raised a brow. "I did buy it so I can make it."

She widened her eyes in mock surprise. "Really? Great. Then you can get that started. We can make my mom's favorite comfort food. Macaroni and cheese pizza."

"You're shittin' me."

She laughed. "No, I'm not. Now if you have a long casserole dish…"

In no time she had everything she needed. As she opened her other ingredients, he stood at the stove. The whole domestic scene tugged at her resolve. As she feared, her attraction to him far exceeded a simple physical need. She liked him. A lot.

Once he finished his part, she put everything together and stuck it in the oven. "It'll need to bake for thirty-five minutes."

He raised his brows. "Can you wait that long?"

She shrugged, feeling a little shaky from hunger. "I'm not sure."

He opened a door on the kitchen island to reveal a wine cooler with a dozen bottles. "Red or white? I don't know what goes with what. I just drink what I like."

So, her beer-drinking hunk liked wine too. He kept getting better and better. "How about red then."

"Red it is. And if you open the cabinet behind you, you'll find crackers."

She brought out some wheat crackers and arranged them on a plate. "This will definitely do."

She looked up when he didn't respond and found him watching her. Her stomach tightened at his gaze, but he returned his attention to his task.

"Good." He uncorked the wine bottle and poured them each a glass, then led the way into the living room.

She followed and made herself comfortable on the couch. The fire spread a golden glow over the furniture and the warmth from burning logs made the room inviting and cozy.

He sat on the couch next to her, but allowed her space. She brought her leg up underneath her and took a sip of wine.

"You better have a few of these too." He held out the plate of crackers.

She nodded and took two.

"You wanted to know more about me. Ask away. This is a perfect opportunity." He sat with his forearms on his knees, angled toward her.

She swallowed hard. What she really wanted to know about was his love life, but she might give him the wrong impression. "How about this house? Did you build it? I mean, it's huge and I didn't realize loggers made that much. I mean, that didn't come out right. What I meant was—"

"That's okay. You're right, loggers don't make enough to build a house like this. I owned a logging company and sold it for a better profit than most would get."

She stroked the side of her glass. "Why? Was the buyer a city person who didn't realize what your company was worth?"

He smirked. "Not exactly. After I sold the company, I found this piece of land and knew in my gut that this house had to be built here. It took a year to complete, but it was worth the wait."

Bea perused the room because looking at him distracted her too much. "It really is a beautiful home. It's almost as large as another of the Larsen's properties, the Boat House Inn."

"Thank you, but it's not quite that big. I kept it very simple, large and open down here with smaller functional rooms upstairs."

She glanced at the stairs. His bedroom would be up there. Would he have a big, masculine, king-size bed? She could almost picture herself naked, spread-eagled as he slowly licked his way up the inside of her thighs before exploring the secret spaces around her opening and finally stopping to play with her clit. Yes, he would play for a long time. She took a gulp of wine, her blood heating.

He put his glass on the pine coffee table before he caught her gaze. "What about you? How long have you worked for the Larsens?"

She loved the color of his eyes. They were happy eyes with the appropriate lines in the corners. Her heart beat faster and she took another sip of wine. "Um, the Larsens?" She tried to concentrate on the conversation because the Larsens and her love life simply didn't belong in the same thought process.

She stared at her glass, stalling for time, trying desperately to get her mind back on the right track. "Let's see, it's been seven years now. When they arrived in town, they took me under their wing. They taught me all they knew about the hospitality business and encouraged my studies in that area. It took a long time and a lot of nights, but I finally earned my degree from the university this past December."

He leaned back on the couch, away from her. "Congratulations, that's quite an accomplishment. I imagine working and studying is hard. Being a logger is more of a 'learn on the job' type of career."

She noticed a tensing in his jaw. There was something about the experience he obviously didn't like. "How did you start with the carvings?"

He shrugged. "After I finished the house, I got bored. One day I was outside fooling around with my chainsaw and before I knew it, I had a six-foot carved bear staring back at me. But he wasn't very good company, so I brought him to Bear Tracks Bar. Tracy, the owner, loved him and gave me free beer for a month."

Zach's withdrawal concerned her. It was as if he wasn't concentrating on their conversation. "I would imagine the bear was worth a lot more than that."

He shook his head. "I don't think so. After a year, I gave her a better one. She had been telling people about me. With the roughed-out bear standing next to the entrance, more people started coming in for a beer and to find out how to get a bear. Next thing I knew, I was setting up shop and built the little cabin out on the driveway."

"Didn't you like your bear?"

He leaned forward. "Let's just say I got better with practice. That first bear was put to good use. I donated him for the town's Fourth of July bonfire."

She put down her wineglass. "It sounds as if he made the ultimate sacrifice for his country."

Zach chuckled. "Yeah, I guess he did. Never thought of it that way."

She liked his smile. He had deep lines etched around his mouth, probably because he smiled so much. How wonderful it must be to laugh as much as he did.

"Bea?"

She started, caught staring again.

"If you keep looking at me like that, you're going to find yourself naked on those sheepskins in no time."

She glanced at the beige softness before the now-roaring fire and shivered. She could imagine the feel of them against her naked skin.

"Come." Zach stood beside her, his hand outstretched.

Did he want her to get undressed? A shiver of anticipation raced across her skin. She took his hand, but didn't look at him as his warm palm heated her own.

He tipped her chin up. "We better check on dinner."

She met his gaze as realization dawned. "Of course, it should be done by now. I hope we didn't overcook it."

He led her into the kitchen, but instead of releasing her hand, he boxed her in against the island counter. "Bea, you need to accept that I will not take advantage of you. However, the chances of us making love tonight are at about one hundred percent. Don't you think?"

Her breath caught in her throat at the baldness of his statement, but she couldn't deny it. Her body completely agreed with him and from the weakening of her limbs and the hardening of her nipples, it was ready to prove him right—immediately. Slowly, she nodded.

His smile lit his face before he bent his head to pull her into a soul-searching kiss. She wound her arms around his neck and his hard body pressed her against the counter. As their tongues entwined, she forgot to breathe.

Abruptly, he stepped away and put his hands into his front pockets, a gesture she was coming to adore. He stared at her as if he had to make a life-changing decision, but then looked away.

He strode around to the stove and turned off the oven. He didn't glance at her. "I'm glad that's settled. Do me a favor and pour us more wine and I'll serve."

Breathless, she managed to nod at his back and went to the living room to retrieve their glasses.

Unsteadily, she poured their drinks and set them in front of the plates. He had put their plates across the table from each other instead of next to each other like he had the last time. Perplexed, she sat as he served.

He took his seat and without looking at her, dug in, but his eyes widened.

She paused with a forkful at the ready. "Is it okay?"

Zach looked at her as he chewed and winked. "This is good."

"You sound surprised."

He took a gulp of wine. "Well, you have to admit, using boxed macaroni and cheese to create a pizza doesn't sound…normal."

She crinkled her nose. "Hey, I grew up eating this, but I guess you're right."

"Of course I'm right."

"Oh please."

Zach laughed. He liked this woman. She was different from other lovers he'd had. Getting laid had never been a problem for him. Keeping it to no more than three times, his magic number, was tough, but it was for their own good. As much as he wanted a lifelong partner, his two deadly engagements had cured him of that dream.

They ate in companionable silence, something his parents often did. When he finished every single morsel, he sat back. "That was excellent."

A light blush rose in her cheeks. "I'm glad you enjoyed it. And you'll have some for tomorrow, if you want. Do you eat leftovers?"

He stood and picked up the plates. "All the time. I think cooking for one is a pain in the— Uh…so I make something big on the weekend and live off that for a few days. Afterward, it's catch as catch can. Bear Tracks Bar is usually the main catch."

Bea brought her wineglass and sat on the stool at the island counter behind him as he rinsed the dishes and loaded the dishwasher. He wished she'd sidle up against him instead of sitting on the stupid stool.

"If you only cook for one, does that mean you're between girlfriends right now?"

He paused before slipping the last dish into the rack. Subtle she wasn't. And it wouldn't be cool to explain he didn't have girlfriends per se. "You're pretty blunt, even for an Italian."

She shook her head. "Oh, I'm not Italian. I mean, yes, my name is and my Rappaccini ancestor was, but there have been so many nationalities in the family, I couldn't claim to be anything but a mutt."

He gazed at her. Black straight hair, prominent nose, deep-brown eyes and olive skin so smooth he never missed an opportunity to touch her. His brain screamed pure-blooded, hot Italian. "Well, I would guess there must have been more Italians than mutts in your background."

She broke eye contact, absently swirling the remaining wine in her glass. "That could be, but it would be difficult to know.

Just like it's difficult to know if you have someone special in your life at the moment. I mean, if you do, she wouldn't appreciate me being here."

The familiar gut reaction made him turn his back on her and move to the fridge. His "someone specials" had died. There was no way he'd risk having another one. "I don't cheat if that is what you're asking." He grabbed a beer, closed the door and faced her. "Do you?"

She squirmed in her seat and finished her wine before she answered. The pause made him wonder what she hid.

"No, I don't cheat. Actually, I haven't had anyone around long enough for that to be a possibility."

She looked him in the eye before she continued. "My one long-term relationship was with my first boyfriend. He went into a coma, but he came out of it. Thank God. I hope he found a great woman to marry. I know he's better off without me."

Zach's mind buzzed. She felt guilty her boyfriend went into a coma. Why? Did she cause his coma? Was there an accident? Maybe she could relate to what he'd been through and understand his limitation on their time together. He found himself wanting to know, but he didn't want to get serious right now. No, he wanted to get naked. He reached his hand out to her. "Come."

Gracefully, she rose from the stool and let him lead her into the living room. This time, when she sat on the couch, he sat next to her, putting his arm around her as they faced the fire. He leaned in to nibble on her ear. "I want you, Bea."

The tremor that passed through her body told him all he needed to know. Turning her head to face him, he initiated a kiss. No sooner had her tongue touched his then his cock hardened. At this rate it would all be over in five minutes, and he prided himself on his ability to please a woman. He forced himself to take control of his body while he enjoyed the sweet recesses of her mouth before nibbling a path down her soft neck. She smelled like oranges, and he inhaled deeply.

"Zach."

Bea's breathy whisper met his groan as he lifted his head away from her collarbone. "Yeah."

She refused to look at him, focusing instead on his cuff where she worried the material between her fingers. "I...I want..."

He brushed back the hair from her face and forced her to look at him. "Yes. You want me?"

Bea smiled shyly. "Could you take off your shirt? I want to see your chest again."

"Your wish is my command." Standing, he unbuttoned the flannel and threw it across to the other couch. "Better?"

She devoured him with her gaze. His chest appeared a golden brown in the fire's light and his pectorals looked harder than granite, dwarfing his dark, erect nipples. She licked her lips. "Are you cold?"

His seductive grin sent chills racing through her body, readying it for what was to come.

"No, I'm burning up. Want to feel?"

"Yes." She stood and ran her fingers through the short black hairs covering his contoured torso. They were so soft against the hardness of his muscles that she wanted to stroke his body for hours. She traced her fingers around his nipples, causing the tips to harden more. Her own nipples ached in response as she dropped her hands.

He took a deep breath, causing his chest to grow larger before her eyes until he released it. Following the dark line of hair with her gaze, she itched to slip her fingers into his blue jeans and cradle the hard cock that moved as she stared. Would it be long or thick or ruddy or crooked or—

"Your turn."

"What?" Startled from her focused concentration, she glanced up to see him raise his eyebrow.

"Fair's fair. I want to see you without your shirt."

Moisture seeped along her folds at his words. She wanted him as much as he wanted her, but in a much different way than her normal sex partners. Her attraction to him had nothing to do with her toxic body. Plus, she liked him. What could she do? She could refuse. He would respect her decision, but she wanted this. How could she keep him from coming inside her, from taking her poisons into his body? She didn't want to hurt him.

"Bea?"

She licked her lips and started to unbutton her sweater. Her mind raced as she let the garment drop on the couch. Hungry for him like no other man she'd been with, she searched for a solution. She pulled the dainty camisole over her head and stood in her lacy pink bra.

He lost his grin as his gaze feasted on her cleavage.

She had to think, but his look, combined with the moisture between her legs, made it difficult for her mind to cooperate.

He gazed into her eyes. "Take off your bra."

Her heart beat so fast she had a difficult time breathing. Placing her hand between her breasts to calm herself, she unhooked the front clasp of her Fredrick's bra. His gaze riveted to where her hands separated the two cups, and she shrugged herself out of them.

"You're beautiful, like the snowfall. Delicate, soft and perfectly formed."

Her heart melted at his words, but she remained still, wanting his hands upon her, and yet afraid of the fire he started within her.

He stepped closer and massaged her breasts as if he knew they had been uncomfortable in their confines. When he touched her areolas, stroking until the skin puckered into ridges, he caused her nipples to harden to painful tips. She ached inside her core for this man's cock. She wanted him to the hilt, filling her.

He groaned. "I could eat you right here."

The image of his handsome face between her legs nearly buckled her knees.

That was it! She could let him lick her to orgasm, an activity she had no time to enjoy with her other lovers. It shouldn't hurt him too much since he wouldn't be inside her and she still had a few days before having intercourse was a necessity. Her quandary solved, she relaxed and smirked. "What are you waiting for?"

"Ah Bea, you're a wet dream come true."

Whether it was his words or the first flick of his tongue on her breast, she wasn't sure, but her body responded, her pussy leaking into her thong. His tongue sent exquisite pings of pleasure to her nipple, and the connection between it and her pussy was alive and well. She grabbed his shoulder as she swayed.

He moved his mouth to her other breast, nipped at the tip, swirled the nipple with his tongue and sucked gently. She moaned at the sharp excitement he created and her knees weakened.

He grabbed her to him, his breath heavy in her ear. She could feel the bulge in his jeans pressing against her above her mons.

She tried to inch herself higher, desperate to feel him rub her clit, but he turned her to face the fire. He reached around to hold her breasts, one in each hand as he nibbled at her neck.

He murmured against her skin, "You're so smooth, you glow in the firelight."

His fingers found her nipples and rolled them lightly. She let her head drop back against his shoulder as the lightning pleasure he produced raced downward, engorging her pussy. He moved his hand over her stomach and into the waistband of her jeans, headed for her thong.

She let her knees bend away in mortification. What would he think of her if he felt how truly soaked she'd become? But he followed her down to the floor, down to the sheepskin.

He chuckled against her back as they knelt there. "Oh no, you're not getting away from me that easily." He pressed his cock into her lower back, above her ass.

She turned her head to speak to him. "I wasn't trying to get away. You made my knees weak."

He nuzzled against the back of her ear, his fingers continuing their homage to her nipples. "Perfect, I like your knees weak."

She couldn't focus with his teeth making little bites along her neck, producing exquisite goose bumps across her skin. "Zach?"

"Hmmm?"

"Wouldn't the furs feel nicer if we didn't have our jeans on?"

He stopped nibbling and pulled back. "Definitely."

Before she could blink, he jumped up, unzipped his jeans and his cock sprang forward, freed from the denim. He stepped from his pants, completely naked.

The man didn't wear underwear. Very sexy. And his straight, thick cock stood at attention, begging for her touch. She reached for him, but he caught her hand before she made contact. He raised his eyebrow. "Fair's fair."

"Okay, but I'll need both hands."

He squeezed first, then let her go. She turned her back on him and faced the fire. Quickly, so he wouldn't see her moisture, she unzipped her pants and pulled her thong and jeans down her butt. Then sitting on the luscious fur, she wiggled the clothes off past her feet.

He knelt beside her, pulled the garments from her hand and threw them on the couch behind him. "If you really want to feel the furs, lie back."

The promise in his eyes told her she wouldn't be disappointed, so she let the softness of the fur envelop her. She didn't expect the erotic feel of it between her legs. "Oh."

He winked at her surprise. "Feels sexy, doesn't it?"

She nodded, unable to speak at the knowing tone in his voice. How many other women had he made love to on these skins? *Stop it.* She had no right. If he had an inkling of the number of men she'd had sex with, he would throw her out in the snow.

He lay next to her on his side. "What is it, Bea?"

"Nothing. Just surprised at how well you know me already."

He smirked as he brushed her hair out over the fur. "I know very little about you, but I hope by the end of the night, I'll know a lot more."

Her body vibrated with a need he caused, and liquid seeped from between her legs and onto her inner thighs. He leaned over and kissed her forehead, her nose and finally her lips, but when her tongue begged for entry into his mouth, he refused. Instead, he trailed licks and nips down her neck.

She pushed her hand through his thick hair and guided him to her nipple, which received the attention her mouth had craved. After causing one peak to be so hard she ached between her legs, he moved to the other, giving it equal attention and an extra bite that sent an electric pulse racing to her clit.

She kneaded her hands into his shoulder muscles as he licked his way to her navel, the seeping between her legs now a constant. Her pussy's anticipation of his mouth had it swelling beyond anything it had ever done. Her heart beat for his kiss, his touch.

He licked her waist and sucked on her hipbone before he moved his hands to spread her legs. As he brought his palms along the insides of her limbs, he stopped. "You're bare."

She could only nod. She kept herself hairless to encourage her one-night stands.

He smirked. "And wet." His thumbs played along the crease of her thighs just outside her throbbing labia.

Her body's instinct for survival always made her ready, but the liquid moistening her thighs now was new. Would he think it strange she was so wet? "I know. You did that to me." Her voice came out husky, sexy.

He quirked a brow at her. "Really?"

Anticipation tightened her throat, making her answer in no more than a whisper, "Yes."

"Then you're going to like this."

He pulled her folds apart and lowered his head. His tongue touched her opening, gliding over it to settle on her clit. Sharp pulses of excitement raced deep into her core. His tongue camped there, laving her back and forth, swirling around her nub, until his mouth covered her. The creative sucking on her clit had her body bowed, strung taut, the pleasure building. She grabbed his hair to push him down even as her hips came up of their own accord.

The sucking stopped with a flat swipe of his tongue and she whimpered, left on the edge of a growing orgasm.

But Zach wasn't finished. His tongue moved lower and the licking continued with a stronger purpose as he reached her opening. His tongue delved inside.

She couldn't think. She moaned as she released his head and gripped the sheepskin beneath her, the soft touch adding to her helpless pleasure. To feel him inside her, this man and only this man, would be heaven. If only it could be.

By the time he worked his way back to her clit, she felt lightheaded from his expert ministrations. Her breaths were short and she couldn't help begging as he held her on the edge, too desperate for release and air. "Please, Zach, I need… Oh God."

Zach's tongue stroked her clit, circling, licking the tiny pleasure point over and over. Then he slipped two fingers inside her.

She came with a scream that would've frightened Canada geese away. Her body bucked and writhed as her release pounded through her and she gasped for breath. The sensation had her vision collapsing to small points as all feeling centered on her bliss. Zach kept her on the pinnacle of her orgasm until her spasms relaxed and her heartbeat slowed. She grabbed his hair and pulled his head up, despite her hips grinding against his hand.

Zach grinned from ear to ear. When he caught her watching, he licked his lips and wiped his chin. "I think you're ready now."

Chapter Four

Bea laughed, letting her head fall back upon the furs. Zach crawled up her body and she tried not to drool as his defined chest came over her. But as his cock brushed her inner thigh, she scrambled from underneath him like a crab. She hated leaving the place she wanted to be more than anywhere else, but what she wanted wasn't enough to outweigh her need to keep him healthy. As it was, she didn't know how sick he might become with her juices soaking into his fingers.

He grumbled. "Hey, where are you going?"

She brought herself to kneel in front of his push-up position. His gaze went to her lap.

She lifted his face to look at her. "Fair's fair."

He chuckled. "I guess it is." He collapsed upon his stomach and rolled onto his back, away from the fire.

As much as she wanted to crawl on top of him and experience a sixty-nine position, she couldn't. She could almost feel his strong cock pushing into her mouth, his hips rising reflexively as his tongue penetrated her pussy, stroking her clit, while her breasts brushed his hard abs. No, she wouldn't chance him sucking on her poisons. Maybe next time they could do it before she came. Next time?

She shook her head as she crawled around him, the soft fur of the sheepskins making her want to roll her naked body across them. When she'd positioned herself between his legs, she paused to take in the view.

His face and chest appeared to move as the firelight flickered across them, transforming his sexy smirk into a grin and back again. His cock moved too, but not with light. As she stared, it jumped toward his belly in short jerks.

"Bea?"

She gazed into his smoldering eyes. "Mmm-hmm."

He swallowed. "If you keep looking at me like that, I'll come without you touching me at all. I'd rather feel your mouth on me."

At his words, excitement played havoc with her stomach. She put her hand to her chin as if pondering the dilemma, but gradually sank between his legs. Her first lick was along the underside of his hard penis. It jerked again as if trying to get away. She bent lower and took one of his balls into her mouth, using her tongue to roll it, test the weight of it. She did the same to the other, thinking of how he had sucked on her nipples. A warmth spread through the folds between her legs.

Pressing her tongue between his balls, she stroked upward over his cock and took the tip into her mouth. She could lick him all night, a luxury she never had the time for with her one-night stands. Those were about her need to survive, but with Zach, she wanted to make him feel good, make him happy.

His hand rested on her shoulder, its tension telling her he anticipated her next move.

She ran her tongue around the ridge of his cock before moving her teeth along the edges.

The pressure of his hand increased.

With her teeth, she stroked down his length, lightly scraping his tight skin.

He groaned.

Pleased he was enjoying her attention, she stroked down again and without warning, she sucked in his tip, bringing his whole cock into her mouth.

His hand on her shoulder shifted to the floor as it fisted.

Beneath her mouth, she palmed his balls, his sac tight and ready. Rolling them within her hand, she ran her mouth up, enjoying the feel of every bump against her tongue. She glanced at his face as her teeth hooked on his tip again.

His closed eyes and rigid jaw testified to the pleasure building inside him. As she sucked down on his cock and up again, his lips parted. His chest rose and fell rapidly. His excitement fueled her own and wetness dripped along her thigh to nestle on the furs beneath her. She couldn't help herself as she increased the rhythm. He buried his hand in her hair and she felt his pulse beat against her tongue. He was close.

Triumph spread warmth throughout her body. She took his hard cock deep into her throat and tightened her jaw. His thighs closed against her face and his hips arched into her mouth as his cum squirted inside, sliding down her throat. She wrapped her tongue around him as she moved, and sucked until his hand on her head stopped her.

She satisfied herself with licking him clean.

The fire gave off very little light, so she sat up to see his reaction. She'd never had a man come in her mouth before since she always needed to orgasm with someone inside her to take the poison from her body and into theirs. She wouldn't mind another orgasm right now, not because she needed to, but because she wanted this man deep within her.

"Hell."

She froze. "What's wrong?"

"I came."

Bea laughed. She didn't remember laughing while having sex before. "Wasn't that the whole idea?"

He opened his eyes and lifted his head. His stomach muscles contracted into hard ripples that reminded her of frost heaves. His gaze roamed her body. "Yes, but I wanted to bury my cock deep inside your pussy."

Uh-huh. As much as she wanted that too, she couldn't let it happen. She shrugged. "Oh well. Guess you'll have to make do."

He dropped his head back to the floor and closed his eyes. "I think you're right, you wore me out."

She stood and drank in the sight of his body, hard even when he relaxed. "Before you go to sleep, can you point me in the direction of a bed?"

He opened one eye. "How about here on the furs next to me?"

Her heart leapt, excitement flaring, and a drop of her wetness ran down the inside of her thigh. To cuddle in the furs with this man would be heaven. Could she? Her logical side stepped in. No. She had limited willpower with him. If she let him inside her, she could never see him again, and she very much wanted to see him again.

She shook her head.

He opened his other eye and followed the telltale drop of her juices as it hit the crease of her knee before continuing down the side of her calf. "So that's a yes?"

She shivered at the hunger in his eyes, but stood fast. "No."

His gaze returned to hers, his resignation clear.

Disappointment and relief tornadoed through her.

He closed his eyes. "Upstairs to the left is a guestroom."

"Great. Thanks."

She tiptoed around him to pick up her clothes, throwing on her sweater against the cooling air. She turned toward the stairs, but his resting body in the light of the dying fire stopped her cold. What was it about him that had her heart pulsing to life along with her libido? She'd had many, many men, but he was unique, at least to her.

Unsure what to make of her attraction, she passed between

him and the fire. The air in the room had cooled, causing her to tense. She stopped and grabbed a log and threw it on the fire. Sparks sprayed everywhere, one jumping the fire screen and landing on Zach's arm.

He jerked awake, sitting up. "Ow!"

She jumped back from the dangerous little missiles herself, her bare heel catching his thigh.

As she fell backward, his arms came around and he rolled with her, slowing her fall. He lay half on top of her, his chest pushing against her covered breasts.

He grimaced. "I take it you've never had a fireplace."

She shook her head, unable to speak at the heat building within her from both embarrassment and desire.

He brushed the hair from her neck and cupped her cheek. "You're a handful, Bea."

Her breath caught at the desire in his eyes. No grin softened his lips. The purpose in his face changed the heat in her body to a roaring fire. His hand on her cheek tensed as he positioned her face for his kiss. At the touch of his lips, she breathed again, his strong, silent command demanded she open her mouth and let him in. Giving up, she twined her tongue with his, wrapping her arms around him and pulling him hard against her body. As he devoured her mouth, the touch of his hardening cock next to her thigh caused pulses of excitement to streak through her body, tightening her inner muscles.

She moved one hand to rifle through his hair, its thick softness similar to the furs at her back. Her mind and body acquiesced to his demands. When his hand left her face and burrowed under her sweater to hold her breast and thumb her sensitive nipple, she moaned in sheer helpless pleasure. To let him have his way with her, however he chose, was a heady turn-on and she floundered in the fantasy.

This was what she'd been missing, to abandon herself to the

ecstasy. His hand reached between her legs, his finger found her clit and circled it as if exploring it for the first time. His touch sent her juices flowing.

The kiss continued, not urgent but controlled, his total mastery of her undeniable. As his tongue swept through her mouth, so did his finger play upon her, building her anticipation, winding her up. Helplessly, she spread her legs wider, pushing her thigh against his swollen cock, her hips thrusting and retreating from his skilled hand. She wanted him to do what he would and gave up her own will in the process as the tension between her legs built.

He played her like a master puppeteer, but with no teasing this time. Her blood raced to the spot where his fingertips rubbed, building and catching fire. He had a goal and he would bring her to it, a full conflagration. His tongue thrust into her mouth, becoming demanding even as his strokes against her clit changed cadence and her pleasure intensified, increasing until arching her hips against him, her orgasm burst upon her.

He caught her scream in his mouth and his finger stopped its movement to press her throbbing nub, holding her on top of her release until he decreased the pressure. He released her mouth and placed a gentle kiss on her open lips before leaving a peck on her cheek. She gulped in precious air as her heart tried to find its normal rhythm. A strange weariness infused her body, weakened her limbs and refused to allow her to open her eyes. Giving herself up to the unusual sensation, she drifted into a comfortable slumber.

Zach couldn't stop touching the hot beauty in his arms. He played with the black strands of hair resting in his palm. Though his cock ached for release, he wouldn't wake her. The way she responded to him confused him.

He'd had his share of lovers, but none had reacted to his sexual skills quite the way she did. None had completely shaved their pussies either. Hell, that was hot. He'd seen hairless labia in porno movies but never in person. Bea's differences didn't end there either. None of his past women had sex with him so soon.

It would be hard to split with her. He wasn't sure that three times would be enough, but he couldn't let her get too close. For some reason fate didn't want him to have a permanent someone in his life and had proved it with Danielle and Lisa. He would have to stay on guard. But there was a sweetness beneath the professional distance Bea occasionally created. And despite her obvious sexual experience, he found her naïve in a strange way.

It didn't matter. He planned to enjoy this temporary relationship for all it was worth and keep both his and her hearts out of it.

Letting go of Bea's hair, he lay back next to her and pulled the sheepskins over them. The warmth from the fire had transferred to the furs and enveloped them in a warm cocoon. He glanced at the fireplace. Not much wood left, but he sure as hell wasn't getting up. They would be cold come morning, but they could always have sex again to produce more heat.

He had worn her out. He grinned as he closed his eyes. Despite a six-month hiatus from sex, he still had it. And he would use it every chance he got.

~~*~~

Bea stretched, luxuriating in the softness that surrounded her body until her toes slipped from beneath the covering. She yanked her foot back under the…fur? She opened her eyes. Oh damn.

Zach had little issue with the cold. He lay on his back, his entire torso and one knee exposed to the living room air. His chest rose and fell in even rhythm. Grateful he still slept, she lifted his hand, which lay possessively on her thigh, and wriggled out from under the sheepskins.

The cool air shocked her and she bent to retrieve her clothes, but when she stood again, she stilled. The sight outside the living room windows captured her breath. If a definition of "winter wonderland" were posted online, the sight before her would be the perfect image. No words needed to define it. The snow sparkled in the morning sunshine, twinkling on every buried branch, rock and banister. The forest valley below proved at least three more feet of snow had fallen overnight and only the sharpest incline escaped its burden. The trees bent low with their loads, one white birch making a perfect arch that reminded her of a wedding bower. She gazed at the scene, enthralled. A hump of snow fell from its precarious branch and drifted in a sparkling cloud to the ground. She shivered at the cold and turned to find the bedroom Zach told her about.

His voice from the floor startled her. "It's amazing, isn't it?"

She looked down at him. No, he was amazing, in so many ways. Lying there on the sheepskins, his hands beneath his head, his biceps pulled taut by his position, had her wishing for a different life. She loved it here with him, but she had limits and the bulge beneath the fur was a clear indication of what he had in mind.

"You have a beautiful place here, Zach. I'd love to stay longer, but I have to go to work. I'm already late and it's always crazy after a snowfall. You know, digging out guests, helping them find other flights or extending their stay, having the porch and walkways cleared…"

She paused, sensing his withdrawal. She tried a different tact and gave him a knowing smirk. "Today is Thursday and as much as I'd like to crawl in there with you, some of us have to work."

His face lightened a little and she breathed easier. She didn't want him upset with her.

He sat up, his stomach muscles tightening as he threw the skins aside. "Okay. I'll start the fire and find you some breakfast. Coffee?"

About to shake her head, instinct kicked in and she nodded.

When she did, he relaxed and turned his back to her to set up a fire in the cold fireplace.

She hesitated as he bent over, his tight butt, smooth, pale and perfect, called to her. *No.* If she wanted any more of him, she had to leave, and the sooner, the less painful. Striding across the room, she raced up the stairs and found the guestroom. She dropped her clothes on the bed and strode into the bathroom.

She stopped and took in the enormity of it. A person could have an orgy in the tub. It was the size of a small pool and sunken into the pine floor. The skylight above it mirrored its size. Next to it stood a tiled shower with no curtain. She closed the bathroom door and locked it, which didn't make sense considering how much Zach and she had done already. This was a new experience for her, this "morning after". Whatever it took for her to muddle through it, she would do, even if it meant locking out the nicest man she'd ever met.

Zach strolled into Bear Tracks and took a seat at the bar. Old George sat at the end as usual and a young couple claimed the corner.

"Hey, Zach. Great game last night. Thanks for the hundred bucks!"

He looked over to see Randy, Steve and Billy lifting their glasses to him.

He waved. "Yeah, it's the least I could do. With that new baby comin', I thought you'd need more cash."

Steve frowned, but Randy and Billy thought the comment hilarious. They had been here a while, probably since happy hour had begun. Zach checked his watch. Eight o'clock.

"Hey, Zach, how's it going?" Tracy plopped a tall draft of Bud Light in front him. Wisps of her gray-streaked brown hair fell into her eyes.

He glanced up into her lined faced and gave her a smile. "It's going, with or without me."

"Ain't that the truth." She jerked her head toward the main room. "Heard you lost a little money at your poker game last night."

He shrugged. "Yeah, but don't worry, I've got enough left over for a few beers."

She propped her foot on the drying rack behind the counter and leaned closer. "You better. So, you want munchies to go with that?"

"Yeah, you better make us some moose balls. Josh is coming and he loves those things."

She stood back. "You've got it. One order of fried testicles coming up."

He chuckled. "Better fried than mashed."

She laughed as she punched the order into the computer and disappeared into the kitchen.

He took a taste of beer. He should install a tap in the house. Beer on tap was so much smoother, but if he did, he would never have a reason to leave his place.

The door to the bar opened, letting in a gust of frigid air as Dr. Joshua Porter ducked under the doorframe and walked in. "Made it."

Zach shook his head. "Late again. Guess you have to buy."

"I'm not late." He took the barstool next to Zach. "This is early for me."

Zach raised a brow. "Hate to tell you this, Josh, but you said 7:30. It's 8:12."

Josh raised his brows. "Damn, I'm good. Less than an hour late."

Tracy approached. "Michelob Ultra, Doc?"

Josh put a finger to his lips. "Shhh, it's just Josh. I'm off duty."

"Whatever you say, Josh."

"That's my girl. What's new, Tracy?"

"Not much, grandchild due in a month and the ex is playing mind games, so basically the same old, same old. How about you?"

Josh bowed his head in an attempt for sympathy. "The usual, working too hard."

Tracy smacked his arm with a bar rag. "Yeah, right. Zach, you got a lying sack of shit for a friend."

He sighed. "I know."

Josh took a gulp of beer as Tracy moved away to wash glasses. "Hmmm, that's good. Thanks for inviting me. I needed an excuse to get out of the lab. What's up?"

Zach took another swallow of beer. "Nothin'."

"Don't give me that shit. It's not hunting season and the ice fishing derby is over, so it must be personal."

Zach shifted in his seat. His friend knew him too well. "Hey, I usually invite you when there's something to keep you entertained. It's not as if my life is that exciting. But I figured, what the hell."

"Mmm-hmm and I'm a crab apple tree. Zach, we've known each other for more than thirty years now. What's up?"

Zach wiped the sweat from his beer glass. "I guess it's a woman."

"You guess?"

"Yeah, I guess. I just met her Monday."

Josh counted on his fingers. "You've known her five days and already you think she's special? That's not your usual *modus operandi.*"

Zach took another gulp of beer. "My what? Never mind, I don't think I want to know. And I didn't say she was special. The thing is, we met on Monday, had mind-blowing sex on Wednesday and I haven't heard from her since."

Josh let out a low whistle. "Sounds like a one-night stand to me, but your limit is three, so you want your two more, don't you?"

Zach looked away.

"Ah, that's it. It's fine for you to call it quits but not her. Okay, I get it. So did you call her?"

Zach shook his head.

Josh tipped his beer and swallowed. "Oh man, you're kidding me. You have some hottie, she is a hottie right, 'cause you always get hotties, and you haven't called her?"

Zach kept silent. His friend, with his elongated face and thin six-foot-four frame resembled Lurch from *The Addams Family* and didn't catch many dates, despite being a doctor and a great scientist.

Josh finished his beer and signaled to Tracy for two more. "I'm flattered you called me, but there's a simple solution to this dilemma, Zach. You know what it is, but for some reason you aren't acting on it. You don't need a biochemical doctorate to know you need to pick up your phone and call her."

Zach took the beer Tracy handed him and watched the foam disintegrate. Great, now he'd insulted Josh's intelligence and still didn't have the guts to call her. "Isn't she supposed to call me? That's usually what happens. You know, women are much more vocal about what they want. If she hasn't called me, obviously she doesn't want to see me again."

Josh set his beer down with a thud, foam sloshed over the side and puddled on the bar. "Wake up, man. Even I know every woman is different. If you want to see her, call her. If you don't, I guarantee you'll never see her again."

Josh could be right. Bea was confident and insecure at the same time. Maybe she was old-fashioned and needed him to call her. "You're right, I'll call her now."

"Good man. While you do that, I'm going to troll for chicks."

Zach pointed across the room. "Uh, Josh, if you want to do that, we'd better go somewhere else."

Josh looked around the small bar.

Zach chuckled as realization dawned on his friend's face. There were maybe fifteen cocktail tables with chairs and the bar. In total there were eighteen men and one woman—the lady at the bar was part of a couple if the way she had her leg on her companion's lap was any indication. The old "make her come at the bar in public" scenario going on. He'd like to do that with Bea. The thought caused his cock to pay attention. Hell. Grabbing his phone, he stalked outside.

The air was sharp and fresh, but cold, so he zipped his hoody. He pulled his wallet from his back pocket and fished out Bea's card. The ever present white Christmas lights on the bar's porch gave him enough light to read her phone number. He dialed and held his breath.

"Good evening, Lakeside Inn, Beatrice Rappaccini."

"What are you doing there so late?" Okay, maybe not the best beginning.

"Huh? Zach, is that you?"

He couldn't help being concerned. "Yeah, why are you working so late?"

She didn't answer him, but he could hear her talking to someone else. Was that a male voice? She had moved on already?

"Hi, I'm sorry, Jared needed to know what he should do now that the bridal reception had consumed all their preordered wine, but I guess you don't really care about that, do you?"

He relaxed. What an idiot he was for jumping to the worst-case scenario. "I don't know. It could be interesting."

She chuckled. "Trust me, it's not. But it's been very busy here and the Larsens are out of town so I'm handling all three inns. I guess it's good experience. At least, that's what I keep telling myself. Still, I'm looking forward to their return."

He paced to the end of the porch. "When will that be?"

"Tomorrow morning, thank God. I swear, as soon as I fill them in on what they missed, I'm crawling into my own bed for a long sleep."

A sinking feeling grabbed hold of his gut. "Oh, so I guess getting together tomorrow wouldn't be good for you."

"I'm sorry, Zach. Tomorrow evening I promised my mom I'd come for dinner."

He nodded to a couple of guys as they passed him to enter the bar. "Well, you shouldn't disappoint your mom. I don't want her to have a bad impression of me."

"Are you kidding? My mom would love you. Actually…"

The silence lasted too long. Zach checked his phone. Did he lose the signal? Wouldn't be the first time among the hills, but nope, he still had service. "Bea? Actually what?"

"If you like, you could come with me. That is if you want. I can't guarantee it will be comfortable, but it will be interesting."

His heart skipped a beat. Meet her mom? This girl moved fast. Was he reading too much into this? "Sure, I'd be happy to. Where does she live?" Hell, what was he thinking?

"She lives in Wrenborough, that's right in between us, so why don't I meet you? Let's say the Wrenborough Depot at five?"

Zach leaned against one of the porch posts. "I can do that. But why do you say the evening will be interesting?" She didn't answer, but he could hear someone else speaking to her, this time a female.

She brought her attention back to him. "Trust me, it's always interesting because I never know which father will be there. Listen, I have to run. See you tomorrow."

"Okay."

She ended the call.

Zach clipped his phone back on his belt and shook his head. She didn't say "which father" did she?

Striding back into the bar, he found Josh chewing contently on moose balls. Zach picked up the basket with two balls left. "Mind if I have some?"

Josh shook his head. "Nope, I'm full."

Zach took a swallow of beer and popped the two balls into his mouth. The tangy taste of pineapple and seasoned moose meat glided across his tongue. A few more would have been nice. He gave Josh a disgruntled look.

Josh ignored it. "Did you talk to Mystery Woman?"

"Yeah, I'm going to see her tomorrow night."

Josh slammed his hand on the bar. "See, what'd I tell ya? I'm a genius."

Zach shook his head. "I think your Harvard degree already made that clear, Josh, but thanks for the nudge. What do you say we hit another place? It's the least I can do. We need to find you a mystery woman too."

Josh polished off his beer. "Yeah, good luck with that."

Bea plopped onto the office chair and closed her eyes. She opened one to check the time. Three in the morning. Technically tomorrow, but she couldn't rest until the Larsens returned.

The evening had gone perfectly for all the guests and special occasions, but for the staff, it had been tough. She must be managing the business incorrectly. That or she'd been lucky to land a crazy night. Either way, she'd done it.

Sitting up, she opened her eyes and looked at the desk filled with paper and started to organize. She found the day's mail under a band contract for an event next week and sorted through it.

She came to an envelope with "To Bea Rappaccini" typed on the outside. That was strange. One of her friends must have dropped it off for her. Curious, she slit it open and unfolded the single page enclosed.

I know your secret.

Huh? What did that mean? She turned the page over. It was blank. Okay, this was strange. What secret? She didn't have any secrets. She had one big secret, but no one could know… She dropped the letter, her breath catching in her throat as a shiver sped up her spine. No. No one could know about her poisonous nature. No way. Yet her fear persisted.

Had she been followed? But even then, a person couldn't know. The only people who knew her secret were her mother, her six fathers and Grandma Beatrice. And the only one of that lot who might be upset would be her father Jim, a headhunter by trade and from what her mom said, quite wealthy. They had no communication with him, but then why would he write her a letter like this? He may have been angry about sharing her mom years ago, but that had nothing to do with her.

Shaking her head, she put the letter back in the envelope and stuffed it in her purse. It was probably a friend joking around about her upcoming birthday. She made it a big secret every year. Yes, that's all it was.

She didn't buy her own conclusion, but what could she do? If someone wanted to threaten her by exposing her unique genetic problem, sending a letter with no instructions didn't accomplish anything.

Great, just what she needed, another pool of water she had no idea how to swim in. First, she had her strange attraction and feelings for Zach and now a mysterious message. The letter left her no recourse but to wait and see what happened. But Zach she would see again tomorrow night and was sure to mess that up. Except for Phillip, her high-school boyfriend, she'd never been on a second date or brought a man to Mom's house.

What she needed was advice. She scanned the semi-organized desk and decided it looked good enough. Kayla had the night shift. Though a few years younger than herself, Kayla had been in many long-term relationships, including an engagement. She had to know how it all worked.

Bea turned out the light and headed for the lobby counter,

hoping no more customers would check in at such an early hour. Kayla would get off at five this morning. Bea had a feeling she would need the next two hours to learn as much as she could on how to do the dating thing.

Chapter Five

Zach spun the steering wheel in the opposite direction as his truck slid across the entrance to the parking lot of the Wrenborough Depot. The large patch of black ice took all control away. Catching clear dirt, he hit the brakes before slowly driving to the side of the building. What shitty weather. The melt-off from the snowstorm had streams appearing out of nowhere and the thirty-degree temperatures didn't help. He hoped Bea drove more cautiously. What happened to spring? At this rate, he'd have another whole month to carve the birch tree for the inn.

He glanced at the clock in his truck. Early as usual. He must be crazy to meet the mother of a woman he'd known for five days. He hadn't met a parent of a woman since Lisa's, and the last time he'd seen them was at Lisa's funeral, closed casket. He shut down those thoughts fast.

Zach tapped his fingers on the steering wheel. And then there was the question of her fathers. She must have a stepdad, but why wouldn't she know which dad would be at her mother's house? If her stepfather lived with her mother, wouldn't he be there? Zach shook his head. Everything about this woman intrigued him.

Was it Bea or their chemistry that had their relationship racing at warp speed? Not that it was a relationship. Though he had to admit meeting the parents indicated that. Why did he say yes? Maybe he should leave. Standing her up was better than sending her the wrong signals. He had been too anxious to see her again. He should have waited until tomorrow.

As headlights shined across his window, his gut tensed. No getting out of it now. Bea's blue Camry negotiated the driveway and came safely into the parking lot. Good girl.

His pulse raced as the streetlight shone through her windshield and illuminated her face. He forgot all about meeting her parents and remembered only her passionate responses to his touch.

She stepped out as he jumped from his truck. The sight of her after two days was like honey to a starving black bear.

She walked toward him. "Sorry I'm late."

He closed the distance between them in a heartbeat and wrapped her in his arms. "No problem. You make it worth the wait."

He pressed his lips against hers before he slipped his tongue inside and reveled in the taste of…strawberry mint? He lost the question as she molded her body against his and released the softest of whimpers.

She pulled her mouth from his and laid her head on his chest. "I wish I didn't have to see my mom tonight."

He stroked her hair, enjoying its fine thickness. "I'm sure she's looking forward to the visit."

She shivered against him.

He eased her back. "Come on, you're cold, and I believe we're already late." He started to lead her toward his truck.

She pulled away. "Wait, I have to turn off my car."

He turned. "Why did you leave it on?"

She opened the door and took her keys from the ignition before she answered. "Habit. I'm always driving myself. This is a treat for me to be driven."

What he'd like to do was drive her right into another orgasm. His truck did have a large bench seat and he could cover her with his own body so no one could see her if they got caught. He could easily picture pulling her pants down over her ass and unzipping his jeans to squeeze his cock between her legs.

Hell, he needed to focus. But once the scene was in his head, he couldn't stop the wave of wanting that accompanied it, or the hardening of his cock. Instead of acting on his impulse, he opened the passenger door and helped her climb into the truck, enjoying the sight of her long legs clothed in tight red jeans with matching high heels. The woman was certifiably hot.

He closed the door and strode around the truck, sucking in deep breaths of frosty air to clear his senses of her intoxicating smell. She wore a type of citrus scent, perfect for lying on the beach naked, which didn't help the tightness of his jeans.

As he opened his driver's door, he made some adjustments, jumped in and started the engine.

She patted the seat next to him. "What model truck is this?"

"A Chevy Silverado."

"It's really big. Four-wheel drive?"

He stared at her. She eyed his truck like she eyed him—with lust. His cock hardened further, actually becoming painful. "Yeah, I use it to plow in the winter. It's good at pushing a lot of snow."

"I bet." She turned her gaze on him and he wanted to take her. Now. Ah hell, he was supposed to be meeting the parents, for Christ's sake.

He cleared his throat. "Where are we headed?"

She broke eye contact and peered out the window. "Continue down Center Street and then we'll take a right."

"Got it." He pulled the truck onto the road, carefully navigating around the ice at the exit.

From the corner of his eye, he caught her reaching for the door handle while her eyes focused on the road. Okay, he'd have to behave on the road tonight. She was a nervous passenger.

She let go of the handle once they hit dry pavement and faced him. "There's something I should tell you about my mother."

He kept his attention on the road. "Let me guess. She's gorgeous, but of course she is. And she's dyslexic. No, she's missing a finger. No wait, she loves eating dinner in the snow."

Bea laughed, the sound filling him with pleasure. "No, but you're getting close."

He smiled, wishing he could keep the moment alive longer. "Zach?"

"Yeah, so what do I need to know about your mom?"

"She was born in the 1960s and has kept that decade alive and well, even though she's now in her fifties." Bea pointed. "Take a right here."

Zach turned down the curvy hill. "So are you saying she's into peace, free love and burning bras?"

"Exactly. Only it isn't so pretty at her age, if you know what I mean."

Zach focused as they glided across a good-sized patch of black ice, Bea's life fascinating him more by the minute. "That's not too bad. You should meet my friend Josh's mom. You'd think you were meeting the mummy."

"That's not nice."

Zach shrugged. "Not really. I say it with complete affection. What's your mom's name?"

"Susan."

He winked at her. "Not Hope or Willow?"

"Nope, just Susan. She was named after the flower Black-eyed Susan. Take a left here."

Zach turned the truck and Bea leaned forward, her white fashionable parka hiding her curvy body. He appreciated the view of her classic profile.

Her long fingers grasped the dash. "You'd think they'd have

streetlights around here. But Mom should have a light on. It's six houses up on the right."

He brought his mind back to the evening ahead of him. "Did you say your father would be here?"

"Yeah, one of them." She pointed. "There, it's that one."

Zach turned. "What do you mean, one of them?"

He couldn't see it, but he could sense her flush. "It's kind of embarrassing. You were right when you asked if my mom was into free love. When she conceived me, she had six lovers."

"What? You mean you don't know which of the six is your dad?"

The motion detector spotlight went off on the garage as he brought the truck to a stop in the driveway, illuminating Bea's sheepish face. "Yeah, and Mom won't find out because five of them want to be my father, so she invites them to the house at different times, except Jim and Charlie. They're married."

The front door of the house opened and a woman descended the steps.

"There she is. That's Mom." Bea scrambled from the truck and hurried across the driveway to hug her parent.

Zach tried to wrap his mind around the six-father issue as he approached, but the idea of having to play nice to six fathers had his neck tensing and his jaw grinding.

"Mom, this is Zach."

Her mom held out her leather-encased arms, six inches of fringe hung from her jacket sleeves. "Zach, it's so nice to meet you."

Her round, warm face welcomed him. He didn't hesitate, but walked into the older woman's embrace and found himself the recipient of a soft bear hug, his cheek brushing against her brown, frizzy hair. He stepped back. She didn't resemble her daughter at all. "It's nice to meet you too, Mrs. Rappaccini."

"Please, I'm no Mrs. Call me Susan. Come on in out of this frigid cold. Andy's inside."

Bea laid her hand on his arm. "I think you'll like Andy. He's a contractor and a very nice man."

Zach snaked his arm around her waist. "I'm sure I will."

So, Andy would be number one. No wonder Bea didn't have any long-term relationships. Who the hell wanted to take the father test six times? He sure didn't.

He squeezed her before letting her pass in front of him at the doorway. He didn't need to dwell on the future. He had her for now and that was fine with him.

They all entered the house, shedding their coats and gloves. A tall, thin man came over to greet them. Bea gave him a hug, her head coming to his chest. He had to be six foot four because Zach found himself looking up. This father had his brown hair tied back in a long ponytail.

Bea did the honors. "Andy, I'd like you to meet Zach."

Zach smiled and grasped the hand held out to him. "Nice to meet you, Andy."

Andy nodded but remained serious. "Same here. Bea doesn't usually bring a guest with her. I guess you must be something special."

Her dad didn't appear to be too happy about that, but when Zach caught a smirk on the older man's face, he smiled wider. "That's one way of looking at it."

Andy gave him a friendly shake. "Sit down. Take a load off. Want a beer?"

Bea watched Zach and Andy. Zach didn't appear intimidated in the least, but then again, Andy was the most laid-back of all her dads. She released her breath. Andy liked him. If Andy hadn't, there wouldn't be any hope for Zach. The toughest dad would be Gerry, but she'd cross that bridge if she ever made it that far.

Bea couldn't help comparing the two men. Zach was a bit shorter than Andy, but he was much more muscular and broad.

Her mother whispered in her ear, "You're drooling."

She whipped her head around. "Shh. Am not."

Her mom placed her hands on her ample hips. "Right, and I'm Janice Joplin. He's really yummy, Bea. I'm so thrilled you brought him."

Bea tugged the beaded belt around to the front of her mom's gypsy skirt. "Don't make more of this than it is. I don't know if I can do this yet."

Her mother caught her hands and held them. "I know, honey. I'll try to be good."

Zach turned from his conversation with Andy to join theirs. "Did I hear someone was going to be good? That doesn't sound like much fun."

Andy chuckled. "Believe me, it can be. Susan doesn't know how to behave."

Susan sauntered over and let Andy wrap his arm around her and place a kiss on her hand. She snuggled against him. "That's why he thinks it will be fun, watching me struggle to be normal." She shook her finger at Zach. "I make no guarantees."

Bea studied the three of them and a yearning grew deep in her gut. This is what she wanted. A normal life.

She and Zach sat on the couch together. As she leaned back, he glanced at her cleavage and a warm, excited buzz commandeered her stomach. She'd been afraid he might be tired of her when he hadn't tried anything in his truck. She loved that big bench seat. He could easily lay her down and cover her, thrusting between her legs while his tongue invaded her mouth like a new country to be conquered. The feel of his weight on her would be heavenly. She squirmed.

His brows drew together. "Are you all right?"

She smiled. "I am now. Thanks for coming."

He grinned back at her, his eyes claiming her. The thrill his gaze sent through her had her stomach tightening and her pussy moistening. She stood abruptly. "Mom, don't you think we should check on dinner?"

Her mom was perched on the arm of Andy's chair. "Honey, I didn't even tell you what I was cooking yet."

"True, but I'm sure it needs to be checked." She lifted her eyebrow at her mom, trying to telepath her need to leave the room.

"I don't think so, I mean…"

Bea could tell the moment her mother's confusion cleared. In fact, she was pretty sure everyone could.

"Oh yes, we better see how my lasagna is doing." Her mom stood and pecked Andy on the forehead. "You never really know about lasagna." She looked at Zach. "Last time I made it for company, we had to call for pizza."

Bea grabbed her mom's hand and pulled her into the kitchen. She expected an embarrassing night, but she hadn't anticipated the reason would be because she got hot over her new lover in front of her parents.

Her mother plopped down at the kitchen table, dinner clearly forgotten. "Okay, honey, I'm here. What's wrong?"

Bea smirked. "Nothing. I want to see the lasagna."

Her mom sat back in her chair. "Why? I made it from your Grandmother Beatrice's recipe. I'm sure it will be fine."

Bea grabbed the potholder from its hook and opened the oven. Susan had a penchant for slipping drugs into her meals and Bea would be damned if she'd let Zach's first experience with her family be a psychedelic trip. She wanted him sober at the end of the evening. Pulling out the rack, she took a fork and broke into the pasta.

Her mom jumped up and grabbed her arm, the bell sleeve of her top dipping into the lasagna. "Hey, what are you doing?"

Bea pulled away. "I'm checking it. Let go." When her arm was free she moved the cheese around. She spotted a green fleck. "Mom, what is this?"

Her mother peered over her arm before stepping back a bit to focus. "That's oregano."

Bea let her voice sound its own warning. "Mom?"

Her mother retreated to her chair and picked the cheese off her sleeve. "Really, its oregano. Ask Andy."

Bea breathed a sigh of relief. She pushed the pasta back together as well as she could and closed the oven. At least she didn't have to worry about Zach getting high off dinner.

Her mom pouted. "I can't believe you think I'd add marijuana to the lasagna."

"If you remember, that's exactly what you did when I brought Kayla over for dinner."

"Yes, but after you told me not to, I didn't do it anymore. You need to trust me, Bea."

Bea sighed. "I know, Mom, I do. I just wanted to make sure you didn't forget."

Her mother patted her hand. "I understand, honey. You're nervous."

Bea collapsed in the chair across the table. "Nervous would be an understatement. I don't know how to do this. Except for Phillip, this has been my longest relationship ever and this is only the third time I've seen Zach."

Her mom rose and went to the sink to wet her sleeve. "Bea, you've let your experience with Phillip stand in your way all these years. I don't know how many times I have to tell you, it wasn't your fault. I just didn't know how to tell you about our problem. If I had given you the talk, complete with all the poisonous details, you would have known not to have sex with Phillip so many times. You know he doesn't blame you. In fact, he called again yesterday."

Bea cringed. Phillip had grown into a nice man from what her mom had told her, but his work at the pharmaceutical company was his life. She was happy for him, but they were in very different places now. And besides she had a…boyfriend? She spoke to her mother's back. "I'm glad Phillip stays in touch with you, but that doesn't help me with Zach. Every time I see him, I want to fuse his body to mine, but I can't. And I have almost no control with him."

Susan turned, eyes sparkling. "Really, that's a good sign. Let yourself go with him, Bea."

She shifted in her chair. Her mom's simplemindedness irritated her. "How can I do that? I care for him already. I don't want him sick, or worse, in a coma."

Susan sat across from her. "Then tell him."

Bea stared. "Oh please. How do I do that? He'll think I'm crazy, if he doesn't already."

Her mom shook her head. "I told all your fathers and most of them stayed. You need to stick to a few men to get pregnant. That's how I had you and look—I still have four of them in my life."

Bea let her head fall into her hands. How did she explain to a "born-again hippie" that men weren't into free love anymore? And from Zach's reaction when she asked about other women in his life, her gut said he wouldn't share her with anyone. "Damn, Mom, the idea of having sex with anyone besides him turns my stomach right now."

Susan reached across the kitchen table and grabbed Bea's hand. "This is not good. You need to release those poisons. If not on him, then someone else. You can't hold them in or they'll kill you. You may not have as much as I do, but you still need to release."

Bea leaned her elbow on the table and rested her head in her hand. "Do you think my daughter will be the one? Dare I hope she will be free of the poisons?"

Her mom squeezed her arm. "I don't know, honey. But look how far we've come since our ancestor created the first poisonous Beatrice. We've all survived. Every Beatrice and every flower. Have you thought about which flower you will name your daughter after?

I was thinking about it today when I heard you were bringing Zach to dinner. What do you think of Daisy?"

Bea's throat closed. All the women of their line had been cursed by Dr. Rappaccini's need for experimentation with poisonous, beautiful flowers. If he had kept to his flowers, none of them would have had such difficult lives. Her earliest ancestors had killed their lovers to survive. Lily had it easy because Dr. Rappaccini had given her a poisonous mate, but that had strengthened the poisons in her daughter Beatrice, who gave birth to Violet. Bea's great-great-great grandmother Violet had turned to whoring. She became the whispered black widow killer back in Italy.

Her mom interrupted her morbid thoughts. "You know, Bea. Once you have a daughter, the need to release the poisons is diminished."

"I know, you've told me. But I don't want to have a child who will have the same issues we do."

Her mom's whole body shivered with excitement. "But, Bea, think. It means you might be able to have a daughter *and* a husband, as long as you conceive right away and he doesn't mind being sick a lot. And if he dies, you would still have been the first to have married. What does Zach do for a living?"

Bea froze, stunned. What could her mother be thinking? That she'd have sex with Zach until he died in the hope she'd conceive before then? Oh God, how could her mother think like that? "Excuse me?"

Her mother had a dreamy look on her face. "Yes, if you married and conceived before having to stop having sex with Zach, then you wouldn't have to sleep with as many men."

Bea stood, catching her mother's eye. "You want me to be the first to marry and then break my vows. Who are you?"

Her mom flinched.

The horror of her mother's idea refused to be contemplated.

"Mom, I'm going to see how Zach's doing. You might want to take out the lasagna. It smells like it's burning."

She stormed from the kitchen, but stopped when she reached the living room and received the full force of Zach's smile. Her whole body melted and she grasped the back of Andy's chair to steady herself. How could she feel so much for a man she'd known such a short time? She didn't even know his age.

Zach's face turned serious. "Are you okay?"

Andy glanced behind him and rose from his chair. "Come here, Bea. Take a seat."

Embarrassed to be caught mooning, she gratefully took his chair.

Andy placed his hand to her forehead. "You're a little hot. Are you coming down with something?"

Bea shook her head. "No, I think it was just the heat in the kitchen. Oh, and you may want to check on Mom. When I left, it smelled like she was burning dinner." She wrinkled her nose as she met Zach's gaze. "It may be pizza after all."

They finished dinner without incident. Zach's occasional touches on her thigh throughout the meal made her anxious to leave, especially when she caught her mother watching him. She couldn't shake the feeling her mom wanted Zach as a son-in-law more for the experiment of it than for Bea's happiness. She must be wrong, but sometimes the way her mom looked at him, as if she couldn't wait to crow that her daughter was the first to have a husband, made Bea uncomfortable. Would her mom even care if Zach died within a year?

Bea squeezed his hand under the table, reassuring herself the reality was quite different.

Andy turned from the counter with a tray of brownies in hand. "Dessert, anyone?"

She preferred to leave and spend more time with Zach. "No thank you. I'm stuffed. Mom, that was great. I'm glad it was only the spillover that burned. Your cheese lasagna is fantastic."

Susan blushed at the compliment and Bea admonished herself for having such mean thoughts about her own mother. After all, she didn't really know what the woman truly meant. Her mother's thought process had always baffled her.

"I'll try one." Zach took a brownie.

Andy sat and both he and her mom added dessert to their plates.

It appeared they would be staying for a few more minutes. She stepped over to the sink and began to load the dishwasher to give herself something to do while they enjoyed the sweets.

Susan broke the silence. "Bea, please call Phillip. I know he's happy to talk to me, but all we talk about is you."

Bea glanced at her mom over her shoulder. "Why? I'm not that interesting, and he has a great life without digging up our past. I'm sure he misses you more. You were his surrogate mother, after all."

She turned back and slammed silverware into the wire rack, peeved her mom would bring up Phillip in front of Zach.

Zach's voice had an edge to it. "Who's Phillip?"

"He's one of Bea's boyfriends."

Bea spun to look at Zach. His face was tense and she'd bet a day's salary his muscles twitched. She rolled her eyes so he'd know her mom was ridiculous. "*Was* my boyfriend." She let her sarcasm reign. "We broke up about, oh, more than fifteen years ago."

Zach relaxed and she turned back to the sink.

But her mom wouldn't let it go. "I don't know, honey. I think he still has a pilot light on for you."

Bea threw the last plate in the dishwasher, though she tried to hold on to her temper. "I don't think so. Drop it, Mom."

She glanced at Zach, but he was busy examining his brownie. Actually, he appeared to be dissecting it.

She turned back to wipe the sink.

Her body thrummed at the sound of Zach's voice behind her. "These are excellent, Susan. Mind if I have another?"

"Not at all, have a few. If you like, you can take some home."

Zach mumbled a thank-you with his mouth full.

As Bea finished, she realized how quiet the room had become. A sinking feeling grew as she turned around and caught the silly smile on her mother's face.

"Mom, you didn't!"

"Didn't what, dear?"

She focused on Andy, but he avoided her eyes. She peered at Zach. He seemed alert, but he also looked guilty.

She whirled on her mother. "Damn it, Mom. You can't keep drugging my friends."

Zach grabbed her hand. "Does that mean I'm your friend?"

The tingles of excitement that raced up her arm at his touch lodged her response in her throat.

He rubbed his thumb across her palm. "I'd like to be more than friends."

Oh God, she would jump him right there in front of her mother and Andy if he kept looking at her as if she were a tall drink of cold water and he had the worst thirst. She glanced at his dish where half a brownie rested and grabbed his plate away, but his hand sneaked around her neck and brought her lips to his in a searing, chocolaty kiss.

Bea didn't attempt to resist despite their audience. The second their lips met, he swept his tongue inside her mouth, claiming every inch of it as his. Her head felt light and the hand that held his dish threatened to drop it. She wanted to give in and let him take her. Heat raced through her at the idea of being pressed between the hard table and his warm body.

Her mom applauded.

She pulled away and grabbed Zach's arm. Andy sat still, a happy grin on his face. "I hate to eat and run, Mom, but we have to go."

Susan remained seated. She beamed, unconcerned she had drugged another friend. "Bye, honey. Nice to meet you, Zach. I hope you come back and visit soon."

Bea murmured, "I bet you do."

"What?" Zach halted.

"Nothing. Let's go." She tugged him into the living room, silently cursing her mother. After helping Zach into his coat, she threw her own on and guided him out the door. At the truck, she searched his pockets for the keys, but he palmed them even as his arms came around her. He pushed her back against the truck and captured her lips.

She melted into him, loving the feel of his leg between hers, rubbing her pussy through her jeans until her clit throbbed with need. His demanding cock pressed into her abdomen.

She pulled her mouth away, breathless. "We have to get you home."

He shook his head. "No, we don't. Don't worry, I only ate half a brownie. I snuck the other one back onto the plate when they weren't watching. It only took one bite to know what was in them. Your mother is a bit heavy-handed with the pot."

Bea couldn't believe it. Thrilled by his cleverness, she pulled his head down for another kiss.

Eventually, she came up for air. "My hero. Let's leave before they realize we haven't departed yet."

Laughing, he helped her into the truck and jumped in. Backing down the driveway, he didn't turn the lights on until they were on the road. "So, your mom's a druggy. Who'd have thought?"

She glanced uncertainly at his profile. "I warned you she loved the sixties."

He chuckled. "Yeah, you did, which is why I was careful when they offered the brownies. I didn't think people did that anymore."

She rolled her eyes. "I'm afraid a lot of Mom's friends do."

He nodded as if that made complete sense.

She stared at him. "You think it's normal?"

He shook his head.

She laughed and butted her shoulder against his.

He brought his arm around her, locking her to his side.

And then the whole world spun out of control, literally. The truck accomplished a complete three-sixty before it slid across the road and slammed into a snowbank. The silence was weighty and Bea panicked. "Zach, are you okay?"

His head lay against the driver's window.

Oh God, she didn't know what to do. She resisted the urge to move him. In the back of her mind, she remembered seeing a television show where they were very specific about not moving an accident victim with a head injury. "Zach, can you hear me?"

His eyes opened and he gazed at her blankly.

"Zach, are you okay? You hit your head."

He reached up and rubbed the side of his temple. "I'm fine." He gazed at her with open appreciation and something more. But then his eyes widened and he grasped her to him. "God, Bea, are you okay?"

She chuckled with relief, the adrenaline rush from the scare making her a little shaky. "Me? You're the one who was knocked unconscious."

His own hands trembling a bit, he cupped her face in concern.

She smiled. "Really, I'm fine. I had your body to cushion me."

He relaxed and looked in the rearview mirror. "We were lucky, the snowbank cushioned us and kept us from hitting that oak." He restarted the engine. "Well, the truck appears okay. I'm sorry, Bea. We must have hit a patch of black ice."

"Are you sure you can drive? How's your head?"

He wiggled his eyebrows. "Perhaps you should see for yourself."

She giggled as he placed her hand on his jeans where the hard length of his cock pushed against her. "I didn't mean that head."

He sulked. "But that's the one that needs the most attention."

Liquid heat seeped through her body as she contemplated acquiescing to his request. She gave a furtive glance out the window. The truck lay off the dark road, facing the patch of ice they'd hit. Giving Zach the oral pleasure he craved while parked on the side of the road where anyone could happen upon them had her body trilling and her blood pounding.

"Well, what do you say, Bea? Care for dessert? I don't think I can wait to get you back to my house."

Either the adrenaline rush from the accident or his desire for her caused a warm pleasure to surround her heart. She scrambled down the seat to unzip his jeans.

His hard cock burst forward, making her thankful he didn't wear underwear. She loved that she could stroke him without wrestling with more clothing. Tilting the tip toward her lips, she flicked it with her tongue.

His arm tightened on her waist as he growled. "Don't tease, woman. I've been good all night, except that kiss in front of your mom and that was only because I wanted inside you so bad. Take me into that sweet mouth of yours. Now."

The desperate need in his voice echoed through his cock as it jumped in her hand. She grasped it hard, sucking the length, surrounding it with a gentle pressure. She stroked it with her tongue and at his moan, her pussy swelled. His need for her was addictive.

She moved her mouth up and down the hard, silken shaft as if she had all the time in the world. He tasted clean and salty as her tongue found the pre-cum at the top. His texture was smooth with small bumps tracing his veins. She craved the taut ridges of his rock-hard cock. She moaned in pleasure as her labia swelled, making her jeans feel confining.

Zach's hand buried into the hair at the back of her head. "I want to take you right here in the middle of the road. You're so hot. But I doubt I could keep from ripping your clothes apart."

She squeaked as she imagined the reckless image of him tearing her shirt from her body and she increased her pace.

Zach's hand in her hair stopped her. "Bea, I need you to zip me up and slowly put your head on my shoulder."

She started to lift her head, but his hand kept her low. Her need to taste his cum clawed at her and she couldn't help the whine in her voice. "Why?"

"We have company."

She groaned and tried to breathe slower. Regretfully, she forced his hard cock under the denim and zipped him.

His hand moved to her back as she sat enough to lay her head on his shoulder. He held her close as the glare of a flashlight reflected off the side-view mirror.

He lowered the window.

Light shined into the truck. "Are you folks okay?"

Zach took a deep breath and looked at the police officer. "We are now. Just a little shaken. I hit a patch of black ice."

The flashlight moved to shine on the road and Bea sat up to look. Sure enough, the entire road on a decline with a bend was covered in the stuff. What luck.

The officer turned back and the flashlight lit her face, causing her to squint.

"Bea?"

She nodded. "Yes. Who are you?"

"It's me, Christopher Ledoux."

Bea released a nervous laugh. Great, just what she needed, the guy who wanted to date her in high school and still did. Could the evening get any worse? "Hi, Chris, could you move that light a bit?"

"Oh yeah, sorry. Are you all right?"

She could already hear the protective macho voice coming into play. Could the man not see she was in the capable hands of a sexy hunk? "Yes, just scared there for a moment, but we're fine. This is Zach Woodman."

Chris nodded and looked at Zach, but spoke to her. "You were at your mother's. You didn't eat any of her brownies, did you?"

She smiled, though she doubted it reached her eyes. "Come on, Chris, we know better than that." Let him think Zach was a longtime relationship. Maybe he'd take the hint.

Chris stared. "Yeah, okay."

Zach tensed beneath her. "If you don't mind, I'd like to try pulling back on the road. Could you wait and make sure we don't need a tow?"

The flashlight swung to Zach's face before taking a measured swing through the cab of the truck. Thankful she had managed to zip Zach's jeans, Bea dared not check to see if Chris' appearance had any impact on Zach's ardor.

Chris shined the light on her. "Okay, I'll wait. Glad you're okay, Bea."

"Thanks for checking on us, Chris."

He tapped the door twice. "That's my job."

As Chris moved back to his patrol car, Zach put the window up. "Ex-lover?" His tone was colder than the black ice they'd skidded across.

Bea pulled away and glared at him. "No. He would like to be, but I've been turning him down as far back as high school."

Zach faced her, his voice anything but contrite. "I'm sorry. It's none of my business."

She peered at him, but his eyes were in shadow thanks to the bright police car lights. She wished she knew what he thought. "That's true, but I'll forgive you this time. Next time, I won't be so easy."

Zach didn't react. He just put the truck into four-wheel drive. The vehicle crawled onto the road, fishtailing as he coaxed it toward the dry asphalt. Finally, the tires found traction.

He brought the window down as he pulled next to Chris' patrol car. "Thanks. Looks like we're good."

Chris nodded and opened his mouth to speak, but Zach waved and hit the gas.

Bea relaxed against the seat. "Wow, that was close."

Zach's jaw was rigid as he remained silent. Was he angry or horny?

She glanced at his lap and her cheeks warmed. She had loved sucking on his cock before Chris arrived. "I'm glad you saw him pull up. That could have been embarrassing."

He turned, his gaze raking over her in the dim light of the interior.

Her breath caught. Horny. He was definitely horny. She laid her hand on his thigh.

The muscle under her hand tensed, but he didn't speak. At the intersection, he turned and passed the Wrenborough Depot.

She watched the building go by and dared a peek. "Zach?" She couldn't help the meekness of her voice. "My car is back there."

His jaw moved, barely. "Yeah, I know."

She studied his profile. "Then how am I going to get it?"

His hands opened and closed around the steering wheel. "You're not. We're going to your place so we can finish what we started. It's closer."

At his words, erotic tingles slithered across her skin and the imp in her moved her hand to slide between his legs. "How do you know it's closer?"

His voice was tight. "It's in Meriden, right, not far from the inns?"

"Yes." Wow, good memory.

He pierced her with a possessive look. "Or if you like, I can pull down the next dirt road and we can do this in my truck."

Her heart sped up to meet the heat of her flesh. He seemed ready to jump her and in a way she wanted him to, but she'd already seen where that got her. "No, my place is fine."

He brought his attention back to the road. "Then you better remove your hand."

Chapter Six

Zach took a cursory look at the small apartment filled with a profusion of plants. The local cop had followed them, though he doubted Bea realized it.

Mine. The command filled his head, leaving just enough space for the lust claiming him. He pulled her into his embrace.

Her quiet gasp inflamed him. He took her mouth in a searing kiss while he cupped her ass, forcing her hips into his granite-hard erection.

She melted, her arms wrapping around his neck as her tongue mated with his.

His heart raced and a clawing need built for the willing woman in his arms. He pulled away, tugging on her shirt. "Off."

She complied, revealing her smooth white breasts beneath a white satin bra.

"You too," she said in a husky voice that strained his control.

Zach undid the top button of his shirt, whipped it over his head and threw it on the table behind him. He unbuttoned his jeans and let his cock breathe. It helped him gain a semblance of control over his raging need to claim her. He growled. "Everything."

Her eyebrows rose, but she licked her lips.

Zach's gut clenched. This sexually alive, yet somehow naïve

woman was his for the taking, and he would take her. Triumph, pure and exhilarating, surged through him, tightening his muscles in anticipation.

She stood before him naked, her stance uncertain, but her nipples hard and begging for his attention. Kicking off his boots without removing his gaze from her ripe body, he stepped from his jeans and crowded close to her, but didn't touch, leaving a mere inch between them. Her soft, short breaths brushed against his neck as the hair on his chest strained to feel the rosy, hard nubs of her breasts. He breathed deeply, inhaling her scent of musky readiness and tangy body perfume. His need climbed and strained against his inaction. Oh shit. Bending over, he retrieved his wallet and pulled out the condom he'd stashed there.

She shivered.

His body tensed, muscles ready. Giving her no warning, he scooped her into his arms. Her softness satisfied his skin's immediate craving, but his desire for absolute mastery of her climbed. "Bed?"

She pointed with a shaky finger and a smile of pure invitation.

He groaned silently as he strode to her bedroom, thankful for the smallness of the apartment. He wanted this woman, now. A streetlight across the road gave the room enough brightness to see. He placed her on the bed, covered her with his body and nudged her legs apart, unable to resist the need to feel her all at once. But he didn't enter her.

Her eyes widened before she moved against him, wrapping her long legs around his.

He reveled in her soft skin and luscious curves, wondering again how he could be so lucky, but at the same time not caring. He took her mouth, exploring its hills and valleys, her fine white teeth and the texture of her tongue. She tasted of wine and sex, and way too good.

Bea moaned.

The sound sent a vibration speeding across his skin, telling him to take her. He broke the kiss and held her head in place so he could explore her neck, licking the pulse he found there. His cock throbbed in time to the beat of her blood as he left that spot to taste the breasts that begged for his attention.

She grasped his head as he swirled his tongue around a pink nipple and her fingers dug into his hair. Her tight, desperate hold sent victory racing through his veins, allowing him more control. He nibbled at the hard peak, scraping his teeth across the very tip, obeying an inner command to give her more pleasure than she'd ever known before.

She let go and tried to wiggle her hands between their chests.

He reacted immediately. Not tonight. Tonight he controlled who gave and who took. He caught her hands together and pushed them above her head. "No touching. I'm going to pleasure you and then thrust my cock into your thick, warm pussy and make you mine. And you're going to let me."

Her eyes opened wide as her breath hitched. She nodded once, her gaze centered on his, her pulse beating a tattoo against her skin. She leaked a warm wetness onto his thigh where it rested between her legs.

Her heightened excitement had him drawing deep breaths to control his raging need to conquer. He looked around the room for something, anything to restrain her. The need to claim her, make her his, pushed his own heart faster. His gaze fell on the belt of a robe hanging on the back of a dressing table chair. He lifted himself from her and grabbed the silken tie.

Her brow knit. "Zach?"

"Yes?" He knelt upon the bed, smoothed her arms above her head and tied her wrists. He watched a shiver of anticipation pass over her body.

She wiggled, testing the bonds around her wrists, drawing his gaze to the full length of her as she crossed her legs demurely. "You make me so hot, I'm almost embarrassed."

At her words, he brought his gaze back to her face, surprised to see a blush creeping from her neck to her cheeks. She was incredible, an innocent sex goddess all his own. He tied the other end of the silk to the latticework in the maple headboard.

Zach sat back and stared. "Beautiful. Open your legs. I want to see your pussy. I love how wet you are for me."

Bea's breathing shortened, but she obeyed. Her legs fell open, revealing the sheen of moisture between her thighs where her thick folds begged to be spread.

His cock jumped in anticipation. His blood pumped downward, leaving but one overwhelming thought behind. *Mine.* This woman had him acting the caveman. He'd feel guilty if she wasn't so turned-on by it.

He smirked with that knowledge as a sense of utter dominance filled his psyche. He lay beside her and leaned on his elbow. Using his finger, he chased lazy circles around her hardened nipples. The sight of the puckered skin filled him with confidence. She was perfect for him.

Bea squirmed. "Zach, please."

He stopped, lifting his brows. "Please what?"

She groaned and closed her eyes. "I need you."

"Really?" He took his finger away and because he could, without warning, he buried it inside her dripping pussy.

Her body jerked up to meet his hand. "Oh God."

The hot wetness surrounding his finger nearly undid him. He palmed her pelvis and pressed her to stillness as he took a nipple into his mouth and sucked. Her racing pulse beat against his hand, causing his own control to waver and his cock grew painfully hard. The tightening of her slick vagina around his finger urged him to let go even as he ground his cock against her hip.

She bucked as a frustrated moan passed her lips.

He lifted his head. "Whoa there. You'll throw me off the bed."

Bea opened her eyes. Her desire starkly visible, desire and determination. "Take me, Zach."

At her words, pre-cum leaked from his cock. His control slipped another notch. Hell, he would have to explore the restraining game another time. Pulling his finger from her pussy, he sat up. Running his hands over the blanket, he found the condom, opened it and snugged it on, but even that slight pressure brought him closer to his orgasm. Quickly, he pushed Bea's legs toward the ceiling, resting her ankles against his shoulders. He set his cock at the entrance to her tight, wet opening, his head spreading her moist folds. He paused, teasing them both.

Bea panted as she stared at him. "Take…me."

"Mine." Zach eased inside. Deeper and deeper he pushed, her warmth surrounding him, sucking him. His cock wanted more, all of her. He brought himself down onto his elbows, forcing Bea's legs farther toward her head, tipping her pelvis until his cock slid to the hilt and touched her limit.

"Oh yes," she whispered. "Take me, Zach. Make me yours."

Exactly what the Neanderthal inside him needed to hear. With a growl, he pulled out and rocked back into her.

Her pussy tightened at his exit. He pushed his way back in, his balls slapping against her ass, his arm and leg muscles screaming for conquest. The adrenaline and friction added to the pulsing sensations spreading through his body. With each thrust he made, his brain said she was his. Faster, he pumped as her whimpers of need changed to small cries of pleasure. Grasping a nipple into his mouth, he tugged hard.

Bea shrieked as her climax took hold.

He stiffened. Her pussy greedily sucked at his moving cock, pulling his own orgasm from him against his will even as his mouth pulled at her breast. His balls pulsed and he came deep inside her. His release sent pleasure reverberating through his body, wringing him out even as he branded her his. Her nipple slid from his mouth and he collapsed, barely holding his chest above her so he didn't suffocate her.

Bea's cries dwindled to soft whimpers and heavy breathing.

He lifted his head. "Bea?"

"Hmm."

"Open your eyes, beautiful."

She did.

"You're mine." The words felt carved in granite.

A shiver ran through her body. "Definitely."

He rolled off her and reached to untie her hands, but she stopped him. "Wait."

He looked down. "Yes?"

"I don't mind being tied."

Zach closed his gaping mouth, her implication clear. Could she read his mind? Or maybe she was attuned to his hardening cock. "Then tied you'll be."

Bea moved her gaze from his face to his cock, where his protection was in tatters, a common sight for her "Um, I think there was a problem with your condom."

"My condom?" He looked down. "Shit! I've never seen anything like that. It looks like it was dipped in acid or something." His gaze returned to hers. "It must have been old. But don't worry. I've been tested and I'm fine, but what about…?"

"Me? I've been tested as well. I could show you my results, but they're in my purse and," she looked up toward her wrists, "I'm a little tied up at the moment."

His brow remained furrowed. "But what about getting pregnant?"

Bea looked away. "We don't have to worry about that." How could she tell him that having his child would be a dream come true but impossible? Her poisons not only destroyed condoms, they destroyed all sexual diseases, and unfortunately, all semen.

Zach moved off the bed. "I better get this mess off me. Bathroom?"

"Over there." She nodded to her left.

"Thanks. Don't start again without me."

She rolled her eyes as he turned and entered her bathroom, his ass making her itch to touch it, but her tied hands reminded her that wouldn't happen soon. What had she been thinking? If he made love to her again, it would be however he wanted. The thought sent a warm glow through her body. But she couldn't orgasm on him again. She really didn't want to make him sick and he'd already had one dose of her.

The running water in the bathroom stopped. Damn, she had to think of something fast. She gave a tug on her bonds, but they weren't moving.

He strode back to the side of the bed and stared.

She enjoyed the light as it bathed his body in an orange glow. As she studied him, his cock moved, already semi-hard.

She licked her lips in anticipation. That's what she wanted. "May I make a request?"

He appeared to think about it. "I guess one request of the prisoner is allowed."

"Can I suck you again?"

His lips tightened. His cock jumped. "Absolutely."

Zach was on the bed and positioned across her chest, his cock head in front of her lips in under three seconds.

His quick acquiescence had her grinning inside. She enveloped the shaft with her mouth and sucked hard, the clean stiffness causing her to moan with pleasure.

"Hold on there." He grabbed her jaw. "There's no rush."

She pouted as she released him. "But I want it."

"Hmmm, maybe if you're good, you can lick it."

She stuck out her tongue. She could make him come this way and save him from another of her orgasms.

He moved his cock parallel to her face.

Slowly, what she hoped was sensuously, she licked the underside, marveling at how fast his balls tightened.

He pulled away.

She tried to reach him, but her tied hands prevented her from contact. Cocking her head, she looked at him in question.

Zach stroked her hair off her shoulders and cupped her face. "You are beautiful."

She returned her gaze to his cock. "So are you."

She felt his chuckle before he climbed off her.

A shiver of panic ran up her spine. "Where are you going?"

He strode to the window. "Nowhere."

Her body craved him again, but she couldn't let him inside her. She had to gain control. She shrugged to release the mild strain from having her arms tied above her head. What an idiot. How could she gain control when she'd practically begged him to keep her tied to the bed?

She watched as he switched on the lamps on either side of her. "What are you doing?"

"I want to see your beauty in brighter light. It seems as if we are always in shadows."

A thrill sliced through her stomach at the image of him studying her in her most private, throbbing place. Did he mean…

The bed dipped as he knelt between her legs. He stroked the inside of her thighs. "You're very flexible. I like that."

She concentrated on breathing, wondering when those fingers would move up. "I took ballet when I was little. Guess that helped."

He smoothed his hands around her knees and down to her ankles.

Despite her attempt at control, her breaths increased when he lifted her legs in the air.

Zach gazed at her limbs as if they were a work of art. "Bend your knees."

She did as she was told, which made her wide open to his gaze. His face was tense with hunger as he stared, causing tingles of anticipation to race through her veins. Moisture seeped from her pussy.

"Pink," he said as he used both hands to spread her labia wide to view her clit and vaginal opening.

Her body was on fire and though her pussy may have appeared to be attempting to douse the flames, it wouldn't. She had to protect him, stay in control. She squeezed herself tight, but her juices still flowed. They dribbled down to the crease of her ass.

She sensed the moment he noticed them. His mouth opened. He let go of her pussy to lift her legs higher, farther than where she had been when he'd entered her minutes ago.

His finger traced the wetness between her swollen folds to her anal opening.

She tensed, but her head swam at the realization she couldn't stop him.

His other hand stroked her leg. "Relax. I won't hurt you."

She tried to obey, but her excitement overrode her wishes. "I've never been touched there."

He tore his gaze from her ass and met her eyes. "Do you like it?"

The strange combination of helplessness and excitement had her swallowing hard and nodding. Her heart beat so fast she couldn't speak. Control. For Zach's sake. She had to stay…

Gently, he explored her, nudging her ass opening. Unable to resist, she moved her hips to push into his touch.

He stilled. "Do you have any lube?"

She managed a whisper as she turned her head to the left. "In there."

He leaned over her body to open the drawer on the nightstand, his cock pressing against the inside of her thigh. "Wow. You have quite an interesting collection here."

Her cheeks heated. What would he think?

He glanced back at her. "I hope you'll allow me to play sometime."

The appreciative look on his face made her want to laugh with relief. Instead she nodded, too filled with pleasure at what they could do together with her special sex toys.

He grabbed the pillow next to her and knelt between her legs again. Tilting her hips, he folded it beneath her butt, positioning her ass in the air for him to explore. More wetness leaked from her pussy. She wanted this man where no man had been before. Of course! She could have him there without poisoning him. Her heart beat with joy as well as lust and she moaned.

He used his finger to smear her juices around her clit, causing her to buck into his hand. "Oh Zach. I'm so hot."

He grinned tightly before pushing his finger into her pussy. "Yes, you are. Hot and wet."

His finger stroked inside her, building her excitement, sensitizing her clit. Then a cool silkiness ran down her crease and across her ass. Her pussy tightened around his finger.

"Bea, you're going to like this. I can tell."

At the tightness in Zach's voice, she whimpered. She didn't want to wait. Anticipation flooded her, tensed her muscles in readiness.

He pushed a different finger against her anal hole. "Relax."

Relax? How? She tried, anxious to feel herself taken there, but she couldn't control her own actions. She made her hands let go of her bindings, signaling the rest of her heated body to calm.

Zach's finger penetrated.

She cried out. Though he didn't move either finger, shocks of pleasure tingled through her steadily. "Make me come, now."

The finger inside her pussy finally moved in and out. Her ass and pussy tightened against both his hands of their own accord. As he started to stroke her anal opening, her blood pounded through her and her limbs grew useless, her pleasure building. Her body, mind and heart gave in, accepting Zach's total possession and she let him take her where he would. As the sensations converged between her legs in waves, she grew lightheaded. Finally, a sweeping orgasm hit her hard, exploding from her center to the very tips of her toes. She grabbed the silken belt that tied her hands and held on as her body rocked with spasms of pleasure.

When her orgasm subsided, Zach removed his fingers.

But her sated feeling dissipated as cool lube dribbled across her butt crease. She opened her eyes to see him lubing his hard cock.

Fear and excitement warred within her. "Zach?"

He glanced up, his face strained with passion. "Mine."

His desperate need for her erased all nervousness and melted her heart. She swallowed as his cock butted against her ass and a welcoming joy permeated her veins.

Zach encircled her clit with his pussy-wet finger. The sharp excitement he caused had her closing her eyes, relinquishing her body to his knowledgeable, caring hands.

He played with her clit while the steady, gentle pressure of his cock increased against her ass opening. She panted to catch her breath as electricity flowed through her body along a now-known path to her inner core. The freedom of the act allowed her to embrace every titillating spark, grasp every shock as it swept through her.

Zach pushed through and filled her ass.

She melted into stillness. Savored being taken.

He remained motionless. "Bea?"

She rasped, "Yes."

"Do you want me to continue?" His tense pectorals and neck muscles revealed his self-imposed restraint.

That he would stop for her had her heart swelling with emotion. Touched, she nodded vigorously so he wouldn't mistake her meaning.

He pushed farther into her, stretching her virgin flesh.

She moaned as the pleasure exceeded the small, uncomfortable strangeness. His finger on her clit played its expert strokes and his cock inside her ass began a slow pace. She pushed against him as he entered her body, gripping her bonds, at his mercy and aroused beyond thought.

Zach's rough breathing broke through her own euphoric senses. He would come inside her. That thrilled her as much as his ministrations to her body. As his cock glided in again, his finger rubbed a gentle circle upon her clit.

Zach moaned. "Oh God, Bea."

At his words, her orgasm sparked through her. She shook with tremors and when a warmness invaded her ass, she peaked, moaning in complete satisfaction.

Zach pulled out. Breathing hard, he leaned over her and released her hands.

She let them drop to the sides as he pulled her against him.

He brushed her hair from her face, his gentle touch warming her from the inside. "Bea, are you okay?"

She sighed as she cuddled into his body, her head resting on his shoulder. "Mmm-hmm. Just spent."

He kissed the top of her head. "Sleep."

Yes, she would, and be content he'd only experienced her poisons once. Maybe there was hope for them yet.

Zach lay awake, recovering from an orgasm unlike any he'd experienced before. The woman in his arms was a wonder. How the hell was he going to break it off after one more time?

He looked at the clock across the room. If the cop was still outside, his superiors may start to wonder. Two hours was a long time to be parked in one place while on patrol. Unable to resist a moment longer, he slipped from the bed and turned off the lamps on either side. Stealthily, he moved to the side of the window.

The patrol car was there.

He smirked. He hoped the cop would be there in the morning when he took Bea for her car. Let the man see their date had been an all-night event.

Zach turned back to gaze at Bea. She was curled on her side, accentuating the smallness of her waist and fullness of her hips. Possessiveness filled his blood again, causing him to stalk from the room. He hadn't expected to take her like that. It must have been the double reminder of her past boyfriends that had him being so aggressive. First, her mom with the boyfriend call, then the cop wannabe boyfriend. He'd never been forceful, but something about her, and her past, rubbed him like deer antlers on a tree.

Finding himself in the kitchen, he opened her refrigerator. Not much food graced the shelves, in fact, less than in his own. Working for the inns must include free food while on the clock. However, the Amstel Light on the upper shelf looked appetizing. Rummaging around for a bottle opener took a little longer, but he succeeded and took a swallow.

She had a small place. Except for the plants, it was barely lived in. A workaholic. He'd rather share her with her job than have himself acting like a grizzly with cubs because of her old flames. It didn't make sense. He hadn't known her a week yet and besides, she'd be gone soon.

Taking another gulp, he sat on the couch and studied the room.

She was a mystery. Incredibly hot and sensual and yet awkward and limited, intelligent and educated, but so down-to-earth he kept forgetting she was only temporary. What if he broke his own rule and stayed with her longer? He didn't see any signs of possessiveness or deep caring yet. In truth, she hadn't made a single move to continue the relationship. That could be a good sign.

Finishing his beer, he walked back into the bedroom and slipped into the bed. He pulled Bea against him. Maybe four sex dates, but then he had to let her go, no matter the strange caveman instinct. He liked her and it wouldn't be fair to test fate by loving her.

Bea woke to the sound of a man vomiting in her bathroom. It took her a moment to remember that Zach had stayed the night.

Dread hit her hard. He was sick because of her. She wanted to cry, but that wouldn't help anything. Rising, she wrapped her robe around herself. In the kitchen she grabbed a water from the fridge and as she stepped into the bedroom, Zach opened the bathroom door.

She handed him the bottle. She didn't like how pale he'd become.

He took a tiny sip. "Thanks, sorry about that."

She cocked her head. "About what? Being sick? It's not your fault."

He gave her a sheepish grin and ran a hand over his face. "Yeah, but I knew it would happen. I'm allergic to marijuana. I didn't think I had enough to get sick. But like I said, your mom is a little heavy-handed with that particular ingredient."

Pot? He was allergic? Relief flooded her. Men became ill because of her poisonous fluids, but she had no idea how. Phillip had gone into a coma, but they'd had sex like bunnies. Since she never stayed with the men she slept with, she didn't know what actually happened to them afterward, but she always kept it to the minimum she needed to survive another week. Unfortunately, it didn't lessen her guilt.

Zach took a sip of water and grimaced. "I'm not sure how long this will last, but you might want to get in the bathroom before I need it again."

Guilt rode her once more for rejoicing at the fact she hadn't caused his pain. "I'm so sorry. Don't worry about me. Let's get you back in bed."

He followed her and lay on the mussed sheet.

She smoothed his hair away from his face. "This is all my fault. I should have checked those brownies."

Zach placed his hand on hers. "Don't blame yourself. I didn't have to eat more than one bite. I'll be fine in a couple hours."

She bent and kissed him on the cheek. "I'll call in and let them know I'll be late for work."

He grasped her wrist as she rose. "Don't do that. I'll be fine, if you don't mind my staying here for a while."

She sat back down. "I need to make this up to you, plus you still have to bring me to get my car. How about you stay here? When I come home, I'll cook you dinner."

He frowned. "How will you get to work?"

She smiled smugly. "I rented this apartment because it's close enough to walk to all three inns. I'll throw on my sweats, grab some clothes and change at the Lakeside. I have a whole set of toiletries there because I often have to sleep at the inn. This way, if you need the bathroom, it's all yours."

Zach squeezed her hand. "Thanks."

She kissed him on the forehead and grabbed some clothes. As she closed the door behind her, she heard him leave the bed and run for the bathroom again. Poor man.

She headed down the stairs to the street. She should be ashamed of her good mood, but the fact Zach wasn't sick because of her excited her too much. How many times could they make love and keep him healthy? Her grandmother would know.

Maybe a visit to Grandma Beatrice was in order. Bea would hear the truth from her. While she could talk to her mother, her instinct said Mom wasn't completely truthful.

Shrugging, she strode up the hill toward the Lakeside Inn. Since it was still early, the sleepy little town had few cars on the road. When she came to the stoplight on Main and Lakeside Drive, she pressed the *Walk* button and waited.

A car pulled up next to her. "Hey, Bea, need a lift?"

She turned to see a patrol car and Chris hanging out his window.

She raised her brows. "Are you still on duty?"

"Yeah, but not for long. I'm heading back to the station to end my shift." He pointed down the road. "Would you like a ride to the inn?"

Bea smiled to soften her rejection. "No thanks. I want to enjoy the crisp air before being trapped inside all day."

She glanced above the patrol car to see the *Walk* light lit. "Thanks anyway."

Bea crossed the street, but could feel him watch her. She hadn't run into him since last year's Rotary Ice Fishing Derby, and now twice in twenty-four hours. He was a good guy, but not her type. In a way she wished she'd dated him in high school, maybe then he wouldn't be interested in her now.

She stepped into the lobby of the inn and strode past the check-in counter where one of the staff helped a customer. Sneaking into the back office, she grabbed her travel case and ducked into the bathroom. In no time, she showered and dove into her work.

She was deep into the monthly billing when Kayla came in for her shift.

Kayla was dressed in a pale-beige silk blouse and tan pencil skirt. Her short fashionable hairdo made her look like a model, but her smile warmed people down to their toes. "Good morning, Bea. How'd it go last night?"

Bea smirked. "Let's say better than expected."

"Seriously?" Kayla sat on the desk. "Okay, I want all the juicy details."

Bea glanced around before she lowered her voice. "Oh, it was juicy all right."

Kayla hit the desk with her hand. "I can't wait. I have to relieve Gary at the front, but as soon as the checkout rush is over, I want coffee and a story."

Bea nodded as Kayla jumped off the desk. "You've got it."

Bea pondered her petite blonde friend as she left. Kayla's advice the other night had been helpful. If it hadn't been for her, Bea would have told Zach she would drive them to her mom's house. That could have been embarrassing. He had obviously expected to drive. It hadn't occurred to her to let a man drive since she'd never had a man to go anywhere with. And the evening wouldn't have been so enjoyable either if not for Kayla's hints on dating.

Picking up the phone, Bea called her grandmother who lived in the town next door and arranged to see her during her lunch break. She didn't feel comfortable spending another evening with Zach unless she could learn what the ramifications might be. She looked at her desk calendar. It had been one week since her last one-night stand, and she'd expelled poisons once this week, so she should be fine for a few days. If she and Zach could make love without him becoming ill, she might have a chance at a relationship.

Her stomach fluttered as hope rose strong and fierce. It had been such a unique experience falling asleep with him. The whole relationship process itself was new, but to go through it with a hunky, kind man was absolute heaven.

The phone rang, jolting her from her daydream. She answered. "Lakeside Inn, Beatrice Rappaccini speaking."

"Hi, Bea, it's Phillip. How are you?"

Her pleasant mood evaporated. Phillip never called her. He spoke to her mother all the time, but not her. On her guard, she went into professional mode. "I'm fine, how are you?"

His tenor voice came through screechy. "I'm really great. Listen, I'm heading back to Massachusetts the day after tomorrow from here at Maine General Hospital and was wondering if you could meet me for lunch. I've made an amazing discovery that I have to share with you."

Bea swallowed. "Me?"

He sounded breathless. "Yes. In fact, you're the only one I can share it with, except maybe your mom."

Huh? "I don't know, Phillip. Kayla has the day off and—"

He became impatient. "Come on, Bea, this is important. More important than work."

Ah, now that was the Phillip she remembered—spoiled. But it had to be serious. She hadn't seen him in four years and that time only because she'd dropped by unannounced while he visited her mom. Maybe he wanted to tell her he'd found the future Mrs. Phillip Sutton. That would be great. "Okay, I'd be happy to have lunch with you. Can you give me a hint? Is it good news or bad?"

She could imagine his boyish grin as he spoke. "Definitely good. I'll see you around noon."

Bea stared at the phone after she hung up. She hoped Phillip's good news had to do with a girlfriend or fiancée. Maybe he wanted to bring her so they could meet. Maybe he wanted Bea's seal of approval. Phillip would need that.

She breathed easier. How wonderful if that were the case. Worst case could be he had made a great scientific breakthrough for the pharmaceutical company he worked for and was given a promotion. Either way, it shouldn't be too uncomfortable.

Kayla bounced back into the office. "Okay, spill."

With Phillip on her mind, Bea blinked as she focused on Kayla. Then she remembered Zach and laughed. "Hold on. Let's go sit where we can see the front. Craig would have our heads if a customer came in and waited more than five seconds."

Kayla gave her a little pout, but moved to the opening that led to the front. "Okay, how'd he do with your mom and her usual marijuana lasagna?"

Bea chuckled and related the switch in menu from a drugged dinner to a drugged dessert. "Then we skidded on black ice and the next thing I know I'm giving him a blowjob."

Kayla licked her lips. "Is he hung?"

"Oh yes, and he doesn't wear underwear."

Kayla wiggled her eyebrows. "A man after my own heart."

"Yeah, but then Officer Chris came upon us, so I had to stop."

Kayla's eyes widened. "Seriously? Did he catch you at it?"

Bea shook her head. "No, but it made Zach so hard we went right back to my place."

Kayla glanced toward the front, then back at Bea. "And?"

Her body flushed with heat. She lowered her voice. "He tied my hands to the headboard and had his way with me."

Kayla breathed, "No."

"Yes, and I loved it. He became possessive all of a sudden. I think it was Chris' doing. Zach is a fantastic lover. Have you ever done anything like that?"

Kayla nodded wisely. "Yes, and I know exactly what you mean. I don't think there is anything I've tried that I haven't enjoyed except—"

Bea leaned forward. "Except what?"

"Wax. I don't like the dripping-hot-wax stuff."

Bea sat back. "What about in your ass, or threesomes, or being watched, or total bondage? Have you tried those and liked them?"

Kayla's smirk was seductive and secretive.

Bea found herself reacting to the image of Kayla doing unique sexual activities. Heat traveled through her body.

Kayla glanced out front. "Oh shoot, be right back."

Bea took a deep breath. What was wrong with her? It wasn't as if she'd never heard of the many variations of sexual acts. She'd simply not been interested before. Besides, she couldn't have indulged unless it had been a threesome with two men, and with a one-night stand that would have been too risky. Her need to expel poisons made sex a necessity, not an experiment. Now her body heated just thinking about the many forms of kink Kayla may have experienced. Bea hoped Zach hadn't created a monster. She didn't want to hurt him.

What was she thinking? She could control her interest in kinky sex. It was the release of her poisons she had no choice with. That always drove her before, but now— The idea of going back to one-night stands after having Zach cooled her blood.

Kayla came back in. "So. Where were we?"

Bea eyed her shrewdly. "You were about to tell me everything regarding your very satisfying sexual perversions, in detail."

Chapter Seven

A few minutes late as usual, Bea waited in the lobby of the Evergreen Retirement Community. She could blame her tardiness on the hotel shuttle driver, but that wouldn't be fair. Besides, her grandmother would make her sit for several minutes before calling her up to the apartment no matter what the reason. Grandma Beatrice was seventy-six and believed tardiness was a lack of respect, so Bea's constant lateness bothered her namesake.

The receptionist broke into Bea's musings. "You can go up now, Ms. Rappaccini."

Bea took the elevator to the third floor of the nicely appointed building and knocked on the door sporting a stained-glass sign that read *Beatrice Rappaccini.*

That very lady opened the door and gave her a warm hug. "Ah, my Bea, come on in, sweetie. Sit. Sit. I'll make us some tea and we can have these lovely Girl Scout cookies I bought from Mrs. Giuseppe's granddaughter."

Bea followed her dainty grandmother to the small kitchen table. "I didn't have a chance to order any this year. Did you buy any Trefoils or Thin Mints?"

The older woman placed her hands on her hips. "Of course. Why buy Girls Scout cookies if not to get at least those two?"

Bea waited as her grandmother set the teapot on the stove and pulled teacups from the cabinet. Grandma Beatrice was a small woman with long white hair caught back in a bun, but her eyes always twinkled with amusement, sometimes at herself and sometimes at others.

"Here you go, dear. Have as many as you want. I bought a dozen boxes."

Bea widened her eyes as she pulled the Thin Mints toward her. "Really? Are you trying to gain weight?"

Her grandmother looked over her shoulder. "Don't get sassy with me, now. I bought them so I had something for my company."

Bea smirked. "So, who is he this week, Gram?"

Grandma poured the water into the cups and brought them to the table. She winked at Bea. "His name is Randal, but I like to call him Randy, if you know what I mean."

Bea's spoon clattered back into the sugar bowl. "Grandma."

Grandma sat and reached for the Trefoils. "Honey, I'm old. I'm not dead."

Bea chuckled and took a sip of warm, sweet tea.

After her grandmother added cream and sugar in her own, she dunked a cookie. "So, honey, what's the matter?"

Her grandmother knew how to get to the point. Okay, so could she. "I think I've found Mr. Right."

Grandma stopped in mid-chew and swallowed. "Bea, really?"

"I think so, but I'm so afraid I'll hurt him. I realized this morning that I have no idea how much is too much for a man to take. I've never been around them after… Uh, you know."

Grandma nodded. "After sex? Yes, unfortunately, it's different for different men. I had one man who could make love with me twice a week and not feel bad at all, but I also had another who became ill after just one time."

Bea's hopes dwindled. "How do they get sick? Do they vomit, have headaches, pass out? I have no idea what to expect for Zach."

Chewing her cookie, her grandma thought for a moment. "It's a lot like a virus with cramping, sometimes vomiting, generally diarrhea and often a headache. Those who are sensitive pass out. I think your first boyfriend did that, didn't he?"

"Yes, we were teenagers and Mom hadn't told me, so we had sex every chance we could for a week. He went into a coma."

Grandma Beatrice patted her hand. "Yes, I remember. Your mother should have told you as soon as you started your monthly cycles."

Bea sighed. "So, I guess what you're saying is, I have to experiment. I was hoping for something a little more definitive."

Grandma shook her head. "Honey, even if I could tell you exactly how a man could handle it, each of our generations is different. My experience is based on a higher level of poison in my system than you have in yours."

"I know. And mom has less than you. She keeps reminding me of how little poison I have. Sometimes she gives me the shivers. Sorry, Gram, but it's as if she has me in a competition and she'll do anything to see me married in order for her to win. I already know I've disappointed her by not having a child yet."

Grandma pointed her finger. "You listen carefully, child. Though she is my daughter, your mother has a tendency to get her priorities mixed up but it's not her fault, it's her genes. And she's not the first in our line to have moral issues."

Bea set down her teacup. "Wait a minute, what do you mean?"

Grandma dunked another cookie in her tea and let it melt in her mouth before answering. "I wasn't sure you noticed, so I didn't say anything before, but now that your instincts have kicked in, you need to know the truth."

Oh boy, this didn't sound good. "What?"

Her grandmother leaned forward. "Just as every other generation of Rappaccini daughters is named Beatrice and the others after a flower, those with flower names have inherited a bit of Giacomo's insanity."

Bea's Thin Mint broke. Did that mean if she had a child, the child would be odd and have moral issues? Her dreams crumbled like her cookie. "Are you sure? Is this an actual fact?"

Grandma shrugged. "It's a genetic phenomenon. But just as Giacomo's flowers were deadly poisonous, so too are the flower children a bit off." Her grandmother tilted her head to the side to punctuate her point. "But like us, each generation gets closer to being normal. Your mom was the best of all of them, but you need to be wary."

Bea shook her head, unable to accept the new information. "Mom may be a little strange, but don't you think calling her insane a bit overboard?"

Grandmother Beatrice sat back and pierced Bea with her stare. "No, it's not. When the original Beatrice died, her father Giacomo hated all men. Lily, Beatrice's daughter, slowly poisoned her own mate with Giacomo's help. But then Giacomo died and Lily's daughter Beatrice died young, after giving birth to Violet, the Black Widow. As a paid whore, she had sex with men until they died. My grandmother Beatrice tried to raise my mother Rose with a full understanding of our situation, but my mother fell in with the wrong crowd and became a pinup girl. Like Giacomo's flowers, she was beautiful, but deadly. When the artist she posed for was discovered dead, they charged her with murder. She died in jail as you know. They said she poisoned herself, but without multiple men to release her toxins, she couldn't survive."

Despite her dashed dreams, Bea noticed the flicker of pain that crossed her grandmother's face. Quickly, she rose and sat next to her. "I'm so sorry. I always thought Great-grandma Rose had an exciting life."

Grandma Beatrice tried to smile, but didn't quite make it. "My mother tried not to kill anyone, but the more popular she became, the more popular she needed to be. Sleeping with the artist set was an easy way for her to be liked. Her need was too great, and they were a dangerous crowd. She always felt unworthy and cursed."

Bea mumbled, "We are cursed."

Her grandmother's hand shot out and grabbed her chin. "No, child. We are not cursed. We are blessed. We have survived from generation to generation, bringing forth one daughter to carry on, and soon, the poisons will be gone. I hope to see a great-granddaughter from you."

Grandma let Bea's chin go and squeezed her hand. "If you do, I will be the first of our line to experience such happiness. We must focus on what we have gained, our small triumphs, not on a past we cannot change."

Her grandmother patted her cheek and rose. "I think I need another cup of tea. How about you?"

Bea glanced at the clock. She should be back at work, but this was far too important. She nodded. "That sounds perfect."

As her grandmother put the water on to boil, Bea wandered around the small one-bedroom living area. She found the picture she remembered in a pewter frame. Her great-grandmother Rose stood next to a Bentley of the period with Grandma Beatrice as a teenager. They could have passed for sisters. Next to that photo stood a picture of Grandma with Mom. Mom wore a mini-dress and white knee-high Go-Go boots at the age of five. Bea had always liked the cute picture, but it took on more meaning now. Actually, the whole hippie lifestyle finally made sense. Her mom could function best within that culture.

"Come over and make your tea, honey." Grandma motioned to the table.

Bea sat and took her tea bag from the darkened water. "So where does Mom fit in with all this?"

Grandma looked tired. "Your mom has tried very hard to do what is right, but her nature makes it hard. The sixties came at the perfect time for *me*. It made it easy to hide my many partners under the spirit of free love. Your mom resented that. She became a self-proclaimed hippie long after we had melded back into society. Luckily, there were other hangers-on. It has worked well for her."

Grandma sipped her tea. Then she wrapped up the cookies and stuffed them back in their box. "Susan has her good qualities, which is more than I can say for Lily or Violet. But there is a selfish streak in her. She wants to see you married. She wants to be the one to have the daughter who broke the mold and nabbed the first husband. It's not so bad, but she'll do anything to make that happen."

Realization struck and Bea shivered. "No wonder she lost it when I said I was going to try in vitro fertilization. It's not about my having a child. She wants me married."

Grandma nodded. "Yes. She called me the day you told her that, ranting and raving 'til I couldn't understand what she said. She hung up and I began to worry. I thought I would hear from you sooner rather than later, but never expected to hear such wonderful news."

Bea smiled. She couldn't help it. When she thought of Zach, her whole family history of craziness and poison dimmed. "Oh, Grandma, he is special."

Her grandmother took another sip of tea. "Special is good. So, is he well-hung?"

"Grandma!"

~~*~~

Bea rubbed her eyes. The liquor inventory didn't add up. She needed it to balance before she left for the day, but it was almost seven and Zach would be hungry by now. Maybe she should go.

112

Kayla walked in. "You still here?"

Bea shook her head. "No, I'm just a figment of your imagination."

Grinning, Kayla leaned against the wall. "Well, get out of my imagination. I have better things to think about, like going home. I'm off tomorrow and I plan on sleeping most of the day away."

"That sounds great. I have to work."

Kayla sauntered over to the desk. "I almost forgot. While you were at lunch, this came for you."

Bea looked at the envelope with "To Bea Rappaccini" typed across the outside. She shivered. "Where did you get this?"

Kayla's brow furrowed. "It was left at the front desk. I'm not sure who dropped it off because I was busy with a shuttle of check-ins. Why? What's wrong?"

Bea shook her head. "Nothing, I guess. But personally delivered mail isn't exactly a common occurrence."

Kayla leaned on the desk. "Well, open it up. See if it's anything important."

Bea hesitated, but she needed to know. She sliced the envelope with the letter opener and took out a single piece of paper. It had one line.

Are you going to kill him?

Bea crumpled the paper in her grip as her stomached followed suit and her breath lodged in her throat. The letter writer knew about her and Zach. She took a furtive glance around the room, as if she might spot someone watching her.

Kayla tried to sneak a peek. "What's it say?"

Bea stuffed the letter into her purse. "Not much and it isn't signed."

Kayla stood back. "You're not going to tell me, are you?"

Bea sighed. "No, not yet. This is the second one of these I've received. They're strange. Do me a favor, if another one comes, look to see who drops it off, okay?"

"Sure. But do you need to call the cops? Are they threatening?"

Bea thought of Chris. Maybe she should ask for his help on this, at least with the first one. "Not really. It could be just a friend playing games. I don't know. It's hard to explain."

Kayla turned away. "Okay, okay, I can take a hint. I'm out of here anyway. See you on Tuesday."

Bea nodded as Kayla disappeared around the corner. Someone knew. There was no other explanation. Someone knew about her poisons and the threat they posed to Zach. Oh God, Zach.

Springing from the chair, she grabbed her coat and headed out the door. She had to see him, make sure he felt better. The inventory could wait.

The cold temperature outside brought her up short. Oh damn. She didn't have her car. Running down the hill as best she could in heels, she pulled her gloves on, her fast breaths making patches of moisture in the air. Would it ever be spring? At this rate, Zach would have the carving done long before the ice melted on the lake. At least he would if she could leave him alone to work on it.

She took the stairs two at a time. When she reached the second floor, she put the key into her door and turned the knob.

"Hi, beautiful."

Her breath caught at the sound of his low voice, but her heart almost stopped at the sight of him. He had a significant shadow on his chin from a lack of shaving and the color had returned to his face.

Zach stepped up to her and cupped her frozen cheeks in his hands. His grin faded. "You're too cold. You should have called me. Now I need to warm you up."

Bea didn't have a chance to disagree as his lips descended on hers. Her purse dropped to the floor and she leaned her body into his. Insulated by the layers of clothes between them, she groaned with frustration.

He stepped back. "Hungry?"

"For you."

He cleared his throat. "The feeling is mutual, but unfortunately, I emptied my stomach here today. It's not going to let me go with missing another meal."

She unbuttoned her coat. "I'll get started on some dinner right away."

His hands enveloped hers. "No, I have a better idea. Let's get your car first because I don't want you walking in this weather again. Then we'll go to my house. We'll pick up a pizza on the way. I want you in *my* bed tonight."

Her fingers under his hand burned hot at his blatant need. She nodded. "Okay."

He smiled before he kissed her nose. "I knew I liked you."

Zach finished his beer and gazed at Bea as she sat back against the couch cushions, a speck of pizza sauce on the corner of her mouth. He leaned over and licked it away.

She moved her mouth to meet his and he parted her lips with his tongue. Now that his stomach was happy, his cock was jealous. He sucked her tongue into his mouth, enjoying her spicy taste combining with his own. He pulled away.

"Oh." She pouted.

Her lips in that position had him fighting not to kiss her again, but he had other plans. "Tell me, Bea. Have you ever had sex in a hot tub?"

She didn't move except for a slight tightening of her crossed legs. He made a mental note. Knowing what he wanted to do to her made her hot. He'd have to remember that.

She looked away toward the fireplace. "No, I haven't. That sounds a little kinky."

He grinned. "Don't you like kinky? After seeing the toys in your nightstand drawer, I thought perhaps you wouldn't mind a little kink."

She snapped her head around, her face serious. "I'm not really sure how adventurous I am. How could I judge?"

He stood. "Don't judge, just enjoy. Take off all your clothes while I open the hot tub."

She leaned over the back of the couch as he flipped on the outside spotlight. Her hands gripped the frame. "You mean go in the hot tub outside, in the cold?"

He stopped on his way through the sliding-glass door. "Trust me, you won't be cold."

Zach tried to walk normally in case Bea watched, but his hard cock made it difficult.

After unbuckling the straps, he pushed the hot tub cover off until it stood against the deck railing. As he turned to go back in, he caught sight of Bea unzipping the skinny skirt she'd worn to work. It fell down her shapely legs to puddle at her feet. She stepped out in a tiny red thong. Didn't the woman realize she was kink from the tip of her nose to the tops of her toes?

He opened the sliding door and strode up to her, enveloping her in his cold embrace.

"Ow, you're freezing." She laughed as he nuzzled her neck while she pushed weakly against his chest.

"Funny, I feel hotter than a bonfire. Here, feel." He brought her hand down to his crotch.

"I stand corrected," she purred as she stroked him over his jeans.

He stepped away. "Okay, off with that and that," he pointed to her bra and thong.

She didn't tease. She undid the clasp at the front and let the bra fall to the floor. Her rosy-red areolas appeared to stand hard, straining toward him. Then she slipped the thong down her legs. He noticed a sheen of moisture stripe down the inside of her thigh. Hell, the woman was already wet for him.

Scooping her up in his arms, he strode outside.

Bea pressed her body against his clothed frame as if she could disappear inside him. "Holy crow, Zach, it's freezing out here."

He licked her neck, since her face was buried in his shoulder. "You don't know cold 'til you've had ice up that wet pussy of yours."

That got her attention. "Oh geez, I think I'm going to come right now."

He squeezed her before he let her legs down into the hot water. "How's that for warm?"

She scrambled in and sat. "Oh, this feels wonderful."

He smirked. "If you like that, wait." He reached over to the controls and turned on the jets.

The sound of her laughter filled his heart.

"This is awesome, Zach. Aren't you coming in?"

He didn't need to be asked twice. Stripping outside in the cold to gain control of his rampant cock, he went into the house naked, dropped his clothes and grabbed two beers from the fridge.

When he returned, he hesitated as he watched her perfect breasts bob near the surface of the water. Beautiful and easy to please. Yup, he was one lucky man…for now.

Stepping in, he handed her a beer. "Better?"

She nodded and took a sip.

He lowered himself slowly, letting his body adjust to the sudden change in temperature. Her eyes devoured him, making him feel like some Greek god.

Once in, he slid over to her. He placed her beer in a cup holder on the side of the hot tub. The tub could hold eight people, but tonight they would use it to its full capacity.

He floated in front of her and settled himself to kneel between her legs, before pulling her face closer for a cold beer kiss. He worked his way down her neck, kissing the area just behind and beneath her ear. At the shiver that raced across her skin, his cock hardened further. He blew on his wet kissing spot.

Bea brought her shoulder up and giggled. "That tickles."

He lifted her to straddle his chest. "Tell me if this tickles too." Taking her breast in his mouth, he sucked.

Her hands settled on his shoulder. "No, that feels heavenly."

He agreed, but didn't open his mouth to say so. Instead, he nibbled and bit lightly on the hardened nub. He could suck on her hard nipples for days. The rough ridges of her areola made him feel as if he alone had the key to her pleasure.

"Oh Zach. That's too good."

He broke away. "Are you hot yet?"

She gazed down at him. "Hot? I'm dying of heat. The cold air isn't doing much now."

"Good." He grinned before he lifted her torso out of the water and sat her on the edge of the hot tub, spreading her legs. "Let's see if I can cool you off."

She reached down and dribbled water over her clit. "I don't think that's possible."

Zach's body heat rose a couple degrees at her action. Her hard nub called to him. He sucked in a breath as much to take in cooling air as to keep his tongue from piercing the pink folds she displayed, his cock jumping in anticipation. No, he wanted something else inside her.

Leaning over the hot tub, he broke off an icicle hanging from the deck. With the melting and freezing the past week, the icicles had grown. This one was perfect, a half inch around at one nubbed end that widened to three inches where he broke it off. The whole icicle was about a foot long, but it began to melt in his grip.

He turned and held it up. "This might help."

Her mouth opened, but she didn't say a word. She didn't have to. The scent of her wet pussy rose over the chlorinated bubbles, causing his cock to grow painfully harder.

He spread her pink, heated labia and brought the tip of the icicle to her opening.

She shuddered.

He glanced up. If there was a goddess of love, Bea fit the role as she perched there. Her eyes closed, her head tilted to the side and her mouth open, her breathing ragged as it passed by her reddened lips. Her nipples puckered against the cold night air and contrasted with the soft, dripping-wet skin of her waist. But it was her engorged folds, just touching, melting the ice at her slit that caused him to moan silently. He pushed the icicle in an inch with one hand. With the other, he gently pressed her clit.

She dug her hands into his shoulders. "More."

His body tightened at her harsh need, more than willing to obey. He moved the icicle farther into her waiting body. The idea of the frozen water filling her had him straining against the eroticism of the scene. His cock dripped pre-cum into the roiling bubbles as his muscles tensed against his own release. Another few inches and he had filled her with ice.

She grabbed his head. "Do it, Zach. Do it."

He pulled the icicle from her body and quickly sank it in again. It wouldn't last long in her heat. Again, he pulled and pushed, watching her body shiver with pleasure, barely holding back his own orgasm as her deep-throated moans filled the air. He pulled out the ice and found but a three-inch piece left. Pushing it in as far as he could, he let go of her clit, stood and pushed his cock into her pussy.

"Oh God."

Bea's whispered words shot through him, but as the coolness enveloped him, he gained the control he needed to finish it right to please her. The friction of her wet canal sent shivers racing through his veins, making him more determined to give her what she wanted. She grasped him to her and bucked her hips, grinding herself into him. He held her head and drove his tongue past her lips, even as his cock struck what little ice remained inside her.

Her movements continued unrestrained. Her moans grew louder, fueling his desire. He rocked his hips into her and she squeezed his cock as if she'd never let go. The harder he pumped, the slicker she became and the suction of her pussy pulled at his control.

Her orgasm hit, her breath lifting in the air as she threw her head back and screamed.

He laughed for the sheer joy of watching her, feeling her ecstasy as she broke apart around him. Pulling her off the tub's edge, he rammed his cock into her, holding her to her peak.

When Bea grew limp, he kept them together and sank into the roiling water. Her warm body, soft and yielding, floated against him in complete trust. Her light grasp on him penetrated his heart and had him wanting something more, something dangerous.

Bea lifted her head from his shoulder and gave him a shy smile. "I don't think I'll ever look at icicles in the same way again."

Zach chuckled. "Believe me. Neither will I."

She played with the hair at the back of his neck. "Have you ever done that before?"

"Use an icicle to bring a woman pleasure? No."

Relief spread through her at his words, but she tensed as his cock moved within her. Holy crap, he hadn't come yet and her poisons were seeping into him. She started to rise, but he clamped down on her hips.

"Where do you think you're going?"

"I thought you might want to—"

Zach held her in place. "What I want is to make you come again."

His strong hold on her melted her resolve. Once more she was completely his to do with as he pleased, knowing full well his strength far exceeded her own. The thought itself had her folds thickening. She had no control with this man and didn't have a clue how to handle that. Even now, her poisons soaked into his body, but she didn't want him sick again. She'd be careful next time or she'd just have to find the will to leave. She stroked along his hardened biceps. "Then I'm at your mercy."

His lips touched hers in the most gentle of kisses and her heart melted alongside her body. She was lost to this man.

He ended the kiss. When he looked her in the eyes, his hand lifted to stroke her hair. The deck lights shone on her face, leaving his in shadow, but she didn't need to see his eyes to know he wanted her. The thick cock deep inside her, filling her with its length, told her all she needed to know. Her greedy body tensed around his hardness, asking for his domination.

Suddenly, he let her go and she floated back into the warm, still water. "What?"

He stood, reached over her and pushed a button on the tub. The water started to bubble again. She hadn't noticed it had stopped.

He sank back into the hot tub. "I want the jets going for you."

She nestled her shoulders under the water. "For me? Why? I don't mind the still water, as long as it's warm."

He grinned. "If I'm right, you will soon love these jets."

"Why?"

Zach pulled her toward him. His hard cock dug into her abdomen. How could he stand being hard for so long and not come?

He kissed her with a passion held in check and she reveled in his control.

Then he pulled away and turned her from him. "Kneel."

She looked back at him with her eyebrow raised, but he nodded, so she obeyed. She grabbed the edge of the tub and knelt. A hot jet spurted against her upper thigh. Zach dropped down behind her and reached around to palm her mound. He moved them a few inches to the right and took his hand away. She pushed back as the jet stream hit her clit, sending a jolt of fire spiraling through her body. "Zach, my God. It's a vibrator."

She felt his chuckle against her back even as he pushed her toward the rushing water. "Not exactly. I'm hoping it will be better than that. Spread your legs for me, Bea."

She did as he asked and the stream rushed against her clit, down along her lips to the opening of her pussy. The erotic feeling stroked her and played against her all at once. Her need and pleasure rose equally, causing her to pant. "Zach, this is… amazing."

"What does it feel like?"

"I don't know. Like…being turned-on. Staying…that way." Was this what it felt like for him when he was hard for so long? She wanted the pleasure promised, but enjoyed each sharp gush of excitement itself. Then his hand snaked from behind her and came up between her legs.

Even as he held her shoulder to keep her in place, two of his fingers penetrated her and the sensations intensified. Her pussy tightened. Her blood throbbed. But he didn't move, just kept still, leaving her on a plateau of sheer sexual bliss. "Zach."

"Yes?"

"I need…"

"What do you need, Beatrice Rappaccini?"

The intense spasms of pleasure pulsing between her legs left her speechless, and she panted to keep air flowing into her lungs.

He touched her ear with his lips. "What is it you need, beautiful? Do you need me? Did you want this hard cock to push into your throbbing pussy? Did you want my cock to slip between your legs and replace my fingers while the jets stream against your clit? Did you want me to hold on to your hard nipple and roll it between my fingers as I pump from behind and the jets pulse from the front?"

Bea's head swam at the images he painted with his words while she grasped the edge of the hot tub to keep her position in front of the jet's stream. Even in the water, her pussy filled with her own special slickness, pulsing for release. Somehow she found the ability to nod.

Zach wasted no time. His fingers pulled out of her, his arm coming around her waist.

She shivered as his cock slid against her ass, along the crease and entered her pussy in one long stroke. The jets on her clit kept her pulsating arousal high. Her pussy tightened around Zach's invasion.

His other hand tweaked her nipple, even as he whispered in her ear, "Ready?"

She swallowed as fire from her breast ran down to the pleasure building in her core.

He didn't wait for a response. He pulled his hips back and plunged in.

She gasped for air as the sudden sensations in her pussy, clit and nipple converged. Zach pushed deeper and she let herself go, her body convulsing around his cock. She shook in his arms as pulse after pulse of stimulation powered through every nerve. Then his liquid heat filled her and pleasure burst through her entire body. She trembled, the sensations too intense as she tried to breathe.

She went limp, too spent to move.

"Bea? Bea?"

She opened her eyes. The warm swish of water enveloped her sated body and Zach held her on his lap, a worried expression etched on his face. She reached up and stroked his brow. "Wow."

He grinned. "Are you okay?"

"Mmm-hmm. That was the most amazing experience I've ever had."

His smile turned cocky. "Good. Remember, you can only have it with me."

Her heart jumped with longing at his words. "Promise?"

He pulled her face up to his and kissed her thoroughly.

She held on to his neck. When he released her lips, she gave him a coy smile. "I think I blacked out."

He kissed her nose. "No, you didn't."

"Maybe not, but all those amazing feelings and the heat and I couldn't breathe. I didn't want to breathe. It was so good."

He stood with her in his arms, the cool air grazing her body as steam rose from them both.

Zach stepped onto the deck. "I need to get you out of this hot tub. I kept you in it too long."

She practically purred. "I don't remember trying to get out."

He nudged the sliding-glass door open and continued across the living room with her in his arms.

"Zach, I can walk. You don't have to carry me."

He didn't miss a step, but continued upstairs and brought her to what she assumed was his bedroom.

He stopped in front of the bed and let her naked, wet body slide along his until her feet touched the warm rug. "You stay here while I get a towel to dry you off."

As he let go, her knees buckled. She grabbed the footboard of the bed to keep herself upright. His lovemaking had worn her out. That never happened. Sex always energized her because she released her poisons.

Damn. She lost control again and now Zach would be ill, unless…unless she felt differently after sex with him because he was immune to her toxic fluids. Hope sprang to life as she watched him return, studying him for any sign of unease.

He brought a fluffy blue towel and gently dried her from the top of her shoulders to the tops of her feet.

He didn't even look tired. When he finished drying her, he threw the towel over his shoulder and pulled back the deep-green quilt. He scooped her up and laid her on the bed. As he covered her with the blanket, she reached out, capturing his wrist. "Where are you going?"

"I'm going to dry off and get you some water. You're dehydrated. I'll be right back."

As he walked to the door, she enjoyed the view of his tight, wet butt cheeks. Nope, he looked fine to her. If he was immune, then she actually could have a normal life with him. She glanced around the room. Then this would be their bedroom. Like the rest of the house, it had warm honey-colored logs that made up the walls, and furniture with greens and rusts in the cushions. The large flat-screen television opposite the bed was the only item not made of natural elements. She'd love to wake up every morning in here with Zach by her side. She could almost picture the warm sunlight brightening the room in the morning.

Zach returned with a bottle of water and a beer. As he walked toward her, she smiled. She hadn't lied when she told her grandma he was well-hung. Damn, but the man had one good-looking cock.

He sat on the bed and handed her the water.

"Thanks."

He didn't move until she had opened it and taken a gulp. She was more thirsty than she realized. Smart man.

She watched his thigh muscles as he moved around to the other side of the bed, but the long scar on his back caught her attention and her curiosity. She could ask about it now. After all, they were lovers. Her body glowed at the thought. She had a lover. She had her own man and he appeared to be fine. No cramping, and she had come on him twice.

He got into bed and pulled her up against him, his shoulder making a nice pillow.

"Zach?"

His hand rested on her waist. "Yeah."

"How did you get the long scar across your back?"

He gave her a squeeze. "Noticed that, did you?"

She played with the dark hair on his chest. "It's not that obvious, but it's so long. Were you hurt?"

He shrugged beneath her. "Not much. It was worth it. I'd do it again."

"Do what?"

"To make a long story short—"

"Huh-uh. I want the whole story. It will pass the time while I get my strength back."

He kissed her forehead, but she still caught a glimpse of his smug grin. She pulled a hair on his chest to take him down a notch.

"Ow." His hand came up and covered hers. "Do you want the story or not?"

She nodded, biting her lip to keep from laughing.

His fingers entwined with hers. "I told you I was a logger. I had a young college kid working for me one summer. He thought he knew more than he did. He was lucky I was at the site that day trying to get my guys to move a little faster. We had a contract we were behind on. I needed to determine how many more men I would have to hire."

Bea's trained business mind took over. "How big of a company did you have?"

He shrugged beneath her. "Depends on how you look at it. By employees, we were big in the late winter when most of the cutting was done. Generally, my gross income averaged a few million. By that standard, it was small."

The inns ran on a five-million-dollar budget. Zach had run a business at least that large. "That's big enough. Was it stressful? I can imagine the number of decisions you had to make every day. I know what it's like with the inns, but luckily I don't own them."

Zach's hand moved to her arm and idly stroked her flesh. "I didn't find it too stressful except when we were behind. I got out into the woods a lot, which has always been a relaxing environment for me."

Bea squeezed the hand that held hers. "So, what happened?"

"I sold the company."

She lifted her head to catch the smirk on his face. "No. What happened to your back?"

"Oh, my back? The college kid, cocky as usual, got in front of a falling tree. I happened to be in the skidder nearby. I threw it into forward, getting under the tree just in time. The kid ended up with only a broken leg, but he would have been killed. Still, can't believe I was there and in the skidder."

Bea squeezed Zach's hand. "And the scar on your back?"

He kissed the top of her head before he continued. "My skidder's top caved in under the tree's weight. I attempted to jump out, but a piece of the bent metal caught my back as I fell."

Bea lifted herself to see Zach's face. "Oh my God. Did you have to go to the hospital?"

He nodded. "Yes, but it wasn't that deep. Still, I did need stitches. It bled through my shirt and the kid thought I was dead. When I got up, he started to cry."

She lay back down on his shoulder. "He was very lucky you were such a quick thinker and willing to put yourself in harm's way to save him."

He shrugged again. "Most of my men would have done the same for each other, though I do think he was lucky it was me in the skidder. The kid had been a spoiled brat, his father a rich man, so he hadn't been a favorite among my crew."

"I hope his father appreciated what you did."

"I'd say he did."

She sensed his amusement and looked up at his face. "What?"

"This kid got his act together after that and his father was so thankful he offered to buy me out."

"What do you mean buy you out? You mean your contract?"

"No, the company. He offered me a ridiculous amount of money for it if I would run it for three more years and mentor his son. I couldn't resist."

She moved her hand with his so she could touch his abdominal muscles. His strength made sense. "Is that when you moved down here?"

"Yeah."

The muscles tensed beneath her hand and a light tingle of anticipation surged through her veins.

She moved her hand lower, but he stopped her progress. "I don't want you to be sore in the morning."

God, what was she doing? This man was too big a temptation. She clasped his hand and lifted it to her lips for a kiss. "You are very thoughtful."

She gasped as he rolled her onto her back, bracing himself on his elbows as his semi-hard cock pressed against her inner thigh. "Not really, I just want more of you tomorrow."

At his words, her worry intensified.

He nibbled at her lips, but she refused to allow him entry. Giving up on her mouth, he paid homage to her jaw, then kissed his way down her neck.

She closed her eyes and sighed, her resolve weakening.

"You're too easy, beautiful." He licked her earlobe.

She turned her head away.

He took full advantage, raining sweet kisses down to her shoulder until she shivered. "You must be cold. Let me see if I can warm you up." He licked her collarbone before wetting a path between her breasts. Then he used his nose to push up under one breast so he could nibble the underside before licking his way to her hard nipple.

Bea's limbs turned to mush even as tension built between her legs. She couldn't let him be inside her again. She didn't want to risk—

His teeth caught her nipple and scratched the surface, pushing coherent thought away. The man was born to pleasure her, she was sure of it. At least her body believed so because her folds throbbed with need and moistness seeped between them.

He took her nipple into his mouth and played his tongue over it before sucking. His touch was gentle yet erotic. She felt like a maiden sacrifice being worshiped in preparation for penetration.

His hips moved his cock along her wet entrance.

With the little strength she could muster, she used one hand to play with the hair resting on his neck. Its silky thickness caressed her skin as she pressed his head more firmly to her breast, but his touch remained light.

Without warning, his hard cock slipped into her pussy, seeking her depths. The lethargy of her limbs lent a curious helplessness to her psyche and his gentle strokes and light kisses made her feel loved.

Loved?

She opened her eyes and pulled on his hair.

He lifted his head to gaze at her, a tenderness in his expression that had the back of her eyes itching. "Zach?" Her voice came out in a whisper, all she could manage.

"Relax and enjoy while I make love to you."

Her heart leapt at his words. It was just an expression. She shouldn't read anything into it. But her body responded to his gentle touches and slow strokes. Her blood sped as a slow, building pleasure grew within her.

She pulled at his head to leave her breast. She needed to kiss him. She didn't understand why, but the need was too strong to deny.

He finally gave in to her and raised himself, leaning his hard chest against her soft breasts where his hair scraped her nipples. But his hips continued their slow rhythm.

When his mouth touched hers, she licked his lips, kissing the edges until he opened for her. She grasped his neck to lock her tongue with his. Her hips moved of their own accord, meeting his, answering his call to be taken. She pressed his ass into her with her other hand. She wanted all of him, every inch.

Breathless, exhausted and on the edge, she held on as his cock drove home and sent her body into spasms of ecstasy while her heart leapt with sheer joy. Her weak limbs tensed as the orgasm rolled through her body, wringing out every last drop of energy.

He gasped, pulling away from her mouth. His seed flowed into her as her name spilled from his lips, filling her with completeness. Pure happiness swarmed through her for the first time in her life.

He collapsed on top of her, panting.

She couldn't help a smug smile of her own.

He rolled to the side and lay on his back, his chest rising and falling in a slowing beat. "You're going to kill me."

Bea's euphoria crashed hard. She gasped as the words echoed in her brain. *Are you going to kill him?* She shivered.

"Hey, are you cold again?" Zach covered them with the thick, green quilt and pulled her against him.

She nestled into the comfort he offered, trying to ignore the dread seeping into her heart. She had yet to discover how immune Zach might be to her poison. Maybe fate had led her to him and she was meant to be with him because he didn't react to her like other men. Maybe he wouldn't become sick. She prayed she was right because she'd coated him with the full force of her poisons three times, but instead of feeling energized from their expulsion, she felt relaxed. God, she hoped that meant he wouldn't become ill.

Zach kissed her hair. "Go to sleep, beautiful."

She kissed his chest in response. What was it about this man that left her with so little control of herself? If she wasn't careful, she could lose her heart to him, but to lose him would be devastating. Pushing the scary idea away, she concentrated on her dream that Zach was immune and they could have a happily ever after. Surely if she believed it enough, it could be so.

Chapter Eight

Bea woke to the sound of Zach moaning. Her gut tensed as dread filled her. She sat up to find he had kicked aside the blanket and lay curled on his side away from her, clutching his abdomen.

"Zach? What's wrong?"

"I don't know. It feels like food poisoning. Are you okay?"

Guilt surged through her. "I'm fine."

"I'm sorry I woke you. I'm in bad shape. You should go." He groaned again, his thigh muscles tensing against the pain.

Tears escaped unexpectedly. Bea swiped them away. Feeling sorry for herself would not help Zach. "Do you have any of that pink stuff? It might help flush your system."

He pointed. "The bathroom. Under the sink."

She jumped out of bed and ran to the bathroom. Finding the bottle, she then brought it back to him. "I'll get a spoon and some water. You'll probably need it."

He didn't move from his cramped fetal position.

She flew down the stairs as another tear wet her cheek. Grabbing her blouse from the living room floor, she threw it on.

She found a spoon and snatched a bottle of water from the fridge. This was all her fault. She should've had enough willpower

washcloth with cold water. She didn't want to lose him when she had just found him, but that was when she thought him immune to her. She had lied to herself and he paid the price. She should be the one in pain instead of him. It was what she deserved.

Back in his room, she sat on the bed. "Here, you have to take this."

He didn't respond.

Setting the two Tylenol on the nightstand, she brought the cold cloth to his forehead, but he shook her away. "Cold."

Her throat tightened as her eyes filled. She wasn't helping.

She tucked the blanket around his body as stubborn tears wet her cheeks. Unsure what to do, she crawled on top of the blanket and put her arms around him. She felt his body loosen. After an hour or so, his shivering ceased and he slept.

Carefully, she moved off the bed and pulled on her skirt. She tiptoed over to feel Zach's forehead. Still too hot. Somehow she had to force the pills into him.

A sound below stopped her reach.

She listened. Footsteps on the basement stairs echoed up to her. Oh God, someone was in the house.

Glancing around the room, she searched for a weapon, anything, a baseball bat, a heavy statue. Zach had to have something up here. She opened the drawer in the nightstand…no gun.

The steps grew louder.

The intruder would be at the bedroom door any moment. Why didn't Zach have a gun mounted on a wall? Didn't all log cabins have guns on the walls? She dropped down to search underneath the bed. Aha. A rifle was suspended from hooks beneath.

Heavy steps sounded at the top of the stairs.

The intruder was big by the sound of the creaking floor beneath his weight. Grabbing the rifle from its rack, she stood in front of Zach and lifted the gun. As a tall shadow fell across the doorframe, she tried to calm her racing heart. Her sweaty palms weren't helping, but she had to make the intruder think she had control of the situation. Oh God, she didn't even know if there were any bullets in the damn gun.

A man appeared in the doorway.

Lurch from *The Addams Family* stood there. Her pretended calm left her. "Stop right there or I'll shoot."

The man put his hands out in front of him as if he could protect himself from a bullet. "No, wait, I'm Josh. Someone called me to help Zach. Was it you?"

Bea sagged in relief and lowered the rifle, though her hands still shook. "I'm sorry, I thought you were an intruder. How did you get in?"

Josh reached in his pocket and raised his keys. "I have a key."

"Oh."

"Can I come in now?"

Bea moved away from the bed. "Please. He's burning up. I couldn't get anything in him, but he was shivering with cold. Are you a doctor?"

Josh nodded, but he had already begun to examine Zach. "I can see you wore him out."

Bea felt herself blush. If Josh knew his medicine, he'd also know poison caused Zach's current condition. She placed the rifle on Zach's dresser and clasped her hands together to keep them from shaking. Josh took a long time to explore Zach's symptoms. She bit at the inside of her lip.

He looked at her. "Poison."

Bea froze.

He turned back to Zach. "We need to get the poison out of his system. Do you have any idea what he might have ingested?"

She shook her head. "We ate the same food."

"Did you use any particular sex lube or flavored enhancements?"

Bea wanted to sink into the fur rug at her feet, her face growing as hot as Zach's. "No. Nothing."

Josh turned back to scrutinize her again. "I don't know what it was, but he needs to get rid of it, fast."

Bea shook her head, ignoring the tears that coursed down her cheeks. "It's my fault. I shouldn't have come here. I didn't mean for him to get sick."

Josh's eyebrows rose. "Well he is, and if you weren't here to call me, I'm not sure he could make it. I'm going to give him something to make him vomit and set up a saline drip for his dehydration. It will be easier to administer the drug for his fever. Will you stay and help me?"

She nodded, unable to bear the thought that Zach could be seriously ill. What had she done? If she had just restrained herself. Stopped him. Done *something*.

Josh removed his fingers from Zach's neck. "Great. Then stay here with him while I run to my car and grab what I need."

She nodded again as Josh left the room, his lanky strides covering the space in half the time it would take her. She went to the bed and brushed Zach's hair away from his forehead before taking his hand in hers. "I'm sorry. I didn't mean to hurt you. Please get better." She kissed his fingers and wiped away her tears. He would be all right. She had to believe that.

Bea sat in the kitchen sipping a cup of tea Josh insisted she have. She'd called work and told them she was sick. Hopefully, no one would go to her apartment to see her car wasn't there. She never called in sick, but she lived in a small town and she could imagine Sharon Larsen dropping by with chicken soup.

Josh entered the kitchen. "He's going to make it."

She started at his voice. "Thank God." Her relief made her want to cry again, and it took all her effort not to fall off the stool as her tightened muscles finally relaxed.

Josh opened the fridge and grabbed a beer.

A beer? Her face must have shown her surprise because he shrugged.

"I need a drink after that. I don't know what got into him, but it was bad. You were right to call me."

Bea looked into her tea as if she could find solace there. "I wanted to take him to the hospital, but he told me to call you."

She sensed Josh inspecting her. He sat on a stool next to her. "So, are you Zach's mystery woman?"

She faced him. Up close, he had a much nicer face than Lurch. It had been his height that frightened her. That and the fact she thought him an intruder. She offered her hand. "I'm Bea Rappaccini. I work at the Lakeside Inn."

He smiled and shook her hand. "I'm pleased to meet you. I think he will wake up soon. Did you want to see him?"

She shook her head and stood. "No, I'd better go. Thank you so much for helping Zach."

Josh gave her a searching look. "I've known Zach since grade school. I wouldn't let anything hurt him if it was in my power to stop it."

Bea gulped at the hint of a threat in the doctor's words. "I'm so glad he has you as a friend. Thank you for helping him." On impulse she leaned over and kissed him on the cheek, then she rushed into the living room to gather her purse.

Josh came around the kitchen wall and intercepted her at the top of the basement stairs. "Did you want to leave him a message?"

She stopped. There was too much she wanted to say, but the best words would be "goodbye", and she just couldn't do that. "Tell him…I'm sorry."

Josh raised an eyebrow, but Bea headed down the stairs.

She could have killed Zach. He deserved so much better. Moving away from the house, she forced herself to place one foot in front of the other, despite the growing ache in her chest. As she walked the path, she couldn't help glancing back at the second story one more time. She liked him too much to be with him again. "Goodbye, Zach."

Bea checked the clock for the fifth time in the last twenty minutes. She couldn't help it. Every minute past noon could mean Phillip had changed his mind. She didn't want to see him, especially today. After witnessing Zach's pain yesterday, she had been on the edge of vomiting herself. Her stomach tightened again. She hadn't been able to eat since she and Zach had finished the pizza before hitting the hot tub the other night. Now she was supposed to eat lunch? What was she thinking to meet with Philip?

The image of Zach curled on his side, groaning, had her diving into her desk for an antacid. The knot in her stomach tightened to unbearable and her eyes misted. She couldn't see him again. She cared too much to cause him that kind of pain. If only she had control when she was with him, but for some reason, she got lost in how wonderful he made her feel. She wanted to have all the crazy experiences Kayla had had, but with him. What a mess.

She glanced at the clock again and wished Kayla didn't have the day off. She could use a friend to talk to. She loved her mom and grandmother, but despite their frank talks, she'd prefer someone closer to her own age, and her boss's quiet concern made her feel worse. Picking up her phone, she punched in Zach's number. At the first ring, she hung up. What was she doing? She had to stay away from him. He might still be ill and with her luck, Dr. Josh would answer.

Her gaze had wandered to the clock again when Gary, the front desk worker, poked his head around the corner.

"Hey, Bea, there's a guy out here asking for you."

She swallowed. It must be Phillip. "Okay, I'll be right there."

She should brush her hair and touch up her lipstick, but she didn't care how she appeared for him. The sooner she met him, the sooner she could go back to work, or rather, the sooner she could go back to thinking about Zach. Her productivity was nil.

Sighing, she rose and dragged herself to the front desk. She glanced around the lobby, but didn't recognize any of the dozen or so people milling around. "Gary, you said there was someone here for me?"

"Yeah, him." He pointed to a man standing with his back to her, staring out the three-story window.

Curious, she approached the stranger. He was built, probably used weights, maybe stood five foot ten. "Can I help you?"

He turned to face her. "Bea, it's me."

She couldn't hide her surprise. "Chris? I didn't recognize you without your uniform and hat. What are you doing here? Is this police business?" Sudden images of Zach being rushed to the hospital flooded her mind and her legs turned to slush. She leaned on the couch for support.

Chris smiled, relieving her of her panicked thoughts.

She'd forgotten how handsome he was. His blond crew cut made his jawline more pronounced and his light-blue eyes reminded her of the sky in summer.

"No. I have the day off. I just wanted to give you a friendly heads-up."

She motioned to the couch and took a seat.

Chris sat facing her. "I heard from a friend of mine at the

Wrenborough Police Department that they ran the plates on your car. I guess you left it at the depot the other night."

Bea could feel her cheeks burn. "Yes, I did. You know how slippery it was, though it's hard to believe with a day like today. They say it will hit sixty degrees. Zach insisted on driving me home. Why did they run my plates?"

Chris shrugged, his shoulders looking bigger in the light-blue t-shirt he wore than in his uniform. "Standard procedure. That's a private parking lot and the department there does a good job of watching out for the businesses in town. I wanted to let you know because if they find it there again, they'll tow it."

"Really?"

"Yeah." His smile went crooked. "Standard procedure."

She chuckled. "Well, thank you for stopping by here to let me know. That was so nice of you."

"No problem. Hey, since I'm here, do you want to grab lunch?"

Bea kept her smile by sheer force of will. "I'm sorry, Chris. I have an old friend who's supposed to be meeting me for lunch. Do you remember Phillip Sutton from high school?"

Chris thought for a moment. Then his eyes narrowed and his muscles bunched beneath his blue shirt. "Weren't you two an item at one time?"

Bea studied her hands. "Yes, but he got sick."

Chris slapped his hand on his knee. "That's right. He's the kid who went into a coma and missed a ton of school. I'd heard he'd come out of it, but I was in the police academy by then. What's he up to these days?"

Bea looked over the couch to check the lobby. She hadn't been anxious to see Philip again, but at least he would go home. Chris was right in town, and she didn't like how awkward he made her feel. "He works for a pharmaceutical company now. He and my mom keep in touch."

Chris rubbed the back of his neck. "Now that I think of it, you didn't date anyone after Phil got sick."

She stood. Okay, enough was enough. "Thanks for letting me know about my car, Chris. I'd better finish the billing, if I can, before Phillip arrives."

Chris stood. "Right, forgot you're on the clock. Well, if you ever need anything, just give me a call."

Bea accepted the card he gave her. "Actually…"

"What?"

She glanced toward the lobby and caught Phillip, in a pale-gray suit, entering the main doors. "Nothing important. I'll call you. It looks as if the billing will have to wait."

Chris turned as Phillip joined them and gave her a kiss on the cheek.

She sensed Chris stand straighter. Maybe because Phillip was so tall. He had to be six four. Great, the testosterone levels elevated another notch. "Phillip, this is Chris Ledoux. He went to high school with us."

Phillip reached out his hand and the two men shook. "I don't remember you, but then again there are a lot of things I can't recall from high school. Luckily, Bea is the bright memory for me."

Chris put his hand on Bea's shoulder. "Yes, she's definitely special."

Bea stiffened. Time to end the posturing. "So, Phillip, are you ready for lunch?"

"That I am." He held his arm out to her.

She gritted her teeth as she stepped away from Chris and linked her arm with Phillip. "Thank you, Chris, for the information."

He nodded at her before Phillip led her to the inn's restaurant. She could feel Chris' gaze on her until she had rounded the corner of the lobby. One down, one to go.

As they settled into a private booth, Bea took a sip of water and dove in. "So, Phillip, tell me about your great discovery. Have you found a perfect match? Developed a new medicine for the company? Oh, have you been promoted?"

He glanced sideways before making eye contact with her, an old habit she'd forgotten he had.

He reached across the table and grabbed her hand. "Bea, it has nothing to do with my job and everything to do with you."

Huh? She pulled her hand away, watching him gauge her reaction. "What is it, Phillip?"

"I've found an antidote." He sat back and waited.

She shook her head. "For what?"

"You."

"Me? What about me?"

He leaned forward and lowered his voice. "Your poisons. I know about your toxic orgasms."

Bea's blood chilled, her heart slowed. "What are you talking about? What poison?"

"My coma. It was the poisons in your orgasm that caused it. I know, Bea. Your mom admitted it to me. She thought if I knew, I could forgive you and then you could forgive yourself."

Bea shook her head. This couldn't be. Phillip couldn't know. Would he tell others? What had her mother been thinking? Fear skidded up her spine as the full implications of Phillip's knowledge penetrated her brain.

The waitress came over at that moment. "What would you like?" She smiled as if everything were normal.

Bea would like her world back the way it had been less than five minutes ago. She couldn't even manage a smile for the girl, so she kept her eyes fixed to the menu while she ordered her usual sandwich. Maybe she could eat it later when she could think straight.

Phillip waited for the young woman to leave. "Bea, it's okay. I forgive you. You didn't know at the time."

Her shock transformed to anger, mostly at her mother. No one outside the family knew their secret. Did her mother have a death wish? Was her mom so determined to see her married that she would risk their very existence? Or worse, was she clueless?

Dread seeped into Bea's heart. She stared at Phillip, who looked away before meeting her furious gaze. Her body shook as she tried to keep her voice low. "You forgive me? There is nothing to forgive. I didn't do anything wrong here."

Phillip sent a furtive glance around the room. "Shh, you're attracting attention. We need to keep this a secret."

Bea laughed, hysteria building in her throat. She dug her nails into her palms to hold on to her sanity. "So, now you want it to be a secret. Now that you're in on it. What right did you have to dig into my family's past? We dated as teenagers, Phillip. Teenagers. There was nothing to it but young love. Damn, it was thirteen years ago."

He reached across the table again, but she was ready this time and pushed back against the seat.

He took the hint. "But I never stopped loving you, Bea. Surely you know that. It took me years to figure it out, and then sneaking samples of your DNA from your mom and using the lab at work to do the experiments. But I knew it would all be worth it in the end."

She shook her head at the stranger sitting across from her. This could not be happening. Her DNA? He stole her DNA. No, her mom and he stole her DNA. "Phillip, I'm sorry if you spent years figuring out why you went into a coma, but you have to understand, this doesn't concern you anymore. I've resigned myself to my fate. I've made peace with it."

Bea couldn't believe she could utter such nonsense. But her limited knowledge of Phillip and his motives had her instinct pushing him away. She needed him to leave, now.

He glanced to the side before looking at her again. "I don't think you understand, Bea. I have the cure. You wouldn't have to be resigned to your fate. We could be together, have children. Remember how we chose names for our kids?"

Bea shook her head. She didn't remember. It hadn't been important for her because their whole relationship had been buried under her guilt, but facing him now, she finally understood it hadn't been her fault. Her mom had never told her. Her mother. She would wring her mother's neck. Grandma Beatrice was right. Her mom's aspirations far outpaced common sense.

What she wouldn't do to have Zach walk in the restaurant right now and sweep her into his arms. Maybe that would finally register with her old beau. "Phillip. I'm sorry, but there will be no 'us'. I've found someone."

She looked down, afraid to see Phillip's reaction. She needed him to understand, but her gut feared he would take revenge. What the heck was she supposed to do here? When he didn't say anything, she chanced a peek.

His smile was wide, confident. Huh? Why did she feel as if she were breaking up with him all over again? That he didn't understand? "Phillip, did you hear what I said? I've met someone special."

He took a sip of water and shook his head. "How long can it last, Bea? A few days at best. If you spend any more time than that, he will die, if he doesn't go into a coma."

He leaned forward, excitement shining in his eyes. "You see, Bea, I realized fate had saved me. By going into a coma, I couldn't have sex with you, which, as the randy teen I was, would have killed me. We were meant to be together."

He sat back, picked up his napkin and laid it neatly across his lap before making eye contact again. "But it's okay, I can wait. You'll see. The only way you'll ever have a normal relationship is with me. Ask your mother. She knows we're right for each other. I just hope you don't kill this guy before you wake up and realize the truth."

The blood pounded through Bea's veins, causing her head to ache. The man was in severe denial, or certifiably crazy, or both. "Phillip, I love this man and I will control whatever I need to control to insure his health." She ignored the twist of pain in her heart at her own words.

Phillip glanced sideways before a Cheshire Cat grin settled on his face. "I'll wait as long as it takes for you to come to your senses. But a word of caution, you're not getting any younger and if we're going to have children, we should get started right away."

Whoa. The conversation had disintegrated and she had no idea how to save it. On second thought, she didn't want to.

She stood. "I'm sorry, Phillip. What we had as teenagers died a long time ago. I didn't realize you still had feelings for me, but I don't love you and I don't need your forgiveness. Find another woman to love. One who can love you back."

Bea took a breath and waited for Phillip's gaze to return to her. "Phillip, don't call me again. I don't want to see you, *ever*."

She turned to leave, but he grabbed her wrist, his grip painful, his eyes narrowing. "We are meant to be a couple, Bea. We will have our family. I have the solution and when you're ready, we can make it happen."

She pointedly looked at his hand and he let go. She spun around and stalked through the door, doom settling over her like the gray sky of yesterday.

As she strode through the hallway, she thought of her mother's machinations and she ground her teeth. Grandma had been right. Ms. Susan Rappaccini had her priorities mixed up to have given hope to the poor, insane man who was Bea's ex-boyfriend. She stopped in mid-stride. Or had her mother created the insanity? The idea was too horrible to contemplate. Her mother had to be made to understand the ramifications of her actions.

Bea moved across the lobby on shaky legs. She headed behind

the desk, intending to grab her phone from the back office, but Gary stopped her.

"Bea, this came for you while you were at lunch."

She glanced at him, saw the plain envelope with the single line of typing on the outside and swayed.

"Hey, Bea, you all right?"

She grabbed on to the counter for support. "Yes, no, I don't know."

"When did you eat last?"

She shook her head, she couldn't remember. "I'll take that."

He handed her the dreaded envelope and she dragged herself into her office. The outside read, "To Bea Rappaccini".

Her hands shook as she used the letter opener to slit it. Unfolding the note, she read. *Does he know about the other men?*

Bea dropped the letter as if it contained a rattlesnake and slumped back in the chair. She wiped the perspiration from her forehead. Had she been followed? As if she didn't have enough problems, someone felt a need to make things worse?

"Damn it." She sat up. She was tired of being manipulated. She needed to take control, like she used to when having a one-night stand. Ever since Zach, she'd let herself be pushed and pulled. The question was, where to start first?

Craig Larsen meandered into her office at that moment. "Bea, you look flushed."

His expression mirrored his concern.

She brought her hands to her cheeks. "I'm not quite myself today."

He frowned sympathetically. "Why don't you go home early? We can handle it. It's pretty slow for a Wednesday. You must have come back to work too soon."

She glanced away from his kind face. "Yeah, maybe I did. Thanks, Craig."

He waved her off as he wandered toward the front desk. "Get some rest. See you tomorrow."

As soon as he left, she grabbed her purse and strode outside to her car, for once unhappy with the warmth of the air. The half-mile it took to drive to the police station wasn't long enough for her to calm her racing blood. She should have done this as soon as she received the first letter. Inside the small building, she stepped to the window.

A young man in police uniform gave her a nod. "May I help you?"

"Yes, is Chris Ledoux here?"

"I'm sorry, ma'am, he's off today. Can I help you with something?"

She curled her hands in frustration. She knew that. What had she been thinking? "No, I'll call him tomorrow."

The young man looked concerned, but she waved him off. "Thanks."

Bea left the station and went to her apartment, her thoughts circling her brain like mosquitoes hovering over water. She may be delayed in slaying that dragon, but her mother was one monster she could tackle today.

She sat on her living room couch and opened her phone, but before she could dial, it rang.

Zach. Or it could be Dr. Josh using Zach's phone, which could mean the worst. Either way, she couldn't answer. After six rings, it went to voice mail. It was for the best.

She had lied to Phillip. She had no control with Zach, which meant she couldn't be with him anymore. She'd have to make a clean break. It meant going back to the one-night stands. The very thought caused her stomach to roll over. But she had at least a week before she needed to contemplate that, a little longer if she used her porous dildo.

Unable to stand the idea of having sex with anyone besides Zach for one more minute, she dialed her mom's number. "Hello, Andy?"

A man's cultured voice answered her. "No, this is Tony. Your mom's outside chatting with the neighbor. What's up, Bea?"

Bea ground her teeth in frustration. "I need to talk to Mom. You're not going to believe what she did. No wait. Tell her I'm on my way over and I'm pissed."

Her dad's quiet voice didn't help her nerves. "Now, Bea, you know your mom, and she's not going to change. What happened?"

"Let's just say she told someone about our family secret, and now I've got a man determined to make babies with me and it's the wrong man." She hung up on her dad, unable to say another word until she had her mother in her sights.

Her grandmother's words came back to her. *It's not her fault, it's her genes.* At this point, Bea didn't care what excuse her mom gave, the woman needed to take responsibility for her actions.

As Bea slipped into her Camry, she squinted. Grandma may have been wrong about the insanity skipping generations because right now she wasn't quite sure what she might do when she confronted her mother.

Chapter Nine

"Relax, Bea, it's not the end of the world."

Bea turned back from her pace through the living room and stared open-mouthed at her mother. "You don't get it, do you? You've made a mess of my life by telling Phillip. The man is insane. Are babies so important to you that you'll take psycho grandchildren just to have them?"

Her mom bowed her head as she sat next to Tony on the couch. The man, chief operations officer of a national catalogue company, was smart enough to stay out of it.

Her mother, however, was another matter. She was as clueless as Phillip. No wonder they connected.

Her mother fidgeted. "I'm sure you're exaggerating."

She gripped her hands tight, aggravated beyond her limit. Her throat constricted as she spoke through gritted teeth. "No. I'm not."

Bea forced herself to unclamp her jaw. "This is the last time you will mess around with my life. You better get used to life without me because I'm not coming over and I'm not calling you. Quite frankly, I need a break from you. If I could move, I'd leave the country."

As she headed for the door, her mom stood, tears tracking down her cheeks. "Bea, you can't. I'm your mother."

Bea stopped and stared into her mother's fearful gaze. Anger coupled with hopeless frustration boiled within her, causing her to sweat. Her mother needed to learn a lesson and this might be the only way to teach her. She strode to the door. "Goodbye, Mom."

"Bea!"

She kept walking, ignoring her mother's tearful crying until she stepped into her car. She looked up before backing out and saw Tony take her mother inside. That must be nice. Thanks to her mom, Bea doubted she'd ever know what it was like to have someone care for her.

Though she had taken control, she didn't feel any better. In fact, her stomach was knotted up like a tangled fishing net and a slow burn had started in its depths. She had to keep Zach out of her life and she'd kicked her mom out too. Maybe she needed to wind down.

Passing her apartment, she stopped farther up the street at Busy Body's. It seemed appropriate.

She sat at the bar and ordered a Toasted Almond. As the first sip warmed her, her body loosened. Finally, some temporary relief, but her stomach growled. When had she last eaten? Waving down the bartender, she ordered mozzarella sticks. She took another sip and let the calming effects of the liquor soothe her frazzled nerves. Maybe she could kill a few brain cells tonight and forget about her mom.

"Hi, beautiful."

Zach? Hope speared her heart as she looked up at the man who'd spoken to her. But it wasn't Zach. This guy had to be a tourist with his polo shirt and khaki pants. One of those suburban white-collar men who thought they had the world by the tail. He screamed arrogance.

The guy leaned on the bar. "I know this may be bold, but you have the most gorgeous eyes."

Although he complimented her eyes, he stared at her breasts. Great, just what she needed right now, an intoxicated tourist hitting on her. "Thanks. Now go away."

He leaned toward her, crowding her space with his Polo aftershave. "Just 'cause you're beautiful doesn't mean you can be a bitch."

She turned away and ignored him.

He wouldn't take the hint. "Hey, I'm talking to you, Miss Priss."

She shook her head. Should she give in to the temptation to spill her drink on the guy's pants? It would be such a waste of money, but maybe worth it.

Another male voice chimed in. "Excuse me, sir, but the lady's not interested."

"And who the blazes are you?" The drunk sounded ready for a fight.

"I'm a friend of the lady and suggest you move along."

Bea turned around in time to see Chris flash his badge. The drunk raised his hands. "I'm not breaking the law here, Officer. I was only trying to have a friendly conversation."

Chris motioned with his head. "I'd suggest you head back to your hotel before I cite you for disorderly conduct."

The guy mumbled beneath his breath, but she couldn't hear him. After he skulked away, Chris sat next to her.

More pleased to see him than usual, she tilted her head at him. "I thought you were off-duty."

He shrugged. "I am. But he's too drunk to realize it."

"Well, thanks. I really didn't need that to end my day." She lifted her glass to him and took another sip of her creamy almond drink, thankful she hadn't had to waste it.

He waved for the bartender and ordered a bottled water. "I thought you were working?"

She sighed. "My day was going so badly I took the afternoon off, but it only got worse."

He picked up his water and took a gulp before he fixed his sympathetic gaze on her. "Anything I can do to help?"

She stopped in mid-bite of her cheese stick. "Actually, there is."

Opening her purse, she found two of the letters, but had no clue which was which. The second one about killing Zach was still at home where she'd stashed it. If Zach was who it referred to? She couldn't be sure about anything right now except that giving that particular letter to Chris would be a huge mistake. She pulled out one of the envelopes. "I've been receiving these strange letters at the Lakeside Inn. I don't know which one this is. One of them came today, in between my fight with Phillip and my fight with my mother."

Chris threw her a look of understanding before he took the envelope and studied it. "Did anyone see who dropped this off?"

She took another sip of her drink. "No, but I have everyone watching."

"Do you mind?" he asked, gesturing to the letter inside.

"No, please do."

Bea ate one whole cheese stick before Chris finished with his study of the paper. "Well, what do you think?"

He looked her in the eye. "I think this could be serious. 'I know your secret' sounds as if this could escalate into blackmail. Would you mind if I took this and talked with a detective friend of mine?"

She bit the inside of her lip. If the secret did refer to her toxic nature, did she want the local police investigating? Probably not, but then again, she'd had it with reacting to the mess her life was in at the moment. She needed to take action. "That's fine, but I don't want to make a big deal of this. That was the first one I received, and there has been no demand for money or anything."

He gave her a stern look. "Bea, you need to take this seriously. Have you told the man you're seeing about these?"

She avoided his gaze. "No, not yet."

"Have you told your mother?"

She shook her head. "If I told my mom the world would know,

which means my dad Gerry would find out and then I wouldn't be able to move without some huge motorcycle dude shadowing me."

She'd meant it as a joke, but Chris didn't smile. "Tell your boss and your dads at least. I don't like this."

She smiled inside at his avoidance of Zach, but that was fine. She didn't have Zach anymore anyway.

Chris slipped the envelope in the back pocket of his jeans then gestured to the appetizers on her plate. "So, are you going to finish those or just play with them?"

She looked at the remaining cheese sticks. She'd managed to eat one, but there were seven cold pieces still on the plate. She pushed them toward him. "No, they're all yours. I think I'll go home now. Maybe if I stay there, nothing more will happen today."

She finished her drink in a couple swallows and stood to leave.

"Bea." Chris caught her by the wrist.

Again? Why did men feel they had a right to hold her back? Her grateful feelings toward Chris vanished in an instant as she pulled her hand away rudely. "Yes?"

"Be careful. Lock your doors and if anything goes wrong, call me. My personal cell is on the back of the card I gave you."

She flushed at her defensive reaction and gave him a deprecating smile. "Thanks. I appreciate it."

But as she walked away, she sensed Chris' gaze on her, even as she opened her car door. Glancing at the bar window, she found him still watching her. She shivered, despite the warm air. Climbing into her car, she closed the door and berated herself for being paranoid. Chris was harmless. He was a cop for goodness sake. She needed to get a grip.

Back at her apartment she threw her purse on the table and unhooked her phone from the outside pocket. The message light flashed at her and reminded her to listen to Zach's or Dr. Josh's message. Did she really want to know?

With a need far stronger than any decision process, she hit her voice mail and listened.

"Hi, beautiful. It's me, Zach. I know we were supposed to have dinner tomorrow night, but Josh says I'm not well enough to go out. What does he know? You'd think he was my mother or something. I'll call you. Bye."

She slumped into the chair at the kitchen table and started to cry. Would her day never end?

~~*~~

Zach paced across the living room, cell phone in hand. "Come on, Bea. Answer, damn it."

Her voice mail message came on. "Bea, you can't avoid me forever. What's going on? Call me."

He hung up and threw the phone on the couch. What the hell? He didn't peg her for a game player. Something was wrong. She'd tell him if she'd decided to call it quits, right?

He turned as Josh meandered into the living room, a plate full of potato salad, cold spaghetti and Greek olives in his hand. "She still hasn't returned your calls?"

Zach gave his friend his best give-me-a-break face and stuck his hands in his pockets. "What makes you think that?"

"Hey, don't attack me because you got sick on your date. It's not my fault she's not attracted to guys who groan in the morning." Josh threw his long body onto one of the couches.

Zach grabbed his phone and clipped it on his belt. "That's it. I'm going down there."

Pulling his attention from the television remote, Josh set it down hard. "Hey, I just arrived. What's the rush? I only have a couple days off. So it's been a week since you last saw her. What happened to your rule of three?"

"I'd decided to go four with her. She's not the needy type. But she needs to explain why she's avoiding me. I want answers and I want them now. Sorry, buddy."

Zach pulled on his leather jacket and grabbing the keys to his Harley, threw them at his friend. "Here, to make it up to you. Why don't you take the bike to Smokin' Joe's? They have a band on Friday nights. Lots of girls go dancing there. I'm sure I'll be back in a couple hours. If she's not at work or her place, then I'll be longer because I'm not leaving until I find out what's going on."

Josh shook his head. "Man, you're all twisted up, but I'll be happy to take the hog for a spin. Maybe I can find a copilot."

Zach hesitated at the top of the stairs. "Be good to her. If you get drunk, ask for a ride, okay?"

Josh winked. "Maybe."

"Smart-ass." He picked a pillow off the nearest couch and threw it at Josh.

"Hey."

Not wanting to know if he'd hit the plate of food or not, Zach ran down the stairs and jumped into his truck. He sent hunks of mud flying into the air as he sped out of the driveway before he bumped onto the main road.

The closer he drove to Meriden, the more confused he became. Bea had been more than satisfied the night they were together. Maybe she wanted more than sex. But she had initiated all of it. Well, maybe not all of it, but she had certainly been willing. If she didn't think anything was wrong with taking their relationship at the speed of light and then slamming on the brakes, he would have to give her a lesson in dumping people. She couldn't just stop taking his calls. She had to tell him it was over. Hell. He didn't want it to be over—yet.

He pulled into the Lakeside Inn and drove to the back parking lot for employees. Good. Her Camry was there. The lady had some questions to answer and he better like what he heard.

Zach strode up to the front desk where a pretty blonde with short-cropped hair greeted him.

"Can I help you?" The invitation in her large round eyes was so clear, it gave him an idea.

"Yes, I'd like a room for the night."

"Did you want a double, king size, or a suite?"

Reading her name badge, he smiled. "Kayla, I think I'd like a suite. Does it have a king-size bed?"

She batted her lashes. "Even better, it has a California king."

"Perfect." He handed her his credit card.

She reached for the card, but held his hand as she asked, "Is that just for one night?"

He smirked. "Yeah."

She pouted as she pulled the card from him and slipped it into the machine behind the counter. "Too bad. But if you decide to stay longer, I see that the suite is available the rest of the week, Mr. Woodman."

He shook his head. "Nope. If I don't get everything done tonight, I won't be staying any longer."

She gave him a puzzled look before she handed him his card and a room key. "That's room 223, go down this hall and take a left. At the end is your room. It has a gorgeous view of the lake."

He didn't plan to enjoy the view. "Thanks."

"Is there anything else I can do for you, Mr. Woodman?"

The invitation in her eyes remained, but Zach wasn't interested. Sure, if he was free he might have been, but he was taken at the moment. He may keep his relationships short, but he never cheated. "No. I'm good. Thanks."

He strode to his room. He would order a bottle of champagne and take the seductive approach with Bea. That might be a better idea than a confrontation. She seemed so clueless about dating. It could very well be that she thought taking a week-long break after incredible sex was normal. He grinned. He'd have to show her how much she'd been missing.

~~*~~

"Earth to Bea. Hello." Kayla sat on the corner of the desk and waved her hand in front of Bea's face.

She jumped, startled. Her heart beat a rapid tattoo in her chest at the interruption of her thoughts. "I'm here. What's up?"

"You don't look 'here'. You've been moping around this place for a week. Why don't you call him back?"

She sat back in her chair and stared at her friend. Slowly she inhaled, held her breath and exhaled. "It's not that simple."

"Okay, okay, I can take a hint." Kayla pouted for a moment, but then her blue eyes twinkled with mischief. "Listen, maybe you need a distraction. This really hot guy just checked in. I flirted with him and he flirted back, but I don't think he's interested. Maybe he prefers brunettes."

She raised her brows. "So, I'm to have a rebound relationship with a guest?"

"Who said rebound? I'm talking about a one-night stand. He's only here for tonight. Besides, you can't go on the rebound. You weren't dumped."

Bea shook her head. The thought of a one-night stand made her nauseated. Either that or it was the poisons building in her body. "No thanks, he's all yours."

Kayla stood and ran her fingers through her short, stylish hair. "Well, I can give it another try. He's not my type for a relationship, but he's built and I certainly wouldn't throw him out of bed."

Bea grinned, pleased to have something to smile about. "Go get him, girl."

The phone at the front desk rang and Kayla sauntered to the

door. "I'm off in an hour. But I may be sticking around for a while." She threw Bea a wink before she disappeared around the corner.

As soon as Kayla left, Bea closed her eyes. Her body had begun to show the signs of her increased toxins. Her muscles were weakening as proven by the number of items she'd dropped in the past twenty-four hours, the hot and cold flashes had started and the dark circles appeared under her eyes. She had one, maybe two days at best, before she'd have to seek out a sex partner. The thought of sex with someone other than Zach made her physically ill.

She opened her eyes and looked blankly at the paperwork on her desk. Either way, she was screwed.

Kayla bopped her head around the corner. "Hey, Mr. Hunk just ordered a bottle of champagne, chocolate-covered strawberries and a whole can of whip cream. Something tells me he won't be alone tonight."

Bea had to smirk at Kayla's pouty face. "Hey, you know all the good ones are taken."

"Absolutely not, they're just harder to find."

"Right." She'd found her Mr. Right, but couldn't have him.

Kayla disappeared again and Bea returned to her work. Next weekend they had three events at the inns and she still had to order the linens for two of them. She promised herself if she could finish that, she could order a sandwich from the restaurant. It would be better than going home to cook for herself.

"Ah, Bea?"

She looked up to see Kayla hugging the doorjamb again. She sighed. "Yes?"

"That hunky guy I told you about earlier? He's at the front desk and he's asking for you by name."

Bea shivered. Could it be her "letter stalker", as Chris had started to call him? At least she wouldn't be alone. Kayla would be at the desk and could always call security. Tensing for battle, she straightened her back. "Okay, I'll be right there."

Kayla stepped farther into the doorway. "Hey, Bea, you good?"

She attempted to smile, but failed. "Good enough."

"Okay. I'll keep him busy."

Once her friend left, Bea stood, but her knees shook. She hadn't had any letters in days and while she had hoped they were done, Chris said the guy was biding his time. Maybe this was it. Pushing herself into professional mode, she set her jaw and resolutely stalked to the check-in desk.

The minute the man turned around, her façade crumbled and her breath left her lungs as if she'd been hit. She grabbed the counter to keep from falling to the floor. "Zach."

He strode around the counter, lifted her into his arms and carried her to the couches in the lobby.

Her body combusted the second he touched her and sweat started to bead on her forehead. Why was he here? She'd missed him like a caught fish misses the water.

He knelt before her, his brows drawn together in concern. "Bea, are you okay?"

She nodded as she touched his face. He'd come to see her. The joy in her heart radiated throughout her body and caused her to quiver. Her senses came to life as she stroked his stubbled jawline.

Kayla approached them. "Here. I brought water. You look like you need it."

She took the bottle. "Thanks."

Her friend pushed the bottle toward her mouth. "Drink."

She tilted the bottle to her lips and drank, but she couldn't stop smiling. Her blood pounded through her and she felt alive for the first time all week.

Kayla turned to Zach. "Hi, I know we met when you checked in. I didn't know you were her Zach."

Zach grinned. "I take it you're a friend of Bea's."

Kayla laughed. "More like an advisor. I told her to call you. She's been miserable."

He moved his gaze to Bea. "That makes two of us."

Her tears caught in her throat and she swallowed hard. "I missed you."

His face taut, his voice came out rough. "Then why didn't you call me back?"

What could she tell him? She never expected him to come find her, which was pretty dumb considering how close he lived. "After you got sick, I didn't think I was good for you."

Kayla interjected. "I'll let you two talk." She turned to Zach. "We both get off in a half hour, but I'll cover for her."

He looked up, distracted. "Thanks."

Bea took a swallow of water.

He took her hand in his and sighed. "I was exposed to some kind of poison. Josh thinks it was skin related, not ingested. I'm just thankful you're okay."

She gulped down more water at Josh's astuteness, neatly avoiding the need to speak.

Zach shook his head. "But you don't look especially healthy at the moment. You have dark circles under your eyes and your face is drawn. Will you share my suite with me tonight?"

Her heart leapt at his thoughtfulness even as her mind cautioned her to decline. "I'd love to."

Zach leaned in and touched his lips to hers, but starved for him as she was, she deepened the gentle kiss by wrapping her tongue with his and grasping the back of his head to pull him closer.

"Hey, you two, get a room!" Kayla shouted across the empty lobby.

Bea pulled away, embarrassed to have kissed Zach so ardently in a public place.

He smirked and stood. "Yes ma'am."

Kayla huffed. "That's Miss to you."

As Zach reached down to help Bea up, panic set in and she hesitated. "Let me put away my work and I'll meet you in your room."

He turned his head, his wariness apparent. "You're not going to disappear on me, are you?"

She shook her head. She couldn't if she wanted to, and she definitely didn't want to. "I'm all yours."

He gave her a curt nod. "Very well, you have fifteen minutes."

She kissed him on the cheek, trying to ignore the sizzling in her veins as she made contact with his skin. "I'll be there in ten."

Not waiting for an answer, she strode across the lobby and behind the counter to her office.

Kayla followed her in. "Well, no wonder you were in mourning. He's hot and so sweet. What were you thinking, leaving him out to dry?"

Bea sank in her chair for a minute to give her weakened knees a break. Now what? If she had sex with him, she'd kill him. She had to find her self-control.

Kayla stood in front of her desk. "Do you realize you have champagne, strawberries and a whole can of whip cream waiting for you as well as that hunk?"

Her mind raced at the possibilities even as a sinking feeling started in the pit of her stomach. She was lost. If she could only find a way to mitigate her poison. Phillip's discovery flashed through her mind, but she rejected it outright.

Kayla put both hands on the desk and leaned forward, a jaunty smile on her lips. "Hey, you should be grinning from ear to ear. Did you hear what I said? Whip cream. A whole can. Let me tell you, sweetie, you can have a heck of a lot of fun with a can of whip cream. I know."

Kayla winked with knowledge and suddenly Bea's heart lightened. "Kayla, would you like to join us?"

Her friend froze for a moment, then a sensuous smirk played across her face. "Hmmm, now that's the most interesting proposition I've had all month and the first one I've had from a woman all year."

Bea's heart thudded as hope blossomed. "Well, what do you think?"

Her friend played with her necklace and moved back to sit in the chair across from Bea's desk. "It does have possibilities for me, but are you sure, Bea? I know you haven't experienced anything like a threesome before."

At the prospect of such a sexual night, Bea could feel her body warm. "No, I haven't, but if I'm going to try it, I'd like to do so with a friend."

Kayla licked her lips and remained silent. A strange occurrence for her.

Bea waited anxiously, her body heating as she thought about the three of them naked on the bed. Would they make it to the bed? What would it be like to touch another woman's breasts, feel her moist pussy, watch Zach pump into her?

Kayla rose. "What about your hunk? Will he want to?"

She stood, her adrenaline kicking in as the possibilities of the evening took shape. "You're the one who told me it was every guy's fantasy. All I can do is ask."

The look in Kayla's eyes was sensual, gauging. She stepped close to her. Then she took Bea's head in her hands and kissed her.

Bea gasped as Kayla's tongue swept inside her mouth. The heady sense of doing the forbidden caused her knees to shake again, and she grasped Kayla's arms for support.

Her friend broke off the kiss, her breathing just as shallow. "Okay. If Zach is up for it, then so am I. I'll go to the bar after my shift. If you want me, you can find me there." She glanced at Bea's breasts and moistened her upper lip. She moved her gaze up to look Bea in the eye and whispered, "You'll enjoy it. I promise."

After Kayla exited the room, Bea took a few deep breaths to cool her overheated body. When she had herself together, she grabbed her brush and detangled her hair. Using the office bathroom, she brushed her teeth and fixed her makeup. Desire sizzled along her skin. The lure of unknown pleasure beckoned her with more strength than the poisons that filled her body. She couldn't wait to get to Zach's suite.

As she strode along the corridor, she wondered what the people she passed in the hallway would think about what she planned for the night. The secrecy of her venture into the kinky side of intimacy gave her a lightheaded, sexual buzz that had her body flush with readiness. As she knocked on Zach's door, she prayed he was in an adventurous mood because Kayla joining them was the only way she could think of to save him from herself. And satisfy her newly discovered wild side in the process.

Chapter Ten

Zach paced the large suite of rooms. The massive shower and the tall bar had him thinking of the many ways he could make love to Bea. He glanced at the clock on the nightstand. Late. She had five more minutes before he went after her. He still wanted to know why she hadn't returned his calls when she was obviously thrilled to see him. He shook his head and continued to pace.

A knock at the door stopped him in mid-stride.

He strode to the door and threw it open. "You said ten minutes."

Bea stepped back. "Hello to you too."

Yeah, he was an ass, but he didn't care. He grabbed her, ignoring her gasp and pulled her into his arms. "I missed this."

He brought his lips down onto hers and left subtlety behind. He forced his tongue into her open mouth. The minty tang couldn't disguise the flavor of Bea and he gorged himself on the combination. As her arms entwined around his neck, he kicked the door closed.

She moaned deep in her throat and pushed her hips against him, which caused his cock to come to strict attention.

Breaking their kiss, he burrowed his hand in her hair and pulled her head back so he could access her long neck. Her tropical scent filled his head, creating an addiction he didn't want to kick.

"Zach. I missed you."

He nibbled at her collarbone, so enchanted by the taste of her skin he barely heard her. "Then why didn't you call me?"

She stiffened in his arms and he cursed his stupid tongue.

Bea pulled away and he let her go, to a point. He kept her hand in his, not ready to part now that he had her again. "Look at me, Bea."

She refused. "I can't. I get lost when I look at you. And when I touch you, I lose all control. I don't like it. I don't know—"

"It's the same for me, beautiful." Zach squeezed her hand. "I don't like it either. I think I could have ten of you at once and still want more. The sex we have is amazing. Why fight it?"

She surprised him by meeting his gaze, her eyes dark and smoldering and filled with…hope? "Would two do?"

"What?"

"Would two of me do?" She spoke fast, betraying her nervousness. "Well, not exactly of me, more like me and another woman."

Zach lost all ability to speak. Did this hot, quirky woman just ask him if he'd like to have a threesome?

She bit at her lip before she rushed on. "I've heard every man's fantasy is to have two women. Is that something you would like?"

If anyone besides Bea had asked him that question, he would assume Josh had put them up to it to play a joke on him, but she looked too serious and way too nervous. Suddenly, a horrible thought hit him like a falling tree. Had she experienced multiple men before? He let go of her hand, grabbed her shoulders and made her face him. "Bea, have you ever done a threesome?"

Startled, she shook her head then looked at the floor before she raised her gaze to his again. Her red blush made her eyes sparkle, but her direct stare, despite her insecurity, was honest. The tension left him.

She hesitated to speak, as if she didn't want to ask. "Have you?

Because if you're not interested, it's okay, I mean, it was an idea I had and I'd heard, and…"

He raised a brow. "Okay, Miss Adventurous, suppose I said yes, I'd like to have hot, forbidden sex with you and another woman. Where are you going to find another woman? You should know right up front, I don't do whores."

Bea continued to gnaw on her lip. If she kept at it, he would have to kiss her to make her stop. "How about Kayla?"

He drew a blank. Kayla? Kayla who? The only people he'd met were her mom and one dad, except for the hotel clerk. "Do you mean the flirty blonde who checked me in?"

She nodded.

He stared at her a minute. The image of Bea's pink pussy in his mouth while the blonde sucked him off caused his blood to rush to his groin. "Sure. Why not? When?"

Bea relaxed, her whole demeanor changing. "Right now. She's in the bar and said to get her if we wanted her. I'll go now."

Zach caught her arm as she started past him. "Hold on there a moment. You already discussed this with her?"

She didn't quite meet his gaze. "Yes. I wanted to give you something special to make up to you for not having called you back. Don't you want me to get her?"

To be honest, Zach wasn't sure what he wanted, but he'd be a fool to pass up such an opportunity, as long as she came back. "Yeah, okay. But I'll go with you."

"Okay."

He opened the hotel room door and as Bea preceded him, he lowered his gaze to her curved ass. Hell. He moved his jean crotch aside to better accommodate a painful hard-on. What was he getting himself into?

~*~

Kayla flirted with Zach as they all stood at the bar in his room having a drink. Bea watched. Her skin seemed to grow more sensitive by the minute. Her loose blouse felt stifling and the heat in her body made her want to turn on the air conditioner, but the two of them seemed calm and cool. Though comfortable with the situation, Zach had to be as new to this as she because he kept touching her in possessive ways. She hoped Kayla would take the lead because Bea doubted she could start anything without making a fool of herself and yet, if they didn't start soon, she would combust.

Kayla chuckled. "So, Zach, I hear you're well-hung."

Bea choked on her wine and Zach rubbed her back, but he grinned at Kayla. "I guess my cock precedes me."

Kayla winked. "Yes, it does. And did you know Bea's got the best-looking breasts in town?"

Zach growled. "And how would you know that?"

A sultry smile spread across Kayla's face. "I don't, but I certainly want to find out."

Before Bea could react, Kayla unbuttoned Bea's blouse and unhooked her bra. The cool air on her bare nipples made her shudder. Kayla reached forward with both hands and held up each breast. "Hmm, these are nice. Mind if I nibble?"

Zach pulled Bea's shirt off her shoulders until it caught on her wrists. He held it down against her back, effectively locking her hands behind her. "No, help yourself. I have." He took a swig of the beer in his other hand, acting casual, but Bea could sense his tense desire as he pulled her back against him.

She was thankful Zach had answered because between Kayla's approaching head and his cock pressed into the bottom of her spine, she could barely breathe, never mind speak.

Kayla's warm mouth covered one breast, expertly licking around the nipple before she bit lightly on the hard nub. Her hand grasped the other one to squeeze it before she sucked hard.

Sharp pleasure raced from Bea's breasts to her pussy. Kayla's sucking and nibbling caused the wetness between Bea's legs to moisten her thighs. She took shallow breaths as excitement filled her veins, her head falling back against Zach as he held her tight against him. But then his hand snaked around her waist to catch her between her thighs, rubbing back and forth across the linen pants she wore, causing a friction that had her clit begging for more.

Zach left off his rubbing of her pussy and stepped to her side, but he kept one hand locked on her shirt, practically offering her to Kayla. With his other hand, he unbuttoned Kayla's blouse. Kayla stopped licking, which gave him better access, but she took both Bea's nipples between her fingers and tweaked.

Though squirming with anticipation, Bea couldn't help but watch as Zach unveiled Kayla's pert breasts. They were smaller and higher than her own, but the areola was much larger and very pink compared to her dusky-rose color. She couldn't tear her gaze from them and an unusual yearning to taste those tight peaks caught her by surprise.

Zach raised his brow at her as if he sensed her interest before he bent over to capture Kayla's nipple in his mouth, pulling Bea's arms tighter behind her back, which forced her own nipples into Kayla's playful fingers. Bea's wetness dripped down her leg as she stared at Zack's mouth moving across Kayla's breast.

Zach's head came up. "Do you want to taste, Bea?"

She started, not sure what to say. Then he spoke to Kayla. "She does have beautiful breasts. Let's show her how much we appreciate them." Kayla released her nipples and Zach took one in his mouth. Kayla joined him to suckle the other. Unable to grasp their heads to her, she pressed her chest toward their busy tongues, craving the intense pleasure that shot through her and drenched her between her legs. Her core ached with need. "Please."

Zach spoke against her breast. "Please what?"

Bea struggled to pull air into her lungs. "I want you both."

Zach looked at Kayla. As they made eye contact across her breasts, Bea trembled.

Kayla and Zach let go and Bea sucked in calming air, but Kayla stepped against her and pressed their bodies together. Bea's wet breasts touched her smaller ones, and Kayla rubbed her nipples back and forth across Bea's tight nubs while Zach moved behind her again and rubbed his cock against the crease of her ass.

He kissed her neck as he pulled her tight against him and undid her pants. Pushing her clothes off her hips with one hand. He let them fall to the floor.

Kayla stepped back and dropped her skirt and thong. Her blonde pubic hair, shaved to a small triangle, pointed the way to her pussy.

Bea tried to move her hands. She wanted to touch the straight, short hair at the juncture of her friend's thighs to see how it would feel, but Zach held her bound. "Spread your legs, Bea."

Zach's deep voice sent chills through her and she did as he commanded.

He pressed his naked cock hard against her butt. When had he dropped his pants?

Kayla knelt down and purred. "Oh, bald pussy. Yum. Have you tasted this, Zach? Is she as sweet as she looks?"

Bea shivered at Kayla's words, but then Kayla flicked her tongue against Bea's clit and all thought fled. Kayla licked and nibbled, grazing her teeth across Bea's throbbing nub.

Sandwiched between Zach's insistent cock and Kayla's skilled tongue, Bea let her head fall back on Zach's shoulder and surrendered her body to helpless pleasure. Zach held her close, her arms pinned between their bodies while he caressed her breasts and played with her nipples. Kayla's tongue and Zach's hands fed the fire building inside her. Bea thrilled at the heady converging sensations.

When her friend pulled back, Bea groaned with need.

Kayla sauntered to the bed. "Zach, bring her over here. I want to get comfortable."

Zach pulled Bea into his arms and stood her next to the bed. Kayla lay on it, her head hanging off the foot. "Come here, Bea. You taste sweet and I'm ready for dessert."

She should be shocked at how turned-on she was, but the idea of Kayla making her come with her tongue had her legs moving forward until she'd straddled the woman's face.

Kayla grabbed Bea's legs and brought them tight against her cheeks. "Much better. Get ready to ride, girl. Are you hard, Zach?"

Zach pressed his cock against Bea's ass. "What do you think, Bea? Am I hard?"

She swallowed. "As granite."

Kayla spoke below. "Good." Then she pushed two fingers into Bea.

Shock waves of electricity coursed through Bea at the suddenness of the invasion, but it didn't begin to prepare her for Kayla's lips as they latched on to her clit and started to suck.

Bea swayed.

Zach unbuttoned her cuffs and took off her shirt. "Bend over and brace yourself on the bed, beautiful."

She did as told, hoping she didn't fall on top of Kayla. Then again, it would be a soft landing and leave her face in Kayla's pussy. What would it be like to lick another woman's juices? She wasn't sure she was ready for that. Heck, she wasn't sure about much at the moment.

Suddenly, something cold hit her ass. She glanced back to find Zach had sprayed whip cream on her crease. He caught her look of confusion. "Lube."

She dropped her head and shivered at the feel of the cool cream slipping over her anal star and down to her slit to meet Kayla's fingers.

The pulsing sensitivity of Kayla sucking her clit as she pumped her fingers caused Bea to reverberate with wanting. When Zach spread her ass cheeks and his hard cock pressed against her anal opening, she whimpered.

Zach stopped. "Are you okay, Bea?"

Her anticipation spiked. "Yes. More."

"My pleasure." He pushed slowly against her until the cream allowed him to glide in.

It was too much. Her senses reeled at the sexual sensations in her pussy, ass and clit. Her orgasm rocketed through her. She screamed as she gushed over Kayla's fingers, her body shaking hard. Kayla pumped into her as Zach moved out and in again, prolonging her pinnacle of pleasure.

Panting, she gasped, "Oh my God."

Kayla chuckled as she released her hold on Bea's pussy, but plunged one more time with her fingers as Zach slowly pulled out. Bea's heart leapt as the final thrill hit before she fell to the side of Kayla, eyes closed, trying to fill her lungs. Her poisons hadn't harmed anyone. She wasn't sure what effects Kayla might experience, but she doubted there had been enough absorption to do any harm. The guilt-free orgasm made her beam with sheer joy.

Zach knelt next to her. It had to be him because Kayla's body lay warm against her other side.

He brushed her hair away from her face and touched his lips to hers.

She welcomed his kiss, opening her mouth to show her gratitude with her tongue.

He pulled away and stood. "You keep kissing me like that and I'm going to come all over you."

She opened her eyes. The image of Zach standing next to the bed pumping himself until his thick cum squirted over her body caught the attention of her satisfied pussy. "That has possibilities."

Kayla sat up. "I don't think so. Bea, you're too damn sweet. I'm hornier than hell now."

Bea watched as Zach perused Kayla's body. He turned around and headed for the bathroom. "Hold that thought."

"Will do." Kayla left the bed. "More wine?"

Bea pulled herself up to sit against the headboard. "No thanks."

"Well, I will. I worked up a real thirst. Oh, stop blushing, I'm sure he's done that to you before."

Bea nodded shyly. It was strange and yet liberating to be completely naked and chatting with Kayla.

Zach strode back in and Bea couldn't help but admire his taut strength. His cock was still hard as it angled away from his body, his balls up tight. "I think I need to give you girls some attention. What do you think?"

Kayla took a large gulp of wine.

Bea purred. "I think."

Now she could focus on him. There was no reason for Zach to experience any of her poisons with Kayla there.

He jumped on the bed and lay on his back, spreading his arms, one hand resting on her thigh. "I'm all yours."

She caught Kayla's attention and motioned with her head toward Zach, then knelt on all fours next to him and licked his earlobe. He turned his head and captured her lips with his.

She melted at the invasion of his tongue before she sidled away. Bea ran her fingertip along the length of Zach's cock. "See, Kayla, I was truthful about how handsome his cock is, wasn't I?"

Kayla moved to kneel between Zach's legs. "I'm not sure. I need to make a closer inspection."

"Please do. I want my man's handsomeness confirmed."

Zach chuckled and his cock jumped.

Kayla took Zach's cock into her hands and stroked down to hold it tight at the base while Bea stared, fascinated. Kayla's tongue darted out and flicked across the top. Bea shivered. A strange excitement whirled through her body like a waterspout as Kayla's mouth slipped down her man's cock.

Bea glanced at Zach and found his eyes on her, his expression worried. He stroked her back in reassurance. She smiled mischievously and lowered her head to his chest. He may be concerned she'd be jealous, but she was too happy she could please him, and not poison him, to worry about Kayla. Besides, it was hot watching and having sex at the same time.

She darted her tongue across his nipple, mimicking what Kayla did to his cock, and his hand moved from her back to her hair. She glanced down to see Kayla licking the underside of his penis and Bea swirled her tongue around each nipple until they were as hard as his cock.

When Kayla sucked Zach in earnest, Bea's pussy swelled and she changed from licking to sucking his hardened nipples. His tense body strained toward her and the hand at the back of her head became insistent. Nibbling at a hard nub, Bea ran her hand into Zach's hair, unable to stop the moan that rose from her throat.

Abruptly, she found herself lifted.

Zach growled. "Sit on my face. I want to taste you."

More than willing, she positioned herself above his mouth so she faced Kayla. She wouldn't have believed it, but she enjoyed watching Kayla's tongue on Zach's cock.

His own talented tongue shot out and encircled her clit as she had done his nipple, dividing her attention. The sharp spasms of excitement had her heart beating erratically.

Kayla sat up. "Oh Bea, I have to have him inside me now."

Bea nodded her permission, unable to talk for the lightning buzzing through her veins.

"Do you have a condom?"

Zach's groan against her clit vibrated every nerve, but his

message was clear. She shook her head at Kayla. Would they have to stop?

"Good thing I come prepared." Kayla hopped off the bed and rummaged in her purse. Bea watched as her friend ripped open a packet to expose a florescent-pink condom.

"Pink?"

Kayla wiggled her eyebrows. "Hey, if I'm providing the protection, I get to choose the color."

She grew hotter as Kayla sheathed Zach in hot pink while his tongue continued its homage to her clit.

The sight of Kayla impaling herself on Zach had Bea's hips moving in response. But Zach held her still, where he wanted her. She licked her lips as Kayla lifted herself, clear liquid coating Zach's cock.

Kayla caught her gaze. "Oh girl, you're going to love this." She took Bea's nipples between her thumbs and forefingers and held on.

Bea's full pussy quivered at the contact. She grasped Kayla's nipples in the same way.

Kayla panted as she moved herself up and down along Zach's length, her juices making him shine a bright pink. "Holy crow, but you two are good."

Watching Kayla's excitement, feeling her hard nubs at the same time Kayla's hands were upon her own nipples and Zach's tongue on her clit brought Bea to the edge. Kayla's breath hitched as Bea pinched her nipples. Excited by her power over the other woman and unable to resist Kayla's growing pleasure, Bea let go of her friend's breasts and grabbed her head. Without thought, she thrust her tongue into Kayla's mouth. The forbidden taste spiked her own need to an overwhelming pitch.

Kayla came. Moaning deep inside Bea's mouth, she crushed Bea against her, breasts smashing breasts, tilting Bea's pelvis against Zach's mouth. As Kayla shuddered, Bea's pussy tightened, almost hurt, desperate for release.

Zach's own growl vibrated against her clit. Without warning, he thrust two fingers inside her, pushed through the suction of her pussy and penetrated her taut euphoria. Her world exploded.

Chapter Eleven

"**B**ea."

The soft female whisper dragged Bea from her sound sleep and she struggled to wake up.

"I'm leaving."

She cracked one eye open to see Kayla crouched next to the bed. Why was Kayla in her… Realization dawned as embarrassment swept through her. She wanted to close her eyes and pretend it had all been a dream, but the persistent whisper wouldn't let her.

"I have today off and I want to make the most of it. I wanted to thank you for inviting me. Zach is a definite keeper." Kayla smiled, her lips spreading from ear to ear, the same lips that had brought so much pleasure.

Bea opened her other eye and kept her voice low. "I know he's wonderful, but I—" This wasn't the time to talk about her silly insecurities.

"You what?" Kayla looked at Zach. His breathing remained steady. "He isn't listening."

She took a deep breath. "I don't know how to keep a man."

Kayla raised her brow. "Last night was a good start. Think of him as your best friend and lover and you'll be fine. Did you tell him about the strange letters you've been receiving?"

"No. Why would I?"

"Because if he's your best friend, you should ask his advice, don't you think?"

Bea sighed. "I don't know."

Kayla rolled her eyes. "Trust me. Tell him. I gotta go… 'Beautiful'."

"Please don't call me that. I'll wear a permanent blush."

Kayla smirked then leaned forward and kissed her on the lips. "But red becomes you."

Surprised by the tingle of excitement at Kayla's touch, she remained motionless while she watched her friend's thin figure leave the room. The door closed with a soft click.

She glanced at the clock. Five fifteen. After last night, she definitely needed more sleep. Rolling over to face the man in bed with her, she found him wide awake, if the lowered brows and tense jaw were any indication.

Uh-oh, maybe he didn't like Kayla kissing her goodbye? "Good morning." She gave him a tentative smile.

Though she could tell he wasn't happy, his growl surprised her. "What letters?"

She shrugged. "Kayla's making more out of it than it really is. I've been receiving letters from an anonymous person, but they don't say much. It's not a big deal."

He sat up and his tone took on a warning note. "Tell me about the letters. Why are they strange? How many have you received?"

Pulling the blankets with her, Bea sat to face him. "All right. They're strange because they aren't going through the mail. They are addressed with just my name and dropped off here at the inn, but no one has seen who's been leaving them. I've only received three."

Zach threw the covers off and stood to glare at the woman in the bed. Could she be that naïve or was she hiding something? He tamped down the hurt permeating his gut. "So, you've received three strange letters and you weren't going to tell me? Exactly how long has this been going on?"

Bea lowered her gaze and fiddled with the blanket. "It started two weeks ago, after I met you. The only person I can think of who might want to send them is Jim, one of my six fathers. He always resented Mom keeping multiple men. I figure he discovered I was with you and wanted to keep me from a serious relationship." She looked him in the eyes. "Because you're the first relationship I've had since high school."

He folded his arms. That he was her first relationship explained why she hadn't told him about the letters, but it didn't explain the crazy protectiveness he felt for someone he planned not to see again. However, her theory about the dad was farfetched. "And who else knows about these letters besides Kayla?"

She hesitated to answer. "Really, Zach, they aren't that important."

"Bea." He kept his tone firm, not willing to let his frustration at her evasiveness be revealed by raising his voice.

She refused to meet his gaze and fisted the blankets in her hands, her agitation obvious. "I gave the first one to Chris. He's a police officer, after all. I thought he'd be able to figure out who sent them."

"Fuck." Zach turned away from the bed and strode to the bar. Grabbing the champagne bottle from the mini-fridge he tipped it up and took a swallow. The woman drove him to drink! He spun to find her staring at him in shock. He lifted the bottle in salute before he took another gulp. Hell, he didn't even like the stuff. He set it back on the bar, hard.

She jumped.

Her nervous gaze made him grit his teeth in an effort to control his rising temper. "Didn't you think Chris might be the one who sent the letters?"

She shook her head in disbelief, her dark eyes wide. "I can't believe that."

He took a deep breath. "Think about it. Who else knows we're seeing each other and wouldn't want us to? I doubt very much your estranged dad would suddenly take an interest in your love life, but Chris wants to fuck you in the worst way. What better way to send you into his arms than with threatening letters?"

"I don't think he would… I mean why…oh. I never would have thought of him."

Though she finally saw what he saw, the slump of her shoulders made him feel as if he'd just told her Santa Claus wasn't real. Could this mature woman be that idealistic? He strode to the bed and sat, taking her in his arms. She melted into him. "I don't know if he's your secret admirer or not, but this is serious stuff. What do the letters say?"

She tensed. "They only have one sentence on them. It doesn't make any sense."

"Let me see them."

She pulled away. "I told you, I gave one to Chris and the other is in my apartment."

He held her by the shoulders. "And the third one?"

She looked away.

He forced her chin up. "Bea?"

She glanced at the stuffed chair in the room, but pursed her lips.

He let her go and strode to the chair.

"No!" She jumped from the bed, bringing the sheet with her, and pulled at his arm as he reached for her purse.

He grabbed it and gave it to her. "Let me see the letter."

She shook her head and looked down.

"Listen, you can give it to me, read it to me, tell me what it says, or I can take it from you. Your choice."

She stared at him, desperation clear in her beautiful brown eyes.

He pulled her into his embrace. Her fear of his reading the letter's message cut a hole the size of Golden Pond in his ego. If she was in danger he had to protect her. Usually he broke it off with women to protect them, but he couldn't leave her yet. "I just want to keep you safe. Can't you at least trust me?"

He could feel her soften against him as she squeezed him hard. She nodded.

He set her back so he could see her face and kissed away the single tear that rolled down her cheek.

She stared at him for the longest time then opened her purse and gave him the letter.

He couldn't have explained the feeling that rose inside him at that moment, but his protective instincts went into overdrive.

He led her back to the bed and sat with her. The typewritten envelope told him nothing except the person knew how to spell "Rappaccini". He opened the letter.

Does he know about the other men?

Zach stared at the question. Jesus Christ. A kick in the gut from a moose would have been preferable to reading those seven words. The paper crinkled as his hand formed a fist of its own accord. He struggled to control his breathing as pain, betrayal and fury washed over him. Did he have the word "sucker" tattooed on his back? He must have missed it last time he looked in the mirror.

"Zach?" Bea's soft whisper claimed his attention. Her wrinkled brow and worried eyes reminded him of his own damning words, *trust* me.

He dropped the crumpled paper, stood and grabbed the champagne bottle off the bar. After finishing off the contents, he threw it in the trash, thankful for the artificial relaxant to his muscles despite the churning acid of his stomach. He leaned against the bar, crossed his arms over his chest and chanced looking at her again.

Bea's hair was messed from their night of play and her hands clutched the sheet above her breasts to cover her exquisite beauty. But her eyes reminded him of a flying squirrel's, wide and afraid. He stared at her, cutting himself slack for falling for her vulnerable act. He should've known, the speed of their relationship, the intensity of the sex. But he wasn't made of steel and doubted any man could have resisted any of it.

Bea didn't drop her gaze in shame. In fact, she lifted her chin before she spoke. "You said I could trust you, so I have. Do you trust me? Do you believe me when I say I haven't been with another man since I met you?"

Zach pushed away from the bar and strode to the sliding door, whipping the curtains open. He needed the outdoors, to take a break from the closed room. The sky was still dark with but a hint of whitening across the lake. The water's calm surface did nothing to quiet his racing thoughts or relieve the tightness in his gut.

He spoke to the glass. "Explain."

Her voice high, the words rolled out in an anxious rush. "I can't. That's just it. I don't understand these letters any more than you do. Yes, I've been with other men before you, just as you've been with other women, but I haven't had sex with anyone since we met. I don't know if the writer has followed me and mixed up his timeline or if he's an ex-lover who's angry, or if it's someone like you said, who wants to keep us apart. But if he wanted to do that, then why not send the letter to you instead of me? The letters don't even tell me what he wants."

At the mention of someone following her, Zach's protective instincts overlaid all his other emotions and despite himself, he couldn't help but remember the night the cop had followed them and stayed parked outside. Could it be that simple? Or was he looking for a way to make her innocent when she wasn't? It didn't matter. He'd told her to trust him and she had. He had no choice but to accept her word and shield her from the cop or whoever was stalking her.

How ironic. He'd gone out of his way for years to avoid staying with a woman too long, so she wouldn't end up dead thanks to his twisted fate, and here he was having to stay with Bea to protect her from whoever sent the letters. The question was, what would keep her from the same fate as his early fiancées?

Zach opened the sliding-glass door and let the cold morning air bathe his naked body. It helped clear his mind and settle his knotted stomach. Her life could be in danger either way. He had no choice but to try to keep her safe.

He sensed her behind him before she laid a delicate hand on his arm. "Zach?"

He took a deep breath of the fresh air, filling his lungs and soothing his quandary. Studying her long fingers as they rested on his biceps, his gut tightened. He had to protect her, no matter what. She trusted him.

Moving his arm from beneath her hand, he turned and brought her into his embrace. Her shudder of relief filled him with resolve. He held her, stroked her hair and warmed to the need building inside him. The faith she had in him humbled him, but doubt for her safety remained.

Bea could feel her heart paste itself back together. When had she fallen in love with this man? She would have to tell him about the poisons running through her body, but she had no idea how to broach that subject. Her mom must have done pretty well with all her fathers. Four of the original six still in her life wasn't bad, but Bea would be damned if she'd ask her mom. She didn't want to mess this up. She couldn't bear to lose Zach now.

She hugged him harder before she lifted her face to look at him. He met her gaze with a warm one of his own before his lips found hers. The heat of her desire for him was tempered with a new tenderness that made her feel vulnerable and…cold?

She pulled away. "Could we close the door?"

He sighed. Turning them both so he could reach the slider, he pulled it closed. "Don't you have faith in my ability to keep you warm?"

She gazed up at him. "I have complete faith, but a short memory. Maybe you should remind me."

He took her face in his hands. "I'd be happy to."

As his lips touched hers, her phone rang. He ignored it, pulling her hips against him to tease her with his hardness. She reveled in his need as he crushed her to him, his mouth devouring hers, causing warmth to spread everywhere.

Her phone rang again.

He pulled away. "I think someone is looking for you."

She turned her head toward her purse on the bed and waited. The ringing stopped.

She returned her attention to him and the ringing started again. "Oh damn." She fumbled in her purse to find the phone. Grabbing it, she flicked it open. "Yes?"

"Bea, this is Chris. Sorry to call so early, but I just finished my shift and wanted to let you know what I've found out about the letter. Can I meet you somewhere?"

She moved next to Zach and pointed to the phone. "I guess, Chris. Does it have to be now?"

Zach's expression turned hard.

She angled the phone so he could hear.

"I'm afraid so because I need to get some sleep."

Bea glanced at Zach. He pointed to the room.

"Okay, can you come to the Lakeside? I'm at work."

The other end was silent for a minute. "You're at work?"

She shivered as the implication became clear. She had walked to work yesterday and left her car parked outside her apartment. Was Chris surprised she was at work because he was outside her place? "Yes, I'm at the Lakeside. I'll meet you in the lobby in fifteen minutes. Can you make it here by then?"

Zach's nod of approval gave her a little confidence.

"Sure. I'm just down the road. See you in a few."

Bea ended the call and stared at Zach. "Do you think he's at my apartment?"

"I know he is. Come on, let's get dressed and see what he has to say."

"How do you know he was at my apartment, you were here with me."

He pulled on his jeans. "Trust me, he was. And wait until you see his surprise when we meet him together."

She buttoned her blouse then slipped on her linen pants. "You'll come with me?"

Zach rolled his eyes. "Bea, you need to get it through your head that I'm involved in this now, and in more ways than one."

Huh? What did he mean by that? She opened her mouth to ask, but he looked ready to tackle a black bear single-handedly. She swallowed her questions and slipped on her heels. "Are you sure about this?"

He opened the hotel room door, an unreadable expression on his face. "I wouldn't miss this meeting for the world."

Zach took Bea's hand as they walked through the hallway toward the main lobby. He grinned. She had no idea she looked adorably messy. She'd forgotten to brush her hair and her clothes were wrinkled from lying on the floor all night. She'd obviously had a fulfilling night of sex. Perfect. Perhaps a kiss was in order.

He checked behind them to see if anyone was around, but the hall was empty. Dragging her to the side, he pulled her into his arms and pushed her against the wall.

"Zach?"

He silenced her surprise with his lips. The taste of peppermint flowed across his tongue as he swept inside her mouth. The thought that she'd popped the candy for her meeting with Officer Chris had his caveman reappearing. He forgot where they were and deepened the kiss, making love to her mouth while his hand crept inside her blouse to find the hardened nipple within her bra. He pressed his cock against her until her hands tightened around his ass, pulling him into her.

She moaned, her hips rocking into him. He had unbuttoned her blouse before he remembered they were in the hall. He stepped away abruptly.

Bea opened her eyes, dazed, until she noticed where they stood. A soft blush covered her cheeks as she closed her blouse. "What was that about?"

He shrugged. "Couldn't resist, I guess." Now she looked thoroughly ravished. Her lips reddened from his kiss, her blouse unevenly tucked into her pants and her hair matted where it had crushed against the wall. Good.

He grabbed her hand, strode toward the lobby, pulling her with him.

"Whoa, Zach, what's the rush?"

If he was right, Officer Chris would be waiting for them. "I want us to be there when your cop arrives."

She ran a few steps to match his stride. "Okay, okay, but it hasn't even been five minutes yet."

"Exactly."

As they rounded the corner, they found Chris standing by the reception desk. His eyes narrowed when he saw them. Zach relished the jealous way Chris took in Bea's appearance.

He stepped toward them, but focused on Bea. "They told me you weren't in yet."

Bea blushed, but Zach smirked as she answered. "That's because I don't start 'til nine today, but I stayed the night."

Chris' gaze took in their clasped hands and Zach couldn't resist baiting the cop. If Chris wanted to know, he'd be happy to tell him. "We spent the night here. After all, it's the best place in town for a romantic evening."

Zach reveled in the knowledge that the man across from him wanted nothing more than to throw a punch, but of course he wouldn't. That would be too obvious in front of Bea.

But Bea was a smart woman and she recognized the standoff between them. "Chris, you said you had news on the letter? Why don't we go over to the couches and talk? I think the less people who know, the better." She nodded in the direction of three guests who walked toward the front desk.

Chris nodded. "Sure, I'd like to tell you in private."

Zach shook his head at the look the officer gave him. "I agree. We should keep it between the three of us."

Before Chris could say anything, Zach started for the sitting area, refusing to let go of Bea's hand, though she tried to disengage. She got the message and gave in. They sat on the couch together while Chris took the chair nearby.

Zach let go of Bea's hand and draped an arm behind her. She leaned forward, her anxiousness obvious in the clasp she had on his thigh. "What have you discovered?"

Chris took the letter from his pocket and handed it to Bea, but Zach intercepted it. He wanted to read this one too. He wanted to read all of them. Ignoring the irritated look from the cop, he opened the letter as he listened to what was so important Bea had to be dragged out of bed at six in the morning.

I know your secret.

Okay, that was short and to the point, but what secret?

Chris explained. "First, we noticed that the person knows how to spell your last name. You have to admit, it's not an easy name to spell. Plus, you don't have your number listed in the phone directory, so that means this person knows you."

Zach squeezed Bea's shoulder. Hadn't he already figured that out?

She gave him a nudge with her elbow. "That makes sense. Were you able to discover anything else?"

Chris smirked. "Yes, we pulled a number of fingerprints from the envelope. We should have the results back in a few days. Of course, yours and mine will be on there, but hopefully the writer's will be too. I also asked the lab to check for DNA on the seal. If the writer licked the envelope, we'll know who it is."

The man wanted to be Bea's hero. No way Zach would let that happen. "The prints sound like a long shot to me. With the front desk people who handled the letter before Bea obtained it, I doubt there'll be any usable ones, and that is assuming the sender is in your database. Plus, if the writer used water to seal the envelope, we'll have nothing."

Chris turned to Bea, ignoring Zach. "Don't worry, we'll figure out who it is. Do you have any idea what the secret is that the letter refers to?"

Though her body tensed, Bea shook her head. Zach studied her. She did know. He'd bet his house on it.

Chris leaned forward and patted Bea's knee. "That's okay, we'll catch this guy."

Zach tensed, unable to keep his cavemen from rising. Moving his gaze to Chris, Zach took his arm from the couch and squeezed Bea's shoulder. "If it's a guy?"

Bea's head snapped around. "You think it could be a woman?"

He rubbed her arm, hoping to reassure her, letting her know he'd be beside her to face whomever it was. "We can't know for sure. It's hard to tell with just one letter." He waited to see if Chris knew how many there were.

Chris sat straighter. His eyes narrowed and a slight smirk curved his thin lips. "Actually, you've had a number of these, right, Bea?"

Zach gave her arm a warning squeeze. No need to let the man know exactly how many. He might slip and mention the number and they would have him.

Bea looked at him before she turned to Chris. "Yes, I have."

Chris' face became stern. Though he tried to appear relaxed, his hands clenched and unclenched. "I think we should take a look at all the letters. If we can't get good prints off the first letter you gave me, maybe we'll get lucky with one of the others."

"Sure. Thanks for all your help with this." Bea stood, taking Zach by surprise. He rose next to her and put his arm around her waist.

Chris appeared taken off guard as well. "Okay then. I guess I better get myself some sleep. Thanks for meeting with me so early."

Bea cuddled into Zach as she addressed him. "Thank you for helping us with this. We really appreciate it."

His heart swelled at her use of the word "we" while a different part of his anatomy swelled as her body pressed close to his. The added advantage to their position was Chris couldn't shake her hand. Smart woman.

Chris said goodbye and left.

Zach was damn proud of her. He turned her in his arms to give her a kiss and instead got the side of her head. "Bea?"

She pulled away and started to pace. "I hate this. I don't know who to trust. Now, I even have to be guarded with a cop? And the two of you, posturing like two dogs fighting over a piece of meat. You don't have to do that, Zach. You already have me. You don't have to rub it in his face. What if he isn't the one writing the letters, but is truly interested in helping?"

Zach grabbed her in mid-stride. "I have you?"

She caught his face in her hands and lowered her voice. "Yes. Completely."

Her words meant more to him then they should, but they were

what he wanted to hear. He clasped her body to him and gave her a searing kiss.

When he broke away, her eyes were still closed.

His good mood faded as he stared at her elegant face. They were getting too close. He needed to put some space between them. "So, what is this secret you're hiding?"

Bea stared blindly at the computer screen. She'd been able to put Zach off until tonight, but he wanted to know her secret. She had to tell him, wanted to tell him, but didn't know how. And what if he didn't believe her? She didn't believe it herself the first time her mother told her. Not until the doctor had explained Phillip's coma had been caused by a strong poison, did she accept what she was.

The purchase order on her screen for two hundred geraniums seemed impossible to complete, so she saved the file and turned off her computer. It was time to go home anyway. She organized her work for her next shift. She and Zach only had tonight because he was heading up to Maine to visit his parents. Would he still want to see her again after she told him about her condition? She needed to make love to him before he left. Would he be willing, knowing he'd be sick?

Her cell phone rang. She pulled it from her purse and checked the caller's identity. Winni Real Estate popped across the screen. "Hi, Dad."

"Hi, Bea, how are you doing? Your mom tells me you've had better days."

She dropped back into her chair. "That's one way of putting it. Did she tell you what she did?"

"Yes, she confessed. I understand how upset you must have been."

Bea rolled her eyes. Mathew Emerson was the ultimate salesman and if her father thought he could get under her skin, he would. "I hear a 'but' coming."

"Well, yes. She's your mother. She tries to do what's right, but you know she doesn't always succeed. Think about how you'll feel when you have a daughter. What will happen when she gets angry at you for a mistake you made and refuses to see or talk to you?"

Oh, he was good. Really good. "I understand what you're saying, Dad, but I'm not ready yet. I have a more pressing issue on my hands that needs my undivided attention."

"Is it anything I can help you with?"

Bea hesitated. "Maybe. You're pretty well-known in town, right?"

She could envision his chest puffing as he spoke. "Well, I try to be. Being the chairman of the Chamber of Commerce and part of the Rotary helps."

She worried her lip before asking. "If I need you to, would you confirm my condition for someone?"

There was silence on the phone.

"Dad?"

"Does this have to do with your new boyfriend?"

Bea crumpled her skirt in her hand. *Boyfriend* sounded so teenager when what Zach was, was a man, a perfect man. "Yes. He's right for me. Andy liked him right away."

"Honey, if he makes you happy, that's all I care about. If he's the right one and you need me to convince him, you bring him on over."

She let go of the material bunched in her hand and closed her eyes. "Thanks, Dad."

"See your mom, Bea."

"I will, eventually."

She hung up and threw her phone back in her purse, then

glanced at the clock. She would have barely enough time to go home, shower and drive to Zach's. Telling him her secret wasn't quite so daunting, now that she had someone Zach could talk to about it, in case he didn't believe her.

She reached to turn off the desk lamp when Craig Larsen stepped into her office. "Oh Bea, I'm glad I caught you. This came for you today. I almost forgot to give it to you."

She stared at the letter in Craig's hand, her heart thumping in her chest. She shook her head and fell back into the desk chair, her knees completely giving way as the air left her lungs. Her head swam, making the white envelope in front of her go in and out of focus.

Craig rushed around the desk. "What is it? Are you all right?"

She pointed to his hand. "Another letter."

He looked confused. "Yes, it's a letter."

"But it didn't come in the mail." She closed her eyes. "Neither did the other three."

He sounded perplexed. "Is it from a friend?"

She opened her eyes. Poor Craig was so scattered he wouldn't recognize a rattlesnake for the danger it was if it slithered across his foot. "I'll take it. Did you happen to see who brought it?"

Craig wrinkled his nose to push up his glasses. "Yes, I did. It was the kid who works at the ice-cream shop in front of our Hillside Inn. You know him. He's the one with the sandy-blond hair and pierced ears?"

Bea stared at Craig. He never noticed anything, yet he'd discovered who had been dropping off the letters? She stood and gave him a hug. "Thank you."

He shrugged. "You're welcome, I guess. Are you coming in tomorrow?"

"No, I have the next two days off, remember?"

"Right. See you when you get back."

As he left the office, Bea stayed absolutely still and concentrated on breathing deeply to stop the quaking inside her body. She couldn't wait to tell Zach about the boy. She doubted the kid had sent the letters, but she'd bet he knew who did. She looked at the envelope on the desk. She could open it at Zach's. After all, she wanted to get over there and then she could share it with him. But even as she had the thought, she picked up her letter opener and slit the envelope. She took out the letter and unfolded it. Hand-sized pieces of paper spilled onto the desk. She read the one line.

He's not happy with you.

Dread filled her as she lifted one of the papers. It was a digital photo printed on plain paper of her talking with a man at a hotel in Boston. She picked up another. It showed her talking with another man she'd met the weekend before. His name was Darren. Another photo caught her walking into a hotel room with yet another man. The next showed her leaving a room with her shoes in her hand. Another was taken through a window and showed her on her hands and knees with Tom, her one-night stand before she met Zach. How the hell did the person shoot that one? Oh God, there had to be a dozen of them!

She'd been followed. A sharp pain in her stomach had her doubling over. She reached for her Tums. Popping four in her mouth, she took deep breaths. As the tablets coated her stomach, she gathered all the paper and dumped it into her purse. *He's not happy.* That had to mean Zach. Oh God. The same package must have been delivered to Zach! She was as positive of that fact as the dread overwhelming her. The question was, did he receive a letter too? Did he open it?

She raced out the door and headed for her car, ignoring the cold air and her lack of coat. How long had Craig had the letter? An hour? All day? Whoever had it delivered to him must have known how scattered Craig was. Either that or it was pure bad luck.

Her hands trembled as she turned the key in the ignition. She drove as fast as she dared along the winding back roads until she reached Zach's. The mud in the driveway had hardened, which made it easy to drive straight to the house. A light shone from inside. Jumping from her vehicle, she ran to the basement door and knocked. Her racing heart had her taking short breaths, forming white puffs against the glass window.

When there was no answer, she tried the door. It was locked. She knocked louder as dread filled her soul. She couldn't have found him just to lose him. Fate couldn't be so cruel.

"Come on, Zach. Open the door. Please."

She pounded on the door with no results. Frustrated and scared, she ran to the side of the deck and took the stairs two at a time. She peered in the sliding-glass door and found him. The photos lay scattered across the coffee table in the living room. Zach sat on a couch, a bottle of Johnny Walker in one hand, a two-page typed letter spread on the cushion next to him.

Bea groaned as he lifted the bottle and took a large gulp.

"Oh God, no." She banged on the glass.

Zach looked up and focused on her slowly. His face twisted in disgust.

"Let me explain!" she yelled as loud as she could, her body trembling with panic. She had to get in there. It wasn't what he thought. She tugged on the door. It didn't budge. The tears flowed from her eyes and her vision blurred. This couldn't be happening. Why would someone do this to her, her only chance, her one hope?

She wiped the water from her eyes with a shaky hand and tried the other slider. It remained in place. She gazed at Zach. "Please, open the door. Let me explain."

He gave her a snide grin before he saluted her with the scotch bottle and took another gulp.

Her stomach twisted hard and she pressed her arm against the pain. She'd lost him. The hopelessness caused tears to come fast, but she couldn't accept it. She shook her head in desperate denial. "Zach, please. Open the door."

He leaned forward and picked up the TV remote, which lay next to the photos.

She pressed both hands against the glass. "Zach, it's not what you think! They're old photos! Please, don't throw us away!"

He looked at her again and sneered, then the television popped on and the volume went so loud she couldn't hear herself.

She stopped pounding on the door and watched as he stared at the television and laughed. Laughed.

Her heart shriveled inside her chest. Her breaths caught in her throat, sore from yelling in the frigid temperature. She grabbed at her stomach, unable to move as defeat settled upon her like a winter cape.

She made herself leave the deck and forced her legs to carry her to her car.

Her tears dried as she drove home, her whole body turning numb. She climbed the stairs to her apartment, dragging herself up as if she were an unwilling sacrifice to a vengeful god. She couldn't go back to her life before. She couldn't do it. She'd experienced what could be, what she wanted with her whole being. She loved Zach.

She dropped her purse on the table, her old table. Her old life. She had a good job, lived in an apartment and had to sleep with a different man every week. She hated that life. She was tired of it. She didn't want it. She wanted Zach!

Bea lashed out and sent a plant flying across the kitchen. Dirt and green leaves scattered over the floor. She grabbed a beer from her fridge. "Happy now, Mom?" She saluted the air with Zach's Bud Light. "Who would have guessed you could be so wrong."

Chapter Twelve

Zach held his hands over his ears. Why wouldn't the pounding stop? He cracked one eyelid and found two large feet standing at his sliding-glass door. Only one person had feet that big.

Carefully, he removed his hand and motioned with his finger to wait before attempting to raise his head from the cool pine floor. Bracing himself on the couch, he squinted and managed to stand, but the pounding in his head reached new levels. Josh had to have a painkiller with him.

With that sustaining hope, Zach made it to the door and flipped the lock. The door flew from his hand as it slid open. Cold air hit his body, numbing the pain for an instant before—

"Why the hell did you throw the floor bolt on the door downstairs? I couldn't get in. Jesus, what the hell happened to you?"

Zach's knees buckled, but unfortunately he stayed conscious as he slumped down again, the hard floor reacquainting him with last night.

"You're in bad shape, my friend," Josh whispered as he hauled him up against the couch.

He didn't plan to give a response to such an obvious statement. Holding his head, he tried to keep his pulse from pounding between his ears.

Josh nudged his arm. "Here, drink."

He sniffed, but smelled nothing so he drank the liquid handed to him.

As Josh walked to the other couch, Zach covered his ears against the sound. He wasn't sure if he blacked out again, but it seemed only minutes later when Josh woke him.

"Okay, enough sleeping on the floor. What happened?"

Zach glanced up to find his friend towering over him. Surprised by the lack of pain in his head, he moved it right and left, then looked at Josh again. "What was in that stuff?"

"Just a little something I concocted in med school." Josh strolled back to the couch and cracked a beer. "I made it to help me pull all-nighters, but discovered it works great on hangovers as well."

Zach pulled himself onto the cushions behind him, still nervous he'd start the blinding pain in his head again. "Hell, you should market that."

"I don't think so. There's a controlled drug in there. I'd prefer not to go to jail."

Leaning forward, Zach grabbed the water bottle Josh had left for him. After a few good swallows, he felt better, but still tired. "What are you doing here?"

His friend stared at him as if he'd grown horns. Maybe he didn't want to know the answer.

Josh picked up his beer and toasted him. "It's Saturday. You offered me your place for the weekend because you had decided to take a break from Bea and go see your mom and dad. Remember? Though why you'd see your parents instead of having sex is a mystery to me."

Bea. The photos. Everything came back in a rush, or almost everything. He ran his hands over his face. "Hell, how many days have I been out of it?"

Josh surveyed him from head to toe. "I'm going to hazard a guess it's been two days since you were sober and conscious. I base that solely on the number and variety of empty bottles I took from your living room. That and the post-office stamp on the envelope I found lying on the floor."

Gut-wrenching pain took Zach's breath away as the photos of Bea with other men flashed across his mind.

Josh strode into the kitchen and came back with another beer. "Here. You look as if you could use one. But nothing stronger, got it?" He grinned. "Doctor's orders."

Zach took a swig and set the beer on the table. "Christ. What an idiot I am. I fell for her act."

Josh rested his long legs on the coffee table and crossed them. "First, who can blame you? She's downright hot. Truly the queen of the hotties, I mean that body is—"

"Hey, you're talking about my girlfriend there. I mean ex-girlfriend." Zach had no idea where his anger came from, but knowing Josh had stared at Bea's body in those photos had him struggling not to reach over and punch his friend. It didn't make sense.

Josh sobered. "Wow, did you fall for this girl?"

Zach shook his head and took another swallow of beer.

Josh eyed him. "You weren't even this messed up after Lisa."

Zach shrugged, unwilling to compare photos of a woman in the act of cheating to his late fiancée's run-in with a moose. Lisa had meant everything to him, but she had been killed instantly when she hit the moose with her car, the animal's large body flying through the windshield. Yes, the pain had been bad, but she was gone, forever. But Bea…the pain in his chest returned. Bea loved him. He would bet his house on it. And she was still alive, in the next town over. His throat closed, making it hard to swallow.

"Hey, Zach. You still with me, buddy?"

He crossed his ankle over his knee in an attempt to appear less affected, but the movement sent a potent waft of Scotch up from his jeans. He grimaced. Hell, he was rank.

Josh set his beer on the end table and leaned back. "So what did she say when you confronted her with the pictures?"

A vision of Bea crying on his deck popped into his head. Had she been here? Christ, he couldn't remember, but a niggling sensation in the back of his mind had him feeling uncomfortable. "I haven't spoken to her about them."

Josh crossed his hands behind his head as if he planned to pick out all the gory details. "So you haven't broken it off yet. Does she know you have them?"

Zach looked at his friend, but didn't see him. He saw Bea at the window asking to come in and he…he… What the hell did he do? "She knows I've seen them but—" He was sure he would remember if he had let her in. He had seen her on his deck and then he— "Oh Christ."

Josh perked up. "What?"

He groaned and dropped his head into his hands. "I was a real ass. I wouldn't even let her in. I didn't want to hear it." The feelings rushed back and with them a need to dull the pain again. He lifted his head and grabbed the beer and gulped. The cold alcohol did nothing for him. He put the half-empty bottle down with a thud.

Josh shrugged. "From what I saw and read, there wasn't much left to learn."

He glanced around the room. "What did you do with the letter and photos?"

"Over there." Josh angled his head toward the kitchen table. "Who sent them? The postmark said Tamwick, but I didn't see a name on the letter."

Zach ran his hands over his face again. "I don't know."

"I'm sure it doesn't matter. Who cares what motivated the person to send that packet? It's not as if you need to talk to her anyway. I mean, it's all there in black and white. Besides, it was time to break it off anyway, right?"

Zach stared at the sheets of paper he could see piled on the kitchen table. "Yeah, right, I guess."

Josh smirked. "Of course I'm right. I told you, I'm a genius."

He took another swig of beer and stared at the leafless trees outside. The scenery didn't soothe him like it usually did, which left getting drunk or working the chainsaw to escape the pain. Since he didn't relish the idea of another head-splitting, timber-falling headache, he might as well work. Maybe carving into the wood would make him forget that Bea still existed. "I'm going to work."

Josh sat forward. "What? It's frigid outside, you'll freeze. Don't you like my company?"

Zach strode to the stairs. "Nothing personal, Josh, but you planned on being here alone this weekend, so feel free to do as you please. Maybe you can get lucky. Me, I've got a carving to finish."

"Bea? You okay? You don't look very good."

She forced her gaze to focus on Kayla, standing in the doorway of her office. "I'm fine, just tired."

Kayla strode in and placed her hand on her forehead. "I don't think so. You're hotter than a tin roof in June."

Bea jerked away. "I have a little fever. Don't worry. I took aspirin. It'll go away. I get these sometimes." Though she tried to avoid them until now. The poison in her system had built up more than she'd ever experienced. She had come by herself last night with her specially made porous dildo, which made it possible for her to go to work, but she needed a man. She just couldn't bring herself to find one. Masturbating only expelled some poison. Most of it seeped right back into her body through her skin. Boy, her mother would be so disappointed in her. No husband, no baby and dead at thirty.

Kayla shook her head. "I don't like it."

She turned back to her computer. "I'm sorry you don't like it, but I have work to do."

Kayla backed up a step. "Now I know you're not well. You never snap. Just because Zach dumped you doesn't mean you can let yourself go. I'm calling my doctor. You need to see someone."

"No!" Bea slammed her hands on the desk and let her head drop. "Will you let me do my work, please?"

Kayla shook her head. Something was very wrong. "Okay, but I'm going to keep checking on you."

Gary peeked around the corner. "Kayla, could you come here a minute?"

Torn between work and her friend, she sighed, but went to the front desk. "What do you need, Gary?"

"This just came for Bea. You told me to let you know when another one arrived."

Kayla stared at the envelope with "To Bea Rappaccini" printed on it. If she gave the letter to Bea now, the woman would have a nervous breakdown. "Thanks, Gary. Did you see who brought it?"

"Yeah, the kid from the ice-cream shop down by the Hillside Inn. He tried to be discreet, dropping it on the counter when I was busy, but I noticed."

"Excellent, Gary. This is very important. I think the police will be thrilled to hear you caught sight of who has been leaving these letters."

Gary puffed with pride, but another customer demanded his attention.

Kayla took the opportunity to peek in on Bea. Poking her head around the corner, she gasped. Bea had fallen from her chair and lay motionless on the floor. Kayla ran to her side. "Bea, can you hear me?"

"Mom?"

Oh shit. Kayla felt Bea's forehead and grimaced at the heat radiating off her. Except for two bright spots of color on her cheeks, her face was pale. Dark circles shadowed her eyes, making them appear sunken. Kayla tamped down her rising fear and cradled her friend in her arms. She pulled Bea's purse off the desk, grabbed the cell phone from it and scanned the contacts. Finding Susan Rappaccini's name, she dialed, proud that her hand barely shook.

Susan answered. "Hello? Is that you, Bea?"

Kayla cringed at the hopeful sound in the woman's voice. "Hi, Susan, this is Kayla. You need to come quick. Bea's fainted and she asked for you."

"Oh my God. I'll be right there."

Kayla closed the cell phone and dropped it on the floor. "It's okay. Your mom's on the way."

Bea struggled to sit. "Mom? No. I can't. She can't."

Kayla propped her against the desk. "Listen, lady. It's either your mom or I'm calling 9-1-1."

Bea's shoulders sagged. "Fine."

Susan left the guest bedroom and wrung her hands. She'd never seen anyone in her family in such bad shape. Praying her daughter would use the porous dildo she gave her until they could figure something out, she entered the living room.

Gerry stopped pacing. "How is she?"

Susan shook her head.

He enveloped her in his massive arms. "Shhh. We'll fix her. Don't worry."

She cuddled her face against his black muscle shirt and almost gave in to the tears smarting her eyes. "She's really bad. It's as if she doesn't care anymore."

Gerry moved her back to arm's length. "You listen to me, Susan. We're going to get our gal back on her feet if I have to kidnap every man or doctor this side of the Connecticut River."

She nodded. He was right. Between them all, they would come up with something. "I just have to figure out who can help her. We can't give her a man, she only wants Zach and he dumped her."

Gerry let go and whipped out his cell phone. "There you go. Now we're talking. I'll call my boys. We'll get him over here right now."

Susan grasped his arm. "No, that won't work because he won't have sex with her. Bea said he thinks she cheated on him. We can't force him to have sex."

Gerry's face fell and his arms dropped to his sides, the cell phone useless in his big hand. "Maybe I could think of something."

Susan smiled sadly, but shook her head. "If only I knew someone Bea liked well enough to have rebound sex or which of her lovers likes her, but I haven't met any of them except Zach and Phillip. Wait. That's it! Phillip loves our Bea desperately. Give me your phone. I have his number on the fridge."

She ran into the kitchen and scanned the many pieces of scrap paper she had taped to the refrigerator. She always kept Phillip's in the upper-right corner, a good place of Karma for long-lasting love. Or at least, she thought it was. "Ha, here it is."

She dialed quickly.

He answered on the first ring. "Hi, Susan, does Bea want to see me now?"

"I hope so. She's in bad shape and I'm at a loss what to do. Can you come by right away?"

"I'd be happy to."

Susan sighed with relief. "Thank you. How long will it take you to get here from there?"

He laughed. "Actually, about ten minutes. As it happens, I'm in town this weekend."

Tears gathered in her eyes again and her entire body trembled as Gerry entered the kitchen. For a moment, she thought she would fall, her knees were shaking so badly. "Thank you, Phillip. I knew you would help."

After hanging up, she kissed the paper with his phone number for good luck.

Gerry pulled her onto his lap at the kitchen table. "What'd he say?"

She wrapped her arms around his neck and stroked his smooth head, a habit that always calmed her. "He's coming."

~~*~~

Susan bit her lip as Phillip came out of the guestroom. "Were you able to…?"

He shook his head. "She won't have me. She's says she's in love with this Zach guy. I thought she'd be over him by now. She should be with me. We're supposed to have a family."

Susan's heart felt like the tree in her backyard, split in half by lightning. She couldn't let her daughter die this way. Yes, she had wanted her to marry, but never expected her to be so heartbroken she didn't care about her own existence. She would do anything to save her. She grabbed Phillip's arm. "There has to be something you can do for her. You said you've been working on an antidote. Please, Phillip. If you love her, for goodness sakes do something."

Phillip patted her hand on his arm. "What I've developed hasn't been tested yet. Bea wasn't interested."

"It can't hurt to try." Susan's voice rose, but she couldn't control it. "She's dying in there! You two can't ever be together if she dies. I know you love her. Please, you have to try."

Gerry stepped up behind her. "Is this true? Do you have an antidote that will release her from the poison?"

Phillip raised his finger. "I do, but I wouldn't be able to guarantee anything. It might even make her worse."

Gerry pulled Susan out of the way. "Do it. Do it now."

"Very well, but remember, I'm not sure of the results."

While Phillip went to his car with Gerry as a personal escort, Susan walked into her guestroom and sat on the bed. Bea had used the toy she'd given her and her temperature had gone down a few degrees, but it was only a matter of time. "Bea?"

Bea opened her eyes.

Susan stroked her daughter's cheek. "Phillip is going to give you the antidote he discovered. You'll be cured and then you can have a normal life."

Bea's eyes brightened in her otherwise pale face. "Really? He would do that for me? Are you sure I won't have to marry him in exchange? He's still in love with me, Mom. If I loved someone that much, I don't think I could watch them have a life with someone else."

Susan lied easily. "No, honey, he just wants you to live. When you love someone that much, you want what's best for them."

Bea turned away. "How would you know?"

Ouch, that hurt. Taking her daughter's face in her hands, she gazed into her eyes. "Because I love you and would gladly give up what I have for you if it would help. I would give Phillip anything to save you."

Bea's eyes started to water and Susan hugged her. "I need you to live, honey." When her daughter hugged her tightly, she couldn't hold back the tears.

"Okay, let's get this show on the road." Gerry carried in a cooler and set it down on the dresser.

Susan wiped her face before she moved to allow Phillip access. "She's all yours, Phillip."

He lifted his brow. "Thank you. You don't know how long I've wanted to hear those words."

Bea had the covers grasped tightly to her chin. "Are you sure this will work?"

Phillip laid a hand on her head. "Trust me. You're in good hands."

As Phillip injected Bea in the arm, Susan watched. Her daughter's eyes widened. "Oh wow. I feel a change already."

Her color came back quickly and her breathing returned to a normal pace. Susan couldn't believe it. If this worked, maybe she could be cured too.

Cured? It had never occurred to her. If her poisons were gone, she could have a normal life, but she didn't want a normal life. She liked her men. She liked having four men who adored her and six men who loved her daughter. She shook her head. Her daughter and she were complete opposites in every way.

Phillip spoke. "How do you feel, Bea?"

Susan looked down again and noticed Bea's flushed face.

"Wonderful, except I feel a little hot. Is this what a hot flash feels like?"

Phillip fidgeted. "That's good, that's good. That means the medicine is working. You know I always wanted to be with you, Bea. I just needed time to find the antidote. But I always watched out for you. I even sent you letters to help you make the right decisions, but you disappointed me. I wanted us to be together forever. But I guess that can't be."

Bea stared at him. "You sent the letters? Why?"

He shook his head. "I was trying to make you see that your life was headed in the wrong direction. We were meant to be together, but you wouldn't listen." He stood. "I'm sorry, Bea. But if I can't have you, then no one should. You were supposed to be mine."

As Phillip left the bedroom, Susan grabbed his arm. "Where are you going? Is it going to work?"

Phillip halted and looked at her in triumph. "Exactly as it's supposed to. Goodbye, Susan."

At his words, instinctual fear skittered around her heart and she ran back into the room. "Bea, how do you feel?"

"Not good. I'm cold now. Really cold and my feet feel numb."

Gerry's face mirrored her own worried thought. Was her daughter having an allergic reaction? She turned to him. "What should we do now?"

He ran his hand over his bald head. "I'm not sure. Maybe we need a real doctor now. If she is cured, she could be having a reaction to the medicine."

Susan twisted her hands. "Gerry, Phillip said if he can't have Bea, then no one can. Do you think he meant…?"

Gerry's eyes rounded. "That bastard! He said that?"

She nodded. Gerry couldn't hear from his left ear so of course he'd missed Phillip's remark. If he had heard it, Phillip would be lying on the floor in agony right now.

"Mom? Mom?"

Susan ran to Bea's side and took her hand. It was like ice. "I'm right here, honey."

"Mom, I'm really, really cold."

"We'll get you another blanket." Susan looked at Gerry. "Grab a blanket from my bed."

Bea squeezed Susan's hand. "Mom, I just wanted Zach. I love him. Phillip ruined it with his damn letters and photos of me." She stared at the dresser before returning her gaze to Susan. "I don't think he cured me. I think he's killed me. Please, Mom, I need Zach. I want to say goodbye."

As the tears rolled down her daughter's cheeks, Susan broke, giving in to the despair that had been beating on the door to her brain. Dropping her head onto the bed, she allowed the pain in, taking her breath away.

When Gerry came back with three blankets, he piled them

on Bea. The shaking stopped and Susan lifted her head to see her daughter had fallen asleep.

Gerry pulled Susan into his arms and escorted her to the living room. He sat her on the sofa.

She pulled away. If she let him hold her again, she'd turn into a blubbering mess. She didn't want to be a mess. She needed to save her daughter. "I don't think this is good. I'm afraid she's dying. She asked for Zach because…because…she wants to say goodbye."

Gerry stood. "Then that's what she'll get. I'll call my boys."

"Gerry, I think I should call all her fathers."

He rubbed his hand over his smooth head. "Yeah, I guess."

She stood next to him. "I mean *all* of them."

He pulled her into his arms and she squeezed him hard. As he tipped her face for his kiss, she caught sight of a tear on his cheek. He might be her big biker dude, but he loved Bea as much as she did, as much as all her fathers.

Gerry hugged her for a moment then pulled away. "I'll get Charlie on the way to this guy's place in case he tries to make a run for it. Do you know where this Zach lives?"

She gave him directions from her conversation with Bea the night she'd been snowed in with Zach. The same night she had convinced her daughter to put her heart on the line. Ignoring the cloud of guilt threatening to break through her defenses, Susan plopped down on the couch. She heard the door slam at Gerry's exit and she picked up the phone. She had to believe between the six of them, one of them could save Bea. She'd start with the farthest away and the one with the most resources. "Hi, Jim, you need to get here right away."

~~*~~

Zach left the downstairs shower in a pair of clean jeans and dragged his butt upstairs to the living room. Josh was sacked out on the couch, which looked like a good idea. It was late afternoon and he'd finished the carving for the inn. A few touch-ups with the detail lines and it'd be ready to go. The sooner he delivered it, the sooner he could cut all ties to anything reminding him of Bea. He didn't give a damn when Ice-Out happened anymore.

After grabbing a beer from the fridge, he collapsed on the other couch. The television was on, but Josh had it on mute, so Zach clicked it off. Taking a swallow of Bud Light, he gazed outside.

The sun lit the open area in front of the deck, but the house shaded the driveway, one reason the ice hadn't melted there yet. The bright scenery did nothing to ease the ache inside his chest, but at least the physical exertion of making the chainsaw obey his commands had tired him out. Maybe he could have a sober, forgetful sleep.

Josh snored and rolled over.

He toasted his friend with his beer then took another swig. Maybe he needed to get out and meet a new woman. He'd never had a woman betray him before, not even his many short-term relationships. Maybe that was the key. He'd stayed with Bea longer than usual. If she hadn't screwed around on him, she could have ended up dead like Danielle and Lisa.

Bea's sexy eyes and brilliant smile hedged into his thoughts. She was too beautiful. He would have been more than willing to satisfy her sexual needs even if they had to spend days in bed. Why did she have to stray? Why did she stay away for days at a time?

He took another gulp. It didn't matter. She'd probably picked up a couple more suckers to sleep with. No wonder she went for him. She obviously wasn't interested in long-term either.

He set the beer on the table and stretched out on the couch. Closing his eyes, he tried not to think of Bea, but found himself sketching her in his mind.

A hand around his throat brought his eyes wide open. "What?" He tried to grab the hand but his arms were restrained.

A bald giant with a goatee bent over him. From the tattoos, earring and black tank with a faded Harley logo on the front, Zach hoped the man had seen his own bike parked in the driveway where Josh had left it.

The giant spoke. "You Zach Woodman?"

Zach glanced at the other couch to see Josh in a similar situation, a hand on his throat and scared shitless. What the hell were these guys doing in his house? Anger built. He stared the giant in the eyes. "What if I am? What's it to you?"

That was the wrong answer if the lack of air getting to his lungs was any indication.

The giant's eyes became slits. "Don't play with me, man. I'm not in a pleasant mood and I have no time to make nice."

When the pressure on his windpipe let up again, Zach attempted a civil answer. "Yeah, I'm Zach. Who are you?"

The hand around his neck left, only to find purchase on his arm to yank him up, the other hands no longer holding him in place. He vaguely wished he had a shirt on.

The giant thrust his chin toward Josh. "Who's that?"

Cooperating seemed like the right way to go for now. "That's Doctor Josh Sutton, a well-known scientist in the state. You don't want to harm him if you want to avoid the police."

The giant glanced at Josh then grinned. "Perfect. Bring him too."

Zach scanned his living room to find no less than six bikers surrounding them, plus one short, stocky guy who looked as if he didn't belong but was completely at home in their company.

Zach spoke to the giant. "Where are you taking us?"

The giant's brows lowered. "You're both coming to Susan Rappaccini's house."

Zach tugged at his arm, breaking the giant's grip. "I'm not going anywhere near there. I don't know what Bea's mother told you, but forcing me to her house is not going to change anything. Bea's a nympho. I prefer not to share my woman."

The jaw-splitting punch caught him completely unawares. For the second time that day he found himself staring at his living room floor. Gingerly, he moved his mouth and spit out a piece of one of his teeth. Holy hell, who was this guy? He didn't have much time to ponder that statement before two of the bikers lifted him by his arms to face the giant.

Oh fuck, he wished he was still on the floor. The fury in the man's eyes made him seriously think his time on Earth was limited. He wished his brain would work faster because he had no idea what he could say to save his life.

The giant approached.

Zach tensed.

The little man stepped in front of him, shielding him from the giant's murderous intent. "Whoa, Gerry. I think Bea would like to see the guy breathing, don't you?"

He would have to buy the little man a drink if he got out of this alive.

The giant wasn't moved. "Come on, Charlie, you heard what he said about our daughter. I don't think she'd mind too much if he was missing a limb."

Daughter? Holy shit! He was fucked. These were two of Bea's fathers.

Charlie shook his head. "I don't think so, Gerry. We need to bring him whole. Then depending what happens, you can always beat the pulp out of him later."

Gerry wasn't too happy. "All right, but no interference later if I decide he needs to be taught a lesson, agreed?"

Charlie nodded.

Gerry turned to his friends. "Okay, guys, let's go. Bring the doc too."

Zach waited until they had all made it to the basement before speaking again. "Uh, mind if I throw on a shirt and boots? I'll freeze my tits off out there."

Gerry stepped in front of him. "Aw, wussy girl has to get dressed to go outside?"

Zach smirked. "I don't know. Are you willing to strip and try it?"

Gerry pulled back his arm when Charlie stepped between them again. "Gerry, why don't you head outside? I'll take care of this."

Gerry grumbled under his breath and stormed out the door, leaving Charlie, Zach, Josh and the six bikers.

Charlie turned on him. "Listen, kid, you got a lot to learn here. Rule number one, don't piss off Gerry." The bikers snickered and nodded.

"Number two, you got two dads here who are ready to break every bone in your body if you don't make their daughter feel better, so you'd be smart to cooperate. I'm not stepping between you and him again. Got it?"

Zach nodded. The man's blue eyes communicated his anger and fear all at the same time. What the hell was going on?

At Zach's nod, Charlie scanned the basement. "Okay, anything you've got down here you can wear. Boys, release him, but watch the bugger."

He had a dirty shirt and socks in the bathroom, but they reeked. Instead he tied his Timberland boots on over bare feet and grabbed Josh's jacket off the wall hook and threw it at him. One of Josh's guys caught it. Zach pulled down his hoodie just as two guys grabbed his arms again and dragged him outside.

As they walked by his bike, he thought of making a break for it. But Charlie must have read his mind. "Don't even think about it. Your baby will never start again unless I make a few changes."

The guys holding him laughed. "Yeah, Charlie's the best Harley mechanic in the state. Too bad you didn't own a Honda."

Zach shook his head. If the whole situation wasn't so serious, he would think someone had set him up to be punked.

Charlie, as it turned out, had a very nice Cadillac Escalade. He and Josh found themselves thrown into it, along with the appropriate musclemen. Gerry and the rest of the guys, thankfully, peeled out on Harleys, leaving four machines in his driveway. That, more than anything else, made him uncomfortable. They would never leave their bikes if they didn't have a plan for coming back. Hell.

Chapter Thirteen

Susan sat on her couch, Tony and Andy on either side of her. Mathew stood in front of them, trying to convince her Bea would be all right. She picked at her skirt, concerned that Jim hadn't come out of Bea's room yet. Did he care? He had come. That had to mean something. She'd forgotten how handsome he was.

The front door opened and Gerry strode in. "We got him."

Susan stood to greet Zach. Tony and Andy joined her as two of Gerry's boys brought him to stand before her. A bright-red mark shone clearly on his jaw. Oh dear. "Let go of him this instant."

They dropped Zach's arms and backed away. She glared at Gerry. "You hit him."

He shrugged. "Trust me, he had it coming, right, Charlie?"

"Yup."

Two more bikers came in with another person, but Zach drew her attention. "Hi, Susan."

She shook her head. "Zach, did they tell you why we needed you to come?"

He glared at Gerry, though he spoke to her. "Nope, not a single clue."

She added her glare to Zach's and Gerry threw up his hands.

"It wouldn't have made a difference. He would still be here. Anyone want a beer?"

Every man in the room wanted one, but Zach.

Susan shook her head. Thank God she and Gerry had sex last night or eleven men in one room would have sent her into a frenzy. "Zach, the reason we brought you here is that Bea is not doing well. I think, I think…" Oh God, she couldn't say it.

Andy put his arm around her shoulders. "What she's trying to say is she thinks Bea is dying."

Susan sniffed. "And her—"

Tony interrupted. "Bea asked for you."

Zach's heart constricted as perspiration seeped along his skin. She couldn't be dying. She was too alive, too quirky, too beautiful. What happened? Bea should be in a hospital with doctors who could help her. His gaze collided with Josh's and Josh gave him a brief nod.

He looked back to Susan, Andy and the other father. "My friend here is an excellent doctor. Would you mind if he took a look at her?"

Susan broke down into tears as she collapsed back onto the couch.

A cultured voice came from the hallway. "Please, have your friend come in. I think she's slipped into a coma."

Susan's sobs pounded on his nerves as he and Josh strode toward the stranger.

The man offered his hand. "I'm Jim Bellante."

Zach shook. He must be the father Bea thought had sent the letters, but Zach's instinct said this man was first-class. Without hesitation he followed him into the room. If Zach had to guess, he'd bet this man or the one sitting next to Susan was Bea's biological father.

When he entered the room, she didn't move. Her face was white and as still as death. A sharp pain grabbed his chest, stopping him in his tracks. He shook his head, refusing to believe what his eyes told him. Making his feet move to her side, he sat in the chair next to the bed and touched her cheek. Oh God, were they too late? "Josh, she's ice cold."

He tried to keep the panic from his voice, but Josh sensed it and took over. "Jim, I need my medical bag, which is back at Zach's. Can you send one of those musclemen to get my car? It's in there."

Jim nodded, catching the keys Josh tossed to him and left the room.

Zach grabbed Josh's arm. "Is she...?"

Josh shook his head as he held Bea's wrist. "No, she has a strong pulse, but something is seriously wrong with her and—"

He steeled himself. "Tell me."

"Jim's right. She's slipped into a coma."

Zach put his head in his hands. Why hadn't he let her explain? Maybe he could have helped her. Maybe she could have gone to a rehab center. They treated people for sex addictions these days. It was his fault either way. He'd stayed with her too long. Fate had already come to take her away too.

"Move."

Startled, he stared blankly at Josh.

"Let me check her vitals. You're in the way."

"Right." He stood and moved to stand against the dresser. Bea had wanted to see him before...hell. What Susan had tried to tell him was that seeing him was her last wish. His stomach clenched. He slammed his fist against the furniture behind him.

Josh jumped, but Bea didn't. "Do you mind?"

He looked down. "Sorry."

The image of Bea crying, begging to come in, floated through his mind. He'd ignored her. He'd never treated a woman that badly. He'd been so caught up in the photos and his own feelings of betrayal he hadn't even questioned the fucking source of the letter or how old the photos were. Christ. She had to live. He was tired of losing the women he loved. Loved?

He leaned back and knocked over a ceramic bunny, probably a decoration for Easter. He righted it a bit farther away from the cooler. Cooler? What was a cooler doing in the room? He peered inside and found vials and unused needle packs. Had they been experimenting on her? *What the hell.* "Hey, Josh, look at this."

Josh came over and read the tiny scrawl on the labels. "I don't know exactly what this is, but it appears to be some kind of antivenom."

"Antivenom?"

Josh held a vial up to the light and shook his head. "I don't think that's right, but I'd say it's along those lines. If I had my lab I could test it, but I don't even have my bag."

Zach realized Josh was as anxious as he and more frustrated. "I appreciate anything you can do for her."

Josh raised a brow. "You mean the woman you never wanted to see again?"

He stuffed his hands into his pockets. "Yeah, well, I'm sure I would have come to my senses eventually."

Josh put a hand on his shoulder. "Of course you would because I was nudging you there. Good thing you have a genius for a friend."

Zach gave him a halfhearted grin. "Yeah, really. You save Bea, and I'll pay you back, promise."

Josh smacked him on the arm. "Hey, that's what friendship is all about, buddy. Paying each other back."

"Right." Zach choked back the lump in his throat.

"Why don't you go sit next to her, hold her hand, do that lovey stuff. I'm going to tell the others what little I know so far. I need to get her to my lab, but it's a two-hour drive. I hope they have ambulances in these backwoods."

~*~

Zach glared at Susan as she lay next to her daughter in the hospital room, a tube transferring her blood to Bea. She wasn't his favorite person at the moment, despite the fact she may be saving her daughter's life. Even as he stood there, Bea's grandmother was on her way to the hospital in Jim's helicopter. As soon as Bea, Susan, Josh and he had arrived in it, Jim called it back for the grandmother.

Zach approached the bed. "Susan, I think you need to tell me and Josh what's going on if you want him to help Bea. I don't mean bits and pieces either. I want the whole story."

She fidgeted with the metal bar on the side of her bed, not meeting his eyes. "Okay, but I need to have Mathew here or you won't believe me."

He kept his tone stern. "They're on the way, but in the meantime, we need to know what's wrong with Bea. They can corroborate your story later. You do want her to come out of this coma, don't you?"

She nodded, but still avoided his gaze. He glanced at Josh, who threw up his hands in frustration. The good doctor wasn't getting answers from her or from the contents of the cooler fast enough. Zach had never seen his friend uptight, but then again, he'd never seen Josh in his work environment either.

He sat next to Susan, leaving Josh full access to Bea. Then he took Susan's hand. "I know there's a reason you and Bea's fathers didn't call an ambulance right away. I know there's something unusual in that cooler, so you might as well tell me. We're going to find out sooner or later and sooner will be much better for your daughter."

She looked at him and he gave her his best smile, despite the pain in his jaw.

She melted. He could see it in her gaze. "Oh, Zach. I knew you were perfect for her. I just didn't expect her to fall in love with you."

His heart sped at her statement, what a backhanded compliment that was. But he kept his face impassive. "So tell me why she's in a coma and why you think your blood and her grandmother's might help her."

Susan glanced away again and sighed. "We are cursed."

"Cursed?" If she thought Bea's condition was about bad karma, he would break something, anything.

She looked him in the eyes. "Yes, cursed. An ancestor of ours, Giacomo Rappaccini, was a great scientist in Italy. He grew beautiful, poisonous flowers, but flowers weren't enough for him. No, he had to experiment on his daughter Beatrice. Her mother had died young, probably from him as well. But he got it right, which was so wrong. His daughter carried poison in her."

Zach held Susan's gaze, but he wanted more than anything to look at Josh and see if such a thing were possible.

Susan continued, her eyes glazing over. "Giacomo's daughter Beatrice fell in love and became pregnant. Her intended discovered he'd been poisoned simply by being with her. So he found a friend to devise an antidote, but when Beatrice took it, it killed her. Giacomo became enraged and performed what we call a cesarean on Beatrice and Lily was born." Susan looked up at him, anger contorting her face, making him wonder if perhaps she wasn't a little off balance mentally.

She grasped his wrist. "Giacomo provided Lily with a poisonous mate and she gave birth to the next Beatrice, complete with double the poison, and so our lineage started." She looked off toward her own daughter. "Each succeeding generation has had less and less poisons." Susan's smile was pitiful. "My Beatrice has the least."

Zach squeezed her hand, but looked at Josh.

His friend mouthed the word "possible" then left the room.

Zach brought his gaze back to Susan. "So what happened to Bea? Why was she given the medicine in the cooler?"

Susan dropped her gaze again. "Could I have some water?"

Zach patted her hand. "Of course, I'm sorry. I'll send the nurse in." He left the room.

After letting the nurse know of Susan's request, he went in search of Josh. But he couldn't find him in any of the unrestricted areas. His friend must have gone to the lab. He sat outside Bea's room to wait.

He hadn't been there more than a minute when Josh came through the restricted area doors. His eyes shone with excitement. "You're not going to believe this. She's telling the truth. I tested her and Bea's blood samples and it's true. Susan's poisons are stronger than Bea's. It's a fascinating poison, not like anything I've ever seen. They may be the only ones to still have such a sample. I need to research this."

Zach stood. "I'm happy you have a new discovery to make, but I have a woman dying in there. What kind of poison is it? Do you think you can give her an antidote?"

Josh's face sobered. "Sorry. I got excited there for a minute, but you're right. There's plenty of time for discovery later. I don't think Bea needs an antidote, in fact, I think that is what caused her coma. The liquid in that cooler is an antidote and she was given a lethal dose. It attacked all the poison in her body, leaving her with little left. The blood transfusion with Susan should help, but I can't let it go on much longer because I also don't want to poison her. You have to understand, I'm just guessing here."

Josh reached for the door. "Or it could be a doubly potent mix of poison and we are currently killing your mystery woman. I've got to find out and our hippie lady needs to start talking."

Zach swore, his blood chilling, but somehow he managed to follow Josh into the room. Focusing on Susan, with a tube in her arm in hopes of saving her only daughter, helped him find the compassion he needed. Besides, he'd already learned intimidation didn't work with Bea's mom, so he pulled Josh back before his friend started an interrogation. "Susan, can you tell me what was in the cooler?"

She brightened. "Oh yes, that's Phillip's. He discovered an antidote for Bea's poison." Her face filled with confusion. "But he gave her too much. He said if she couldn't love him then no one could have her. That's when I got scared. He loved her so much. He said he had written her letters, but she ignored them. I'm surprised Bea would be so rude."

Zach heard Josh's sigh of relief. "Thank you, Susan. Why did you find it hard to tell me all this?"

She shrugged. "Most people don't believe it. We have to stay away from regular doctors because they try to cure us, but many things don't work on us or have the wrong effect."

She shivered and Zach realized she was talking from experience.

"Trust me. You're in the right hands now. I'm just glad Josh was with me when Gerry showed up."

Susan wrung her hands. "I'm sorry about that. He loves Bea so much and needed to do something to help. I'm glad Charlie was with him though." She cupped his cheek with her hand. "How is your jaw?"

He wiggled it around and gave her a smirk because it hurt less than a smile. "I'll recover."

Josh clicked off a machine. "Susan, I'm going to stop the transfusion. I don't want to give your daughter too much of your blood. It's significantly stronger in its poisons, but I may call upon your mother when she gets here if Bea needs more. Hers will be stronger, I'm assuming, and I wouldn't need too much."

Josh unhooked the intravenous tube. "You may be a little lightheaded as I've taken a full unit, so I'm going to have a nurse bring you to get some orange juice and something to eat."

Susan nodded then looked at her daughter. "Zach, you'll have to ask Bea about the rest."

The rest? "What do you mean?"

The nurse came in with a wheelchair, interrupting them, but

before Susan left with the young woman, he stopped them. "What do you mean by 'the rest'? Is there something we should know that will help save Bea?"

She shook her head. "No, but it will explain a lot. And it won't be relevant unless she wakes up. Ask her how we're able to live with the poison, if she—"

Zach put his finger to her lips. "I will."

When the door closed, he made himself comfortable in the chair next to Bea and glanced at his friend. "Josh, when will you know about the antidote?"

"It will still be another hour or so."

Zach stared at Bea's face. Was there color back in it, or was it his own hopeful thoughts? "Come on, Bea, I came to you, now you have to come to me. Fair's fair."

"Zach, go find something to eat." Josh made a note on Bea's chart.

He shook his head, he far preferred Bea's silent company. Besides, there was no way he would walk past that waiting room again. Too many people, and they didn't all get along, especially Susan and Bea's grandmother. That old lady was one sharp woman and a force to be reckoned with, but when she flirted with another doctor, he'd had to keep himself from laughing. "Do you think you'll need to use the grandmother's blood?"

Josh shrugged. "I'm not sure about anything here. I'm giving it my best guess. The antidote is pure genius, but the dosage would have killed her. I'm going to play it safe and wait a little longer."

Zach squeezed Bea's hand. At least she wasn't as cold as she'd been.

The nurse popped her head in. "Excuse me, Dr. Sutton, but Ms. Rappaccini has a new visitor. She says her name is Kayla Weeks."

Zach smiled. "Finally, a normal person."

Sighing, Josh went back to his calculations. "I guess you can send her in."

Kayla came through the door and Zach left his chair to give her a welcome hug. "It's good to see you."

She lifted her brow. "Really? Has it been that bad?"

He pulled her over to Bea. "Yeah."

She took Bea's hand. "Oh, honey, what's happened to you? You need to wake up and make this man yours. Don't wait forever or someone else will steal him." Kayla looked at him excitedly. "She squeezed my hand."

He rubbed her shoulder. "Josh says that's just reflex."

Josh cleared his throat.

Zach glanced at his friend. "Oh, sorry." He turned back to Kayla. "This is Dr. Josh Sutton. Josh, this is Kayla."

Kayla pushed her hair behind her ear and offered her hand. "Hello. Zach didn't tell me Bea had such a handsome doctor or I would have come hours ago."

Zach peered at Kayla to make sure she wasn't poking fun at his friend, but she gave Josh a hot once-over and licked her lips.

Josh, on the other hand, actually blushed. "It's a pleasure to meet you, Kayla."

Zach coughed as the two remained standing, hands clasped. He couldn't believe it, but then again, everyone had different tastes. "Kayla, Josh is a very close friend of mine and he's been going nonstop for the last twenty-four hours trying to help Bea. Could you do me a favor and escort him to the cafeteria so he can get a bite to eat?"

"I'd be happy to. And when I get back, I think I'll organize the people mess you've got going on in the waiting room. You boys definitely need my help with Bea under the weather."

Zach looked at the ceiling and thanked whoever watched over them for sending Kayla. They did need her.

She linked her arm around Josh's. "You ready, Doc? Let's get some grub. I'm hungry too."

Josh glanced at Zach. "You should eat as well."

He shook his head. "I'll let Kayla find something for me. You guys can bring it back. I'm not leaving this room."

"Okay. We'll be back soon." As Josh opened the door for Kayla, his gaze riveted to her ass.

Zach shook his head. Never would he have matched the two of them together. Then again, they had just met. His own night with Kayla made things a bit awkward, but if Josh liked her that was all that mattered.

He sat next to Bea and took her hand. If the attraction was anything like what he had for Bea, it could last a lifetime. His jaw tightened. He just hoped Bea's lifetime hadn't already passed.

He kissed her hand and felt a reflexive squeeze. The touch grabbed at his heart and tears formed in his eyes. What was that song? *You don't know what you've got 'til it's gone?*

Hell. He was in love with the woman holding his hand. Now if she would only wake up so he could do something about it.

Zach woke to someone brushing fingers through his hair. He opened his eyes and lifted his head from Bea's bed. The sight that greeted him made his heart constrict, even as a tear made its way down his cheek.

Her eyes were open. She gazed at him with such love, he thought he would explode with joy. "Hi, beautiful."

She smiled. "Hi. I'm so glad you came."

He smiled wider despite the pain on one side. "I couldn't stay away. Bea, I'm sorry I was such an ass."

He moved forward and kissed her, loving the feel of her arms as they surrounded him. Her lips were warm and her face flushed. He broke away. "How do you feel?"

"Like I was beat up." She touched his jaw. "Looks as if you were too."

He glanced away. "Just one of your dads being a dad."

"Gerry."

He looked back at her. "Yeah, how'd you guess?"

She smirked. "Because while any of them might want to hit you at some point, Gerry's the only one big enough to leave a mark."

Zach held her face in his hands. He couldn't stop touching her yet. "Yeah, well, he was scared and worried. You almost didn't make it."

She peered beyond him. "I'm in a hospital?"

"Jim flew us here in a helicopter. This is where Josh works. He needed his lab to figure out what was wrong with you. Do you remember anything?"

Her eyes lit up. "Yes, it was Phillip. He sent the letters." Then her face fell, but her gaze remained fixed on him. "Zach, you have to let me explain the letters."

He brushed her hair back from her face. "It's okay, Bea. We can get you help. They have rehab now for people with sex addictions."

The slap to the back of his head caught him unawares. He rubbed the abused spot. "Hey, what was that for?"

Bea's lips pursed and her brows drew down. He wasn't sure he'd ever seen her angry before.

"Because I'm not addicted to sex. I'm shocked you would believe such a thing just because Phillip wrote it."

He squirmed when she put it that way. "Well, what was I supposed to think?"

She lowered her gaze and picked at the blanket. "I was going to tell you that night. Remember, my secret?"

"Your mom told us about the poisons. That's why Josh was able to save you. Your mom and your grandmother both gave you blood infusions to balance the toxins in your body." His hand curled tight of its own accord at what could have happened. "Your boyfriend Phillip gave you an antidote, all right. It wiped out all the poison in your body and it was too much."

Bea covered his fisted hand with hers. "How much did she tell you?"

He tried to relax his hand, but the fact that someone had tried to kill Bea had his body fighting him. "She said you needed to tell me how you lived with the poison."

Bea's shoulders fell. "Oh."

He leaned over and kissed her on the lips, then on her forehead. "It can wait. There are a dozen people worried about you. As much as I hate the thought of sharing you, I need to let them know you're awake. Are you up for it?"

She took a deep breath and gave him a tentative smile. "I guess I have to face them eventually."

~~*~~

Bea grinned as Kayla ushered in her next visitor.

Zach remained by her side. He had been very patient, but her time would come to tell him the facts. She wasn't sure if he would think her worth keeping and her fear grew as the time lagged on.

Kayla started to close the door to the hospital room then stopped. "Fifteen minutes. I'll be timing you."

Jim Bellante waved her on. "That's fine. It won't take me long to say goodbye to my daughter."

Bea glanced at Zach in question, but he shrugged.

Jim sat next to her bed. "Bea, I have to leave, now that I know you'll recover. I need to return to my wife and family."

She lost her grin. "But I haven't seen you in almost a decade."

She couldn't help the whine in her voice. This father had always been an enigma to her. She wanted to know him better.

He patted her hand. "I know, but I will always be here for you if you ever need me. I gave your friend out there all my contact information since it's obvious your mother never did."

Bea winced. Mom hadn't fared well during this whole ordeal, both emotionally and in her family's judgment. "Thank you so much for flying me here. Dr. Josh said I wouldn't have made it if they'd driven me."

He smiled. "I'm glad I could help. I would stay longer, but my children are much younger than you. Teenagers." He said the word as if it explained everything.

He looked at Zach then back at her. "You, on the other hand, are grown and have someone quite capable of watching over you. Remember, anytime you need me or if you have big news, contact me." He glanced at Zach again, making it clear he expected to hear something soon.

Bea twisted her fingers around her father's hand. "I will, I promise."

Jim stood and kissed her on the forehead, then spoke to Zach. "Take care of my girl."

Zach rose and shook her dad's hand. "I will."

Bea's heart hitched. She watched her dad leave then turned to Zach. "I wish he could have stayed longer. I don't know anything about him."

Zach took the seat her father had occupied. "Don't you think you have enough family?"

At Zach's raised eyebrow she laughed. "I guess you're right. Some kids would hate having six fathers, but I've learned something from all of them. From Charlie I learned patience and common sense. You know I didn't inherit those traits from my mom."

Zach nodded in agreement.

"From Tony, I became good at math. He always helped me with my homework. Andy taught me to relax and appreciate the little things, like the mourning doves at sunrise. He also taught me how to organize my time to get as much done as possible so I could enjoy life. Mathew showed me how to see the positive in every situation, which I needed with my, ah, condition." She nibbled at her lip. She still had to tell Zach how she lived with her poisons.

He squeezed her hand. "What about Gerry? Can we forget about him?"

She whipped her attention to his face to find a giant smirk. He wasn't serious, though she wouldn't blame him, considering the blue bruise coloring the right side of his jaw. "Actually, Gerry did teach me a few things. He taught me not to judge those different from me, to accept people for who they are and most important, he showed me what unconditional love is like."

Zach leaned over her bed and placed his hand on the side of her face. "Unconditional love?"

She wet her lips. "Yes. That's what I feel for you, Zach. I love you with my whole being."

His lips were on hers in an instant, the kiss gentle, sweet and loving. Her heart tripped as she used her hand to cup the back of his neck. Opening her lips, she invited him in.

The hospital room door opened and they broke apart.

Grandma Beatrice strode to the bed, a big smile on her face. "About time you two got it on." She studied Zach's face and nodded. "You need to get to work now, young man. She needs sex and she needs it now. That is, if you want her to walk out of this sterile place." Grandma glared at the room. "Humph, I hate hospitals."

Bea cringed at Zach's confused expression. She better tell him now or someone else would. And Grandma was right, she needed him soon.

Grandma Beatrice peered at Zach. "Come down here, boy, and give me a kiss goodbye."

Zach obliged and kissed her on the cheek. Then she stepped up to Bea. "Have courage, young lady. Everything in life worth having is worth suffering for. You've suffered and found someone worth it all. Take care, sweetie."

With a quick kiss to Bea's cheek, Grandma Beatrice turned to leave.

Bea stopped her. "Wait, Grandma. How did you slip past Kayla? I thought she guarded my door like a pit bull?"

Grandma rolled her eyes. "It wasn't that hard, hon. Everyone else is gone and she's hanging all over your doctor, so my guess is that you two will be alone for a while." Grandma wiggled her eyebrows before disappearing around the door.

Zach chuckled. "I like your grandmother. A one-track mind, but I still like her."

Bea took a steadying breath. "Is that the last person?"

Zach grinned. "I don't know. I lost count."

She smacked his forearm.

He grabbed her hand, bringing it to his lips to kiss her palm, his eyes never leaving her face.

A shiver raced across her skin. "Zach, we need to talk."

He brought her hand down and sighed. "I know. I need to apologize for the way I treated you last week."

Bea gazed into his eyes and wondered what planet he came from. Of course he was upset. Maybe they could have worked it out if she had tried to reach him again in a few days. But no, she had to punish herself until she was too sick for sex. Even now, the idea of having sex with another man made her want to vomit. "I know the letters and photos were a shock to you, but they were to me too. I don't know what your letter said, but the photos were enough for me to know you wouldn't understand. I want you to know every one of those pictures was taken before we met."

Zach squeezed her hand. "I should have known. I questioned your letters from the start, that someone didn't want us together. I should have realized. Still, it was hard to see you with another man, men."

Bea looked away. "I'm sorry you had to see that. I know you've been with other women, but I would hate to see proof, especially like that."

He turned her face toward him. "Maybe you can make it up to me by getting in the same position from that photo. Then we could erase your memory of that particular episode."

His kind features warmed her soul. She wanted nothing more than to leave everything as it was. But she couldn't. He had to know if they had any chance of a relationship, which she still wasn't sure was physically possible. She played with the blanket in her hand.

He stopped her hands with his own. "Bea, what's wrong?"

She sighed. "I have to tell you about how I'm able to live with the poison in my body."

He shook his head. "Oh, that can wait. After all, like your grandmother said, we have some time alone right now." He raised his brows at her in imitation of her grandmother.

She tried to smile, but failed.

His face turned serious, but worse, his body tensed as if expecting a rejection. "Why not?"

She pulled her hands from his and laid one on his arm to soothe him and keep him there. "What my grandmother said was correct. If I don't have sex soon, I won't be able to leave this hospital."

Zach's brow furrowed. "I don't understand, I mean I'm more than willing, but why do you have to?"

She took a deep breath. "Because intercourse is how I'm able to expel my toxins and keep them at levels low enough for my body to tolerate. I have to orgasm with a cock inside me to release the bad stuff."

Zach pondered that. "So the men from your past, you were using to survive?"

"Yes."

"Why? Why not simply keep one man and have him at your beck and call?"

Bea touched his cheek. "Because when my poison leaves my body, it soaks into yours. Remember getting sick that morning after we made love all night?"

"How can I forget, but that was only once. We made love many times and I didn't get sick."

"Because the other times, I was careful. I made sure I didn't come with you inside me more than once. Don't forget you were sick the night after we ate dinner at Mom's because you had been inside me when I orgasmed, not because of the marijuana like we thought. But the night at your house, I talked myself into believing you might be immune. I let you take control and it was amazing, but then you suffered for my selfishness. I have no control with you, Zach."

Zach made to stand, but she hung on. He stared at her hand on his arm. "So you poisoned other men until you met me."

"Yes." She desperately looked for a clue to his feelings. His face remained unreadable.

He looked her in the eyes. "Do you know how many times you need to do this to stay healthy?"

"I do. At least three times a week. Less than three orgasms a week and the poison builds too high. That's why my mom sent for Phillip. When you wouldn't see me, I couldn't stand the thought of another man touching me. My body became toxic to itself. Phillip supposedly found an antidote, but I guess that didn't work."

Zach pulled out of her grip and she swallowed a whimper at the loss. She couldn't lose him. He had her heart.

He stood and began to pace. "So that's why you have six possible fathers."

Bea's answer was soft. "Yes."

"Your mom handles the problem by sleeping with the same group of men so no one man gets too sick."

She nodded.

He kept pacing. "Does coming in other ways, like we did, help?"

Bea shook her head. "A little, but not much."

Zach stopped and put his hands in his pockets and stared at Bea. "In other words, for us to have a relationship, the only way to keep you alive would be for me to get sick."

Bea nodded again.

"Holy hell." He'd finally saved a woman he loved, a woman who had put her own life at risk to remain faithful to him, but for it to work, they would have to trade off being sick. He looked at the ceiling. "You have a sick sense of humor."

Bea sat forward. "What?"

He looked back at her. "Not you, fate."

She raised her eyebrow, but he didn't elaborate.

He leaned against the wall opposite the bed. "There has to be a way we can make this work."

Bea's face brightened. But when a tear rolled down her cheek, he crossed to her bed and pulled her into his embrace. "Beautiful, what's wrong?"

She spoke to his chest. "Nothing. I'm just so happy. I thought you wouldn't want me anymore and I'd have to live that other existence. Honestly," she pulled back to look at him, "now that I love you, I don't think I could do it."

His heart twisted at the depth of her feelings. She would rather die, literally, than face life without him. Humbled, unable to speak, he brought her back into his embrace, catching her lips to show her how he felt.

Her body, so soft against his, made him want to strip and crawl into the bed with her. Why not? They had privacy. One orgasm wouldn't make him that sick, and she needed him if they hoped to check her out of the hospital and back to his place.

His mind made up, Zach pulled away, grinning at her groan. He pulled the t-shirt Josh had given him over his head and threw it on the other bed in the room. Then he unzipped his jeans.

Bea's voice halted him. "Zach, what are you doing?"

"What do you think I'm doing? I'm making love to you."

"But—"

"No buts about it. I'm making love to you. I'm going to slide this cock," he pulled his cock from his jeans to show her, "into your wet, swollen folds and find nirvana as you convulse around me. And there's nothing you can do about it."

Bea's bright eyes revealed her desire and his cock hardened. Not needing any more encouragement than that, he bent to untie his boots.

"But, Zach."

He stood back up and slid his boots off, shaking his head at her. "I told you, no buts."

She pointed behind him and raised her brow. "I just thought you might want to close the curtain over the window to the hallway."

He turned, thankful he hadn't dropped his jeans yet, though his cock, hard and upright, hung out. Stepping to the curtain, he closed it and turned, a mock frown on his face. "Are you happy now?"

Bea giggled. "No. Not until you stop teasing me and bring that gorgeous piece of man-meat over here. My pussy is already wet and oh so empty. Want to see?" She spread her legs beneath the sheet.

In a second his pants were off and the sheet tossed as he climbed into the bed. "Let's see exactly how wet you are." With those words, he positioned himself between her legs and pushed into her in one long stroke. Her slick moistness enveloping his cock made him feel as if he'd come home.

Her squeal of delight hardened him further. He held her still, her head between his hands as he waited for her to open her eyes.

When he didn't move, she looked at him.

"I love you, Bea. We will figure this out."

Her mouth opened and he stopped any words with a deep kiss. He didn't want to think. He wanted to feel, and this lady could make that happen. There would be time for thinking later, though his gut told him it might not do them any good. With determination, he pumped into the woman he loved, showing her with his body how much she meant to him.

Chapter Fourteen

Bea paced before the great windows in Zach's living room. If she bothered to stop and look, she could enjoy the budding of the maple trees, but she couldn't stand still. The weather continued to grow warmer and Zach worked on the finishing touches of the carving. The completed birch tree appeared alive, but the two "critters" as Zach called them, had yet to be finished.

She went back into his kitchen and opened the refrigerator. Kayla said Josh had called and asked her to arrive around three. Should she take the cheese out yet? They could be late. Deciding to leave it, she popped a chunk into her mouth and closed the fridge. Maybe she should let Zach know the time. He needed to shower before coming upstairs.

Ugh. She walked back into the living room. Ever since yesterday when they received the call, she'd been a bundle of energy. What could Dr. Josh have found? Four days had gone by since she'd come back to Zach's to recover. Though still weak, she had already gained a little weight back, but her toxins were building. And Zach couldn't afford to get sick with the carving due. The radio said Ice-Out could be any day with the plane flying over the lake every two hours now.

The door closed downstairs, startling her. "Zach?"

"Yeah, it's me. I'll be right up."

His baritone voice alone softened the edges of her over-sensitized nerves. She strode back into the kitchen and pulled out the cheese. Grabbing the cracker tray, she brought them both into the living room. She walked back to the kitchen to open a bottle of wine. As she tried to dig the bottle opener into the cork, she noticed her hands were shaking.

Zach's arms came around her.

She calmed and dropped the corkscrew. Somehow his presence made everything feel possible. She sighed. "Can you help me with this?"

He turned her around.

He was stark naked. "Zach, they'll be here any—"

He pressed her into the counter as his tongue sought entry between her lips and his hard cock begged for entry to her pussy. The hot sensation of pure desire made her knees weak. She wrapped her arms around his neck, crushing her hardening nipples against his wet chest.

He broke their kiss. "Did that help?"

She pulled out of his arms, smiling. "Yes, it did. But you better get some clothes on. Kayla won't mind, but I doubt Dr. Josh will be happy."

"He's just Josh to me."

"I know, but it's fun to tease him. Now go."

He turned to leave but she squeezed his ass cheek. "Think they'll mind waiting?"

He spun around so fast, he caught her off guard. Picking her up, he set her on the counter island, away from the wine. "Who says they'll have to wait?" Throwing up her long denim skirt, he pulled her thong off and held it up. "Did you ever think of going without these? I'd prefer it."

Bea giggled as Zach wiggled his eyebrows. He had taught her so much, how fun sex could be and what it felt like to have someone to love. "I'll have to think about it."

He growled. "You think too much as it is. You need to feel."

Zach pushed her shoulders down, forcing her to lie back. Then he pulled her butt to the edge of the counter. "Hmm, I never realized what a perfect level this counter is."

She linked her hands behind her head. "I did."

He looked at her. "Really? What a sexually active mind you have."

She smirked. "No more than yours."

"Touché." Zach winked before bending over and spreading her thighs.

He planned to make love to her pussy as she had first imagined and her folds slickened with the knowledge.

His tongue found her opening and he licked away at her juice, sliding in between her labia. When he moved his sensuous kiss to her clit and circled it with his tongue, her excitement rose, building where he feasted. Her body weak, yet taut, arched toward him of its own accord.

Leisurely, he inserted a finger into her swollen pussy. She bucked, wanting more as her need pulsed. He pulled his finger out just as slowly while his tongue continued its constant tease.

She moaned. Knowing Zach loved her added a new dimension to their lovemaking. They were connected now and she trusted him with his own safety. Even if she lost control, he would be careful, knowing she didn't want to poison him. That knowledge alone freed her to enjoy without guilt this time. The issue of the number of times and his reactions to her still loomed large, but she put it aside to enjoy his touch.

He didn't change his rhythm, but his other hand opened a drawer beneath her.

What was he doing?

She heard metal. He must have pulled out a cooking utensil. The soft strokes around her clit slowed, keeping her on edge, but the anticipation of what she would feel next made her blood race.

Something cool and blunt touched her opening. She didn't know what it was, nor did she care as the cool, hard metal pushed into her pussy's entrance. She grabbed on to the edge of the counter above her head and tried to thrust her hips forward, but Zach was in complete control and kept the object from going deeper. She panted, tightening inside, craving the fulfillment he could give her. Settling her hips back to the hard counter, she gave herself up to his power. The unknown utensil caused tingles to suffuse her entire body.

Zach pulled his tongue away.

She whimpered before she lifted her head to look at him.

He absently stroked the inside of her thigh as he met her gaze. "Do you trust me?"

"Completely."

Grinning, he gradually pushed the object into her, spreading her, filling her until she feared to move an inch. It touched her cervix and she melted, her head falling back to the counter as her body registered she was at his mercy, under his care, loved.

Zach used his other hand to burrow under her sweater and pop her breast out above her bra. He rolled her nipple between his fingers. Her need to arch into his hand was strong, but she resisted, though her pussy tightened around the object as his fingers produced sharp cravings. Then he lowered his head and stroked his tongue along her clit, upward and back.

Her pulse beat hard where his tongue played her, each sensation building on the next. She struggled to keep her hips still like he wanted, but the pleasure encompassed her. She tried to relax into it, even as the sensations increased.

He kept her core filled, but with no movement. She was speared, taken. Her body's excitement gained momentum, spreading through every fiber from wrist to calf until her orgasm burst upon her, filling her limbs and psyche with sweet satisfaction.

Zach removed the utensil and lowered his head, but she guessed his intention and grabbed his hair, fear slicing through her euphoria. "Don't."

He lifted his head as she let go. "It's just a lick."

She sat up, pushing her breast back within her bra cup. "I know. I'm sorry. I just don't want you sick."

He sighed. "I better get dressed."

The fun of the episode melted away. Deflated, she jumped down from the counter. Turning back to the wine, she found her thong looped over the neck of the bottle. The humor of the image lightened her spirits a little, and she opened the wine with a slow and steady hand. After pouring herself a glass, she took a seat on the couch. This time, she focused on enjoying the scenery. Zach was right. It was a balm for the soul.

Footsteps on the deck stairs had her placing her wineglass on the table.

Zach appeared in the living room in a dark denim button-down shirt and black jeans, which made him appear sexy as hell. He pointed at her. "You sit, I'll let them in. But you better stop eating me with your eyes, or they're going to know what you're thinking about."

She gave him the hint of a smile. "You mean if they notice anyone else in the room besides each other?"

Zach shook his head and opened the door to their guests.

Bea stood and Kayla practically knocked her over with a bear hug. "How are you holding up?"

She looked past her friend to Josh, and at her raised eyebrow, he nodded. Kayla knew. The two of them had been talking on the phone every day. Now Bea knew part of what they found to talk about. She squeezed Kayla before pulling away. "I'm fine right now."

Kayla gazed at her with pitying eyes. Bea couldn't stand it. She stepped around her to give Josh a brief hug. "I'm very interested in what you discovered. Please have a seat. I'll get the wine."

Josh raised his hand to stop her. "If you don't mind, I'll have a beer." He turned to Zach. "Do you have any decent beer?"

Zach motioned her to sit and headed to the kitchen with Josh right behind him. "Yeah, Bud Light, but I think I have some snooty beer in here just for you."

Josh chuckled, his voice carrying into the living room. "Hey, you have any ice cream left?"

Zach coughed. "Maybe, but it's all for me."

Ice cream? Why would Josh think they had ice cream? They hadn't eaten anything all afternoon. The only time they had been in the kitchen was when… Oh. Her entire body filled with heat.

Zach strolled back into the living room. "Bea, didn't I call dibs on all the ice cream?"

She gave him an exasperated look. The ice-cream scoop had been her dildo not thirty minutes ago, which caused her pussy to moisten again. Zach must have left it in the sink.

He winked.

She looked away before Kayla caught on.

Kayla sat on the facing couch. Josh handed her a glass of wine before sitting next to her. Bea wished her and Zach's relationship could be as carefree. What was it with her that she always wanted what she couldn't have? She sat stiffly and took a sip of wine as Zach joined her and linked their hands together.

After a large swallow of beer, he spoke. "Okay, Josh, spill it. What did you find out and can it help us?"

At Zach's use of the word "us", Bea relaxed into him, the warmth in her heart calming her limbs.

Josh grinned. "Do you want the good news or the bad news first?"

Zach put his beer bottle down hard. "Josh, this isn't funny. Tell us."

Bea squeezed Zach's hand in gratitude. She'd been on pins

and needles all day and had been about to strangle the good doctor, not a smart move considering he was her only hope, or at least a possible hope.

Josh turned serious. "I know, Zach. It's just that Bea looks as if she's about to shatter. I thought a little levity would help, but I guess not. All right, I'll give it to you straight."

Bea glanced at Kayla and the sadness in her eyes almost undid the tight hold Bea had on her emotions.

Josh leaned forward and captured her gaze. "I discovered the antidote for your poison is exactly that, a cure."

Bea couldn't help the sigh that escaped at the news. Could her days as a poisonous lover be over? It was too much to contemplate. She ruthlessly stifled the feeling of joy before it spread. Josh's face said all was not as good as it appeared.

She cocked her head. "How come I feel a 'but' coming?"

Josh nodded and turned his attention to Zach. "The problem is the antidote attacks all the poison. That means for Bea to survive the antidote, we need to bring her poison levels low enough to prevent the drug from killing her like it almost did before."

Her stomach dropped as her mind processed Josh's words. She managed to hold back her tears, but couldn't control the shaking of her head.

Zach looked between her and Josh, his brow wrinkled in puzzlement.

She begged Josh with her eyes, imploring him to tell Zach. She wouldn't be able to without crying.

Josh sighed and took a swig of beer. "What that means, buddy, is Bea has to orgasm many, many times on a man to lower those levels."

Zach shrugged. "That's fine. I'm able and willing. You know that."

"I'm afraid the amount of poison she needs to release would kill you. Besides, even you couldn't have sex that long without Viagra."

Zach glanced at her and she could tell he still hadn't realized the extent of the cure.

He turned his attention back to his friend. "How many times?"

Josh didn't bat an eyelash. "My best guess is nine orgasms should do it."

She moaned. "Nine?"

Zach tensed beside her and released her hand. He stood and put his hands in his pockets. "So, you're telling me in order to save Bea, I have to let her have sex with other men?"

Kayla jumped in. "But it doesn't have to be a lot of other men, Zach. I'm sure Bea could do it with say, three plus you. Don't you think, Bea?"

She should answer, but the thought of another man touching her had her frozen. Her stomach formed a familiar knot, but this time nausea took hold.

Kayla continued. "You need to look at it as a medical procedure, right, honey?"

Josh stared at Zach. "Listen, I could set it up at my hospital. I can recruit three men from the local area for a 'study' and let them know they will be having sex with a beautiful woman who they have to make orgasm at least twice. You could be first and last."

Zack turned his back on them all and strode to the sliding glass door. He opened it and let the warm spring air flow into the room.

Kayla touched Bea's knee. "It could save your life." Kayla wiggled her eyebrows. "Think of it as another sexual adventure."

Bea shook her head. "I don't think I could stand another man's hands on me. I'd be more apt to vomit than come."

Zach turned at her statement, his love for her visible in his eyes. She held his gaze.

Josh stood. "I could give you a hallucinogenic. You could believe every damn guy was Zach. I would also have to monitor your vitals and keep nutritional fluids pumped into you. That much sex will take a lot out of you. You'd have to do it as fast as possible to bring those toxins low enough."

Josh moved next to Zach and put his hand on his shoulder. "Believe me. I've been here through Danielle and Lisa. I know what losing them did to you. But, I also know if you love this woman and want a chance at a normal life with her, kids, the whole thing, this might be the only way based on what I've discovered."

Zach pulled back. "What do you mean, 'might'? Are you saying even if we go through with this, it still may not work and we'd be back to where we are now, only with three men between us?"

"Yeah, I'm afraid so. I can't believe I was able to figure this much out in so short a time. Remember, time is something we don't have. If you have a better idea, I'm open to it."

Zach looked at her.

She couldn't stay still a minute longer. She ran to him and he took her in his arms. Burying her face in his chest, she let the tears come. She heard Josh and Kayla step around them, but didn't care.

Josh spoke. "We're going outside. You two talk about this."

Bea felt Zach's nod as the door closed behind their friends. She pulled back to look at him. "What do we do?"

He tilted her head back with his hands and kissed her long, hard, desperate before he pulled away and shoved his hands back into his pockets. "I don't know."

She paced. "I can't stand the thought of other men touching me. How am I supposed to have sex with three strangers when I love you? Even with Josh's drugs, I can't imagine being able to orgasm." She turned and faced him from across the room. "You've spoiled me. I'd be no good with anyone else."

Zach grinned. "Really?"

She strode to him and folded her arms across her chest. "Really."

He made a move toward her, but she stepped back. "Zach, I can't do this."

He halted. "But what else can we do? I don't want to lose you, but I'm not sure my insides can handle getting sick every day."

Her shoulders slumped as her arms fell to her sides. "It doesn't have to be every day. Maybe every third day?"

He grabbed her arm and brought her into his embrace. "No. I'm going to want you every day. And I'm going to want a beautiful little girl with dark hair and eyes to match."

She went limp in his arms.

He squeezed her against him as his shirt became wet from her tears. Why couldn't he fix this for her? Picking her up in his arms, he sat on the couch and cradled her. "Bea, I love you. I want to grow old with you. Please, so we can have a life together. I think we have to give us a chance and do as Josh suggests."

She lifted her head, her chocolate eyes shimmering with tears. "I know. I don't want to have a little girl who one day might have to do what I have done. I always hoped she wouldn't, but it could happen. Now that I have you, I realize I couldn't do it."

Zach's heart squeezed at Bea's observation. To bring a daughter into the world who would have to sleep with men to stay alive would be too cruel. It reinforced his gut feeling that they had to do this. But deep down, a piece of him would die inside. Still, better to give up that piece than have a Rappaccini daughter.

He pulled Bea close, holding her against him, hoping when the time came, he could find the strength to let the woman he loved have sex with three men. He'd give his own blood to replace hers if it would save her, but that wouldn't work. If her having sex with strangers was the only way, he'd do it. He had to. He couldn't lose her. He refused to let fate win again.

She lifted her head from his shoulders. "I hope Josh has amazing drugs."

He gazed into the dark-brown depths of her eyes. "Yeah, maybe he could give me some too."

Bea surveyed her room in the quaint bed-and-breakfast near Josh's hospital. It had a beautiful four-poster canopy bed, a couch with coffee table, dresser, armoire, the overstuffed chair she sat in and a rocking chair in the corner. Josh said it was the biggest room with an en suite bathroom complete with Jacuzzi tub and separate shower. The doctor had gone out of his way to help them by securing the entire place. Even if the cure failed, she'd find a special thank-you gift for him. And if cured, could she get pregnant? It hadn't happened yet. It would be just her luck to have been born sterile. Maybe after they made it through tonight, she'd have Josh run tests. No need to raise Zach's hopes.

Then again, maybe it was like her mom said. She needed to be with the same man or men or... Oh God, what if she got pregnant by one of the men tonight? She wanted Zach's baby, not a stranger's. Panic seized her and she jumped from the chair.

At that moment Zach walked in with Josh. "You share everything with me. Don't give me any of that doctor talk you use on your patients."

Josh smiled. "I wouldn't dream of it."

"Yeah."

Bea grabbed Zach's arm. "What if I get pregnant?"

Zach grinned for a moment before what she said registered. Then a look of horror crossed his face.

He turned to Josh. "What if she gets pregnant? We don't want another man's kid. Is there a way to protect her and still have this work?"

Josh rubbed his chin. "Jesus, I can't think of any way to ensure that. Bea, have you ever become pregnant before?"

She shook her head, her heart pounding at what could happen. If tonight didn't destroy her and Zach's relationship, she was positive another man's child would.

Josh opened his lab coat and sat in the rocker.

Zach stood over his friend. "Well?"

Hesitating, Josh steepled his fingers. "When I talked to Bea's mom and grandmother, they had an unusual amount of sex just before they got pregnant. That could be because they had expelled so much poison, it didn't kill off all the sperm. If that is the case and not just coincidence, we need to rearrange the lineup so you're the last to have sex with Bea. That's when her poisons will be at their lowest, which would increase the possibility of a pregnancy and the chances you would be the father. All earlier sperm should be eliminated by her poisons."

Bea looked to Zach. He seemed less convinced than she was.

Josh stood and pulled a notepad from his coat pocket. "This is the best I can do, Zach. If I could make any guarantees I would, but I'm way out of my league here. And unless you want Bea to become a specimen for our boys in Washington to play with, my guess is this is the best chance we have."

Zach stuck his hands in his pockets. "I know. Thank you for all your help." He glanced back at Bea. "We do appreciate it."

She nodded as she swallowed hard, her fear of losing Zach growing by the minute.

Josh gave her a cocky grin. "Now, let's give you some of my psychedelic drugs. You're in for the ride of your life. No pun intended."

Bea waited for Josh to leave before she touched Zach on his shoulder.

He turned around to face her, his worry clear.

She stroked the stubble on his chin. "You aren't convinced either, are you?"

He cupped her cheek before brushing his lips against hers. "I need to talk to Josh to clarify something. I'll be back."

Her gut told her she wouldn't like what he was going to say, but she held her tongue. If she lost Zach tonight or weeks from now, at least she'd tried. She prayed the drugs Josh gave her could obliterate every man's face from her mind, otherwise the whole experiment would fail. She wanted Zach and only Zach and if she couldn't have him, she didn't want anyone.

~~*~~

Zach stood next to the dining table where Josh sat. "This can work, Josh. I know it. Even if it doesn't, I don't care. I can't let her have sex with other men. Neither of us can handle that. I know you can figure out some way for me to be the only one." He punctuated his statement with a fist to the table.

Josh shook his head, but Zach persisted. "You yourself said all of this is a guess, so make your best guess for saving my life and let's get to it."

Josh ran his hand through his hair. "You'd really die for her?"

Zach nodded, his throat too tight at the thought of not growing old with Bea.

"Jesus, let me think." Josh cracked his knuckles. "You want to be the only one in her bed and I'm supposed to keep her from killing you. Don't you think she'd have a problem with this?"

Zach put his hands in his pockets. "Yeah, a big problem, but you've already given her the drugs to make her hallucinate. Afterward, she'll think she dreamed it was me, not that it actually was."

Josh pulled his notepad from his pocket. "If you're with her all night and take her poisons nine times, how can I keep you alive?" His brows knit as he concentrated. "When Bea called me to your house that morning, how many times had she orgasmed on you?"

"Three maybe four times, I guess."

Josh's scribbled on the pad.

Come on, smart man, I know you can do this.

Josh looked up and leaned back in his chair. He pierced Zach with a steady gaze. "You'll do whatever I say, right?"

Relief unknotted Zach's stomach as he sensed Josh's capitulation. "Yeah."

Josh studied his notepad. "I still need to pay the three studs in the other room and not with hospital money."

"No problem, I'll write you a check."

Josh scribbled down another calculation then returned his gaze to Zach. "Okay, here's what we'll do. Remember, no playing around, she has to have you inside her every time."

Zach nodded as pure elation suffused his body. The other men would no longer be in the picture. He'd do whatever it took.

Josh continued. "I'm going to give you the same nutrients I give her. After she's had three orgasms, I'm giving her an experimental drug that's still in the testing phase. It's like Viagra for women because this will take a lot out of her. For you, you have to let me know after you've had two orgasms. I'll give you Viagra because you'll need your cock to stay hard for a long time, and Zach, I can't guarantee your penis won't become painful and raw. But remember, this is about her, not you, so focus on that. Got it?"

"Yes. Do you think you can counteract the poison I take in afterward?"

Josh smirked. "Better than that. I think I can give you the same antidote in similar doses to kill it as you take it in. I have it measured in her nutritional injections. I'll make the same cocktail for you."

Zach slammed his hand on the table. "I knew you could do it."

Josh stood and came around to clasp Zach's shoulder. "Buddy, this is all a guess. I'll do my damnedest to keep you alive, but I don't know jack shit about this. You have to know that."

"I know. Thank you anyway, even if you can't save me. Think of it this way, if I die, I'll die a happy man."

Josh squeezed. "Not if I can help it. Now get your ass in there and take care of your woman."

Zach grabbed Josh and gave him a bear hug then raced upstairs. As he reached Bea's room, he hesitated. If he died tonight, was leaving her alone with the possibility of a child the wrong course of action? Was it fair to her? Compared to the alternative? Without a doubt. He'd trust Josh and if he didn't make it…he brought his hand to his tightening chest and took a deep breath. If the worst happened, Josh would be sure to take care of Bea for him. There was no choice. She was his. They deserved a chance.

The tightening in his chest loosened. Yes. His woman. And now it was his duty to make love to her until she climaxed again and again. It was a tough job, but someone had to do it, and that someone was him.

He just hoped he'd live to talk about it.

~~*~~

"Hey, beautiful."

"Zach?" Bea watched the man strolling toward her, unbuttoning his shirt.

"Yeah, it's me."

Concentrating was difficult. "But I thought you were going to wait."

He smiled as he dropped his jeans. "Josh has it all figured out, don't worry. Relax and enjoy."

She tried to remember why Zach was supposed to wait, but the drugs in her system played havoc with her mind. As he climbed naked into the bed, she no longer cared why. She wanted his hard body pressed against her. She tried to pull off her t-shirt, but couldn't make it to go the right way.

Zach brushed her hands aside and lifted the shirt over her head. She touched her nipples. "Much better."

He wiggled his eyebrows. "I agree."

But he still didn't touch her as she held her breasts for him to see. So she played with her hard nubs, enjoying the streaks of pleasure hitting her pussy and making her wet.

Zach went to work on her pants. She stood, weaving a bit as he pulled her feet from her clothes. She spread her legs, placed her finger on her clit and pressed it hard to slow the sensations, but her lust was out of her control. She moved her finger back and forth, making her clit harder as slippery moisture leaked from her opening. "I want you, now."

He pulled her against his hard body and she squirmed, trying to feel all of him at once. "Zach, I'm so hot for you."

He turned her around, bending her over the bed. "Let me just check and make sure."

As her face met the mattress, he dropped to his knees and licked through her wet folds. The speeding shards of excitement coming from his tongue threw her into overdrive. She moaned. "Now, Zach. I want your hard cock deep inside me now."

He chuckled. "Yes ma'am."

She reached between her legs to touch her clit, circling the nub, climbing toward her peak. Zach pushed at her opening with his fingers, spreading her nether lips. Frustrated, she tried to push back against him, but he held her hips in one place as he rose.

She groaned, "Zaacch."

His cock brushed her pussy's opening. "Tell me, Bea, do you want me to fuck you?"

She clutched at the covers, her pussy throbbing, aching so much it hurt deep inside her core. "Yes, please, oh please, Zach, now. I want you now."

He drove his cock into her hard.

At the sudden invasion, she shattered. Screaming with release, she convulsed around him. He wasn't gentle, thrusting hard, holding her stimulation at its peak as he created wave after wave of pleasure until her orgasm gradually receded. She squeezed her pussy.

Zach's fingers bit into her hips. "Oh, don't do that yet. You'll make me come."

She froze. "You didn't come?"

He pulled out and she turned to face him.

He made her sit on the bed. "Nope. I'm waiting for the right moment."

Her release energized her, so if he thought he could play hard to get, he was dead wrong. She climbed onto the bed and sat cross-legged. The drugs Josh gave her made her bold, but Zach would forgive her. She stroked her right breast and rubbed the nipple between her fingers. "I hope that moment comes soon or I'll have to pleasure myself."

She watched his jaw tense as she slipped her other hand between her legs and rubbed her clit. It felt so good and yet so bad to have him watch her. He turned away and bent over, giving her a close-up view of his ass with his balls hanging between his legs. Her excitement intensified.

When he faced her again, he had nipple clamps in his hands. Already the remembered feel of them hanging off her peaks had her pussy flowing again. She purred. "You found my toys."

"Yeah, and I want to play too."

"I always thought it'd be better with two people." She let go of herself and scooted to the side of the bed to make room for him.

"You've only used these by yourself?"

She nodded. "You don't think I'm a prude, do you?"

He laughed, his full-hearted laugh. The sound made her warm inside and had nothing to do with sex. Her heart swelled.

He crawled onto the bed and dangled the clamps in front of her. "Come here. I want to play with you."

Bea rose on her knees and thrust out her chest. "I'm all yours."

~~*~~

Zach brushed the hair from Bea's face before lifting the robe off the chair and tying the belt. They'd already made use of that chair, the bed, the tub, even the floor and they were only halfway through. He glanced at the clock. One o'clock in the morning and Bea had begun to tire.

He quietly opened the door and slipped out. He heard Kayla's voice as he approached Josh's room. The two of them had not even had a date, but Josh's help with Bea's and his dilemma and Kayla's friendship with Bea kept throwing the two of them together. Knocking, he turned the knob and opened the door.

Kayla was sitting on the edge of a dresser, while Josh leaned back in a chair, his feet crossed next to her.

Zach shook his head. "You two still talking?"

Josh smirked, but Kayla frowned at him. "Honey, what's wrong with a little conversation?"

Sinking into the overstuffed chair in the corner, he faced them.

Josh brought his feet down. "How are you holding up?"

"I'm doing okay, but I think she's tiring."

Josh leaned forward. "That's good. That means my theory is right. She told me she feels energized after she releases her toxins. If she's tiring, that means there's less in her system. How many times so far?"

He held up one hand.

"Excellent." Josh clapped his hands.

Zach peered at the clock. "I think we need more nutrients. She's also a little too lucid for my comfort. You may want to slip her another hallucinogen. If she realizes what I'm doing, she'll end it."

Josh peered at him. "And how are you feeling?"

"Good enough."

"No, I think it's time for a little Viagra with a splash of antidote."

Zach stood. "Fine. Whatever it takes. By the way, what made you decide it needed to be nine orgasms, why not four or fourteen?"

Josh had already headed for the door to prepare the drugs, but he stopped halfway through it. "According to Bea, she needs three orgasms a week to survive, so I determined the number of orgasms per day versus her levels of toxicity and the elapsed time for them to build minus the amount of antidote in comparison to the poison in her body for that time period."

"Huh?"

Josh shrugged. "I guessed."

Zach stood stiffly as the tension in his muscles built. Anger colored his tone. "You guessed?"

Josh nodded. "Plus, I figured it would be better for her to have too many than not enough or she would have to do it all again."

He opened his mouth, but Josh disappeared around the door.

Kayla jumped off the dresser, drawing his attention. "Zach, he's doing his best. He may not show it, but he's nervous as hell."

Zach slipped his hands into the pockets of the robe as he tried to relax his jaw. "And you know this how?"

Kayla placed her hand on his arm. "Come on, Zach, I can read him as easily as I can read you. You're scared to death this won't work and you won't be around to save her."

The knot in his stomach grew, making him wish he hadn't asked. "Listen, I haven't talked to Josh about this, but in case I don't, if—"

Kayla put her finger against his lips. "Only good thoughts, Zach. Bea has lots of people to care for her, but she needs you more than she needs air. So keep your hope alive and get your cute ass back in there and remind her why she loves that rock-hard body of yours so much."

He grinned. "You think I'm rock hard?"

She smacked him on the butt. "Definitely, but I prefer lanky, sinewy muscles to your bulging biceps, honey, so don't be getting any ideas."

He blew her a kiss on his way out the door and didn't stop until he reached Bea's room. Josh met him with needles, pills and a Bud Light.

Zach took a gulp of the beer. "Gee, I love ya, man."

Josh rolled his eyes before handing Bea a glass of wine.

She wasn't as high as earlier because she held the quilt close to hide her nudity where before she had flaunted herself.

She looked past Josh at him. "I missed you. Where'd you go? I'm not that tired yet."

If her raised, wiggling brow was an indication, she was ready for more. "Good, neither am I. I think we could set a world record here. Too bad we didn't think of it sooner. We could have had officials from the *Guinness Book of World Records* here as witnesses."

Bea's gaze switched to the darkened window, its drapes wide open. From the heat that suffused her cheeks, Zach realized the idea of being watched by strangers turned her on. Wow, his Bea on drugs was wilder than he ever expected.

He sat on the bed next to her and put his arm around her as Josh checked her vitals.

She glanced at Josh. "Eh, what's up, Doc?" Giggling, she leaned into his shoulder. He'd never seen this side of her. He doubted she'd ever seen this side of her either.

Josh let go of her wrist. "You're doing great, Bea. Just keep humping like rabbits and we might lick this thing yet."

She burst into laughter and Josh gave Zach a sympathetic look. "I may have given her a larger dose than she needed." He paused before closing the door on them.

Zach frowned, suddenly wondering if Josh had done it on purpose. But his attention was seized by the hand on his cock.

Bea knelt on the floor, her hands under his robe, her face leaning toward him as his rock-hard penis rose to meet her descending mouth. To hell with Viagra, he had Bea.

255

Chapter Fifteen

Bea stretched as light kisses rained down her naked back, blazing a path to her ass. Hmm, she could wake up like this every day. She opened one eye to view the clock. 3:38. How could Zach keep going?

As his tongue licked under her butt and moved to her folds, she moaned, not sure if pleasure or exhaustion were the cause. "Zach?"

He spoke against her clit. "I'm busy at the moment."

She changed her tone. "Zach."

He lifted his head away, leaving her folds wet from his tongue. "Yes."

"I'm exhausted. Don't you want to rest?"

He shook his head. "Uh-huh. One more time and then we can rest. Come on, beautiful, I know you can do it."

She rolled to her back. "No. I don't think I can."

He pulled himself up next to her. He didn't look good. His skin was pale and the lines around his mouth were too deep. Even his hair appeared ragged and limp. Warning bells sounded in her brain, but she couldn't grasp why. The stupid fog remained in the back of her head.

Zach brushed the hair from her face. Maybe she looked like crap too. They'd made love so many times she couldn't remember the number. It felt like one long orgasm. Not that she had a problem with that.

She captured his hand in her own. "I don't know how to tell you this, but you look like crap."

He grinned a little, making the lines deepen too much, scaring her. "Yeah, I feel like crap, but I'm going to make you come one more time even if it kills me."

She shuddered. In the back of her mind Zach's words rang prophetic, but she couldn't remember why. "No. You don't have to make me come again to prove you love me." She lifted both hands to cup his face. "I know you do."

Zach let her bring his face forward for a gentle kiss. He nibbled at her lips.

She moved her hands to the back of his neck. "Do I taste good?"

He pulled away and leaned over her, staring at her pussy. "You'll have to tell me."

His head lowered and his tongue swept deep inside her thickened entry, causing heady sensations to pulse from there to deep inside.

He lifted his head and pulled her to a sitting position. Without a word, his mouth descended on hers. His tongue swept across her own. Her instinct to capture it could not be denied. A strange flavor met her taste buds, her own liquids. A wave of pure lust flowed through her limbs, but when Zach shivered, the warning bells went off again.

She ended their kiss and touched his face as another slice of fear trickled through her brain. "You're burning up."

He raised his brows. "You make me hot."

She scooted out of his arms. "Lie down."

He shook his head.

Holy heck, did the man have a one-track mind? Why did he insist on making love again? There had to be a reason. What was it?

He reached for her, but she slid off the bed. "Okay, okay, we'll make love again, I promise, but this time I'm in the driver's seat." She changed her tone to stern. "Now, lay your ass down."

His eyes widened, but his cock jumped before he lay on his back, his arms behind his head. "As you wish."

Bea couldn't believe she had this hunk of a man all to herself. He loved her and he was hers. An image of her naked in black leather boots with him tied to the bed jostled her memory and the rush of excitement that came with it buckled her knees. She knelt on the bed as she contemplated ropes on the posts. He'd used them on her, it would seem fair was fair.

She perused his strong body from his tight calf muscles to his overdeveloped pectorals, but her lust lessened as her gaze entwined with his. The love shining in his bright-green eyes had her swallowing hard. Her heart hitched.

Zach didn't grin or speak, just bared his soul in his gaze.

Gently, she covered his body with hers and spoke against his lips. "I love you."

His arms encircled her and they shared a tender kiss. She had to show him how much she loved him.

Zach raised his hand to her cheek and stroked. "I love you too, Bea. More than you'll ever know."

Something in his words, his touch, had her wanting to cry, but that didn't make sense. If only the fog in her brain would go away. Anxious to show him how much she treasured him, she inched her way down his body.

Lovingly, she kissed the stubble on his jaw, the tendons of his neck, the bulge of his shoulder. Her tongue came into play as she reached his nipple. She circled the small nub until it hardened tight, its salty taste from their love play an aphrodisiac. Taking his nipple between her teeth, she tugged before scraping across its tip.

His hand tightened where it rested on her arm and she could feel his heartbeat pulse faster.

Pleased to be able to excite him, she pulled the nipple into her mouth and sucked.

Zach's chest rose against her lips and she grasped his shoulders as she worked her tongue on the nub in her mouth. When she let it go, he relaxed into the bed.

She ran her hands through the hair on his chest, mesmerized by the ripples of his abdomen as it moved under her touch. With her mouth, she pulled at the line of hair down the center of his stomach until she arrived at his thick cock.

She cupped that pleasurable piece of anatomy between her hands and glanced at Zach's face. His eyes were closed, his breathing fast as he waited in anticipation. She wouldn't disappoint him. Lowering her lips over his cock, she took as much as she could into her mouth before she surrounded it with her tongue and slowly sucked upward along his tight skin.

Zach groaned and buried his hand in her hair.

His pleasure fed her own and she continued her attention to his cock as she lifted his balls. She opened her throat to him, taking him as deep as she could. He tasted sweet from the whip cream they had used earlier. His cock moved against her tongue, causing her pussy to tense in response.

Zach's hand held her still.

She moaned in frustration. She wanted to bring him to his orgasm.

"Bea."

His roughened voice stilled her own need.

She loosened her mouth and let him pull her up to lie on top of him, his hard penis pressing against her inner thigh.

He brought her lips to his and devoured her with his tongue, his command clear. She belonged to him forever.

The message surrounded her heart. Blissfully, she moved her hips to position her slick pussy above his tip. With a sigh, she descended, his cock pushing through her thick folds, her tight walls, deep into her body, fully, completely, making her his.

He broke the kiss on a whispered word. "Yes."

That one syllable rebounded through her limbs, fueling her desire. She pulled her hips up and rode him. Her blood pounded between her legs as her breaths grew shorter. Sharp shards of pleasure radiated from her pussy to the rest of her body as she pushed and rubbed harder and harder. Her nipples, caressed by Zach's chest hair, added slivers of fire to her already heated body.

Zach sucked upon her lower lip, teasing her with his tongue, adding to her stimulation. He lifted his hips and pressed them to her groin.

She arched into him, rubbing her breasts against his hard chest as she wrapped one hand around his neck. "Zach."

He gazed at her. "Yes, beautiful?"

"I need you." She couldn't help the catch in her voice. The desire to be closer to him far outweighed her lust.

His jaw tensed. The passion in his eyes caused her own to rise, but with a desperation she couldn't understand.

He nodded. "Whatever you need, I will give you."

He pressed her ass into his hips, helping her stay close. Bea ached with a need to crawl inside him. Tears slipped from her eyes.

Zach stopped. "Bea, what's wrong?"

"I don't know. I just have to touch all of you."

Zach kissed her cheek. "It's okay. I'm right here."

She grasped on to him, burrowing her arm underneath him.

He lifted his other arm to hold her around the waist. "I'm all yours, Bea. Forever."

She lifted her face to kiss him and poured every ounce of love she had into the mating of their lips. When he broke away, he gave her a quizzical look.

She stroked his hair at the back of his neck. She couldn't explain how she felt, she simply had to hold on to him.

Zach turned his head and kissed her forearm. "You're coming down, sweetheart. Don't fight it. It's the drugs Josh gave you. I'm right here. I won't go anywhere."

Her memory returned with the force of a Mack truck and with it the reason they were making love. Her heart cried out at what must have occurred. Had he seen her with the other men? She needed to show him how much he meant to her. She couldn't lose him.

Zach must have sensed her tension because he began dropping soft kisses along her cheekbone, causing her mind to relax and her pulse to accelerate. Without warning, he rolled them over, his cock moving inside her at the movement.

Having him on top of her calmed her anxiousness. But as his mouth found her nipple another need increased. She dug her hands into his shoulders as he teased her hard tip. He left her nipple and gazed into her eyes as he pulled his hips back and pushed through her pussy to the hilt.

Bea's world spun out of control. Her memory flooded back as her body began to peak. Fear pumped her blood as Zach's cock sent electricity sizzling through her veins. She grasped his arms to hold herself together while she rocked into him to meet each deep thrust.

Zach moaned, his pace increased.

Grasping him hard, she rubbed against him, squirming to have every inch of her skin touched by his, meeting his pounding with her own.

He went rigid and as his cum flooded into her, he threw her into her own climax. She couldn't breathe. Wave after wave of pure pleasure washed over her, starlight twinkling behind her eyelids, his love for her blanketing her with comfort.

Finally, she gasped for air and eased her hold on him, but he didn't lift off her as he usually did. She smirked. He must have been as affected by their lovemaking as she. The lack of poison in her system had made her desperate, or maybe as Zach said, the drugs wearing off had colored her emotions. But she must have had sex with other men and even if she didn't remember it, Zach would.

The need to reassure him surfaced hard. She turned her head and kissed him on the ear. "Zach?"

He didn't answer.

She smiled. She had worn him out. Pushing on his shoulders, she shook him. "Zach, I know you're tired, but can you move a little? I need to breathe."

He gave no response.

Dread crept up her spine, feeding her adrenaline. "Zach?" She pushed him off to the side, his limp cock sliding from between her legs. Sitting up, she tapped his face. "Zach, wake up. Can you hear me? Zach?"

He lay as still and pale as death. Oh God. She shook her head. "No. No. Zach, what have you done?"

As denial left her, hysteria built.

She screamed.

~*~

Zach heard the whispers first, but the gentle touch on his cheek had him pushing away the dazed fog of his mind. As he opened his eyes, his gaze rested on…Josh?

"Hey, look who's decided to join the living." Josh set down his notepad, but not before Zach noticed his hands shook.

Was something wrong? Oh hell, he was in the hospital. He looked to his right to find the person who had pulled him from his sleep. Bea's bloodshot eyes attested to her tears and he grasped her hand. "What's wrong?"

"What's wrong?" She wiped her hand across her eyes, but her voice grew in volume. "What's wrong? I'll tell you what's wrong. You scared the hell out of me. You lied to me and tricked me and then passed out. I thought you were in a coma."

With quick insight, Zach grasped the horror he must have put Bea through when he'd lost consciousness. But in all honesty, he hadn't planned to pass out. He squeezed her hand, but she pulled from his grasp. The motion left a pit of dread in his stomach as deep as a marsh. "Bea, I'm sorry."

She stood and started to pace. He noticed Josh had beaten a hasty retreat. Great, just when he needed the backup. "Bea, listen. I couldn't do it. I couldn't let another man touch you. I would still love you, but it would have killed a part of me."

She stopped and stared incredulously at him. "A part? I almost lost all of you. Damn it, Zach. Never mind the scare you gave me, Josh aged ten years in the last ten hours."

"I know, I owe him everything."

Bea spun around. "And what about me? If you died or even slipped into a coma, I'd die too. I love you too much to go back to sleeping with strangers just to stay alive."

Zach shook his head. Wasn't she cured? "Bea, even if I did die, you would still be able to live a normal life. Don't you see, that's why I did it. I'd give up my life if I had to so you could be normal." A heady feeling of success rushed through him. "Though I'd much prefer to live it with you."

Bea halted in her tracks. "Oh God, Zach." She ran to him.

He gladly embraced her. She felt so good. Her citrusy smell enveloped him and filled him with completeness. Yup, now his life was perfect. He'd finally beat fate. He stroked her hair, loving the texture of its fine silkiness on his palm. But something nudged his brain, sending fear through his limbs. Did she finish the cure? "Bea? Did Josh give you the large dose of antidote he said he would?"

She nodded, but didn't lift her head to face him, instead she kept it buried against his chest. Her assurance calmed his initial fear, but as he held her, he noticed a growing wetness on his hospital gown. "Bea, what is it?"

After a few moments, she lifted her head. "Josh doesn't know if I'm cured yet. He said he can't know. The only way to be sure is for us to make love and see how you feel."

Zach grinned. "I can do that."

She pulled out of his arms and sat back in the chair next to the hospital bed. "Or we can wait over a week and see if I collapse, and what if that happens? What if I'm not cured? What if this didn't work? Don't you see, falling in love with you has messed everything up."

Zach gazed at his stunning woman and tried not to laugh. She loved him and stubbornly wanted to keep him safe. What man could ask for more? He took her hand. "Beatrice Rappaccini, will you marry me?"

Joy lit her eyes before her body slumped and her hand slipped from his. Another tear slid down her cheek. "I can't. Not unless I'm cured."

He tried to sit up and found he could, though he'd admit to a weakness he'd never had before. "Come here." He lifted his hand.

She sat on the bed and faced him. He brought her hand to his lips. "Don't you see, I don't care if you're cured. I love you. I want you in my life forever. I almost lost you once and I can't risk that again. If I have to be sick once a week, then so be it. Maybe Josh can work on that antidote. He needs a project anyway." He cupped her cheek. "Marry me, Bea."

She turned her head and kissed his palm before meeting his gaze. "Zach, I love you too, which is why I can't marry you until I'm sure being together won't endanger your life. After I met you, I knew I couldn't hurt any more men. I'm certainly not throwing that decision out the window now that I have you. You mean everything to me."

He searched Bea's eyes for any sign she might weaken in her decision, but she had made up her mind. He sighed. "Very well. Then I guess we better test this cure of Josh's and see where we stand because," he snaked his hand behind her neck and pulled her to within inches of his lips, "I'm never letting you go."

He closed the distance between them and urged her to open her mouth. When she did, he claimed her as he claimed her soul, with everything he had in him. This woman was his life. She would be his forever. As her hands rifled through his hair, her tongue mated with his and his cock responded. But his head swam with lightness and he fell back upon the pillow.

"Zach!"

The panic in Bea's voice had him fighting the darkness. He opened one eye. "Sorry, just need a little more sleep." With no more strength left, he let himself be carried away to dreamland.

~*~

Bea parked her vehicle next to Charlie's Escalade. Josh had kept Zach in the hospital for two full days, claiming dehydration and nutritional needs, but he wouldn't meet her gaze when he gave his explanation, which had her wondering what he hid. She stepped from her car and picked her way through the soft ground. Though she wore hiking boots, thanks to their latest stretch of warm weather, the mud was far worse than the first time she'd arrived at Zach's. At least she wore more practical shoes this time.

She'd meant to give Zach time to settle into his old routine, but she couldn't stay away. She had no idea whether it was because she loved him or her body craved him. But it didn't matter because she couldn't resist his unique pull on her.

The two men were huddled around Zach's Harley when she came to the valley opening. Charlie was on his haunches using a tool of some kind and Zach hovered over him, making sure Charlie fixed her up right. Of course, Zach had to be shirtless and sexy as if she needed more reason to be attracted to him.

He spotted her and a huge smile lit his face. "Hey, Bea. About time."

He left his prized Harley and strode through the muck to grasp her in a bear hug and twirl her around.

She couldn't help her laughter. "Zach, put me down."

He let her feet sink into the ground, but he held on. "Uh-uh. Not 'til you give me a kiss to rival my hug."

A challenge to her mind had to be met. Pulling on his neck, she brought his mouth to meet hers and slipped her tongue between his lips. As she devoured him, his hands roamed her body. The heat in her rose and found the place between her legs. She wanted him inside her. Now.

"Ahem. That's my daughter's throat you have your tongue down, boy. I'd have to say I'm not that pleased by it."

Bea pushed away from Zach as her cheeks heated in shame. How could she have forgotten Charlie? He stood with a large wrench in his hand as if he thought he might need to use it.

She forced a laugh. "I'm sorry, Dad. I didn't mean to ignore you." She gave her father a kiss on the cheek.

He wrapped her in a bear hug of his own. "You be glowing, girl. I do like that."

She gave him a genuine smile. Though he refused to be one of her mother's lovers anymore, he still liked being her dad. "If I'm glowing, it's because of this man." She stepped next to Zach to link her arm around his waist, but her feet went out from under her.

Zach never let her hit the ground. Holding her aloft in his arms, he brought her to where the bike stood parked on solid, dry earth.

Charlie followed. "Yeah, I guess if he makes you happy, I can let it be. He obviously has good taste both in women and bikes. But if he ever makes you unhappy…"

Bea sensed Zach stiffen beneath her at the threat. She looked her father in the eyes. "Don't worry about that, Dad. He'd never test the wrath of my six fathers again." She smirked at Zach. "Right, honey?"

He gave her a lopsided grin that told her she would pay later for teasing him, but he nodded. "Anything you say, beautiful."

The warmth that spread through her had nothing to do with his magnificent body and everything to do with his heart. "Uh, Zach, you can put me down now."

"Right." He let her feet hit the ground, but kept a possessive arm around her waist.

She didn't mind at all. "What are you two doing with the Harley?"

Charlie wiped down his tools before loading them in his toolbox. "What didn't we do? I've got this baby purring like a kitten." He looked at Zach, who moved to help Charlie pick up. "You'll find you get better gas mileage and an extra burst of RPMs in fourth gear. Bring her up to speed next time you ride and then let her rip down a good mile straightaway and she'll take care of you all season."

Zach handed Charlie his tire pressure gauge. "Thank you. I owe you one." He extended his hand to shake.

Her dad shook his head. "Naw, we don't carry debts among family." He gave Zach a quick hug before bending to pick up his toolbox.

Zach moved forward fast. "Here, let me bring that to your vehicle."

"Fine with me." Charlie turned to Bea. "You take care, girl. Let me know how things turn out."

She nodded solemnly. Charlie understood what she was up against. How did other women manage with only one or two fathers? She needed every single one of hers.

Zach returned as Charlie backed out of the driveway. "Did I pass father test number five?"

She took his hand in hers. "Yes, you did, as long as you keep me happy."

"Oh, I know how to keep you happy." Zach picked her up and strode toward the house.

Bea grabbed hold of his neck and planted a wet kiss on his cheek. "Does keeping me happy include strawberries and whip cream?"

He brought her to the door and let her feet go, but held her close against his chest. "It includes anything and everything, Bea."

Her heart skipped a beat at his sincerity and a niggling fear wormed its way into her brain. "All I need, Zach, is you."

His lips brushed hers. "And all I need is you." His eyebrow raised. "However, I did buy these new vibrating nipple clamps I thought you might like to try. But if all you need is me?"

Bea laughed before she hit him on the arm.

In a flash, he spun her around and pinned her against the basement wall. "Hitting me already? Does that mean you like it rough, beautiful lady?"

The tone of Zach's voice had her libido going from zero to sixty in half a second. Her limbs melted against his hard body as he pressed her against the concrete wall. "What I like is you, rough boy. It's been two long days."

He reached his hand beneath her Henley and unclasped the front of her bra. Licking her neck, he answered, "Two days and sixteen hours, but who's counting? All I know is I need to slide my cock into your moist pussy right now."

Bea tried to breathe past the lightning flash of excitement that pulsed by her heart and down to her groin. But Zach's mouth had found her breast and his nibbling teeth had her arching into him, her need for air fulfilled only by panting. She grasped his shoulders as one of his hands unbuttoned her jeans and snaked its way between her thighs.

If he hadn't been pressing her into the wall, her knees would have buckled already, but one hand pinned her, holding her up. His mouth began to suck as his finger pushed open her pussy and slid inside. Bea moaned in pure pleasure.

"Zachary?"

The strange voice filtered through Bea's cloud of euphoria at the same time Zach froze.

The voice came again, a distinctively feminine voice with a slight Maine accent. "Zachary, is that you under the deck?"

Zach straightened. "Hell. It's my mother."

Bea wanted to disappear into the wall at her back, but she doubted even that would help. Zach began to turn but she grabbed his arms. "Wait." Despite the shame flooding her, her panic gave her strength and he hesitated when her nails bit into his arms.

He glanced at his biceps. "Great, now I'll have nail marks to prove what we were doing under here."

She glanced at his face to see if he was angry, but his grin remained.

She let go. "Let me at least close my bra and button my jeans."

He nodded, his grin widening. He was *enjoying* this.

Another voice reached them. "Zachary, is this any way to greet your mother?"

The stern male baritone added to Bea's frustration, which caused her fingers to slip as she attempted to button her pants. Zach pulled her shirt down over her waistband to hide the button and grabbed her hand. "Come on. I want you to meet my parents."

Bea stumbled once, her knees still weak, but Zach held on to her and gave her a reassuring smile.

It didn't help.

Except for talking about the logging company, Zach had never indicated what type of relationship he had with his parents.

As they came to a stop in front them, he put his arm around her waist and brought her close. "Mom, Dad, this is Bea. I told you a little about her on the phone last week. Bea, this is my mom Ginny and my dad Nathan."

Bea tried a tentative smile. Zach's mom appeared friendly, but his dad had Andy's height and Gerry's build with a weathered face. Before she could say "hello", she found herself in a Chantilly Lace-perfumed hug. She looked over Ginny's shoulder at Zach, who crossed his arms and winked.

Ginny stepped back. "It's so wonderful to meet you, Bea. The only girlfriends my Zachary has introduced us to, before you, were his fiancées. I'm so thrilled to meet you."

Fiancées? Zach had fiancées? "Thank you, Mrs. Woodman. It's nice to meet you too. I hope you can tell me more about Zach. It would appear he's left a few details out." She raised her eyebrow at him and felt vindicated when he had the grace to flush.

He gave his mom a kiss on the cheek and a welcoming hug. "It's not as if I knew you were coming. Why the sudden visit?"

Mrs. Woodman stepped back and beamed, making her round face glow. Bea liked her already. She reminded her of what Mrs. Santa Claus would look like, if she existed.

"Dear, I had a hunch you needed to see us. You know I always follow my intuition."

Mr. Woodman shook his head like a man used to his wife's idiosyncrasies and held out his hand. "Do you have a last name, Bea?"

She shook his calloused hand. "Yes, Rappaccini."

He raised his brow, reminding her so much of Zach that she relaxed a little. "I imagine that gets spelled wrong more often than not."

Zach pulled her back against him and gazed at her. "No worries there, Dad." He switched his gaze to his father. "It's going to change to Woodman very soon."

Bea pulled out of Zach's grasp at the same time his mother clapped her hand on her leg. "I told you, Nathan, didn't I? I know my baby when he's in love."

Bea stood stiffly, trying to control the boiling in the pit of her stomach. "Actually, that's not a true statement."

Ginny gazed at Zach with such hope Bea felt like the Grinch who stole Christmas, but she wouldn't start her relationship with Zach's parents on a lie. She glared at him.

He shrugged. "I did ask her to marry me, but she turned me down."

"What?" Zach's mom rounded on her so fast Bea took a step backward.

Zach grinned.

Wonderful, make her the villain. Bea faced Zach's shocked mother. "Mrs. Woodman, it has nothing to do with Zach. I have some health issues I need to take care of and until I'm sure Zach will be happy with me as his wife, I'm not ready to commit."

Ginny grabbed Bea's hand in her own and headed for the basement door. "Oh, my poor dear. You must tell me all about it. Maybe we can help. You know, Zach has a very good friend who is a doctor."

Bea looked over her shoulder at Zach as his mother led her toward the house. His perpetual grin said he enjoyed the pressure he'd placed on her. But when he shrugged as if he hadn't done anything, she decided upon a little revenge. "Tell me, Mrs. Woodman, does this doctor friend specialize in sexually transmitted diseases?"

~*~

Zach led Bea outside. The temperature had dropped, giving him a reason to bundle her in his Chamois shirt and keep her close. He didn't understand why she had to go back to her little apartment when he had plenty of room in the house for all four of them. He tried again. "Bea, you don't have to leave."

She sighed. "Yes, I do. It isn't right."

He squeezed her shoulders as they strolled toward her car. "My parents won't mind."

She stopped and tilted her head up to meet his gaze, but her face remained in shadow. "I mind. For me to stay the night with you shows a lack of respect, and I do respect them. Besides," she lowered her face, "I have no control around you. If I screamed, I'd be more embarrassed than when they caught us under the deck."

He pulled her close and lifted her chin. "There's something else. I can tell. What are you afraid of? I know it's not my parents. I can't believe you let my mom think you have a sexually transmitted disease."

She shrugged. "It served you right for telling them you asked me to marry you. Now what if it never happens?"

He squeezed her to him as a sliver of doubt slid under his confidence. "It's not about whether you'll marry me, it's about when and how we'll handle our sex life. Wait, that's what's bothering you, isn't it? You're afraid that when we make love, I'll get sick."

She didn't say anything.

Frustration burned its way through his gut. He dropped his arms from around her and stepped back. "You don't think what we have is worth fighting for, do you?"

She shivered. "No, that's not it. I just can't stand the thought of putting you into a coma. Is that wrong?"

He lifted his hands. "But we don't know that's what will happen. Don't you think we should find out if that's the case first? Don't you think we should tackle this together? After all, it affects us as a couple, not as individuals."

She crossed her arms over her chest. "But it's my problem, not yours."

Huh? Where the hell did she get that idea? "Excuse me? I thought the only reason it's a problem for you is because you love me. You can't separate the two, Bea."

She dropped her arms and shook her head. "I know, I just can't shake my fear."

He put his hands in the pockets of his jeans. "You don't even know if you should have this fear yet. Is there something you aren't telling me? Is your body craving a release and that's why you want to have sex? Or is it your natural inability to resist me?" He grinned.

"Oh Zach." She pushed her arms through his and hugged him to her. "I don't know. I know I want to make love to you so much I'd be happy to do so in my car, right now, even with your parents waiting for you to return. But I don't know why I want to. It's always been different with you. You're the only one I've ever let have complete control."

He tugged his hands from his pockets and cupped her face. "Total control? I like the sound of that."

As she opened her mouth to respond, he descended upon her, thrusting his tongue between her lips like he wanted to thrust his cock between her legs.

She moaned. Her breasts flattened against his chest as she squeezed herself to him.

He pulled her head away and forced the end to their kiss. "Bea, we will make love. And we will find out if Josh's cure worked. And then we'll decide what to do. Now, do you want to come back inside and test your cure tonight?"

She shook her head. "Not tonight. Let's wait until your parents leave because when I come for you, I want to let myself go."

He couldn't argue with that. "Okay. They will probably leave tomorrow." He took her hand again and continued their stroll to her car. "But when I call, I expect you to come over immediately, and Bea?"

"Yes?"

"When you arrive, come naked."

He felt a shiver flow across her skin. Good. He wanted her hot for him. Hot enough to fry her fears.

They arrived at her car and he gave her one more fiery kiss for her to remember. He held her car door open while she started the engine.

She looked up at him. "I have to work tomorrow. Please tell your parents I enjoyed meeting them."

He cupped her cheek and brushed his thumb across her skin. "I will. And I'll call you the minute they leave."

She swallowed hard. "Please."

Zach closed the car door and stood in the darkness as Bea drove away. The woman was a walking contradiction. God help him, he loved that about her.

As he turned to walk back to the house, he readjusted his jeans. At least it was late enough that his parents would soon go to bed. He could stay up and sketch his favorite subject. Perhaps he could even draw a particular position he'd like to try.

Ignoring the rubbing of his pants on his hard cock, he sprinted back to the house.

Chapter Sixteen

Bea shoved the last bill into the inbox and grabbed her brush from her purse. She couldn't believe how fast the day had gone and now she would see Zach, in front of a hundred or so people. Her need clawed at her, but was it for release or for him? Not knowing drove her crazy. She could understand why Zach's parents had wanted to stay for the unveiling of the carving, but she wouldn't make it much longer without him. Maybe she could sneak him into a room for a few hours.

The image of her, Zach and Kayla on the bed came unbidden to her mind. She groaned.

"Bea, are you all right?"

She snapped her head around to find Kayla standing in the doorway. She swallowed hard before responding. "Yes, just can't believe it's time already. What a busy day."

Kayla sat on the desk. "Are you dying to see the carving? After all, it's what brought you and Zach together."

She clipped her hair back for a more professional appearance before answering. "I'm excited, but I've already seen most of it. Trust me, it's impressive."

Kayla pouted. "Do you think Josh will come down?"

"Zach didn't say he was. Do you really like him?"

Kayla glanced away. "He's different. I like that."

Bea lowered her brush. "Wow. I didn't see that coming."

"What? I just want to find out more about him that's all. It's not a crime."

"No, of course not."

Kayla jumped off the desk. "Hey, you better hurry up. Your dad is already here."

"Right." Bea threw her brush in her purse. She'd best go outside to the great porch at the front of the inn and make sure everyone was ready. "Could you find the Larsens? They may not realize what time it is."

Kayla nodded and left.

As Bea entered the lobby, Zach strode in.

She forgot to breathe. He wore a black suit with an ivory shirt and a Jerry Garcia tie. His shoulders appeared enormous, but the clothes fit him to perfection. Wow, her man cleaned up nice.

He stopped in front of her. "I missed you."

"I—"

Zach kissed her and dipped her so fast she couldn't tell which made her more lightheaded.

Having devoured her thoroughly, leaving her legs weak, he set her upright again. "Hi, beautiful."

"Oh gosh, Zach. People are staring."

He surveyed the lobby and shrugged. "So? I bet they're jealous."

She linked her arm with his and smiled. "Yes, of me, because I have one amazingly handsome boyfriend." Bea's heart glowed at the phrase. To be able to use the word *boyfriend* in the present tense was such a new experience. She warmed every time she had the chance to say it.

As they strolled toward the exit doors, Zach bent his head and whispered in her ear, "Fiancée."

She stiffened, fear racing up her spine at his reminder. He

must have sensed her reaction because he squeezed her hand before opening the door for her.

As they stepped onto the porch, Bea's gaze swept the gathering of people for her father. Spotting him, she tugged Zach's arm. "Come. I'd like you to meet my father, but whatever you do, don't mention marriage or Mom will hear of it."

Zach smirked, making her nervous. What was the man thinking now?

Bea stopped next to Mathew, who was surrounded by a handful of people from town. She recognized a few, but he knew everybody. He had their undivided attention and cut a fine figure in his business suit. The graying at his temples made him appear quite distinguished. "Hi, Dad."

He stopped in mid-sentence and turned. A broad smile lit his face. "Bea. How's my honey bee?" As he gave her a hug, she cringed. She'd forgotten he would call her that in front of Zach.

When Mathew let go, she did the honors. "Dad, this is Zach, my boyfriend. Zach, this is Mathew Emerson."

Her dad hadn't missed the importance of the introduction, but then again, he rarely missed anything. "It's a pleasure to officially meet you, son. It takes a heck of a person to capture my Beatrice here. She's not an easy one to handle, but if you need any advice, feel free to give me a call." He handed Zach his business card.

She'd always wondered how he did that. It was like a magic trick. A business card appeared at his fingertips from out of nowhere.

Zach took the card and shook her dad's hand. "It's nice to meet you as well, sir. I understand you will be speaking at the ceremony?"

Her dad puffed with pride. "Yes, yes I will. I'm the president of the Lakes Region Chamber of Commerce this year and it is my honor to be a part of all this. I love to see a great business like the Lakeside Inn add a piece of fine artwork from a local company."

Zack raised his brows. "Not sure I'd call myself 'a company', but I'm happy I could help. If it wasn't for this carving, I would have never met your daughter."

Mathew nodded sagely. "This carving will always have a special meaning in our hearts."

Bea glanced around, now was a good time to move along. "We'll see you at the ceremony, Dad. I need to introduce Zach to a few more people."

"Of course, of course. You have work to do. I'll be over in a few minutes."

After they met with the Larsens and the organizer of the Lakes Region Craft Fair, Bea steered Zach toward the carving, which stood beneath a red piece of material, hiding it from view. Zach touched the cloth. "Hell, this looks a lot better than the blue tarp I kept over it."

Bea cocked her head. "Why wouldn't you let me see the carving after you finished the tree and the animals were roughed out?"

He strolled around the statue as it stood to the right of the main door of the inn. "I wanted it to be a surprise. I added one additional detail to the original sketch. I'm hoping you'll like it."

For the first time since she'd met him, Bea caught uncertainty in Zach's eyes. Could it be the artist in him that felt insecure or something else? She touched the carving. "I know I'll love it. You're a wonderful carver. Besides, I love everything about you and as Dad said, this statue will always mean so much to me."

Zach pulled her into his embrace and kissed her gently, lovingly.

When he released her, she noticed the Larsens approaching. It was time. They would love Zach's work and she couldn't wait to see their faces when they saw it unveiled. She stepped back with Zach as the Larsens took their positions before the microphone stand. Craig winked at her and she nodded. Everything was ready.

She and Zach stood on either side of the carving, ready to pull off the material. She couldn't see him, but she could sense his anxiousness.

Sharon Larsen opened with a welcome and then Mathew spoke. They introduced Zach, who didn't have to speak, but he waved to the crowd. The director of the Lakes Region Craft Fair spoke next and finally they were ready.

On the count of three, she and Zach pulled the material down over the front and let it fall to the porch floor. A gasp went through the crowd of a hundred people. A second of silence followed before they erupted with cheers. The clapping overwhelmed Craig as he tried to speak and explain the carving.

Bea's heart flipped over with pride. She glanced at Zach, and his ever-present grin was back. Her eyes watered as she gazed at the man who had created such a perfect and detailed piece of work. At his arched brow, she stepped back to take a better look.

The carving couldn't be described in words. The tiny branches of the birch sprouted leaves that seemed as if they would blow off in the wind. The beaver's fur appeared so soft she had to keep herself from bending down to feel it. And the woodpecker, with his wings wide and his beak opened, looked ready to do serious damage to the plodding beaver.

She switched her watery gaze back to Zach, sure that nothing could be as beautiful as he, not even the carving. But he lifted his eyebrow again.

The crowd settled to a dull roar and Craig tried again to explain the carving's story. Bea continued to admire it when she caught sight of an indentation on the left side. Not wanting to stand in the way of the audience, she slipped around the back and stood next to Zach.

She gasped. Craig hesitated in his speech and looked at her. She waved him on before turning back to the carving. Zach had included a heart, much like she had drawn in grammar school, only this one was special. Inside the carved heart were the initials BR + ZW, TLA.

Bea's heart swelled. True love always. A phrase as a child that seemed mushy and dramatic, but today it took her breath away. Pure joy flooded her veins even as fear pestered her spine. She turned to Zach.

He mouthed the words she'd just read as he placed a hand over his heart. She gave him a tremulous smile and whispered, "Always."

He pulled her against his side as they waited for the ceremony to finish. When people started to head inside for refreshments, she faced Zach. "Can you stay for a while? I could find us a room and we could test Josh's cure."

His face lit, but as he opened his mouth to answer, his dad joined them and clapped him on the shoulder. "Zach, this is brilliant!"

Bea stepped away as others crowded around Zach, praising his work, asking for his card or giving him theirs. She could envision every business in town with a Zach Woodman carving on their threshold. The town might even become known as the town with the great wooden carvings, which could increase tourist traffic. Her education must have stayed with her for her to be thinking in that vein. Maybe a chat with her dad Mathew couldn't hurt.

Zach looked at her over the heads of those gathered around him and shrugged.

She chuckled. As the most humble man she knew, he seemed lost among the accolades. She pointed inside and he nodded in understanding. As she walked away, she had the sinking feeling that time together would not happen for another night.

Her frustration grew. Instead of fearing the result of their lovemaking, now she wanted to know, desperately needed to know. Today she had committed to being with Zach always. Now she had to know what that future would be like and somehow, some way, come to terms with it.

~~*~~

Bea threw the pen onto the desk. What the hell was wrong

with her? She should be excited, thrilled, elated, to see Zach tonight. Instead she couldn't concentrate and the blasted columns wouldn't add up.

She stood and walked around her desk to stare out the window. It had been five days since the supposed cure took place. Now anticipation warred with anxiousness, causing her to reach for the Tums again, though it was only eleven in the morning. Chewing a couple of the chalky tablets, she crossed her arms over her stomach. Great, at this rate she'd arrive at Zach's crippled with stomach pain.

She turned and leaned against the sill. When Zach had called a couple hours ago to let her know his parents had left, she'd been excited, but her mind wouldn't stop thinking about tomorrow morning. Then they would know what the rest of their lives would be like. She brought her finger to her mouth and chewed on her nail. Pulling her hand away, she swore. "Damn it."

If only she could focus on the night ahead instead of the morning after. She would be arriving naked and that thought alone should have had her blood heating, but the fear returned and turned her blood colder than the depths of the lake in spring. Maybe if she checked on the caterer for the evening's—

"Bea, you have visitors." Kayla leaned against the doorway, a pile of receipts in her hand and a frown on her face. It appeared her own irritation had become contagious.

"Who is it?"

Kayla pushed away from the door and sat at the side counter. "It's your dad and that cop."

Bea tensed. Chris was here? Why? She'd left him a message letting him know they'd discovered the letter writer. And her dad? "Kayla, which dad?"

She sighed. "Tony."

Bea squeezed behind Kayla and rested her hand on her shoulder. "I'm sorry I'm such a bear today. Gary has the front. Why don't you take a break from the receipt work and find us both a cup of coffee? After I'm done, maybe we can talk about Josh."

Kayla's shoulders fell. "Yeah, I could use some more caffeine and the chat. Thanks."

Bea strode into the lobby to find Tony talking to Chris, in his uniform this time. They stood to the side of the front doors, away from the front desk. "Dad?"

Tony switched his gaze to her and she glimpsed a melting in his dark-brown eyes before he distanced himself and resumed his usual professional aura. "Bea, I understand you called Chris about the letters Phillip wrote you."

She stared at Chris, who appeared uncomfortable, as well he should be. He'd contacted Tony behind her back. She turned to her dad. "Yes. I didn't know Phillip had sent them and asked Chris for help. But when we discovered they were from Phillip, I let him know he didn't need to waste his time."

She caught Tony's glance toward Chris. Her dad already realized he may have been used for other than clearly revealed purposes. "I see." He paused.

That's what she liked about Tony. He didn't ruffle easily. He took his time to think through his options.

He locked gazes with her. "Since Philip's machinations did no harm, we don't have anything concrete we can charge him with."

She agreed. In other words, they couldn't reveal Phillip had tried to kill her with an antivenom.

Tony continued. "However, I do believe Phillip is a threat to you. Would you agree, Bea? Based on the letters you received and your last conversations with him, would you say he may be dangerous? I would venture to say he's showing signs of insanity, but that is between the three of us. I'm no expert in that area."

Tony faced Chris. "Would it be possible to obtain a restraining order against Phillip?"

Chris hesitated. "I'm not sure. Since Phillip didn't actually cause Bea any physical harm…"

Bea had to agree. "I do believe Phillip is a threat, but, Dad, didn't Mom tell him I died when I went into the hospital?"

"She did, but you know your mother is not the best liar. I'd feel more comfortable if we could do something legally."

Chris jumped in. "I agree, Bea. You need to be protected."

Her irritation climbed another notch and she couldn't let the comment go. "I am protected, Chris. I have Zach." She ignored Chris' fallen face and returned her attention to her father. "Maybe you could have a chat with Phillip's employer, professional to professional. I understand Phillip has been using their lab for personal reasons. The company also sends him to Maine a lot. Perhaps his boss could keep him closer to home in Massachusetts. It's not a guarantee, but it would limit his opportunities to bother me."

Tony seemed pleased. "I agree it's no guarantee, but it's another hurdle in his path to you. And in the meantime, Chris, if you could check into a restraining order and see what we need, I'd like to pursue that as well."

"Yes sir. I'd be happy to help with that."

Chris was so anxious to do what he could. She shouldn't have thrown Zach in his face. Chris couldn't help it if he was a little overzealous. She laid a hand on his arm. "Thank you. I appreciate it." She spoke to her dad. "If worst came to worst, we could always ask Gerry to pay Phillip a visit. Gerry would—"

Chris interrupted. "I don't want to hear this. Maybe talk about that option privately?"

Bea sighed. "If only Phillip would find someone else to fall in love with. Someone who could return his feelings, then we could all go back to having normal lives without strange letters and weird potions, and being followed, and—"

Tony put a hand on her shoulder. "It's all right, Bea. Chris and

I will handle this. You stay close to Zach until we see how Philip reacts, okay?"

She nodded, too wound up to speak.

Tony shook hands with Chris. "Thank you for your help. I appreciate it."

Chris stood a little straighter. "My pleasure. Anything I can do. Take care, Bea. Call if you need anything."

As Chris walked out the lobby doors, Tony took her hand and led her to the couch by the great window and sat her down. His business façade evaporated and revealed the warm man beneath. "Beatrice, you're preoccupied. What's wrong?"

She fiddled with the button on her sleeve, debating what she could tell him. Of anyone in the family, he could keep a secret from her mom the best. Her insides knotted up and she instinctually reached in her pocket for her Tums.

Tony caught her wrist. "Tell me before you land in the hospital with bleeding ulcers."

She looked at his hand on her arm, the exact same skin color as hers and wondered for the hundredth time if he was her biological father. But then again, she and Jim had the same skin color, as did many of Grandma Beatrice's lovers.

Unable to handle any more stress, feeling the love and concern emanating from him, she caved. "Zach has asked me to marry him."

Once again Tony held his silence as he mulled over the ramifications of her statement, but it wasn't long before he spoke. "I'm guessing you'd prefer if I didn't tell your mother."

She snapped her gaze to his to find him smiling and took a deep, calming breath. She gave him a halfhearted grin. "That would be an understatement. I think I'd need a restraining order on her if she discovered I turned him down."

Tony's eyes widened. "Oh, that I didn't expect. What is it? Are you afraid?"

She nodded. "We still don't know if Dr. Josh's cure has worked, and I'm afraid of what our lives would be like if I'm not cured. I don't want to tie him to me when he deserves so much more."

Tony opened his arms. "Come here."

She leaned into her dad and he held her. "Beatrice, you have to understand, Zach made that decision when he asked you to marry him. Just as I made the decision to stay with your mom despite having to share her. I could have found someone else, much like Jim and Charlie did, but I chose her and you over a 'normal' life. I've never regretted it. Not once. You can't protect Zach. He has all the facts and he still wants you, flaws and all. That's called true love."

True love always. She squeezed him to let him know she heard because to speak would cause her to cry, and technically, she was still at work.

Tony sat her back. "It's not as if Zach doesn't know exactly what he's getting himself into, right?"

She rolled her eyes.

"And you do love him, right?"

She swallowed the lump in her throat. "More than I thought I could ever love."

Tony took her hand. "Then I think you should give his proposal serious consideration. I would give you my blessing because I know he would take care of my little girl."

She was hardly little. Heck, she should have made this man a grandfather by now and given him a real little girl to spoil.

Tony pulled away and stood. "I'm sorry, Beatrice, but I have to go back to work now, and I think you do too." He lifted her chin. "Are you going to be all right?"

"Yes. Thank you."

He bent and gave her a kiss on the forehead before striding across the lobby and out the hotel doors.

Bea sat for a moment. Tony could be right. Zach knew what his life would be like with her as a wife. Well, not exactly. They wouldn't know that until tomorrow. And tonight she could show him how much she loved him. She needed to focus on that. Whatever happened afterward, they would face together.

Feeling better, she strolled toward the front desk. As she passed it, she noticed the trash can with a large printout hovering across the top. Sticking her hand in her pocket, she pulled out her bottle of Tums and dropped it into the garbage, taking the paper down with it.

Now maybe she could be the friend Kayla needed.

~~*~~

Bea slowed her car at the blue police lights flashing behind her. Oh, this wouldn't be good if they pulled her over. She wore nothing but her robe and a pair of black leather high-heeled boots per Zach's request. As she pulled to the side of the road, her heartbeat increased to match the rhythm of the blue flashes.

When the policeman raced by, she dropped her head onto the steering wheel. What had she been thinking? Wiping her sweaty hands off on her robe, she sat back and turned the car onto the road. Now that the surprise snowstorms had stopped, the roads were clear. She loved that the days were becoming longer and warmer. Soon the brown of the scenery would give way to the full green of already budding trees. She couldn't wait to see Zach's valley come alive.

As she rounded a bend in the road, she depressed the brakes. The flashing blue lights had stopped in front of her, but had been joined by red ones as well. Traffic came to a stop on the two-way road. Was there a back way she could go if she turned around? Had she passed the side street next to the Tamwick post office yet or was it farther up the road? She didn't want to see the crushed vehicles of the accident four cars ahead of her. More cars stopped behind her, blocking her in. She was stuck. Stuck and almost naked.

She hoped no one was seriously injured. She tried to see ahead at what might be happening. Was someone being moved on a stretcher? In the dim light of dusk, she couldn't be sure. A police officer walked back toward the line of cars. The first driver opened his window and spoke with the cop. Then the police officer came to the next car.

"Oh no."

She examined her back seat to see if she'd left a bag of clothes there from changing at the inn, but no such luck. "Damn it." She quickly crossed the robe over herself as tightly as possible and tied it hard. As he strode toward her vehicle, her stomach dropped another notch. It was Chris, of course. She rolled down her window.

"It will just be a moment, ma'am. We need to…" He looked inside her car. "Bea?"

"Hi, Chris. Is someone hurt?"

He hesitated.

Oh no, now what? "Chris? Tell me."

He put both hands on the door. "No, no one is badly injured, but the damage to the cars has blocked traffic."

She let out her breath in relief. "Oh, thank goodness."

His tone became stern. "It's not all good news."

Surprised by what sounded like anger in his voice, she studied him through the shadow of the closing day. Oh boy, his eyes glittered like gunmetal as they took in her robe. "What's wrong?"

"Your mother caused the accident. She's high again."

"Oh geez."

He backed away. "You might want to come down to the station and bail her out. I'd suggest you go home and change first."

Ouch, that hurt. She watched as he went to the car behind her before another policemen came by with a flashlight. He used it to motion for her to turn around. She reversed into the shoulder and drove back onto the road, heading in the wrong direction, away from Zach.

Embarrassment at Chris seeing her behind the wheel in her robe combined with her frustration at needing to make love to Zach. She banged her hand on the steering wheel. "Thanks, Mom."

When she arrived home, she called Zach.

"Hey, beautiful. Where are you?"

"I'm at my apartment. Mom's been arrested. She was high and caused an accident. Looks as if I'll be bailing her out." She sighed.

Zach chuckled. "You have to bail her out? Did she call you?"

How could he think her situation funny? "No, as a matter of fact, I was stuck in the line of traffic waiting to go around the accident my mom caused when Officer Chris came to my car and found me driving in nothing but a robe. He happily told me I would need to rescue her."

The silence on the other end of the phone had Bea reeling in her temper. "I'm sorry, I need you so much and it seems as if we'll never find out if we can have a normal life."

"Listen, Bea. I don't want you going to the station alone. I'm on my way. Stay there and if your mom calls, tell her we'll be right there."

She plopped on her couch and loosened her robe. "Zach, you don't have to do that. She's my responsibility."

"Uh-huh. She has four men who can take care of her. And I don't want you going to the police station by yourself. Besides, I've already left Tamwick and I'm entering Wrenborough, just stay where you are."

A feeling of comfort began in her stomach, releasing the constant tension there. He would take care of her? The idea had her smiling. "Okay. I'll stay right here, exactly as I am."

"Good. Wait. Exactly how are you?"

"I'm sitting on my couch in only my robe and my high-heeled, black leather boots."

She swore she heard him swallow. "You won't start without me, will you?"

She opened her robe to free a breast. "I guess that depends on how long it takes you. Bye."

She chuckled to herself. What fun would starting without him be? She could do that any evening. She wanted him. Her fear for their future returned, but she pushed it aside. She had Zach now. He would take care of her and she would take care of him, in so many ways.

Bea tied her robe closed and strode into her master bathroom to pull out extra towels for Zach. Tonight they would spend together. In the morning they would discover their fate.

Sashaying back into the kitchen, she checked the fridge. A six-pack of Bud Light sat on the top shelf. She had decided to keep it in stock in case Zach stopped by. But she hadn't remembered to buy any whip cream or strawberries. She pulled out a new bottle of Bailey's Irish Cream and poured it over ice. She'd just closed the refrigerator when a knock sounded at her door. He must have sped all the way.

She left her drink on the counter and opened the door.

Chris stood in the doorway. And he hadn't cooled off in the last half hour either.

Bea pulled the robe tighter around her. "Chris, what are you doing here?"

He moved forward, forcing her to back away. "I thought you were coming down to the station to bail out your mother."

Who did he think he was, ordering her what to do? "I decided that if Mom called me, I would go. But Mom can call Andy, or Mathew or Gerry or—"

Chris strode into the living room and peered into the bedroom. "So your mom's not as important as your boyfriend? What's happened to you, Bea? You used to be a good girl."

"I happened to her." Zach's voice behind her startled her. She made to turn around, but he held her in front of him. "And I'm going to take care of her. So you can go back to the station now."

Chris spun at the sound of Zach's voice. His hands tightened into fists and the muscles in his neck stood out in stark relief. "You. Ever since you came into her life, she's had trouble."

Bea opened her mouth to speak, but Zach's pressure on her arm kept her silent.

Chris stalked into the kitchen. He lifted the glass of Bailey's and snickered. "A lady's drink. You need to drink to achieve satisfaction, Bea? I could satisfy you without the booze." He tipped the glass upside down over the sink. "But you ignore me. Why, Bea? What's wrong with me?"

Zach answered for her. "You mean besides the fact that you stalk her and sit parked outside her apartment at night when you're on duty?"

Chris flushed.

Bea couldn't believe it, but Chris didn't deny it. His need for her had grown as she became more involved with Zach. Of course, Chris had always lived off competition in high school. She should have realized it before. He didn't want her, he wanted to beat Zach and she happened to be the prize. "Chris, it has nothing to do with you. I simply refused to be involved with anyone here in town. I want to keep my professional life separate from my personal. This town is too small." The partial truth came easily.

Chris wrinkled his brow. "So you're saying if I lived in Concord, you might have dated me?"

She snuggled against Zach, finding his solid warmth behind her reassuring. "There's no maybe about it. I would have definitely dated you."

He stood a little straighter. It seemed as if he wanted to smile. "I could move?"

She shook her head. "I think it's a little late. I'm very taken."

"I can see that." For the first time, Chris lifted his gaze to meet Zach's. Then he seemed to come to a decision. "Well, I guess your mom can call Mathew or Tony. I doubt at this time of night Andy would be fit to drive. Sorry for the intrusion."

Bea tried to follow Chris' train of thought, but the man headed toward them as they stood in front of her doorway.

He offered his hand to Zach. "Take good care of her."

Zach shook. "I plan to."

Chris waited a second, staring hard at Zach. Then he brushed past them, closing the door behind him.

For some reason she wanted to laugh. She turned in Zach's arms to find him grinning from ear to ear. He gazed into her eyes. "You were brilliant! How did you know all this was about him competing against me and not about you?"

She wrapped her arms around his neck. "I didn't at first. But when you mentioned the stalking, all the pieces fell into place. Do you think he'll leave me alone now?"

He pulled her tight against him and growled. "He better."

She wiggled her body, her instincts singing with the triumph of having won the better man. "If he doesn't, we can always threaten to go to his chief. I don't think using the patrol car to spy on a woman falls under 'other duties as assigned'."

Zach grasped her ass with both his hands and ground his cock against her mons. "Frankly, I don't give a damn what his duties are. All I know is I have a hot, naked woman in black high-heeled boots in my arms and she needs to be satisfied."

Bea opened her mouth to Zach's kiss.

He groaned as his tongue thrust to explore hers.

She broke away, pulling out of his arms. "And I know how I want to be satisfied." She turned her back on him and sauntered into the bedroom.

Resisting the urge to see if he followed, she untied the robe. She stopped by the bed and pulled the belt from the loops before turning around to face him.

He was right in front of her, his clothes gone. His gaze roved over her cleavage and down to the bare juncture of her thighs. She used her finger under his chin to lift his face and held the belt aloft. "Fair's fair."

Chapter Seventeen

Zach's look of surprise mixed with uncertainty gave Bea a sudden rush of victory. She had him right where she wanted him and she laughed at his hesitancy. "Are you nervous?"

His confidence returned with his grin. "Why? Should I be?"

She shook her head even as she wrapped the belt around both his wrists. "No."

"Bea?"

His breathing increased and her body's excitement rose to meet his. She finished the knot and slyly gazed at him. "Yes?"

He grabbed hold of the edge of her robe and pulled her closer. He bent his head and nuzzled her ear. "Leave your boots on."

Tingles of excitement rode her skin from neck to thigh as her pussy contracted. She stepped back. "Come on. I want you on your back."

His shit-eating grin faltered and his Adam's apple moved downward, but he still managed to control his voice. "Whatever you say, beautiful. My body is here for your pleasure."

Her heart slowed and her body cooled at the reminder of the men she had used to survive. Though they hadn't been permanently incapacitated, they'd probably been terribly ill.

Zach crowded her and raised his tied hands to stroke her cheek. "What is it?"

She attempted a smile. "Nothing. Just old thoughts. Hopefully, ones I need not concern myself with anymore."

Zach lowered his lips to within an inch of hers. "Never again."

As his mouth claimed hers, anticipation returned. His hands found her right breast and tweaked the nipple. A sharp need pulsed into her pussy, making her moist. Using her desire to fuel her control, she pulled away, but her body wasn't happy with her decision.

Zach held out his hands. "Are you sure you don't want to be the one tied?"

Power surged through her at his ploy. "I'm sure. I want you my way."

He shrugged good-naturedly. "It doesn't hurt to try."

She tugged him to the bed. "Lie down on your back, please."

Zach stretched out on the bed and obligingly lifted his arms above his head. Quickly, she tied the belt to the headboard, but not fast enough to avoid him licking her rib. Her body responded to his touch by sending a rush of heat to gather at the juncture of her thighs.

She stepped back and gazed at him. She could never tire of viewing his rippled stomach and granite-hard chest, but his massive thighs and the tall cock twitching between them beckoned her.

He spread his legs. "Want a closer look?"

What a tease. Two could play that game. She shrugged, but didn't answer him. Instead she removed the robe from her shoulders and let it slide to the floor.

Zach's entire body tensed. His cock pushed up into the air, calling her.

She placed one black leather-clad foot on the bed and leaned in. She gazed at the cock that would bring her pleasure, but she didn't touch. Instead, she stroked her own thigh with one hand while stroking his thigh with the other, not caressing the places they both craved her to touch.

"Beautiful, if you keep that up, I'm going to come right now."

She shook her head. "No, you won't because I haven't told you to yet."

He raised a brow at her, but she ignored him and took her hands away.

The fact was, she would come soon too and she didn't plan to be standing next to the bed at the time. She crawled onto the firm mattress and knelt between his legs, spreading her own, her thigh-high boots resting against his knees. She used one finger to stroke along her swollen folds, spreading her own moisture over herself before she touched his tip and slowly coated his cock head. She repeated the action again though her heart's rhythm increased, causing her breaths to shorten.

Zach's body looked harder than the granite ledges of Mount Washington. His neck muscles strained as he lifted his head to watch her.

She stopped. "Here, let me move the other pillow for you."

She leaned over him and maneuvered the second pillow beneath his head, but as she adjusted it, his mouth latched on to her breast.

She couldn't move, the excitement racing from breast to pussy bringing her to the edge of an orgasm. Somewhere deep down, she found the strength to pull away.

Zach groaned as her nipple tugged out of his mouth.

She couldn't waste any more time. She needed this man like she needed life. Readjusting herself, she straddled Zach's hips and let her wet nether lips glide along the length of his hard cock, every inch teasing her. She couldn't resist. Pulling up, she placed his cock at her entrance and slid down, impaling herself fully. Her sigh of completeness filled the air.

Zach lay still, his body as hard as the wood he carved, his eyes closed.

She didn't move, just gazed at him and waited for him to look at her. When he did, the passion she read in his eyes almost toppled her. With deliberate movement, she took both his nipples between her fingers and rolled them.

Zach's hips lifted from the bed, pressing his cock deeper into her.

The feeling of fullness within her pussy had her pushing back, grinding forward and back against his hardened cock. She rested her hands on his chest, even as her hips continued to move. The building tightness where their two bodies connected fed on the friction as her clit rubbed along the skin of his cock. Without thought, she increased their rhythm, caught in the swirling pleasure of their mating.

Zach's body strained against hers, pushing upward as if trying to bury himself inside her. The pressure built. He pulled in and out and she rode him back and forth like a bucking bronco. Her folds spread apart as he stabbed inside. Her clit ached with sensitivity as the rubbing stroked against it.

She gasped for air, unable to stop herself from the sheer pleasure building inside that forced her hips to move, pounding against him until he groaned her name. The spurt of warmth inside her pussy sent her into climax, her body shaking with ecstasy. She couldn't catch a breath and didn't want to as wave after wave of satisfying heat flowed from her inner core to her fingertips.

As Zach slowed, she brought more air into her lungs. She tried to calm her body and finally crumpled on top of him.

He turned his head and kissed her ear before putting his arms around her.

Huh? She lifted her head. The piece of wood latticework she had tied Zach to was gone.

They'd broken her headboard.

She rested her head back on his shoulder and giggled.

He wrestled his hands from the belt and stroked her hair. "What's so funny?"

She lifted her head. "I was trying to decide which father I should ask to help me fix my bed and what the reaction might be if I told him how it broke."

Zach raised his arms behind his head. "And why can't I fix your headboard? I'm the one who broke it, though it was your fault. But more importantly, I'm pretty good with wood."

Bea smirked at her foolishness. "Oh yeah, I forgot."

He lifted a brow. "Are you going to want to bring this bed to Tamwick after we get married?"

Bea tensed, but relaxed again as her mind spun at all it would mean for them to be married. Not that she'd said "yes". Suddenly, it hit her. Of course he'd think about such details. He'd been at this point in his life twice before. "Zach, what happened with Lisa?"

His face fell and he brought his arms down, but he laid one across her back. "Didn't my mother tell you?"

Bea lowered her head and kissed his chest. She could tell he didn't want to talk about it, but she needed to know. She glanced at him again. "All she would say is you were brokenhearted and that it was the second time she'd seen you like that. Actually, she warned me if I broke your heart she'd make me wish I were dead."

Zach grunted. "My mom is still trying to protect me."

She couldn't help fiddling with his chest hair, but kept her eyes focused on him. "She said that's when you bought the property in Tamwick."

He sighed and looked beyond her, as if recalling it all over again. "Yeah. I had to leave."

Bea waited.

Finally, his gaze returned to hers. "You really want to know?"
She nodded. "Please."

He moved his hips and she caught the hint. Sliding to his side, she snuggled in and rested her head on his shoulder.

He settled his hand on her waist. "I thought Lisa was the one. She was smart, pretty and very outgoing. We were in love."

He paused and Bea stroked his chest, but he caught her hand in his. "It was my birthday. She said she had a surprise for me, but I was behind on a contract so instead of taking the day off as we had planned, I went to a site. At the end of the day I was driving down the logging road with my men and came upon Lisa's car. The guys wouldn't let me near it, but I could see. She'd hit a moose. The animal's body was still lodged through the front windshield of her Ford Taurus. She was dead."

Bea squeezed his hand. "Oh, Zach, I'm so sorry."

He stroked her palm. "She'd been coming up to surprise me. They found the doctor paperwork in her purse. She was pregnant."

Bea's heart pounded and a tear seeped from her eye onto his chest. There was nothing she could say to that.

He took a deep breath. "We were living together by then, the wedding plans started. She knew I would be thrilled."

Bea wanted to take his pain away. She kissed his shoulder and let go of his hand so she could hold him. "I'm so sorry."

He shrugged. "It wasn't the first time I lost the woman I was going to marry. After high school, Danielle and I had planned to marry. That was the first time I changed plans to be with the woman I loved so I could work on a site. You'd think I would have learned from that. She went to the lake without me and drowned. If I had kept my commitments to them— After that I vowed to never spend more than three nights with any woman to avoid any strong feelings. I was bad luck and it was the only way I felt sure I could keep the women in my life alive. But then I met you and three nights wasn't enough. I don't think three million nights would be enough."

Bea wrapped her arm around him and squeezed. What he must have thought when she'd gone into a coma. She shivered.

He patted her ass. "Hey, beautiful. What do you say we take a hot shower? I need to celebrate my ability to keep you."

Bea sat up and smiled seductively. "Only if you promise to wash me."

He pretended to think about it. "I guess I can do that. You'll have to show me how, though. I've never washed a sexy woman before."

Bea scrambled from the bed. "Really?"

He strutted toward the bathroom. "Yup. Always liked keeping my showers to myself, but in your case I'll make an exception."

Bea glowed. She'd be his first shower mate. She couldn't say the same, but that didn't matter anymore. Ruthlessly, she pushed her past aside and followed Zach. "Do you think you could help me with these boots?"

He turned to face her. "It would be my pleasure."

She sat on the toilet seat cover and lifted her leg.

Zach placed her foot on his thigh, not far from his hardening cock. "You know what I imagined the first time I took your boots off?"

She shook her head, anxious to hear.

He removed the first boot and patted his thigh for her to lift the other one. "I imagined doing this." Zach held on to her ankle while he used his other hand to slide two fingers into her pussy.

Bea gasped as white-hot desire shot through her and she tightened around his fingers. Her natural response was to pull her leather-clad leg back, but Zach held on.

His other hand, however, did not remain still. He turned his fingers inside her and curled them toward him. Bea's heart raced as she leaned back against the tank, unable to breathe steadily. Then he did it. His fingers hit a magic spot inside her and cries of pleasure tore from her throat as she grabbed his arm. Her body shook with the unexpected explosive orgasm that rippled through her.

Zach removed his fingers and dropped to his knees before her. He thrust his tongue into her drenched pussy and licked. She continued to shake as she convulsed against his tongue and reached down to bury her hands in his hair.

As her breathing returned to normal, he finished licking her clean and knelt back. "What do you say to that shower?"

Dazed, she was thankful he didn't wait for an answer. Instead, he pulled her leg up again, and removed her other boot. Then he bent over and turned on the water, giving her an enticing view of his ass with his balls hanging between his legs. She couldn't resist. She cupped his sac, stroking it with her thumb.

He froze. His thigh muscles tensed.

She found the strength to lean forward and kiss his tight butt.

His head dropped as he stood at the side of the shower, water pouring into the tub.

Caressing his balls, she stood and curled over him. "I can't get enough of you, Zach."

He reached between his legs and separated her hand from his sac before he stood and took her into his arms, pressing pre-cum into her abdomen. "The feeling is mutual. I can't wait to get you into my shower. There's a lot of room in there and two showerheads."

She pressed into him. "I like the sound of that. Mine is kind of old-fashioned, but it has a tub, which I like."

He ran his hand under the flowing water. "I suggest we inspect your shower more thoroughly." He scooped her into his arms and stepped in.

Bea squealed as the warm water hit her face before he let her legs drop. She sputtered. "Your turn." She angled the showerhead at him.

He laughed. "Hey, I'm new at this, remember?"

She smiled and moved the head back. "Okay. I'll forgive you."

He grasped her to him and maneuvered their bodies into the spray together.

The warm water flowed over her skin and made Zach's chest hair flatten on his thickly defined chest. God, he was gorgeous. She picked up the soap and lathered his pectorals, encircling his nipples and moving farther down his body. As she arrived at his pubic area, she played with the dark hair, making the soap lather.

His penis moved.

She smirked. Ignoring his stiff cock, she slid her hands down his muscled thighs, washing between them and soaping his balls.

He fixated on her hands, his face tense with anticipation. She watched him as she encircled his cock with slippery soap. He expelled a breath. Her body, attuned to his, vibrated in unison. Excited, she stroked him and his face grew taut. She could give him a soapy hand job right now.

But even as she encircled his tip with her fingers, his gaze caught hers and he lifted her. "Huh-uh. I want to slip inside you."

With a shaking hand, she dropped the soap in the holder and directed the spray to rinse him off.

She cradled his face in her hands. "Take me."

His pupils dilated as he spun her around. She found her back against the tile wall of the shower. Its coolness, a stark contrast to Zach's heated body, pressed against her as his mouth came down to ravage hers.

Her mind grasped that the new experience for him had him hot for her, and her body hummed at the knowledge. She let him take her, grabbing his ass as he tugged her hair to maneuver her mouth where he wanted it.

When he broke off the kiss, she was thankful he had her pressed against the back wall because her legs couldn't hold her anymore.

His mouth found her nipple and she held on to his shoulders. He paused, breathing hard. "God, Bea, I can't get enough of you either."

A shiver raced across her skin at his words, filling her heart and her pussy with warmth. "Good."

Zach moaned, her only warning before he seized her hips and shoved his thick cock into her waiting opening. She gasped at his penetration. Sensations spread from between her legs to send waves of heat through her limbs.

He pushed her farther up the wall of the shower. She lifted one foot onto the side of the tub to allow him better access and his cock slid in a few inches deeper.

He caught her mouth with his, his tongue raiding her senses as his cock raided her body.

She anchored on to his shoulders as he pumped into her, pressing her between himself and the tiled wall. His complete command spiked her arousal and her pussy tightened around him.

Zach gasped.

His movements became frenzied and her body responded to his need. As her back pressed hard against the shower wall with each deep thrust, the angle of his cock rubbed against her clit, building her excitement to a fever-pitch.

His heavy pants gave way to a growl and her pussy contracted around him as his cum pumped into her, sending her into her orgasm.

Whimpers escaped from her throat as she shuddered with her release.

Zach's head had found her shoulder, but he lifted it. Concern riddled his expression. "Are you okay?"

Her senses finally came back. She could actually feel her pulse beating in her clit as it slowed. She gave him a huge smile to reassure him. "Oh yes. More than okay. Spectacular."

He chuckled as he let her slip down to stand in the tub. "That good?"

She nodded as her knees buckled.

He caught her. "Whoa, stay with me."

"I can't, my knees are too weak."

Zach smirked. "Hmm, if you're that weak then I guess I can't wash you. Better put you to bed."

She laughed as she pulled away and stood on her own. "No way. You promised."

He lifted an eyebrow. "As I suspected. You're stronger than you let on."

Bea reached for the soap and handed it to him. "Here. Get to work."

Zach saluted. "Yes ma'am." If this was the toughest chore she ever asked him to do, he had a lifetime of bliss to look forward to.

He turned her around. "Put your hands on the wall. If you want me to wash you, you have to hold yourself up."

"Gee, Zach, you're so demanding."

Once she'd braced herself, he lathered the soap. Gently, he massaged her shoulders before running his soapy hands along her arms to the tips of her fingers. Next he washed her back. The citrusy scent filling the moist air was a double dose of Bea to his senses. He ran his hands along her spine, reveling in the silky smoothness of her skin. As he reached her ass, he knelt and massaged her perfect curves. Unable to resist, he pulled one cheek aside and ran a soapy finger down her crease.

Her legs trembled. "Zach, I'm not going to be able to stand much longer."

He moved his head and allowed the shower spray to run over her ass before kissing her there. "If you can't stay standing, I'll have to stop."

She groaned. "You don't play fair."

He grinned. "Nope."

He continued to wash her, running his hands down her long legs, careful not to go anywhere near her sweet pussy. He grasped her foot. "Lift." She did and he lightly massaged her before doing the same to the other foot.

He stood and pulled her away from the wall, moving her to face the spray.

Bea's head fell back against his shoulder. Her wet, silky hair plastered to his chest. He grasped her to him and nestled his hard cock against her ass.

"Oh Zach. I'm not sure I'm going to last."

He brought his lips to her ear. "Yes you will, because I said so."

At her groan, he brought his soapy hands around her and kneaded her breasts, spreading lather across her chest. The need to ensure her nipples were clean spurred him to rub the hard nubs between his fingers.

Bea started to slide downward, but he held her nipples between his fingers.

"Oh." She stood straighter. "You've got me so wet."

He moved his hands around her slender waist and over her tummy, fighting his cock's demand to enter her at once. "Then I better clean you. I wouldn't want you to be dirty inside your pussy and nowhere else."

He stopped at her mons. "Spread your legs for me."

She opened her legs and he quickly moved his finger to soap her labia and clit. The woman was pure female and he loved the feel of her pussy. He'd like to spend an entire day playing with it.

Bea moaned. "I'm going to come."

He brought his lips to her ear. "Then come."

With his tongue, he licked her neck and nibbled while his finger played on the hard nub at her entrance. Dropping the soap in the dish, he used his other hand to circle her nipple. She was like a finely tuned instrument and he her musician.

Bea's pants grew louder, her whimpers coming steadily. She was close.

Removing his hand from her breast despite her moan of frustration, he positioned his cock between her legs and pushed inside.

Bea yelled as her pussy contracted around him.

He kept playing with her clit, sustaining her orgasm and fighting his own. Her hips bucked and swiveled, but he stayed with her, giving her all the pleasure he could. Bringing this woman to orgasm gave him immense satisfaction. He wanted to make her happy for the rest of his life. He had to convince her.

As her pussy relaxed, he pulled out, unwilling to come again so soon. He didn't have Josh's drugs tonight to keep him going and if he had his way, they'd make love all night, no matter what tomorrow brought.

Brushing aside his concern, he moved forward, allowing the shower spray to sluice over Bea's breasts down to where his finger held her clit. He moved his hand to catch the water in his palm before he cupped her. "Time to rinse."

She began to sink in earnest this time, but he held her around the waist while he continued to rinse between her legs. Eventually, he reached forward and turned off the water. With one hand, he opened the shower door then picked Bea up in his arms.

Her head dropped to his shoulder and she mumbled, "You wipe me out."

As if his ego wasn't already big enough, her words sent him over the top. They were meant to be together. With his love flowing through every movement, he set her on her dressing table chair and toweled her dry. He used her comb to brush her hair straight. He'd like to pamper her more often.

Bea must have gathered a second wind because she sat straighter as he worked on her luxurious strands. Their silky feel begged for his touch and he couldn't resist. After he finished with the comb, he ran his fingers through her hair, enjoying its feminine softness.

Bea turned toward him in all her naked glory. "You're wonderful."

Zach shook his head. "I think you have that backward."

Bea stood, pulling her hair from his hands. "I couldn't resist you, you know. That's why I kissed you the day we met."

Zach stepped around the chair and closed the space between them.

She looked into his soothing green eyes. "And it wasn't because I needed release. I had never been attracted to a man before you. It had always been my poisons."

"Bea, you—"

"No, I need you to know. It has always been different with you. And the feelings grew and I wanted desperately to have you, but I didn't want to hurt you. I still don't want to hurt you, but now I could never let you go and I know that's wrong of me."

Zach bowed his head and kissed her. At the touch of his lips, her thoughts dispersed.

When he broke away, he cupped her face. "I love you too and we'll make this work. I promise."

She couldn't help but hug him to her. Her love permeating every corner of her body.

Zach stepped away, took something off the dressing table and bent to one knee. "Beatrice Rappaccini, will you marry me?"

He lifted an open black box. Inside lay a small square-cut diamond surrounded by tiny rubies.

"Oh Zach."

His voice grew deeper. "You don't have to answer me now. I know you need to find out what happens to me tomorrow, and that's one of the reasons I love you. But I wanted you to know I'm serious. The ring is not huge, but it was my grandmother's, and if you don't mind it being small, I'd like you to wear it."

Bea shook her head at the uncertainty on Zach's face. How could he doubt her? "You know I want to marry you, and I think your grandmother's ring is beautiful. I just don't want to tie you to someone like me with all my issues, if they still exist. You deserve so much better."

Zach stood and took her hand. "Bea, I want you to be my wife." He slipped the ring on her left hand. "And I want you to wear this until you say 'yes' and then forever after that."

Her breath caught as her heart filled with joy. A surprising peacefulness enveloped her. She stared at the ring on her finger, her hand in his and a strange feeling of rightness settled in her soul. She looked up to find love shining in Zach's eyes.

Grasping his hand, she led him to her bed. Whatever happened tomorrow didn't matter anymore. She would be his wife and together they would find a solution to any problem thrown their way.

She stopped at the edge of the bed and faced him. "Zach, I would be thrilled to be your wife. Yes, I'll marry you."

"All right!" He picked her up and swung her around until she couldn't breathe from laughing.

As he set her down, he gave her a gentle kiss, but when he broke away, he smirked. "What did it, the ring or my eloquent words?"

She pretended to ponder that before placing her hand on his chest. "Neither. It was your heart."

He covered her hand with his before lifting it to his lips for a kiss that turned into a lick and soon he was sucking on her fingers.

Bea squirmed as her already moist pussy swelled with pleasure. They were going to have to figure something out if she still had her poisons because she could never stop making love to the man who held her heart in his hands.

Bea woke and reached for Zach, only to find the bed empty. Dread filled her bones as she listened for the sound of vomiting. Intent on hearing noises in the bathroom, it took her a moment to notice the salty scent of bacon coming from her kitchen. How could that be? She didn't have any bacon in the house. Grabbing her robe, she belted it with the wood from her headboard still in it and ran to the kitchen.

Zach stood at her stove, stark naked, while he watched bacon cooking in the oven. Bea's gaze went from the oven window to his smooth, round ass in a split second and the need to touch him overrode anything else. Quietly, she stepped behind him and grabbed his butt.

"Whoa, careful there, beautiful. You might distract the cook."

As he turned to face her, Bea gazed into clear, green eyes and a mile-wide grin. "Does this mean you're feeling okay?"

He looped his arms around her waist. "I feel great! I even went to the store so I could make you breakfast. I showered when I got back because you were still sleeping, but I got hungry. I guess becoming engaged is tough work."

Bea threw herself at him, laughing with abandon. "I can't believe it! Oh Zach, this is huge. We can have a normal life!"

He hugged her to him before he loosened his grip. "I don't know how normal it will be."

At the seriousness in his voice, she leaned back to look at him. Water pooled in his eyes and her heart tightened with fear. "Why, Zach?"

"Because I love you too much for this to be normal. I think it can only be incredible for us."

Her own tears started with her relief. "I agree. What we have is extraordinary and always will be. I love you, Zach."

"I love you too," he broke into a grin, "soon-to-be Beatrice Woodman." He pulled her in for a toe-curling kiss.

Her limbs grew mushy and her body ready. She wanted him inside her, but a smoky smell distracted her.

She pulled away. "Zach, the bacon!"

He spun and turned off the oven, but smoke had already filled the apartment. The fire alarms went off, sending their piercing tones throughout the small space.

Bea yelled to be heard. "Zach, I'll open the windows, you get the batteries out!"

He nodded as he climbed on a chair and pulled the alarm down.

She ran to the window and threw it open, allowing the warm spring air to flow into the room. Yes, they would have an extraordinary marriage. And if she didn't miss her guess, a lot more burned food because they couldn't keep their hands off each other.

With the noise stopped and the fresh air flowing in, she turned to see Zach coming toward her, his ever-present grin firmly in place. "Now, where were we?"

Epilogue

Bea looked up at Zach. He stood behind her chair in his living room, grinning.

She faced the animated group in front of her. "Okay, so let me make sure we're all on the same page."

The noise level didn't diminish in the least bit. Kayla spoke to Charlie and Gerry. Mathew's hands were everywhere as he pontificated to her future in-laws and Grandma Beatrice, while her mom had Tony, Andy and Josh's attention riveted. The only one not present was Jim.

Zach noticed her dilemma. He put a hand on her shoulder and squeezed.

Quickly, she covered her ears as he produced a shrill whistle.

Everyone went quiet and looked expectantly at them.

She tried again. "Okay, I just want to make sure we're all in agreement on the wedding before we give you our surprise gift."

Mathew leaned against the stairway. "Hate to tell you, honey bee, but we already know you're pregnant."

Bea placed her hand on her barely rounded abdomen as they all chuckled. She still couldn't believe she would be having a baby. "Very funny, Dad. No, we have a gift for all of you, once I'm sure you'll behave."

Gerry shut his open mouth.

She didn't want to know what he'd planned to say, especially in front of Zach's parents. "Now, I have booked the M.S. *Wavemaster* out of Stone Cove Beach. Gerry, you and your friends will escort me on the Harleys. Charlie is driving me and Mom to the landing in his antique car and then to the Lakeside Inn for the reception. Mathew, as justice of the peace, is performing the ceremony. Ginny has agreed to sing at the service and Tony's swing band will play at the reception. Josh, you're the best man—"

"Damn right I am." Josh crossed his long legs and glanced sideways at Kayla.

Bea gave him a mock frown. "Hey, no swearing in front of the baby."

He pouted, but kept quiet.

Bea continued. "Andy is a groomsman. Grandma Beatrice is my matron of honor and Kayla, my bridesmaid. Mom is walking me down the aisle. I've asked Jim and Craig Larsen to do readings."

Andy spoke up. "What about Nathan here? What's he going to do?"

Bea slumped. How could she have forgotten her future father-in-law?

Zach answered. "That's a good question. Dad, what role would you like to play in this production?"

Nathan put his arm around Ginny. "I was hoping to sit back and enjoy the spectacle, but I guess if you need me, I'm agreeable. It's not as if the birdhouses I sell will be of any help, unless you plan on having birds at the wedding."

Bea's mom clapped her hands together. "Oh, birds would be so beautiful. What do you think, Bea?"

Nathan saved her from answering. "Actually, Susan, they would probably shit on the guests and spread a lot of loose feathers."

Her mom slumped back on the couch.

But her mom's excitement did give her an idea. "Mr. Woodman, do you think you could build us a box for the wedding cards? Maybe it could look like a birdhouse?"

Nathan grinned. His resemblance to Zach at that moment provided her with an image of how Zach would age and she warmed with happiness.

Zach studied his father. "Dad, what are you thinking?"

"I'm thinking you need a box that is modeled after this house. And I'm thinking this box will need to be used for something practical after the wedding, like maybe a breadbox."

Touched, Bea smiled warmly. "Thank you. That will mean so much to us." She glanced at Zach to see a very different look on his face—humility.

Gerry broke into the tender moment. "So, do we all agree?"
Everyone nodded.

He stood. "Good, because I wouldn't want to have to twist some arms."

Bea shook her head and used her best parenting tone. "Gerry, there will be no talk like that. This celebration is one we've been waiting for, for a long time."

Grandma Beatrice interjected. "Yeah. Some of us longer than others."

People chuckled, but then Tony caught everyone's attention with his soft-spoken voice. "So, Bea, what are the gifts you brought us here for?"

Zach came around her chair and sat on the arm.

Bea looked into his eyes as he took her hand. Every time she thought about it, she choked up, and he knew it.

He answered for her. "It's only one gift that we all have to share."

Gerry groaned and Charlie hit him.

Bea smirked. "Oh no, you'll like sharing this. Grandma, Mom, it's so amazing, I can't believe it." She paused, letting her gaze connect with every expectant face. No one seemed to breathe. "As you all know, the Rappaccini women have given birth to girls for over a century."

Grandma nodded. Mr. and Mrs. Woodman took in the new information.

Zach spoke. "We went to the doctor's today."

Bea waited a moment then burst with her news. "I'm going to have a boy!"

The silence lasted but a second.

Gerry swore, half in awe. "Holy shit, I'm going to have a grandson."

Charlie piped in, "I can teach him how to fix cars."

Andy turned to Susan. "He's going to need to know construction. I can help him build a tree fort."

Bea lost track of the conversation as everyone spoke at once. Zach put his arm around her. "I think my parents are a bit overwhelmed, but I can tell my father is going to demand his grandpa time."

She took a peek at Nathan to see him more animated than she'd ever seen him as he spoke to Mathew about teaching her son how to carve. She moved Zach's hand to her stomach. "He's going to be spoiled rotten. We better make sure he has lots of siblings."

Zach winked. "I can help you with that."

The noise in the room grew until Bea noticed yelling and it wasn't pleasant.

"Gerry's a perfectly good name!"

"Huh, that has no finesse to it. I think Mathew sounds more impressive."

Grandma Beatrice had to add her two cents. "They may want to name the baby after Nathan here."

Bea tapped Zach's leg. "You better tell them before Gerry decks someone."

Zach stood and whistled again. The room went silent. "I think you should know we have already decided on a name."

Susan couldn't hide her surprise. "You have? You can't name him after a flower, you know."

Bea put her hand over her eyes at her mother's remark while others chuckled. The Woodmans looked lost, and Tony tried to explain quietly to her mom why the flowers were no longer needed.

Zach continued. "We have decided to name our son after the one man who made his existence possible. Josh, if you don't mind. We would like to name our son after you."

Josh's face turned bright red, as did his neck, but he stood and took the two steps that brought him to Zach. "I'd be honored."

The two men hugged and Bea couldn't keep back the tears any longer. As the room erupted into cheers, she found herself in her soon-to-be husband's arms. She never would have believed she could have a husband, never mind a son. Only her grandmother and mother could understand how unbelievable it all was. Only them and the man in her arms.

Zach pulled back and kissed her. She could feel his love from her lips to her toes.

She couldn't wait to tell her son their story. He would be a Woodman, but one day when he was old enough, she would tell him what it had been like to be a Rappaccini.

The End

Read on for a preview of Masque.
http://www.lexipostbooks.com/masque/

Rena Mills plans to turn an abandoned abbey in Nova Scotia into a haunted bed-and-breakfast, but Synn MacAllistair, the self-proclaimed Ghost Keeper from the 1860's has other plans that include taking her through the seven Pleasure Rooms and freeing 73 ghosts.

Read on for an excerpt from Masque

Chapter One

Cape Breton, Nova Scotia

People. Living, breathing people.

Synn MacAllistair grasped the embrasure of the parapet, his heart thudding as he stared at the vehicle crossing the stone bridge over the moat. It came to a stop at Ashton Abbey's massive gate.

He waited. The great iron grille, chained and padlocked against intruders, would be considered a significant deterrent to entering. *Open it. Damn it, open it!*

The vehicle remained stationary. No one exited the large red monstrosity.

Impatiently, he pushed away his hair as the breeze whipped it across his view. What were they waiting for? If they needed an axe to break the chain, he'd gladly provide them with one.

Another smaller vehicle rolling parallel to the west wall caught his attention. It crossed the bridge and parked behind the larger one. More people?

A man stepped from the small conveyance and shuffled to the gate. Synn leaned farther over the battlement, anxious to see if their time had come. The joyful sound of clanking chains floated up to him on the breeze.

Finally! About bloody time. He swallowed hard to keep the yell of triumph from escaping his throat. No need to scare their new guests.

The man below hurried back to his transport and, without hesitation, backed across the bridge and left faster than he'd arrived.

Synn peered down at the red vehicle, still as a brick, its black windows making it impossible to see inside. A door opened and a woman burst onto the cobblestone entrance. She bent over and spoke to someone else still inside. Her blonde hair hid her face, but her ass, covered in men's trousers, was small, her legs lanky. A woman? A woman dared enter a haunted abbey? He tried to grasp the concept.

His plan was to convince a man to enjoy the pleasures of the flesh, but there had to be a man to convince…unless a couple entered the Abbey. Couples enjoyed the Pleasure Rooms as well. If he could persuade a couple to participate in the Masque then his companions could still be freed.

Peering hard, he watched and waited. After what seemed another decade, a door on the other side of the red contraption opened. He held his breath, willing the occupant to have broad shoulders, a beard, anything to indicate a man.

A long, slender leg stretched out, a black high-heel shoe of delicate design at its end, and a feminine hand grasped the side, but remained stationary.

He growled with frustration. "Bloody hell. What am I supposed to do with two women?" He hadn't expected women. The Abbey overflowed with spirits. Only men should dare enter. How were blasted women going to help him? He paced away from the wall, but quickly returned. Could there be more people inside the vehicle?

He waited, his patience long gone, not that he ever had much, but damn, it'd been a hundred and fifty years. That would strain the patience of an archangel, something he definitely was not.

He glared as the leg moved and within a moment's breath, the woman unfolded herself from the conveyance.

Synn stared, frozen in time for once, drinking in a beauty far surpassing any painted Aphrodite he'd ever gazed upon. Her long, wavy brown hair captured the sun, shining like fine brandy. Her figure, as lush as any Greek goddess, swayed sensuously in her short dress. Her arms were bare and the smallest of noses held her dark glasses in place. He stepped back, away from the crenellation, his heart racing, his mind whirling with ideas.

He paced the length of the wall. A vision was about to enter his stone prison. A woman fit to be worshiped with every salacious touch he'd ever learned. His cock hardened beneath his pantaloons. Amazed, he stopped and looked down at it. After so many years of having no needs—for food, for sleep, for relieving himself—the last he'd expected to feel was the need for a woman. He shook his head. It defied logic. But if his body could respond, then he could participate, guide a woman through the Masque.

The creaking hinges of the gate brought him back to the wall to see the backs of the two women entering the Abbey courtyard. Two women. Vivid memories of his happier days with the prince caught him by surprise and gave him hope. As he strode across the wall-walk and down the stone staircase, his mind raced with possibilities. One after another they were discarded as he floated to the landing on the second floor. But a new plan began to form as the great pine doors opened.

If she hadn't been in heels, Rena Mills would have jumped over the threshold as she and Valerie pushed open the twelve-foot doors of Ashton Abbey. Their creaking sound didn't bother her. In fact, she'd be sure those hinges never saw oil for the rest of their days. They made a perfect first impression for a haunted bed-and-breakfast.

Valerie shook her head. "You love that noise, don't you?"

Rena grinned sheepishly as she stepped into the two-story stone entry the size of her parents' house and spread her arms wide. "It's perfect. I can't believe it. I'm actually going to make this happen. Can't you see it, Valerie?"

Her friend raised her eyebrow. "If you say so."

"I do." She examined the stone floor beneath her feet before touching a wall. The hard rock under her fingers was cool and rough. Her stomach somersaulted as success filled her veins. She could do this. Ashton Abbey resembled a castle and tourists would love staying here. All she needed was a little plumbing, a little electricity, a functioning kitchen, and a few ghosts. "Seriously, Val. You can see the potential, right?"

Valerie gave her a hard look. "You don't have to do this, Ree. You don't have to prove anything. That jerk is full of himself. So all your success has come while working at your family's company or at Bryce's. That's simply because you are a good event planner. Look at me. I've worked for my dad's company all my life. That doesn't mean I don't know my shit."

"It's not about Bryce. I have to prove this to myself." She wished Valerie could understand.

Her friend threw up her hands and stalked away. The woman was too confident to have any idea how it felt to be unsure. Rena sighed. The fact was, her ex-fiancé had a point. All her jobs had been obtained through her parents or him. After two months of being out of work, this was her only option. Now she had to make her new haunted abbey into a successful bed-and-breakfast, not simply to prove she could, but because she had every last penny on the line.

As she perused the large entry with its double staircase leading to the next floor, her jubilance returned. The abandoned building was so much more than she'd expected for the price. She looked up at the semicircle windows near the ceiling, which let in sunlight, but she didn't see any spirits. "I hope the real estate agent hadn't exaggerated about the ghosts. If this place hasn't sold because it's haunted, then I better see some dead people pretty darn fast."

"Uh, Rena?"

She glanced behind her to see Valerie had stepped into the next room. Turning, she strode through the doorway to find a grand dining room, with green-and-gold paisley wallpaper. She stopped and smiled. "Oh, this is too good to be true." Valerie had pulled aside one of the curtains from the fifteen-foot windows to let in the sun, and it reflected off an elegantly set table.

"Over here."

Her friend stood at the head of the table, a deep frown on her face. "What is it? Did you find something?" She started down the length of the long table set to feed twenty-four. Her stomach twitched with excitement at the sight. She stopped to look at the place setting Valerie stared at. "What am I looking for?"

Valerie shook her head. "Do you see anything unusual here?"

She peered at the setting. The silverware had an elaborate P etched into it, but other than the fact it had multiple plates as if set for a formal occasion, she saw nothing out of the ordinary. "No. Should I?"

Valerie sighed and crossed her arms over her small bosom. "How long has this place been empty?"

She shrugged. "I don't know. Over a hundred years or so? From what I hear, colored lights can be seen shining from the windows at night, but there's no electricity. I guess the Abbey got lucky with ghosts and I'm going to make that work for us."

"And is there a caretaker of some sort?"

"There is one family here who has taken care of the grounds

for eons. I can't remember their names, but it's an old widower and his son. Why?"

Valerie dragged her finger across the plate. "Do they take care of the inside as well?"

"No, we are the only ones to enter inside these walls in a hundred and fifty years. Isn't that amazing? Why, what are you getting at?"

Valerie lifted her finger in front of Rena's eyes. "Then why is there no dust?"

Her brain came to a halt as she grasped Valerie's point. Taking another look around the room, she saw no cobwebs, no dust, not even a chair out of place. She returned her gaze to Valerie. "Clean ghosts?"

Valerie raised her brow. "Did you read about that in your research?"

Rena picked up the plate and examined it, not comfortable meeting her friend's eyes. "No, but I didn't exactly do research. I watched a few shows on television and discovered people will pay to go to a haunted hotel. There has to be an explanation. Maybe someone has been living here and no one realized it."

Valerie crossed the room to the windows. "You mean behind the padlocked gate?"

She joined her friend, puzzled, ready to believe in ghosts who cleaned. "What are you looking at?"

"These curtains. If they're a hundred years old, shouldn't they be dry-rotted and in shreds?"

A shiver ran across Rena's skin. "Oh, damn. This is stranger than a simple haunting." She ran her hand along the forest-green velvet of the curtain. The material, strong and thick, had a beige cotton backing. This didn't make any sense. She turned to examine the rest of the room. The chairs around the massive table also had velvet in their backs. She stepped closer to one and ran her hand over the material. The softness was irresistible…and new.

Coming Soon

Pleasures of Christmas Past
A Christmas Carol: Book 1
(http://www.lexipostbooks.com/pleasures-of-christmas-past/)

Coming November 2015

Though Jessica Thomas is thrilled to land the job of novice Spirit Guide, she's been assigned a hot, arrogant Scottish mentor who confuses her heart. But what should concern her more, is will he protect her soul?
Available for order

Cowboy's Best Shot
Poker Flat Series: Book 3
(http://www.lexipostbooks.com/cowboys-best-shot/)

Coming April 2016

A cowboy who has lost so much.
A woman who never had it to begin with.
Is this their best shot for happiness?

Also by Lexi Post

Passion of Sleepy Hollow

(http://www.lexipostbooks.com/passion-of-sleepy-hollow/)

Cruise into Eden (The Eden Series: Book 1)

(http://www.lexipostbooks.com/cruise-into-eden/)

Unexpected Eden (The Eden Series: Book 2)

(http://www.lexipostbooks.com/unexpected-eden/)

Cowboys Never Fold (Poker Flat Series: Book 1)

(http://www.lexipostbooks.com/cowboys-never-fold/)

Cowboy's Match (Poker Flat Series: Book 2)

(http://www.lexipostbooks.com/cowboys-match/)

For updates, sneak peeks, and special prizes, sign up to receive the latest news from Lexi at http://eepurl.com/D3MqT

About Lexi Post

Lexi Post is a New York Times and USA Today best-selling author of erotic romance inspired by the classics. She spent years in higher education taking and teaching courses about the classical literature she loved. From Edgar Allan Poe's short story "The Masque of the Red Death" to Tolstoy's *War and Peace*, she's read, studied, and taught wonderful classics.

But Lexi's first love is romance novels. In an effort to marry her two first loves, she started writing erotic romance inspired by the classics and found she loved it. Lexi believes there's no end to the romantic inspiration she can find in great literature. Her books are known for being "erotic romance with a whole lot of story."

Lexi is living her own happily ever after with her husband and her cat in Florida. She makes her own ice cream every weekend, loves bright colors, and is never seen without a hat.

www.lexipostbooks.com